SHADOW OF THE SON

IVAN OBOLENSKY

SMITH-OBOLENSKY
MEDIA

Published by Smith-Obolensky Media, DBA of Dynamic Doingness, Inc.

www.smithobolenskymedia.com

www.ivanobolensky.com

ISBN: 978-1-947780-17-0

Library of Congress Control Number: 2021909927

Publication date: June 21, 2021

Printed by Kindle Direct Publishing in Columbia, South Carolina, in the United States of America

OTHER WORKS BY IVAN OBOLENSKY

Eye of the Moon

(Latin American Spanish adaptation: *El ojo de la luna*)

For Ivan's nonfiction articles on the social sciences, visit:
https://dynamicdoingness.com/our-articles/

For his other writings, visit his blog:
https://ivanobolensky.com/blog/

SHADOW OF THE SON

THE SEQUEL TO *EYE OF THE MOON*

A novel

Ivan Obolensky

To Mary Jo, for her encouragement and believing.

LIST OF CHARACTERS
(in alphabetical order)

Alice: John Sr.'s half-sister. Formerly married to **Lord Bromley**, whom she divorced. She later married and divorced **Arthur Blaine**. Alice died under mysterious circumstances when **Johnny Dodge** and **Percy** were ten. She had no children.

Anne Dodge: Mother to Johnny and married to John Sr.

Arthur Blaine: Mining magnate and Alice's second husband, whom she divorced.

Bonnie Leland: John Sr.'s half-sister and **Maw**'s daughter.

Brunhilde von Hofmanstal (Bruni): Daughter of **Elsa** and **Hugo von Hofmanstal**. Works for her father as an attorney.

Cobb: Dr. Angus Maxwell-Hughes. Lord Bromley's doctor.

Dagmar: The cook at Rhinebeck. Married to **Stanley**.

Elsa von Hofmanstal: Wife of Hugo and mother of Bruni.

Hugo von Hofmanstal (the baron): Longtime friend of Lord Bromley and John Sr. He was briefly engaged to **Mary**, Percy's mother, before marrying Elsa. She and Hugo have two children, a daughter, Brunhilde von Hofmanstal and a younger son, who lives in Europe.

Jane: Kitchen staff member, who works with Dagmar.

John Sr. (John Dodge): Married to Anne Dodge and father of Johnny. He owns Dodge Capital, an early Hedge Fund.

Johnny Dodge: Grew up with Percy, son of Anne and John.

Lord Bromley: Former husband of Alice.

Malcolm Ault: Longtime friend of Alice, Lord Bromley, and the Dodge family.

Mary: Percy's mother and close friend to Anne Dodge. She lives in Florence, Italy with her husband, **Thomas.**

Maw (Mary Leland): Matriarch of the Dodge family. She married John B. Dodge, had John Sr., and later divorced. Her last marriage was to a southern banker, who died. She is the mother of Bonnie Leland. Known to the family as *Maw* and *The Crone* in the corporate world, she has the economic resources of a small country.

Percy: The narrator of the novel. He grew up with Johnny in the Dodge household.

Raymond: John Sr.'s personal chauffeur.

Robert the Bruce: English bull terrier formerly owned by Johnny Dodge and now owned by Maw.

Simon: Household staff member, who works with Stanley.

Stanley: The head butler of Rhinebeck. Married to Dagmar, the cook.

NOTE TO THE READER

It has been three years since *Eye of the Moon* was published. In novel time, *Shadow of the Son* picks up shortly after *Eye of the Moon* ends. It is Part II of the narrative. Although the second novel can be read on its own, the reading experience of *Shadow of the Son* is very much enhanced if *Eye of the Moon* is fresh in your mind. One can better appreciate the many fine points and nuances that carry over and weave through the overall story.

It is up to you, the reader, of course, but that is my recommendation.

Once again, I wish to reiterate that this is a work of fiction. The characters, their histories, and dialogues are works of my imagination.

I hope you enjoy this tale. Thank you for reading.

J ohnny Dodge and I had returned to New York after settling my affairs and moving myself and my forensic accounting practice out of Los Angeles. It was a Wednesday morning in the spring of 1977, and I was sitting in one of the client chairs in Johnny's office at Dodge Capital when his phone rang.

Johnny answered and then passed it across the desk. "It sounds like the baron, looking for you."

I took the phone.

"Percy?"

I recognized the voice. "Baron."

"Call me Hugo."

"Hugo ..."

"You need an office."

"I do. It's next on the list."

"Well, get it done. On another matter, meet me at 21 at 7:00 p.m. tomorrow. We'll have dinner, just the two of us. We have some things to discuss. Don't be late."

"I wouldn't dream of it."

"Very good," he said and hung up.

Hugo was the Baron von Hofmanstal and my future father-in-law. He and I were technically on a first-name basis, but I tended to call him by his title. Hugo would correct me, but only sporadically. My addressing him as baron, I thought, stroked his already prodigious ego. He was, after all, small of stature and a little round, but then so was Napoleon. Hugo looked like the former emperor and had a similar presence. He was at once charismatic and intimidating. He also had a cruel and violent nature. Hugo enjoyed dueling, hunting, deal-making, and crushing those who dared to cross him. As a rule, I was careful not to give offense, and with Hugo I was doubly so, but I had yet to formulate a consistent protocol as to when to call him Hugo, or when to address him as baron. It was one of many things that I was trying to work out as I wrestled with the fact that he and I would be seeing a great deal more of each other. Such a relationship was not without its advantages. For a start, there was his daughter and my fiancée, Brunhilde, or Bruni to her friends. I handed back the phone.

Johnny took it. "You were thinking of her again," he said, looking at me across his desk. He was in his typical office attire, dark suit, cream-colored shirt, and dark blue tie with small white polka dots. His hair was golden blond and worn somewhat long, as was the fashion.

"I was indeed. You're jealous, of course."

"I don't think so. Enjoying that future father-in-law of yours?"

"Okay, maybe not. Hugo wants to dine with me tomorrow at the 21 Club."

"Just the two of you?"

"Just the two of us."

"Excellent. Perhaps he'll confess his darkest secrets, now that you're part of the family—or almost."

"I doubt it, but I'll tell you what I can."

"Make sure you do. On another subject—one I hesitate to bring up, but one I must, since it's the next item on our list—the office. How would you feel about renewing our partnership?"

This was a decision that couldn't be put off any longer. Johnny was my best friend. He and I had grown up together in the Dodge household, where I was a long-term resident since my mother and stepfather were often abroad. We had formed a trading partnership, but that had imploded thanks to Johnny's grandmother, better known as "Maw" to the Dodge family, and in the corporate world as "The Crone." Johnny had worked out a deal with her whereby both of us had been compensated for her deliberate sabotage of our little enterprise. Since then, I had thought a great deal about renewing our partnership and had finally concluded that now was a time for new beginnings.

"All right. I agree. We give it another go."

"You're sure?"

"I'm sure. It was a happy time for both of us, other than the ending. But with the understanding that I continue my forensic accounting practice for now. My fees will hopefully cover the overhead while we gather assets. It's also a cross-selling opportunity."

"Agreed, but subject to change once we're established."

"Fair enough. Your dad will have to be informed, and he might not be pleased at losing you to private practice."

"I wouldn't be too sure about that. Frankly, I could do with a chance to stretch out a little, and he would no longer have to worry about what I'm doing all the time. It could work for both of us. I'll broach the matter and get his agreement. He and Mother are heading up to Rhinebeck this afternoon. I could head up there as well, inform them tonight, and be back tomorrow?"

"Sounds good. As for the office, let's start with something functional and not too ostentatious."

"I would have to disagree. A good location and a sophisticated presentation can be quite effective in overcoming investor reluctance. Too spartan an appearance, and the public will think we're operating on a shoestring and can't afford their business."

"Too extravagant, and we *will* be operating on a shoestring."

"True. But I have some good news. Our old offices are available. How about I give the leasing agent a call and set it up?"

"All right."

Johnny was reaching for the phone when another call came in. He picked up, listened for a moment, and asked, "Who's calling?" After a pause, he said, "One moment" and put the caller on hold.

"I don't know if you want to take this. The caller says he's Bruni's husband."

"That's unexpected."

"What do you want to do?"

"Speak with him."

"Are you sure that's wise?"

"No, but news travels fast it seems, and some things can't be avoided indefinitely."

Johnny passed me the phone and took the line off hold.

"So you're Percy?"

The voice on the other end had a French accent and sounded far away.

"Yes, I am."

"My name is Bernard Montrel, Bruni's soon-to-be ex-husband. Listen, for I have little time. I harbor no ill feeling toward you, as unlikely as that may sound. I doubt there was much you could have done to avoid the position you're in. I

4

was in a similar place. How dire it was I had no way of knowing. You face similar perils, which is why I tracked you down. Someone must say something. Trust no one in that family. Their loyalty is only to themselves. She will wrap you in silky threads and spin you round and round, before she sucks you dry. Remember, I had the courtesy to give you fair warning. *C'est tout.*"

The line went dead.

2

"Trouble?" asked Johnny.

"Without a doubt."

"Why am I not surprised? Tell me."

I repeated what Bernard had said. Johnny didn't answer right away but rocked back in his chair and looked out the window at the office building across the street.

"I think this qualifies as an 'Iago' moment," he said at last, turning to face me. "There is poison in the man's words. If you were Othello, I'd advise you to ignore him completely, but you're not. You're my friend, and as your friend, my loyalty is only to you, irrespective of the state of your future marriage or other relationships. You may not like what I have to say. Should I continue?"

"Disliking what you have to say wouldn't be particularly new, would it?"

"I suppose not, but this is different. I know how I am when I'm involved with someone. I can barely see straight, let alone listen to reason. Speak against the one I love, and I struggle to contain myself."

Johnny's love affairs had been a surprising source of trouble. They were incessant, tumultuous, and created endless difficulties for both of us. I was the one he turned to for advice, which he invariably misinterpreted, misconstrued, or plain ignored at critical moments.

"I understand," I said. "I was always careful about commenting on your love affairs for that reason. We are different in that regard, but I get your point. It's personal."

"Remember when we first met the von Hofmanstals, and our heads were filled with suspicions about them?"

"I think I was more than a little paranoid at the time."

"Indeed, but remember we were right in our initial assessment. The baron did want Alice's treasures and was there to obtain them. The parents, on the other hand, told us more than once that they were good people and worth knowing. My suspicions were quieted, but, in truth, never laid to rest. Now, don't get me wrong, I think Bruni is a good match for you, and I have a high opinion of your future in-laws, but they have their own agendas. Their family is not my family. And Bruni's former husband presented no hard evidence other than his opinion, but if it were me, I doubt I would have expended the time and effort necessary to find you. Other than a genuine attempt to warn you, I can see no other motive for tracking you down. Would you agree?"

"It's quite likely," I answered. "Although I sensed some vindictiveness in his words."

"There might be some of that. Talk to your butler and majordomo. If Stanley says Bernard's claims are nothing, then dismiss them from your mind, and I'll do the same. But should Stanley think there's something to it, I'd definitely want to know what he would advise."

"Perhaps this weekend."

"Sooner is better. In fact, I recommend we drive up to Rhinebeck now. You can talk to Stanley, revisit your property, and I can speak with Father. After that, we can all have dinner together, and you and I can drive back tomorrow morning. Besides, there's always Dagmar's cooking to feed the soul, an opportunity not to be missed. She might have some words as well."

"Why now, when I'll be there on Friday?"

"I'll get to that. My further advice is speak to Bruni. Tell her about the phone call, but I think the chat with Stanley should be a private one. Not because I distrust her, but because it will allow a more free-flowing conversation that may not be possible this weekend when she'll be there."

"No Bruni then."

"That's what I recommend."

I had some reservations about going back earlier than I had planned, but returning now seemed the better choice given the nature of the call.

"Very well. I agree. It would be a prudent move. That being said, I'm more than willing to welcome whatever von Hofmanstal secrets, machinations, or eccentricities exist. I made that decision when I decided to marry Bruni. It's part of the package, and I accept all its implications."

"That's as it should be. More information has never been a problem. It's the lack that causes difficulties, from what I've seen. You have a chance to lay any and all suspicions to rest, and that can only be good."

"Or inflate them."

"That, too, but, if it were me, I'd rather be forewarned, than not. Wouldn't you?"

"Yes."

"That's settled then. I'll get my assistant to arrange a car and make an appointment with the leasing agent. On another matter, which this last call brings front and center, you will be getting married, and our relationship will change. Both of us will have to adapt, and that may be hard. Whatever happens, I don't want to become a pain or a burden to you."

"I doubt that's possible. We're entering a new configuration is all, and since you and I are partners again, I'll likely spend as much time with you as with Bruni. I'm not worried about that aspect, even if you might be."

"I am, a little. Still, I feel better having mentioned it. Now, I'll speak to my assistant and give you some privacy to make your call."

As Johnny left, I reached over his desk and dialed the baron's office. Bruni was his in-house attorney. A receptionist answered and put me through to my fiancée after a short wait.

"Percy, it's been so long."

"A couple of hours, but it seems like forever."

"It does. Time slows when we're apart. What's up?"

"I had a couple of interesting calls. The first was from your father. He wants to meet me for dinner tomorrow at 21, just the two of us."

"Lucky you. You'll have the sole?"

"Since he's paying, absolutely. I also had a call from your ex."

"Oh? What did he have to say?"

With that question and tone, Bruni had switched to her professional mode. I repeated what he had said in full.

She paused for a moment. "Bernard is skillful. He's managed to let you know that he accepts that he and I are done, while sowing a seed of doubt between us, hoping it will grow. He's trouble, but we won't have to worry about him much longer. You should also know that my family, your family-to-be, *always* has an agenda. There will never be a time when there isn't something cooking. My father would go mad if that wasn't the case. Both my parents like you a great deal, which means you'll be part of whatever it is they have in mind, and I want that as well. By the way, last night was delicious, but tonight I have to work. Expect me very late."

"That may prove a benefit. I should also tell you that Johnny and I have decided to renew our partnership, but he wants his father's blessing. John Sr. and Anne will be in Rhinebeck tonight as part of a long weekend. I thought I'd drive up with Johnny and return tomorrow morning. I'll also have a chance to speak to Stanley, check out Alice's apartment, and make any needed adjustments before you and I drive up on Friday."

"I think that's sensible. I also feel that a partnership with Johnny's a good idea. You're good for each other. Besides, I have to look over a monstrous business proposal before a meeting tomorrow. I might even sleep at the office."

"At your desk?"

"There's a bedroom here. It's tiny, but there's a shower, and a change of clothes."

"I'll miss you."

"And I'll miss you. I can't wait to drive up with you on Friday. By the way, I wouldn't read any ghost stories before bed tonight."

"Not a chance. I intend to sleep like a baby."

"Talk to you tomorrow. Love you."

"Love you."

3

I hung up the phone. While I waited for Johnny to finish making arrangements, I thought about Rhinebeck. Inevitably, that started the train of thought that had drifted in and out of my mind ever since I'd left. I wanted to savor the timeless beauty that awaited me, but I was uneasy. As the chauffeur-driven limousine had swept up the drive, I had heard someone calling out, imploring me to come back. The voice had been clear enough to cause me to twist and look behind, but as I peered back through the swirling fog in the car's wake, I had seen no one.

At the time, I had debated whether what I'd heard was real or my imagination playing tricks on me. Over the years at Rhinebeck, I had occasionally heard peculiar sounds or vague murmurings at the edges of my hearing in late afternoons. Whispers would move among the shadows in the drawing room, behind the curtains in the library, or pass me as I climbed the stairs to the top floor. I would turn, or follow, but always they moved off until I couldn't hear them anymore. I had spoken to Johnny about them, but he would shrug his shoulders and say, "I haven't heard such things. It could be your imagination, but maybe not. The place is strange, what can I say?"

Johnny may not have been able to confirm the things I'd heard, but he and I both agreed that there was something odd about the west wing where Alice, Johnny's aunt, had lived and died. Growing up, we had entered her apartment only when invited, and such occasions had been brief and far between. After Alice had died and passed to places we could only imagine, we had sometimes felt we were being watched. A chill would settle over the house, and cheery spaces would grow dark and gloomy. The staff would be on edge and inclined to whisper. Even Stanley would be affected, his normal ghostlike service more tentative and unsure. Dagmar in her kitchen would snap at anybody who was moving slowly, which, according to her, was everyone.

Johnny and I never knew what caused such feelings, only that the house was unsettled and disturbed. We would be good as gold until the feeling dissipated, and we could gravitate to our normal antics with little to fear, other than being assigned more chores when we went too far.

From my first visit, the house had projected an aura of mystery and a brooding watchfulness. Deep currents moved beneath the surface. I remembered Rhinebeck's dark gray exterior looming out of the fog on a threatening afternoon in December just before Christmas.

Johnny had briefed me on the estate's many secret hiding places, but most of all, he had wanted to introduce me to Alice, his favorite aunt. Not only did she have an uncanny ability to thwart mischief, he informed me, but an alarming prescience that was vaguely comforting. He was unable to articulate such feelings at the time, other than to warn me to guard my thoughts, as he was willing to bet his aunt was able to read minds, including mine. I considered the implications and was more than a little intimidated from the outset.

If she could read my mind, then she would know how tentative my existence was, and how I yearned for a sense of belonging. She would also know the loneliness and the darkness that lay within my soul, and that was more than I was willing to convey to anyone. I fretted over this as I endured the long drive to meet her.

We had turned down the sloping driveway to the squared roundabout that marked the entrance. I watched the front door open, and a tall woman with jet-black hair stepped out wearing a thin, cream-colored dress that seemed to defy the bleakness of the weather. She stood alone at the top of the steps as she waited. She smiled as the car approached, but for a moment I saw a flicker of something else. It might have been that she too anticipated our meeting with a sense of trepidation. I wondered at the reason. She knew Johnny and Raymond, Mr. Dodge's chauffeur, therefore that passing emotion must've been due to meeting either the new nanny or myself. That I could elicit such a feeling was inconceivable, but in that brief moment of vulnerability, my heart went out to her. I saw that she, years older and an adult, was as alone and fearful as I was.

As we crunched around the driveway toward the front door, I watched a man in a somber morning suit step out, drape a dark blue shawl about her shoulders, and then step to the side. The car stopped, but Johnny didn't wait for Raymond to open the door. He flung it open himself as the nanny squawked, and he dragged me along in his enthusiasm to be the first to introduce me to his aunt.

Johnny bounded up the steps with me in tow and announced, "This is Percy. He's staying with us."

The lady smiled and leaned slightly toward me as she held out her hand. Still caught in that precious moment of impossible connection, I stepped in close and hugged her waist. She laughed and said, "Whoa, little man. Here we do things a little differently, but I thank you just the same. I'm Alice."

I stepped back a little flustered, but as I looked into her dark eyes, they sparkled with a pleasure that seemed to focus only on me.

"My name is Percy," I said, looking up at her.

"Yes, it is. And this is Stanley," she said, turning toward the man in the dark suit next to her. Something passed between them, and then he looked down at me. I stuck out my hand, but he didn't take it. I let it drop to my side. He examined me with bright blue eyes that could have hidden any emotion, or none at all. He didn't speak but only nodded. And so Stanley, a few seconds after Alice, entered my life as I had entered into his.

"Dreaming again?"

I jumped. Johnny had entered and stood at the door observing me. I shuddered and said, "I was thinking."

"Ah, yes. You do seem a tad jumpy. Tell me about that in the car. It's out front."

———————— ❖ ————————

4

A chauffeur from the limo service opened the rear door for us and went around to the driver's side. He started up and threaded through New York City traffic, while Johnny and I stretched out in the back. Once we were on our way, Johnny rolled up the dividing window and asked the driver a question. He didn't answer.

"He can't hear us, so we can speak freely. Now, you seem agitated. Speak to me."

I hesitated before answering and looked at the passing scenery instead. Once again, I asked myself whether what I'd heard as I left Rhinebeck had been real or imagined and was unable to make up my mind. On top of that, I had begun to recognize the possibility that I was hopelessly ill-prepared to manage an estate the size of Rhinebeck. What would happen to the intangible legacies and those who depended on me should I fail?

Fail and nothing would be forgiven, Dagmar had said, and that there would be consequences. But what exactly and from whom, I didn't know.

Over the years, I had come to believe that whatever lay at the mystical center of Rhinebeck was not altogether friendly. I had always sensed a reluctant neutrality that could be withdrawn at any time. My awareness of that something had frightened me growing up, particularly in the dead of night when I would awaken for no reason other than that something had disturbed my sleep.

I had ignored such provocations as best I could, but I was not always successful.

When moonlight streamed through the single round window of my room, and I had been awakened, I would peer out from underneath the covers at the familiar shapes of my desk and chair. Nothing would appear out of place, but I could never be sure. My imagination would grapple with the things I couldn't see, and I would pull the covers over my head to quiet it. Sleep would eventually find me, but not before I had distressed myself to exhaustion. Other times, when there was no moon, I would sit up in the black and whisper softly to whatever listened, "Go away." Silence or a breath of air would be the answer.

After many such occurrences, I couldn't contain my anxiety any longer. I mentioned what I had experienced to Johnny. His answer was simple. "Make a bargain," he told me. "It's what I did."

I took his advice and cut a deal of sorts. That night, whispering to the darkness, I agreed to say nothing to anyone about the moody perturbations that would awaken me, but only if I might be left alone. It seemed to work. The incidents grew less frequent. I thanked Johnny for his advice a week later. He shook his head as if to say that the walls might hear us and then nodded in agreement. We didn't speak about it after that.

Back in the present, I sighed and looked out at the countryside. I did feel agitated.

Finally, after a long pause, I turned to Johnny. "I've been a little reluctant to return to Rhinebeck, if you must know. That may be surprising, but there it is. I heard someone, or something, call out to me as we drove away the last time. It could have been my imagination. I chose to disregard that call, and now I'm returning. I don't know what will happen. Also, the intuition that I had when I was last at Rhinebeck has gone."

"Gone?"

"Disappeared. Its silence began the same time we left."

"That is troubling. What do you think is going on?"

"I really don't know. I'm in uncharted territory."

"What exactly happened when we left? You never told me any of this."

"I didn't mention it because I wasn't sure I really heard anything. As we were driving away, a voice called out for me to return. I sensed an urgency and perhaps a longing. It was sharp but indefinite at the same time. I couldn't tell precisely the direction it came from."

"I see," said Johnny. "I didn't hear any such thing, but that doesn't mean that you didn't. If you want my honest opinion, I don't know too many people who can change careers, discover Lord Bromley is their father, become engaged, take on an estate the size of Rhinebeck, promise who-knows-what to keep it going, have the von Hofmanstals as future in-laws, and not feel out of sorts. That amount of change is enough to drive anyone 'round the bend. You may be experiencing a simple case of nerves, even if what you heard was real."

"Possibly, but I'm concerned."

"I know you are. You think that you'll fall short. You always do. But really, Percy, you can't lead by seeing catastrophes at every turn … not if you ever hope to win. You *will* make mistakes. It's normal. You're now the custodian of Rhinebeck. Right or wrong, leaving for California to pack up your stuff and move here was essential for you to assume that role. Correct?"

"Yes, but I didn't turn back when perhaps I should have. Now I'm worried that I may have doomed this endeavor from the start."

"Listen to yourself! Really, Percy, the future isn't written in stone. At least it wasn't last I checked. You need to settle yourself. I've seen you in such moods before. Why don't you take a nap while I look over some papers? I doubt you've been getting much sleep, and catching up on it can only help. Have you mentioned any of this to Bruni?"

"No, I haven't. I barely knew how to express it until now."

"Fair enough. It will keep. Get some sleep, and when you're rested, we'll talk some more."

"I'll try. And thanks for listening."

"Of course."

As I settled into the car's soft leather, I thought to myself that sleeping was a good idea. I might need all I could get, judging from my previous visit.

5

I slept until Johnny woke me. I felt better and said so.

"See?" he said. "You needed the rest, and by the way, you sleep with your mouth open."

"No, I don't."

"Yes, you do."

"Maybe."

"It's a fact, but I'm glad to see you looking better. We'll be turning into the driveway in a minute or two. Any last words?"

"None. I don't know what to expect, but that's typical, I suppose."

"It is. All will be well, you'll see."

I wasn't going to argue the point. My worrying had only succeeded in wearing me out. I sat up and looked ahead as the car turned onto the private road. The early afternoon was breezy with high clouds. Sunlight played through the moving canopy of leaves and dappled the asphalt in dancing patterns that the car rolled over and left cavorting in its wake.

We turned down the gentle slope to the front of the house. The door opened, and out stepped Stanley in his customary morning suit. I let out a sigh of relief. The car crunched to a halt, and the chauffeur opened the door for me as Stanley came down the steps.

He gave me a flicker of a smile and said, "Welcome back. A little earlier than expected, I see."

"Yes, I can't seem to stay away. It's good to see you, Stanley."

"And I you. Some refreshments will be available shortly in the drawing room."

"Wonderful. After that, I need to ask your advice."

"I'm at your service."

Stanley welcomed Johnny and led the way through the front door into the calm that lay beyond it. We passed the ticking grandfather clock by the entrance to our left with its five ships of the line on its face that tilted back and forth counting out the seconds and, to the right, the long table with a vase filled with fresh gladioli sitting by the bust of Alexander. Stanley opened the door to the drawing room and said, "I'll be but a moment."

As he left, dust motes danced in the bright sunlight that streamed through the French doors across the room and made elongated golden rectangles on the carpet. It was cheerier than I remembered. Johnny followed close behind.

"See?" he said. "Everything's still here. Nothing to worry about." He wandered about the room. I simply stood in the center and breathed.

Stanley slipped in with two flutes of Cristal on a silver tray.

"Some refreshment," he said as he served us. He turned to me. "I'll be available in my office for consultation once you've settled. Dagmar would like to say hello, but first things first. Unwind from your journey. Whatever is on your mind will keep. You're home, where you belong."

After he had retired through the dining room doors, I stood in front of the Constable and admired the gray, clouded sky and pastoral countryside in the painting. It was mine, now. I never would have imagined it. I turned to Johnny as he came up beside me. "Cheers," I said and clinked his glass.

"Cheers," Johnny responded.

"It's been an eventful couple of weeks. I was so overjoyed to see the house still here with Stanley waiting to greet me that I almost gave him a hug."

"Yes, I noticed that, but luckily you didn't. I can't imagine how he would have taken it."

"I can't either. One day I will, to see what he'll do." I looked around again. "I'm so happy to be back."

"I am, too. Excellent champagne, by the way."

"Yes," I said. I wondered whether drinking Cristal exclusively was financially prudent.

"The Cristal decision was one of your better ideas," commented Johnny, reading my mind. "But I note the clouds of fiscal responsibility beginning to form. I suppose that's the difference between a guest and a host. Change it if you must, but let's drink up and enjoy ourselves for now. We're partners again. It's a good day. To our new partnership," said Johnny as he raised his glass.

"To our new partnership," I said, raising mine. "Who would have thought?"

"Who would have thought, indeed," said Johnny. "On top of that, you're engaged. Could you ever have imagined?"

"Not at all. The world has turned upside down, yet here we are. Life is strange but utterly marvelous. Thank you for all your support, by the way, in case I failed to mention it."

"That may have been the case, but you're very welcome. On top of that, there's more to come."

"I think you're right. We should talk to Stanley and Dagmar sooner rather than later, and before your parents show up."

"Father said they'd arrive late in the afternoon. We have some hours yet, but by all means. Waste not a minute."

We placed our empty flutes by the bar and headed for the kitchen. Dagmar was there, bustling about. I went up to her and gave her a hug. I didn't care about the propriety of it. She cooed, placed me at arm's length, and looked me in the eye for a long second.

"I see we have some things to discuss, but I must make additional preparations for dinner tonight, now that there'll be four. Run along. We'll talk later. Stan's in his office."

I could have been ten years old the way she spoke to me, but I didn't mind. She was a source of affection and attention that grounded me even now. We left Dagmar to her kitchen and went down the hall to Stanley's office. He was at his desk, leaning back in his chair.

"So much for relaxation," he said. "That took all of fifteen minutes. Although it is still early in the day, I think a glass of my private reserve will settle things down quite admirably." He swiveled about and prepared three glasses of amber liquid in cut crystal glasses. He handed two to Johnny and me and raised his. "Let us savor this rare brew and each other's company. Good health."

The smoky taste was better than I remembered. After a suitable time to reflect on the quality of the drink, Stanley looked up in my direction. "You wish to consult me. I assume Johnny is privy to your thoughts, since he is here beside you. Where would you like to begin?"

I thought about what to say for a second and started in. "First, my thanks for taking the time. I have two issues...."

I outlined the phone call with Bernard and Johnny's thoughts on the matter as well as my own.

Stanley nodded. "You wish to know if there is something to his warning. And the second issue?"

I told him what happened when I left Rhinebeck and my anxieties since then.

When I had finished, Stanley reflected for a moment. "I think it best if we start with the voice you heard driving away before taking up the other matter. Her ladyship had an experience that might be of interest. It won't answer entirely, but I can tell you what I can."

Johnny sat forward at this. Any information about Alice was always welcome.

"By all means," I said.

"It was not long after her marriage to Arthur Blaine had disintegrated in the jungles of Ecuador. As I mentioned, her return without him was marked by periods of elation followed by depression and rage. It was a difficult time for both of us. She found a means of alleviating her suffering in substances that affected the mind. For myself, I had to struggle not to interfere. Although I suspected that she longed for relief, I was mistaken. She rarely did anything without a greater purpose in mind.

"One day she asked me, out of the blue, as we were discussing various household expenses, whether I believed in other dimensions.

"The question was both interesting and troubling. There were stories I had heard in Scotland when I was very young that seemed to indicate that time is not the same for everyone. There are legends of castles, villages, and individuals disappearing altogether, never to be seen again, while others disappear only to come back into existence from somewhere else.

"I told her I knew that Rip Van Winkle was one such local legend, and that I had heard stories of these things, but I had never experienced the phenomenon myself.

"I remember her sitting behind the desk in her study when she leaned back and asked me, point blank, 'Stanley, have you ever heard voices in this house?'

"We had finished looking over the accounts, and as I looked up to answer her question, I realized that the accounting had been an excuse to ask me this question in particular. I don't know how I knew that, but I did. I asked her to explain. She looked away and then back again. 'I have started hearing murmurs and occasionally distinct voices.'

" 'Recently?'

" 'Yes.'

" 'I haven't noticed any voices per se. That isn't to say that there haven't been occurrences. Occasionally, I have sensed that I'm being observed, but when I turn to see who is there, I see no one.'

" 'Ah' was all she said. I had no reservations about talking to her of such things. Our discussions had been many, and she knew a great deal. In addition, our talks gave me insights into how she was getting on. I believe she knew this and encouraged them. I asked, 'Do they frighten you?'

" 'The voices? No, not really. It is not what they say, or even the fact that I hear them, but rather my incessant questioning of my own sanity because I do.'

" 'What has occurred?' I asked. and she told me that she had recently experimented with a substance called N-dimethyltryptamine. It had extraordinary hallucinogenic properties, although remarkably brief. She said that the drug was not a drug per se but a naturally occurring molecule found in the human pineal gland. The sensations generated were intense but strange. She felt compressed at first, like she was enclosed in a tight skin. The constricting sensation intensified to an extraordinary climax, at which point she burst from the membrane that held her and found herself somewhere else, in a world of a different color, orange predominately. There she found people who seemed as real as you and me. They were eager to talk and enthusiastic upon meeting her, but she quickly discovered they were not the ones she needed to speak to. All they seemed to want was the connection. They knew nothing of her plight. Although she relished the experience, she ceased her experiments with it. She started hearing the voices shortly after.

"I asked her if there was a connection, and she replied that she sometimes wondered if there might be another world placed next to ours, separated from us by walls within our minds. Occasionally, she thought they weakened, and that we could hear others making their own ways, oblivious to us on this side. She posited that each side processes living in different fashions.

" 'Like another dimension.' I commented.

" 'Exactly,' she answered.

"Our discussion ended at that point, and I returned to my duties. Over the years, I've thought about that conversation. I think she is correct. There may indeed be other worlds superimposed onto ours. There are physical locations, not just mental states of being, that seem to facilitate interactions of a peculiar if not mystical nature. Perhaps our minds are like radio receivers tuned in a specific way. Should the tuning change, what will be our perceptions? There may also be interference patterns generated that distort normal or uniform space and time in certain places. I have always wondered about the role of ancient and modern ceremonies happening in only select locations in that regard. Perhaps, some souls and venues are more 'in tune' than others and certain physical points amplify that experience. This property may be one such location."

Stanley smiled and looked at me directly. "What you may have heard was a warning that you were moving beyond the area where such interference patterns, if that is what they are, present themselves. For more specifics, you might wish to confer with Dagmar."

"Thank you for that information. I will speak with her. Perhaps we should now take up Bernard's warning?"

"Very well. I've done some further research into the von Hofmanstal family since your last visit, using several of my contacts who are familiar with the family and have intimate knowledge of their history. I have collected what I've found into a file should you wish to peruse it. It might save time if I summarize what I've discovered. Would that be acceptable?"

"By all means," I answered.

"Very well, let me begin by saying that the von Hofmanstals are an ancient family with Austrian roots whose conduct, given their long history, has not always been exemplary. Regardless, I doubt there exists a family, having wielded real power for an extended period, that hasn't been forced to bend what might be considered best practices in the interest of expediency, if not survival. Each will have bodies buried here and there, deeds that must be glossed over, and progeny best left off the family tree. The von Hofmanstals are no exception."

I shifted in my chair as Stanley continued.

"They are secretive, calculating, and opportunistic, but nonetheless successful. Their activities before and after the Second World War are sufficient proof of their pragmatism and skill in strategic thinking.

"For example, as Hitler came to power, the old baron knew that a time would come when he would have to make a choice between supporting or resisting the growing influence of National Socialism, for which the family had much to thank. The family's wealth and importance had grown with their substantial investments in several German pharmaceuticals during the thirties. The funding of Temmler Pharma proved particularly lucrative thanks to the recommendations of Fredrich von Hofmanstal, Hugo's older brother. He had a brilliant mind and wanted nothing more than to be a scientist. Since Germany had the best schools, he was sent there. He specialized in toxicology and later teamed up with the physiologist Otto Ranke. His advice was widely sought after, and as Fredrich's star rose, Hugo was sent west to England to hedge the family fortunes should his brother's success and Germany's resurgence turn out to be temporary. This proved remarkably far-sighted.

"When war eventually broke out, Hugo remained in London helping the Allies, where he became vital in the movements of supplies and materiel. Like his brother, his star rose, and with it, his ability to influence decisions about the redistribution of property once the war ended. As to what ultimately happened to Fredrich, little is known. He was listed as missing in action and presumed dead after the abortive German siege of Stalingrad. His body was never recovered, and efforts to uncover his fate came up empty-handed. The title passed to Hugo at the death of the old baron.

"My point here is that the von Hofmanstals weathered a crisis that was far greater than themselves by never fully committing to one side or the other despite ethical, ideological, or moral considerations. They look to their own advantage, and the family legacy is kept in the foreground, irrespective of the political, economic, or cultural climate. As to what that legacy is to be, I don't know precisely, although there are a few hints. The family has been collecting artifacts of a dark nature for some time as well as joining forces with those who hold similar items. Those who are in the position to afford such things are not without influence. Perhaps gathering power to themselves is all it is, but maybe there is more. They are taciturn by nature, so their objectives are not easily deciphered.

"In addition, the von Hofmanstals eschew publicity as a policy except when absolutely necessary. That in a nutshell is the nature of the family you will be marrying into. What I have said is not meant to denigrate them, but a statement of the facts as I know them. They are powerful, and power is as addictive as it is dangerous. All great families have similar designs and issues. I doubt that is news, yes?"

"Nothing particularly new," I answered. "Perhaps I'll ask the baron tomorrow at dinner as part of my own due diligence."

"Really?" said Johnny. "I would like to hear what he has to say about that."

"I would, too," added Stanley. "But I would take care. Once you are in the know, such knowledge cannot be taken back, and that can sometimes lead to unpleasant choices."

Johnny shifted in his chair. "Dead men tell no tales. Perhaps that's what Bernard was hinting at."

Stanley smiled, leaned back and steepled his fingers. "I wouldn't go that far, at least not yet. There are a few things you should know, however; not about the family in general, but about your fiancée in particular. I had intended originally to say nothing about any of this, but now I think I must. I would not want you placed at a disadvantage, should this information surface at an awkward moment, and take you unawares."

"What information might that be?" I asked. I had a sinking feeling.

"It concerns two deaths that took place during your fiancée's early years."

———————————•———————————

6

"Two? Bruni spoke of the accidental death of a governess. What's this about a second?" My world wobbled on its axis.

Stanley continued. "There were two deaths. Both were governesses, and it was the second following shortly after the first that raised troubling questions and necessitated Brunhilde being whisked off to the United States to stanch further developments. When added together, the cases paint a disturbing picture, but facts tell only part of the story. They omit the necessary context that is required to fully grasp an event and allow rightful condemnation or exoneration of the parties involved, even when the party is guilty of the act. Please know that it is not my intention to cast doubt upon your fiancée's character. From what I have seen, she is a fine lady, intelligent, personable, and empathetic. The deaths may have been accidental and not deliberate, as was bandied about at the time. It is all too easy to jump to conclusions. Allow me to tell you what I know and give you my thoughts when I'm finished."

"Please, go on." I glanced over at Johnny, who wore a thoughtful expression.

"The facts are these. Two governesses died while bringing up your fiancée, both within a few months and at the same location. The first was the result of a slip and fall down the main staircase of the von Hofmanstal castle in Austria.

Brunhilde was twelve at the time and the only witness. On that day she was in residence with a few staff while her parents were away on business. Those present heard a scream, came running, and found the governess sprawled at the foot of the stairs. When it proved impossible to revive her, the doctor was called. He pronounced her dead and informed the police. The subsequent investigation found that the unfortunate nanny had taken a misstep, tumbled end over end to the bottom of the stairs and broken her neck. The death was ruled accidental.

"Three months later, the parents were away once more when another governess fell several stories from a high window. Brunhilde reported that they had both been reading in her personal library, when the woman heard something below in the courtyard and rose to investigate. She threw open the window and looked down. Unable to see clearly, she clambered onto a chest that was set below the windowsill. While leaning out, she lost her balance and toppled through headfirst. Her shriek cut off abruptly when she struck the paved courtyard below with a report that witnesses said sounded like a gunshot. Brunhilde told authorities that there had been a moment when the nanny almost regained her balance, and that she had lunged for the flailing woman in an effort to save her, only to have the woman's clothing slip through her fingers.

"While Brunhilde's recollection of events was the primary source as to what happened in the first instance, this wasn't the case in the second. A maid was cleaning the parents' room when she chanced to look out precisely when the governess fell. Although she did not have a clear, unobstructed view, she contradicted Brunhilde's account by saying that she saw the daughter push the governess from behind. This version of the mishap spread as only a sensational rumor can.

"Who was to be believed? Was it a crime or an accident? The castle, the village, and the surrounding community were initially divided, but opinion gradually swung against Miss von Hofmanstal for two reasons.

"The first was that she asserted that there were no ill feelings between herself and the new governess; however, this statement was contradicted by several members of the castle staff, who stated quite emphatically that they had overheard arguments, some loud and angry, between the two.

"The second was the suspicious delay in the second witness coming forward. Many of the locals imagined that the von Hofmanstals had tried to suppress the maid's allegations. The maid was also outraged by the lost opportunity to voice her version of events, and rather than meekly accepting the official report of death by misadventure, she told her story to the papers. It was a journalistic coup. Her account sold like nothing else, and several tabloids leaped on the bandwagon. They each reported in different words that the von Hofmanstal daughter had killed her current governess, and likely the previous one as well. They quoted the maid as saying, 'Something must be done. None of the staff are safe. I fear for my life.'

"With that very public betrayal, the maid was dismissed, but rather than the public viewing the sacking as a logical consequence, her discharge was seen as a reprisal for voicing what she had seen. Views in the matter grew heated and loud.

"The growing negative sentiment and the sensational newspaper reports were not without aftereffects. Whether motivated by the growing popular interest, their own sense of outrage, or the opportunity for public distinction and recognition, momentum gathered in favor of an official re-examination of the findings submitted in both investigations.

When news of this hit the wires, headlines announced that the outcome would likely find what the public knew all along: that a spoiled and vengeful Brunhilde von Hofmanstal had pushed both governesses to their deaths in fits of childish petulance.

"At this point, the public relations situation had spiraled completely out of control. The family had always wished to remain anonymous, but now they had a nightmare scenario on their hands.

"Seeing there was no winning the battle in the minds of the public, the family resorted to the tried-and-true method of simply buying the scandal out of existence. They compensated and retired the witness, as well as her entire family, to another locale in spite of what she had done. They bought silence wherever possible, both internally and externally, at whatever the cost. They convinced the local police and judiciary to suppress any attempts to reopen the investigations in exchange for substantial stipends. They even met personally with the editors of several of the papers that had taken up the story and threatened suit. In one case, where the editor refused to let the matter drop, they bought the paper in its entirety, and fired him.

"Through the family's tireless efforts, the contrary news dried up, the official findings were reconfirmed, and the public's attention moved on to other things. With some semblance of calm restored, they quietly transferred their daughter to a boarding school in the United States, where she remained out of public view and far from any further media attention.

"After several years, Brunhilde returned to Austria without even a mention. The nanny affair was dead as far as the public was concerned.

"Although all of this may be alarming, it was what happened to the maid several years later that I find particularly disturbing."

7

"I bet she was killed, wasn't she?" asked Johnny. A strained smile crossed Stanley's face.

"Perhaps she was. One day, she simply disappeared. Months later, her partly decomposed body was discovered in a forest clearing not far from the town where she and her family had been relocated. It had lain there for some time open to the elements and had been partly consumed. More to the point, the tongue was missing. She was identified by a locket around her neck that she had worn since childhood.

"The von Hofmanstals were of course suspected, but there was no evidence to connect the family to the grisly find. In addition, the manner of her passing acted as a harsh warning to those who might have been inclined to make accusations or come forward with additional information. The crime, if it was a crime, remains unsolved to this day."

"Do you think Bruni—or her parents—did it?" asked Johnny. He quickly looked at me. "I'm sorry, Percy. That was callous."

"It was," I said, "But it is the question, isn't it? The whole matter is disturbing, but unproved one way or the other. Is that not correct, Stanley?"

He nodded. "Doubt is not a wholesome sensation. I would counsel that further evidence is needed before drawing a firm conclusion. In the end, you may have to ask her yourself, but the moment to do so would have to be well-considered. I'd be interested to know the answer, if you should ask the question."

Stanley looked at me. I could tell he was troubled. I felt the same, where before I had been ambivalent and listened to his story with a growing sense of alarm. Bruni had a dark side. I knew that. To me, it was part of her allure. Nonetheless, Bruni liked to control her own narrative and often omitted the parts she felt did not cast her in the best light. These flawed, occluded bits that she chose to hide would come at me sideways in the form of surprises, like the news of the second nanny. I had hoped she would realize that I would always give her the benefit of the doubt. Now, I felt a growing sense of dismay and apprehension. What else was there? Was it possible that she could be a murderer? Had I misread her so completely? I knew that I could be extraordinarily naïve. It was a terrible weakness that I had recently discovered, and if unchecked, could lead to my own destruction; but I did not sense in her a nature so violent and imprudent that it would allow for such an outcome. Nonetheless., Bruni was made of hardened steel like her parents. I loved her, but whether my love could stand against the onslaught of my suspicions, I had no answer.

I looked at Stanley. "I'll speak with Bruni about all of this, but as to when, I don't know. Perhaps I'll ask the baron about the whole affair tomorrow. Johnny? Any thoughts?"

"I would say that the von H's are quite the family, but having heard some of our own history over the last couple of weeks, I'm not surprised we're on friendly terms. I can tell you one thing: if ever I have to walk down a long flight of stairs with Bruni, I'll do so arm in arm, with a tight grip. I know such dark humor is in bad taste, but I'm worried. There is much about her that we don't know. Asking Hugo might be a start, but what if he takes offense? The repercussions could be catastrophic."

"It's possible," I answered. "But I doubt the baron is unaware of the rumors. Trust is a mutual enterprise. Perhaps he can explain. Still, all this is ancient history. Is there anything more recent that might confirm or substantiate Bernard's warning? Do you know anything about him, Stanley? I certainly don't."

"Not a great deal, although I asked an old contact in Provence about him the other day. He told me that Bernard Montrel was born in Algiers, educated in France, and now manages several successful businesses that he has expanded from there to the rest of Europe. He has a reputation in many circles as a playboy and is rumored to have lost and won over twenty million francs in a single night at the Casino de Monte Carlo in Monaco, where he resides. My friend also heard that the baron and Mr. Montrel were involved in a business transaction that soured and was being overseen by the daughter. Whether before or after their elopement, he couldn't say. Other than that, I know nothing more recent that would give credence to the warning. Unfortunately, we must end at this point. I have duties to perform that are beginning to press."

"Of course. Stanley you've been more than helpful," I said.

He stood as we heard the gravelly crunch of tires on the driveway at the front of the house. Stanley, I was glad to see, was as alert as ever.

8

W e filed out of Stanley's office, through the kitchen, and into the foyer. There, we were joined by Simon to help with the luggage. Stanley opened the front door and went down the steps as Raymond was opening the door for Anne Dodge, Johnny's mother, who got out and looked about her.

She saw Johnny and me and smiled. "Darlings, what a pleasant surprise. We weren't expecting either of you 'til Friday." She kissed Johnny and then me, stepping in closer.

"You're early," she said.

I smiled and said, "Johnny and I came up for the night. He has something to discuss with his father. We're heading back tomorrow morning. How are you?"

"Looking forward to a long weekend. You and Bruni are still coming up on Friday, yes?"

"Of course."

"Well, good. I believe John has some news."

John Sr. came up beside Anne and said, "Can't keep away, right?"

"Something like that," I said.

"It's good to see you. Your being here has saved me making a telephone call. I have some information you'll want to hear, and I take it from your presence that you might have some news as well, but we'll speak more on that in a bit."

After we had finished exchanging greetings, Stanley herded us into the drawing room and excused himself. He returned wheeling a cart of champagne flutes and two bottles of Cristal in silver ice buckets. I realized that I was now the host. I moved toward the bar, but Stanley had the flutes filled in no time. He excused himself once everyone was served and ghosted away, silent as always.

Once more I was made aware that although little had changed on the surface, underneath everything had. What happened and when was now on my shoulders, even though Stanley and his crew kept everything moving seamlessly. I wondered at Johnny's parents' ability to take such vicissitudes in stride. I had detected not a hint of rancor, only their deep affection. I wondered how I would have felt if our positions had been reversed. I turned away to refill my flute at the bar and think on other things. John Sr. followed me.

"May I refill your glass, John?" I asked, sensing his presence and turning toward him.

"Absolutely. Cristal is a wonderful indulgence."

"Yes, it is, but I may have to reassess that decision."

"Let's hope not. Although, to be honest, I'm relieved that such decisions are no longer mine to make. It's what Alice wanted, after all, and that can only be good. You should know that Anne feels the same. The estate is in good hands."

"Thank you for your confidence, although I think it will take some getting used to."

"It will, but give it time. On another matter and relevant in that regard, I am sorry to say that the maintenance trust is still short the 1.5 million agreed to by Hugo and Lord Bromley. The funds were supposed to have been wired in this morning, according to our agreement. When they weren't, I rang Hugo to ask about the delay. He told me that he'd gotten off the phone with your father, who had stated in no uncertain terms that he wanted to see you, speak with you, and feel the treasures in his own hands before any funds would be delivered. In keeping with that intention, he's on his way to this country to do that."

"Good God! I'm not sure which piece of news is worse."

Alone, each was distressing; together, they were staggering, their ramifications overwhelming. Not only was the money being delayed, but I would likely have to meet a man I didn't want to know, even though he was my father. In addition, I would have to convince him to honor his part of the deal. How was I to do that? I cringed at the thought.

When I had received the estate the other week, I had learned that the maintenance trust, which was supposed to provide the funds necessary to keep the estate running, was insolvent and required an additional $4.5 million to make it self-sustaining. Johnny and I had chipped in the two million from the restitution we had received from Maw, Johnny's grandmother, for deliberately sinking our partnership. John, Sr. had added one million, half the amount he owed the trust, leaving $1.5 million yet to be raised. After some negotiations, the baron and my father, through his representative, Malcolm Ault, had agreed to purchase Alice's treasures for $1.5 million, split between them, while also agreeing to keep them at Rhinebeck, a stipulation that I had insisted upon, based on Alice's bequest. The deal had required a formal agreement that Bruni and I marry, a point that allowed the baron and Lord Bromley to join forces rather than bid against each other. That had proved the easiest and most enjoyable part of the negotiations. Now, I had my father to deal with. I had heard much about him that was disturbing. A dark, sadistic, and malignant cunning lay deep within him.

John Sr. continued, "I wish I had better news. It also puts you in an awkward position. Do you invite him here, or don't you?"

"Exactly. The baron and I have a dinner scheduled tomorrow night. Perhaps that is what he wishes to impart. My father coming here will create extraordinary complications."

"Stanley won't like it, and I might go so far as to say the estate won't like it, either."

"Yes, I agree. I'll have to consider what to do, although I can't see a way around not inviting him. I noticed that Hugo didn't ante up, either."

"Hugo has the money, rest assured, but he won't budge until your father has put in his share. It's the way Hugo is, I'm afraid."

"It's a game of who will go first. The estate certainly needs those funds."

"It does indeed, and to resolve the matter, I suggest you invite them both to Rhinebeck this weekend. You can also speak to Hugo about the situation over dinner tomorrow night and how best to proceed. He and Bromley have been playing games for years. The trick, as I see it, is to shift their focus away from each other and onto something else, but to do that you need more players. My mother is in town this weekend and so is my half-sister, Bonnie. It's up to you, of course, but I'm sure they would be interested in the outcome, and neither of them will let Hugo and your father hog the spotlight for any length of time. It changes the game for a start and puts the two rivals on the back foot."

"It's a good idea, and I think the only option available at this time. Can you find out if Bonnie and Mary are willing to come up for the weekend?"

John, Sr. smiled. "They are available, but you'll have to be the one to make the invitation. I'm sure they'll be only too happy to accept. I have it on good authority."

"I'll ring them tomorrow, and thank you, John, for your advice."

"Don't mention it. You're in a tricky position. Anything I can do to assist, I will. All you have to do is ask."

"Thank you for that. By the way, have you ever met my father?"

John Sr. paused before answering. "Yes, I have. It was not a happy meeting. I'll tell you about it in the library after dinner."

Anne slid up beside her husband. "I hate to interrupt, but I'm tired and feel like taking a nap. Will you join me?" she asked, looking at John Sr.

"Of course," he answered. He turned to me. "We'll see you for drinks later."

As they left, I looked around for Johnny, who was gazing out the window at the grounds. I came up beside him.

"Care for a walk?" I asked. "I have news."

"That makes two of us. At least I don't ever have to grab the leash for that damn dog."

"Oh, I wouldn't be so sure of that."

9

J ohnny and I slipped out the French doors and onto the south lawn. The shadows of the trees had lengthened, and the small, puffy clouds that dotted the sky sent dark patches skidding across the freshly cut grass.

"You know something. Tell me," Johnny said as we walked.

"I will, but I need a moment first."

"Fair enough. Smoke?"

Johnny offered me his pack. I took one and lit it. Johnny lit one for himself. We walked and smoked in silence as we made our way down to the canopy of leafy trees that lined the south boundary of the lawn before heading west along it, and then diagonally back to the bench behind the cypress trees. I tried not to think of anything in particular but concentrated on the woods, the grass underfoot, and the sky above. Regardless of the problems coming at me from all directions, my surroundings let me know that they would be here long after I was gone. The thought calmed me as we reached the bench and sat down.

"Mother commented that the estate may have a funding issue," Johnny said.

"She's right, but that's not the half of it. Hugo told John Sr. today that my father wants to speak with me personally and touch the treasures with his own hands before he puts in any money. To make matters worse, he's on his way here."

"To Rhinebeck? Good God! Stanley's going to have a cow!"

"That was my first reaction, although it depends on whether I invite him. That being said, I can't see a way around not doing so. My father won't put up the money until his demands are met."

"Why am I not surprised? It reminds me of that Bertie Ajanian disaster. We arranged that splendid financing, but each time we sat down to sign, he would read over the contract and say, 'But what about this point?' Or 'I want a better guarantee.' Or 'I want a credit of thirty thousand because the funding is taking so long.' We'd spend days working out a solution only to have him do the exact same thing again and again. It was like one of those horrible Oriental tortures I'd read about where the victim was made to believe he would be rescued any day but had to offer up a body part to keep himself from being killed outright. I ended up hating that man."

"I remember that all too well, and then he signed with someone else. I often wondered if that had been the plan all along. I thought he was a jerk. I wonder if my father is playing similar games?"

"It's possible, but to what end? Frankly, I wish we could tell both of them to stuff it."

"I do too, but one and a half million is a chunk to pull together right now, and then there's my engagement. If we blow them off, and Bruni and I decide to go through with our marriage, there will always be a residual animosity between the baron and myself. He wants control of those treasures, and he's a man who always gets his way. He could make things very unpleasant. Perhaps that's what happened to Bernard Montrel?"

"You still love her, don't you?"

The question seemed out of the blue, but it wasn't. Johnny didn't have to say what he was thinking. If Bruni were out of the picture, we would be free to explore alternatives, but he knew me well enough to keep that thought to himself for now. I would have to consider that at some point, and likely we would discuss it, but the shock from what Stanley had divulged still had me reeling. I wasn't ready to think about it. My world was spinning, and the simple fact of loving her was a way to make it stop.

I sighed. "I do. I also haven't heard her side of the story yet."

"Quite right. I think we need to do some serious planning—and soon."

"I agree. John Sr. suggested a get-together this weekend and that I invite Bonnie and Maw to balance the potential friction between Hugo and my father. That, of course, assumes that I invite the man, something I hardly know how to do."

"I know what you mean. I also see where your dog comment came from. Don't think I'd forgotten about it because I didn't mention it immediately, but onto more pressing matters. How you can make Stanley go along with the idea is something I hardly know where to begin. It might even be impossible."

"We'll have to think of something quickly. He has a way of finding out things and predicting them long before they happen. He might even know already. In fact, I see him coming this way."

"What?"

We watched Stanley through the branches that hid us from the house, heading in our direction with a resolute stride. I had never seen Stanley outside the house other than at the front steps greeting guests. That he was on the south lawn and approaching the cypress trees was unusual enough for me to suspect that he had gotten wind of his nemesis's possible visit this weekend.

As he rounded the trees, Johnny and I stood up.

I greeted him. "Stanley, I don't think I've ever seen you out here."

He gave a stiff smile. "When no one is in residence, I find this an ideal spot to reflect. It is soothing. I'm here now to pre-empt any potential uncertainty. I have had physical altercations with Lord Bromley in the past. I find his duplicity abhorrent, his bullying despicable, and his dark soul repugnant. To say that I dislike him would be an understatement. However, I place the needs of the house before any such personal feelings. Should you wish to invite the man, I stand behind your decision. Do what you must. You will always have my support. My only advice is to be extremely careful. He is a rogue and untrustworthy."

With that, he gave me a nod and walked away, but before he rounded the cypress trees, he stopped and turned. "One other matter: the rules of the guest-host relationship are sacred. In ancient Greece, it was called *xenia*. So important were those matters of conduct in the distant past that the father of the gods kept them as his sole jurisdiction. We honor those precepts here. Know full well that should a violation occur by either party, there will be consequences."

He nodded once again and made his way back to the house.

Johnny and I were speechless until Johnny broke the silence. "Good heavens! That was unexpected, but at least that solves one of our pending issues. Thank you, Stanley."

I agreed. "I wonder how he knew?"

"It's classic Stanley, I'm afraid. Ask him, of course," Johnny continued. "But I'm pretty sure it's a trade secret. You do need to ask him about those consequences he mentioned, and what they are specifically. If memory serves, the host has the obligation to ask no questions until the guest is fed and accommodated, and the guest has to be cordial and not take advantage of the host's hospitality, but that's all I recall on the subject.

"The good news is we don't have to worry about Dagmar poisoning the broth or Stanley sticking a knife in your father as he walks up the front steps, although I suppose that is subject to change, depending on what Lord B. chooses to do. Stanley unleashed would not be a happy thought, but we must move onward. We have an hour or so before drinks, and I remembered that you have no clothes here. The suit you're wearing will suffice, but change the tie. I have several. Will you be sleeping upstairs or down?"

"I thought I'd sleep downstairs and check out the firmness of the mattress in Alice's bedroom."

"Really? Well, better you than me," Johnny said with a smile.

"I'm afraid so."

"If you get scared, know that your room upstairs is available. Speaking of which, I think we should wend our way up there now, grab a yellow pad, and go over the several issues we have going. What do you say?"

"Onward and upward, but I'm beginning to appreciate how Sisyphus must have felt."

"He had only a rock to worry about. You, my friend, have weightier problems."

47

ohnny sat on the leather couch with his yellow pad, writing up his notes on the issues that now confronted us. As per usual, Johnny took the lead when it came to planning. Some things would never change, and likely just as well, I thought. He was good at it, and I was feeling unsettled.

While he wrote, I wandered about the common room where Johnny and I had spent much of our younger years. Rows of books lined the walls from floor to ceiling, interrupted by several doorways. The one to the south led to my former bedroom, Johnny's was to the north, and a governess's residence and bathroom lay to the west. The eastern doorway opened onto the narrow stairs that led up to our sanctuary. I pulled out various titles and put them back as I thought about Stanley and his announcement that he would not object to my father's visit. Coming to no immediate conclusion, I sat down in one of the comfortable reading chairs as Johnny finished.

He looked up. "Very well then. I've listed the major issues we need to work through. Are you ready to begin?"

"By all means."

"Excellent. First on my list is the funding shortfall. Both the baron and your father need to honor their agreement, but I sense there are other issues and perhaps other motives behind the delay. As a first step, you must get written invitations to them for a visit this weekend starting on Friday. As a side note,

I would add a personal invitation to the baroness. Elsa likes you, and frankly, we may need her help with Hugo. I would deliver all of them to the baron when you dine with him at 21 tomorrow night. He can pass along the one to Lord B., since we have no idea where he is, and it is likely that Hugo has the resources to find out and get it to him. Agreed?"

"Agreed," I said.

"Next, you must ring up Maw and Bonnie. Father's idea of inviting them to distract Hugo and your father from their rivalry is a good one. He has their phone numbers. The surprise factor of their being here this weekend, although small in the grand scheme of things, may force an adjustment to both of their agendas and allow you to re-exert some measure of control. It's the best we can hope for at this point. Does that make sense?"

"It does. I'll take care of both, first thing tomorrow."

"Excellent. Thirdly, you will have to inform Stanley and company that what was once a quiet weekend in the country has now escalated into a formal affair totaling nine guests plus yourself. With any luck, it will help keep everyone on their best behavior, at least as much as can be expected. I also noted that this weekend will likely be expensive, but I think you must shelve any thoughts of economy, given the circumstances. I would set a bold course. More staff will be required and on this, you must speak to Stanley and Dagmar regarding how to proceed. I should also point out that this is your first experience at being a host of a major shindig, and I would ask their advice about what you need to do and the protocols that must be followed. I would also take the opportunity to get the fine points on that guest-host thing that Stanley mentioned. With me so far?"

"Absolutely, I agree."

"Next, in spite of any uncertainties, Bruni will have to assume the duties of hostess. I've noted that you will also have to speak with her about Stanley's revelations, but that will likely have to wait. As hostess, she will have to handle some potentially awkward moments, such as speaking with her former lover and future father-in-law. I suggest you review with her how she plans on dealing with him. I noted that you might need to consider that as well."

Johnny gave me a long look, as if to ask if I was up to the challenge. In addition, the mere thought of meeting the father I had never met, and the infamous Lord Bromley at that, had me feeling distinctly ill. I knew that as the meeting approached, my agitation would only increase.

"I have no idea what to do. Let's table that for now and let me work on it. As for Bruni, the woman's a professional negotiator. She'll likely handle the situation far better than any of us. What else?"

Johnny paused as if he wanted to say more but checked himself.

"Fair enough," he said at last. "There is time, but I want to hear what you decide regarding your father—and soon. Next on my list is the seating at meals. Although seemingly minor, the arrangements will have to be seriously considered. Mother is a master at such things. Lastly, speak with Dagmar tonight. Probably after dinner would be best. She might be able to explain what's been happening to you."

"Let's hope, but likely a little later than immediately after dinner. I asked John Sr. if he'd ever met my father, and he said he had. Apparently, it wasn't a happy meeting. He said he would tell the story over brandy in the library."

"He met Lord B.? I didn't know that."

"Nor did I. You should also add to your list getting your

father's permission to leave the firm, which was the primary reason for our visit."

"Good heavens. What with all the excitement, I quite forgot. I'll put it down. Okay then, lastly, and on a more mundane note, I have extra toothbrushes, razors and all that sort of thing up here so you won't do without."

"Very thoughtful, Johnny. Thank you. All doable for the most part."

"For the most part, with one or two exceptions. Now, even before our little talk I noted that you had something on your mind."

I sighed. "I've been thinking about that conversation with Stanley. He agreed to my father's arrival far too easily. I expected a massive fight. He stated he's putting the good of the house above his personal feelings, and I'm sure he is, but my father's presence here might be one of those lucky breaks that he's been anticipating for years. He's usually several moves ahead of us mortals, and he's had a great deal of time to think about such an opportunity possibly unfolding."

"Your devious mind is working, I see. I noted that as well. I hope he doesn't off Lord B. until after the funding is secured. Although, come to think of it, if you are his sole issue and stand to inherit in any case, what would it matter?"

Johnny paused and tapped his number two pencil on his teeth. "You know, this scenario might be exactly what Stanley's been hoping for. He has both a calculating mind and the necessary patience to capitalize on such a serendipitous opportunity, which means it's been gone over from every conceivable angle. Under normal circumstances, I would applaud such initiative, but Lord B. is your father and your guest. The host-guest dynamic is a pretty severe constraint, unless—"

I interrupted. "Unless my father really had something to do with Alice's death, then Stanley could make a case for retribution, and justify setting aside the guest-host constraint."

"Exactly. Your father's continued health would depend on whether he played a part. Fascinating. I probably shouldn't be speaking this way. Neither of us should, but intellectually it has its merits."

"I don't know what to think. At this point, it's all conjecture, and yet what we're thinking has a strange feel to it."

Johnny said, "It does. For Stanley to act, he would have to know that Lord Bromley was complicit and had deliberately played a part in Alice's demise. Since her immediate cause of death was quite by accident, I'm not sure how he might reach such a judgement."

"I'm not sure, either, unless he already has the necessary evidence, but that wasn't all I was thinking. It's not my father I'm worried about. It's Stanley."

"How so?" Johnny asked.

"My father will have anticipated such a move and perhaps has a plan of his own, wouldn't you think?"

Johnny sat up. "You're right! Stanley could be in danger himself! After all, he's the only man I know who's managed to give Lord B. a taste of his own medicine. In fact, your father's sudden condition to release his funds only after he sees Alice's treasures is a rather cunning way of arranging such an outcome. We're definitely in over our heads."

"It would seem so, and by inviting him, I will have set all this in motion."

Johnny looked at his pencil for a moment. "Maybe, but maybe not. From what I can tell, the most likely outcome between the two is a Mexican standoff. Think about it. They're evenly matched in the planning department, so neither party has a measurable advantage, but given their history, neither can feel secure enough in the other's presence to stand down and put aside whatever it is they have in store for each other. It would be like two professional gunfighters facing each other with weapons drawn but neither is able to pull the trigger without mutual destruction, hence a stalemate. Would that be so bad?"

"No. That might be the best, as well as the most likely outcome. I feel a little better. But remember, it's usually some unexpected event, like someone opening a door at the wrong moment that starts everyone shooting."

"You've watched too many movies," said Johnny, "but you have a point. Perhaps there is more involved here than we know."

"Like larger forces are at work."

"It would be a stretch, of course, but stranger things have happened here."

"Too true," I said. "Which is why I get the feeling it doesn't matter whether I invite my father or not. He'll be here."

"I agree. Invite him. Don't invite him. Makes no difference. There are so many variables and dynamics in play at this point, with the stakes so large that all we can really do going forward is to weather the storm while trying to maintain a sense of humor. It's going to be one hell of a weekend."

I laughed. "No doubt. I feel better having talked about it."

"And on a happier note, it's time to head down for dinner, but do change the tie. You might even want to chuck it."

"What's wrong with it?" I asked. "It looks perfectly fine to me."

"It's brown."

"There is that."

After changing my tie for one of Johnny's, we made our way to the drawing room for drinks.

——— ◦ ———

11

J ohn Sr. and Anne were already down and chatting by the bar. I decided I could use a vodka tonic with a splash of gin. I went over to the Constable to gaze at it and reflect.

One day I hoped I could simply relax and enjoy the ease of country life, but that seemed a distant possibility. For now, I was only too happy to forget the issues that consumed me and partake in the rituals that marked the Rhinebeck of my past.

Since tonight's dinner was informal, it would be served at 7:15. That specific time was more the result of custom than anything else. Only formal affairs, like those of this coming weekend, would begin at 9:00. Yet in spite of tonight's informality, I noted that John Sr., Johnny, and I each wore suits and ties, and Anne wore a black dress suitable for a fine dinner in the city. I supposed that too was habit, but by donning more formal attire, we assumed the manners that went with and a corresponding respect for the finer things in life that included civilized conversation and the delights of Dagmar's kitchen.

While Johnny and his father chatted about markets, I went over and asked Anne, who was standing alone, how she had enjoyed her nap.

"Marvelously," she said, turning towards me. "I sleep better in this house than any other. I don't know why that is, but it has always been the case. I understand from John that we are to expect a number of guests this weekend."

She was drinking a rather large whiskey, which was unusual. I decided not to comment.

I said, "I believe there will be ten of us, although I've not been able to extend all the necessary invitations. I presumed that you and John will attend, since you were planning to be here in any case."

"Yes, we'll most certainly be here. I doubt anyone will decline, and from the looks of it, I should think it has the potential of surpassing even our recent anniversary in the tension department. Will Elsa be coming?"

"She'll receive her own invitation."

"How very thoughtful. She loves a personal touch. I'm sure wild horses couldn't keep her away."

"She is a force unto herself, so how could I not?"

"Very wise. I also understand your father might be making an appearance." Her lower lip quivered.

"Yes, that's in the cards as well."

"Stanley has agreed?" she asked, wide-eyed.

"He told me that the good of the house outweighs his personal feelings on the matter."

Anne took a large gulp of her drink and sighed. There was hardly any left. "I suppose that's something, although I can't say exactly what."

"Nor can I. I can't really refuse my father's arrival, considering what's at stake. It's one of the reasons that the guest list has expanded. Maw and Bonnie will hopefully be here as well."

"John mentioned that. I'm glad you took his advice. I would also ask Dagmar how she feels about the matter. She will need to be seriously on her game this weekend. Not that I have any doubts, but she can sometimes be a bit free with her concoctions if she's out of sorts and hasn't been consulted."

"Really? You know about those?"

"Oh, do I. Provoked, she makes Stanley look like a pussy."

"A what?"

"Well, maybe that's not the right word, but you get the idea."

"Can you give me an example?"

"Well, I suppose. I'm not breaking a promise … at least I don't think I am. Although I did say to Dagmar that I wouldn't mention it to anyone, but since she's now your staff, I don't see how I can simply not tell you. Perhaps we should stand over by the corner so I can see the door. Stanley has extraordinary hearing, and I would rather have him not overhear me telling you about it."

Anne moved somewhat unsteadily to the far end of the room, and I followed. She placed me so she could look at the door over my shoulder. I wondered how much of her behavior was the result of drinking on an empty stomach, and how much was legitimate concern.

"I know you think I'm being silly, but if you'd seen what poor Charlotte looked like after she swallowed whatever it was Dagmar had prepared, you'd understand. The two had a falling out years before, but Dagmar remembered her. It was all rather shocking. I thought poor Charlotte might lose her mind permanently. She'd wander around at all hours of the day and night with the oddest expression on her face. She couldn't sleep for months after, but there was nothing I could do because that was between her and Dagmar. I wasn't about to interfere, I can tell you. Still, what happened was my fault, really. I thought I had run the guest list for that weekend by Dagmar, but I learned only afterward that I hadn't. Silly me.

Anyway, I only half-liked Charlotte to begin with, but still, it was uncalled for. I mean really. Anyway, what were we talking about? Oh, yes, consulting Dagmar. One moment I was all set to do it and then poof! Gone. Just like that ... right out of my head. You will remember to talk to her, won't you?"

Anne squinted her eyes as she waited for me to say something, like she was trying to focus. She looked unnaturally pale and rocked gently back and forth and then side to side, like a tall tree in a shifting breeze.

"Of course I will. Are you feeling all right?"

"No, not really. Not really at all, in fact. I think I should sit down. I'll take your arm, if you don't mind."

I helped her get seated on the couch and sat next to her.

After a moment to collect herself, she said, "I'm usually rather even-keeled, but this Lord Bromley business is upsetting. The thought of that man actually staying here this weekend has had me terrified ever since I heard of the possibility. Now that it's confirmed, I feel physically ill. Have you consulted Dagmar about him?"

"Not yet. I intend to after dinner."

"You must, but that's quite beside the point." She shook slightly and her voice rose. "Inviting that man and having him sleep in this house? Really, Percy, *whatever* are you thinking? Have you any idea of the consequences? Have you lost your mind? It's ... it's ..." Her lower lip quivered in earnest, and then she held her face in her hands before bursting into tears. Her shoulders shook until she shuddered and took hold of herself. In a soft voice she said, "I'm sorry. It's ... Do you have a handkerchief?"

John Sr. and Johnny had heard Anne's outburst and had come quickly over to the couch. John Sr. sat down on her opposite side and took her hand. "Anne, whatever is the matter?"

"I need a hanky," she replied.

Johnny provided one. She blew her nose loudly and balled it in her fist. "I must look a fright. To answer your question. This Lord Bromley business has unsettled me. John, can you take me upstairs? I need to lie down."

John Sr. helped Anne get up from the couch and while keeping a hold of her arm, gently guided her to the door. When it closed behind them, Johnny asked me, "What the hell was that about?"

"I think it was the combination of a stiff drink on an empty stomach and news of my father's arrival. When I confirmed he was coming, she said she felt ill."

"What is it about this man? He hasn't even arrived, and already there's upset everywhere." Johnny's voice rose. "Everyone seems to have an issue with him. What will happen when he's actually here?"

I looked at my friend. He was agitated in spite of our last conversation. I was sure it was due to his mother's distress. Johnny and I had rarely seen her in such a state. I paused a moment and said softly, "I assume that's a rhetorical question, but I'll answer it. I don't know what will happen. Nobody does, but he's going to show up here because all of us need him to. He is both the problem and the solution. We must get a grip and put aside our feelings, myself included. This is a business transaction. Well, not completely. In my case, I need to see the man, even if it's only to confirm that I'm not like him, but regardless of that outcome, we're closing the deal by Sunday once and for all. You and I must keep that in mind even if everyone else can't seem to."

Johnny paused, took a breath, and seemed to come back into himself.

"Sorry, Percy. You're absolutely right. I need to get a grip. This is business. Everything else is a distraction."

"Yes, it is. You and I have had our share of dealing with all sorts of clients, even the trying ones. Wasn't it you who pointed out that the more money the client had, the more demanding they are?"

"I did, but I think I said *more of an asshole* instead."

"You did. We've completed some dicey transactions with several very hard cases to everyone's satisfaction, and we will again. My father will likely be no different in that regard. I do hate to see your mom upset. I love her and seeing her distressed is the last thing I want. I'm sure she'll be all right in the morning. You'll see."

Johnny smiled. "She will, of course. It's times like this that tell me why you're my partner. There's hope for us yet."

John Sr. entered and came over.

"She'll be fine. I put her to bed. A good sleep will do her good. Sometimes that's all you can do. Ah, there's Stanley. It looks like it's gentlemen's night this evening."

Stanley announced that dinner was served and held open the double doors to the dining room. The table had been arranged with three places at the end nearest the dining room doors and farthest from the kitchen. Stanley and his staff had adapted immediately to Anne's absence without my having said a word. I sat at the head of the table, John Sr. to my left and Johnny to my right. Tonight, the place settings had white embroidered place mats, heavy silverware, and fine white china. Two large silver candelabras were all that lit the table, giving the dining room a restful orange-yellow glow. Each of us relaxed.

In the past, whenever I had felt cold and alone, Dagmar would seem to know. Her remedy at dinner time was always the same: Scotch broth followed by a savory beef stew. It always picked up my spirits. When Stanley served Scotch broth for the soup, I knew that stew would follow, and it did. It had been a grim day, and although I felt neither cold nor alone, I appreciated the thought. Both were exactly how I remembered. Together they filled me with warmth and a feeling of contentment. Because the portions were large and filling, small balls of raspberry sorbet completed the meal.

When we had finished eating, Johnny said he felt much better. I agreed. Even John Sr. was smiling.

"John," I said, "I think we should retire to the library."

"I quite agree," he answered.

As the two filed out ahead of me, I caught Stanley's eye and stayed behind to tell him that I would like to speak with Dagmar in a bit. In parting, I said, "Thank you for letting me know that I'm free to decide what to do. I've made the decision to invite my father rather than allow him to simply show up. In addition, there will be a total of nine guests this weekend, not including myself. Mrs. and Miss Leland as well as the three von Hofmanstals will be here. We should go over the arrangements at some point. You and I need a plan."

"Tomorrow would be best for us to sit down together, Stanley said. "This weekend is likely to be unique, and such things are best taken up early in the day rather than late at night when our fears come to visit us more often than our hopes. I have spoken to Dagmar. She will be available when you're ready."

"Thank you. Is there anything I need to do about where I'm sleeping tonight?"

"All is prepared. You're in the west wing. I will wake you in the morning."

"Thank you, Stanley. If I don't see you before the end of the evening, have a good night."

"And you too, sir." He seemed about to say something but refrained.

With that, I departed to the library.

12

“ I met Lord Bromley in person some years ago. It was Hugo who introduced us,” said John Sr.

We had each settled into comfortable leather chairs. The ritual of pouring brandy and lighting cigars had finished, and John Sr. began.

“Percy, Anne was quite upset by the news that your father will be visiting and with good reason. Each of us has a history. I am hesitant to tell you the specifics, but both of you are mature enough, I think, to put aside any feelings you might have for her and recognize that Anne was once a young woman, likely no different than those you have met and gone out with. Sometimes that is difficult to appreciate. Age makes us appear worn out, but our hearts and minds are fundamentally the same.

“This weekend will be a test for all of us. It will be for me, for Anne, as you will discover, for Stanley, and for both of you. Some men are put on this Earth to test us. They overturn much of what we think is correct, appropriate, or even civilized. They grate upon our sense of rightness, and yet they are successful, and from all accounts, suffer only rarely. They overturn our ideas of divine justice, or even ordinary justice.

“In the financial world, we meet many of that type, and often have to work with them. We say we shouldn’t, and we would certainly rather not, but economics is remarkably democratic in that regard. We all must make a living, and I find it perverse that such personalities are often the very ones we *must* do business with.

"The maintenance of this house is a case in point. It takes money. Lots of it, and unfortunately those hardened souls are often the very people we need to deal with to make that happen. Nothing comes free, and it's more a question of how *far* we will compromise our standards, rather than *if* we will. Such men are pitiless, and they will maneuver us to give away far more than we would like, and in many cases, far more than we can afford.

"To succeed, we often feel that we must beat them at their own game, which means that over time we end up looking in the mirror and see their image staring back. We turn hard, callous, and brutal because that is what's required. We become what we despise the most as that other personality takes over our lives, including how we deal with family and with friends. I say this because Bromley is that kind of man, and to deal with him effectively you, Percy, will need to embrace a hardness I doubt you will enjoy. Do you understand that?"

I looked at John Sr. through the cigar smoke. "I can't say I am prepared. The closer the time comes, the more anxious I seem to get."

John Sr. nodded. "It will not be easy for you. The question is, must we become like them to defeat them and succeed? I don't think so. There is an answer, and it has been around for some two thousand plus years. In all my looking, I have yet to find another. Do you know how the ancient Greeks dealt with bad men?"

"Tell me," I said.

"There is an old, old story. It goes like this. A house was robbed. Several men were caught by the locals, but no one knew who specifically committed the crime. A wise man was asked to adjudicate who was responsible. He was well known by many and was considered a bit of a magician—at the very least he was thought to be blessed by the gods with an uncanny intuition. He gave each of the men a stick of wood of the same length. He told everyone present, including the suspects, that the stick of the guilty man would grow overnight by an inch or more as he slept. He had each placed in separate cells. In the morning, the wise man was easily able to identify the criminal."

Johnny asked, "So, you're telling us that the guilty man's stick grew an inch like he predicted?"

"Quite the opposite, in fact," answered John Sr. "The criminal had bitten off an inch, to be sure it hadn't grown."

"Very clever," said Johnny.

"Very clever, indeed, but in that story lies your answer. We must outwit them rather than become them. And rest assured, Bromley is a bad man. I will now tell you of our meeting.

"It was some years back. Anne and I had been married for several years. I was at Hugo's castle for a night on my way to a meeting in Geneva. I often stopped at Hugo's, not only to see him, but as a means of breaking up a business trip and turning it into something more. Anne was with Elsa in Paris, and I was to meet her there when I completed my business.

"My first impression of Lord Bromley was that of an energetic man, who was both handsome and engaging. His clothing was immaculate; however, his manners were less so. When he learned my name as we were introduced, he scoffed and said, 'You're the man that married Anne? I would have expected her to do better.'

"Hugo told him to be civilized while in his house. The man shrugged and said, 'You're quite right, Hugo. Sorry about that, Dodge. Long trip.' He turned and asked Hugo if his people could take care of his bags and show him to his room. Hugo saw to it and came back. We had been sitting in the main hall in front of the fireplace having a drink when we were interrupted by Bromley's arrival. Hugo sat down and sighed. 'I'm sorry about that, old friend. Bromley can be such an ass. He was supposed to arrive tomorrow. You will have to put up with him. Will that be a problem?'

"I'd known of him of course, but this was before I had learned the full extent of his dealings with my sister—well, I won't go into it other than to say it was lucky I didn't know it at the time. Had I known, I'm not exactly sure what I would've done. I guess I'll find out this weekend, but our meeting then was without that knowledge, and I was willing to set aside the opinions of others and make my own.

"I remember being at once conflicted in his presence. He was so dapper, smooth, and magnetic. His apology was in all respects sincere and delivered in a way that only the English can pull off, like he had just committed a foul, but with the expectation that once apologized for in a civilized manner, it was meant to be forgotten. The odd part was that I went right along with it. I was repulsed, and yet I was curious. His comment about Anne was wounding, but what was absent, it seemed to me, was the deliberate intention to do so. It was odd, and I told Hugo that. Hugo shrugged and said that was Bromley.

"After a minute, I asked Hugo once again what Bromley was referring to with his comment about Anne, and Hugo looked wary. He knew something, but I could tell by his expression that he was reluctant to tell me. Now, Hugo and I, even at that time, had been friends for a long while. I have put my life in that man's hands on several occasions. There is great trust between us, and we can be extremely frank with each other. He told me he would tell me, but only when I was leaving, not before. I answered that it was obvious that Bromley and Anne must have had an affair, or a relationship of some kind, and Hugo said rather cryptically that there are all kinds of relationships, some more wholesome than others. At that point Bromley entered the room.

"We had dinner, the three of us. In spite of the awkward beginning, it turned out to be an entertaining experience.

"I am not a particularly jealous man. I don't know why that is, but I am not. What Anne had done before she and I met was hers. I played no part, and any relationships she might have had, I was quite able to put aside under the heading of 'before.' The 'after' belonged to me, and I will always be grateful for that blessing. I don't think I am belittling her by saying that I was not her first lover. Perhaps I should not be talking about this, but we are adults, and people are people.

"I suppose all would have ended well, and this would be all I have to tell you, but Bromley had brought his own car and offered me a lift to the train station. I agreed. I had not pushed Hugo to tell me what he knew for the simple reason that I felt it would upset him, and such is our relationship. I would rather err by not pursuing a hurtful subject, even if it was about Anne's past. Bromley had a Porsche sports car. He drove it immensely fast and with the top down. There was little chance for conversation. I got out with my bag, but before he drove off, he said to me as if we were discussing the weather or a horse, 'That girl of yours enjoys the whip. Something to put in your file. Safe trip.' And off he drove, as if there was nothing in the world the matter."

I looked at Johnny. He had a lost look on his face. John Sr. caught his expression as well and said, "I am sorry you had to hear that, but it is what we don't know, those things that are so unknown we can't even conceive of them, that are most likely to cause us harm. It was certainly true for me at that moment as Bromley drove off. If either of you would prefer to take a break at this point, I can do that, but know that there is more."

Johnny said he wished to visit the bathroom but would like to hear the rest of what his father had to say. I elected to stay.

When Johnny had left, I said, "This is hard on him. He is quite sensitive when it comes to her."

"He is, but as I said, this man will test us all. Don't think for a second this won't come up. He'll find a way when Johnny is the most vulnerable to spring it on him and then what? Johnny explodes and exactly at the wrong time. Action. Reaction. With the truth known, we no longer need react to the collapse of what we thought we knew when it is confirmed. We are less likely to be compromised. I have debated telling both of you, him in particular, but a little pain now will prevent a great deal later on, when you will have need of all your faculties—and believe me, you will need them this weekend."

Johnny entered the room. He looked out of sorts, but he had a resolute expression on his face, and that was the best I could hope for.

"I'll continue with my story," said John, Sr. "I did not immediately seek out Anne but decided to keep Bromley's comments to myself. I canceled the trip to Geneva, including my business there, and went in search of your mother, Percy. She lived in Florence, and I went to see her to find out what Bromley knew that I didn't. She told me what had happened, but only after a great deal of effort and emotional turmoil.

"The story she told was this. In her final year at school, Anne had had a dark period. She and Mary were roommates in Lausanne. Anne had been depressed but had seemed to make an unexpected recovery. She was less gloomy but more prone in the opposite direction. She would take constant risks, even in as simple a matter as crossing the street. She would giggle at her close escapes from being run over. She had also started drinking early in the day, and Mary grew alarmed. One afternoon, Mary came back unexpectedly to the room they shared, and Anne was in the shower. Anne stepped out, not knowing Mary was there. Mary saw that much of Anne's body was covered in welts, as if she had been struck forcefully many times. Anne tried to cover herself, but Mary saw what she saw and demanded to know the answer. Anne explained that she was seeing a man, and that by feeling pain, she felt better. In fact, she liked the sensation very much. I will spare you the details. Mary then did a very brave thing. She confronted the man in person and threatened to expose his abuses to the school unless he left her alone. An agreement was reached, and that was that. Hour by hour and day by day, Mary helped Anne through her crisis.

"She hardly left Anne alone until she recovered. Anne in many ways owes Mary her life. They graduated from the school and moved to Florence to study art and work in the auction business. There, they learned the ins and outs of the art world. What Mary hadn't told Anne was that she had fallen under the man's spell, and they had become lovers. She kept her affair secret and made sure that Anne had no further contact with him. That man was Lord Bromley, your father, Percy, whom Anne hasn't seen since. As I said before, we will all be tested."

Johnny threw his cigar into the fire and stood up. "I think I'll kill him," he said through gritted teeth.

"Sit down!" commanded John Sr. "Haven't you been listening?"

"The guy's an abomination!"

"That he may be," John Sr. replied.

"I'll still kill him," said Johnny, scowling as he sat back down.

John Sr. took a drag from his cigar before continuing. "Do you know why I have only a single painting in my office and no other, Johnny?"

"What has that to do with anything?"

"You've seen it. Describe it to me."

"It's a large Lichtenstein of a smoldering wreck in the far distance and the words 'This is going to cost me!' in one of those cartoon bubbles from someone in the wreck."

"That is correct, and do you know why I have that painting, and only that painting, on my office walls?"

"No, I don't."

"I have it because of my decision to cancel that meeting in Geneva. The bitter truth is I was played. Guess who drove to Switzerland and picked up the deal that I'd abandoned?"

"My father," I said.

"What?" said Johnny.

"Precisely. I never want to forget that. Bromley showed up at the exact right time and said the exact right things, and what did I do? I let my heart rule my head, and it cost me personally a large sum. It cost Dodge Capital many times more than that. He knew exactly what he was doing. This is the man who will be coming to this house and come he will. It's time to settle accounts, but it won't be done with emotion. It will be done with brains, because in the end that is all we really have to keep us from becoming like those we dislike most. Johnny, your mother did what your mother did. Was it wrong? How can we know? We are not her. She has her shortcomings, as do we all, but she is the complicated woman that I love, and that is good enough for me. And it has to be good enough for you, too, Johnny."

I watched Johnny take hold of his rage. Finally, he nodded and said, "I'm sorry, Father. And I'm sorry Percy. We're in so much trouble."

"Maybe," said John Sr., "but maybe not. We need to work together, and above all, we need to play smart. It's either that or become like him, and then we'll all go to jail for having killed him."

13

I left father and son together in the library and found Dagmar in the kitchen sitting at her table, the spot she reserved for serious conversations.

"Dagmar, I'm sorry if I've kept you up."

"Not at all," she said. "I was making tea. Please sit down."

Dagmar laid out a service. When all was prepared, and the tea poured, she seated herself and said, "You're back earlier than expected. Stanley has spoken to me of your concerns. Perhaps you can tell me more specifically?"

I briefly sketched out the events of the last week.

Dagmar looked thoughtful when I had finished, although I had told her much that she likely knew already. The kitchen was the information center of all that concerned Rhinebeck. What was known there was often surprising in its details, but Dagmar as well as Stanley understood that taking the emotional pulse of those in their charge and managing the fluctuations, was as important as the accumulation and processing of information. Dagmar looked at her hands and then at me before she spoke.

"If you're looking for what to do specifically as to the several points you mentioned, I cannot tell you, although I have some thoughts, and perhaps some words that you should heed. Would you like to hear them?"

"I think anything you say would be helpful."

"Very well. I'll be brief, for it is late. In regards your fiancée, the most useful tool to have in a kitchen is a sharp knife. Your lady has a hard edge, and she has likely done things that many would object to. She is both smart and beautiful, and that is as much a burden as a help. Likely she has had to use that hardness to keep her place in the world. Her ladyship was no different in that regard. If I had to choose a life's companion, I'd pick a sharp knife with a hard edge to have by my side. I keep no dull knives in my kitchen, and you shouldn't either, but yours is not my kitchen."

Dagmar paused and sipped her tea.

"Now, this weekend is likely to be filled with tension. I'll keep that in mind when I prepare the menus, which I would rather you leave in my hands. Stanley has briefed me on the participants and his decision to allow your father to set foot here. I make no objection on that point, but as to the running of the house, the less you need to decide on, the better. Leave everything to us—all of it. Your wits are best applied in other directions, judging from what you've said."

Dagmar continued, "In that regard, Johnny will need minding. He's a good boy, but loses his way when it comes to women, particularly his mother. He broods, like you. Keep him busy, even if you have to make up tasks for him to complete. It happens often enough. A kitchen maid feels low, boyfriend troubles, who knows? I will have her make the dish again, not because she got it wrong, but because she didn't get it right. Her attention was on her hurt. I'll shift her mind until all that's left are the working hands. No sorrow goes out to those that eat what I prepare, unless I choose it. Being in charge is as much about finding suitable work to do as managing what is done. Does what I've said make sense?"

"It does," I said. "I'll leave all the arrangements for this weekend up to you and Stanley. I'll also speak with Bruni. You and I are of similar minds regarding her, but I doubt it will be easy. She is not for the meek, but as you pointed out, there is a price to everything."

"I am pleased to hear that, although I fear you may be tested. Understand that it is our own willingness to accept what we've received that determines how we feel, and whether we are truly happy with it. Now, you wish to know whether your intuitive gift will return?"

We had arrived at what was foremost in my mind.

"Will it?" I asked.

"It is the question. Gifts and aptitudes of the kind we're speaking about are strange things. They can slip through our fingers if we're not careful. Often when they're gone, they're gone. Having said that, I may have a way, but know that such a method is by no means guaranteed. What you may receive might be different from what you expect. Consider carefully your decision before you choose. Is that understood?"

"It is."

"Very well. Before we spoke, I gave Stanley something to leave by your bed. Drink it before you sleep and remember: all remedies can harm as well as heal. I've answered your questions and said what I've had to say. I will say good night now as I'll be up early."

14

I stopped by the library to see if Johnny and his father were still up, but the lights were out. I went in, poured myself a small single malt, and lit a cigar. I sat in one of the leather chairs in front of the fireplace and gazed into the orange glow of the dimming coals. I smoked, drank, and considered what to do.

John Sr. had said that I might find a way out of my labyrinth by being clever and bright. The truth was I had always felt that Johnny had those qualities in far greater quantities than I. Often I was jealous of his brilliance. The troubles he created for both of us were the result of a mind that needed excessive stimulation to feel alive. I was smart enough to see that need in him, but not clever enough to avoid its consequences. Rather than learning to think for myself, I remained content to be an audience of one, even if the price of admission included being dragged onto the stage as a participant in his adventures as if they were my own.

Our relationship had changed when I had fled to California, but having returned, I still depended on him a great deal. This was not necessarily a weakness, I realized. Utilizing the talents of those around me was not something to be cast aside merely to prove my own specific worth; nonetheless, tonight's decision was mine, and mine alone. I was elated by the possibilities the opportunity might afford me, but equally anxious as to the possible results.

The dilemma was familiar. I was often too afraid of losing to take many chances. Decision-making, I had once naïvely reasoned, ought to be established on a firmer foundation than trusting to chance and subjective probabilities, but reality had proved altogether different. Success, I discovered, depended as much on luck and on taking calculated risks as hard work. It was a truth that I'd protested, and my many attempts to better myself at risk-taking had only perfected my capacity to worry and grow anxious.

The intuitive gift I had received when I was last at Rhinebeck had changed all that. It had allowed me to understand that luck ebbed and flowed through everything, and with it something else. I could see the patterns that lay before me and was able to risk more while worrying less. I had also felt wonderfully alive and connected to the world.

I debated whether that intuition had been a crutch—another excuse to give up thinking for myself to avoid personal responsibility. Perhaps it was, but like the relationship between Johnny and me, I needed to strike a better balance. As I considered that, I knew that I would give anything and everything to regain that sense of certainty. I thought to myself that if death was the only long-term outcome, then why not be brave, and trust that all would turn out well? It surely beat dying incrementally each and every day.

I arose and threw my cigar into the fireplace. It was now or never. I left the half-finished drink for someone else to clean up. I was certainly paying people enough to do so. I'd had enough of being afraid.

I walked down the hall from the library and stopped for a moment before the door of Alice's apartment. I had some trepidation about sleeping in what used to be her bed, but it was either that or climb the several flights of stairs to my old room at the top of the house. There was also the drink that Dagmar had concocted that Stanley in all likelihood had placed on the nightstand. I reaffirmed my decision and opened the door.

Once again, I admired the tasteful mixture of gray and black and the unusually thick carpet. Stanley, or one of the staff, had left the light on for me in the sitting room. The hidden library beckoned silently, but waking Stanley because I set off an alarm was something I didn't want to do. I turned off the light and made my way to the bedroom through the connecting door. The lights were on, and the bed turned down. On a side table was a small, cut crystal glass containing a dark liquid placed in the center of a small white linen napkin. Beside the drink were two modest but ancient-looking volumes. I took off my jacket and tie and draped them over the chair in front of the table and mirror that Alice had used to apply her makeup. All her cosmetics, brushes, and combs had been removed. The picture of Alice in fancy dress wearing the Egyptian necklace had been placed there instead. I picked it up. She gazed back at me from beneath the glass inside a polished silver frame. I touched the surface above her face and thanked her for all she had done for me. I said a silent prayer to help me, if she could, and put the picture down. A pair of pajamas and a bathrobe had been laid out for me. Stanley had thought of everything.

Having changed and gotten ready for bed, I sat down on the side closest to the little table and the drink. As usual there were no directions or indications of what would happen if I drank it. Perhaps that was just as well, I thought. I picked up the glass and sniffed it. There was a hint of alcohol, which meant it was a tincture of some kind, but I couldn't anticipate its taste from the smell. I looked at the liquid closely, but other than being opaque and reminding me of black coffee, the contents gave no further information, even after holding the glass up to the light. Resolved to carry through, I downed the mixture in one swallow. The taste was one I wouldn't recommend: a hint of mint and cinnamon perhaps, but with a strong, earthy aftertaste. I waited for an effect, but there was none.

Stanley had placed a two-volume set of Coleridge's *Biographia Literaria* for me to read. To my delight, they looked to be first editions published in 1817. There was a note in Stanley's spikey script beneath them advising me to read chapter XIV concerning the "willing suspension of belief." I thought that entirely appropriate. I lay down on the bed and began to read Coleridge's lengthy prose. Whether it was his words or the tincture, I felt myself slipping away. I was barely able to switch off the bedside light before I felt myself falling.

15

I awoke disoriented and barely able to move in what appeared to be early morning. I was lying on my back looking up at the dark trunks of cypress trees that stretched up toward the streams of gray clouds that scudded above.

Where am I?

I lay still to try and orient myself. I watched the wind gusts whip the treetops and heard the surrounding grove moan and sigh in answer. The trees bent and straightened in a syncopated rhythm above me, calling out to each other for reassurance in stuttered groans.

If I'm quiet as a mouse, I thought, *no one will find me.*

I felt confused and shivered from the cold. Behind my head and very close, I heard a single heavy footfall as it compressed the surrounding twiggy brush and afterward, nothing. I held my breath. The trees swayed above to keep me company as a large raindrop hit my forehead. The drop rolled and slipped between my eyebrows into my right eye. I didn't dare move.

Don't even blink. Be still as the dead.

I heard what may have been another step, farther away. Whatever it was had moved off—at least I hoped it had. I lay unmoving, wondering if the fading steps were a ruse, another trick to lull me into a sense of feeling safe and thereby make me give away my hiding place. I waited, listening.

After a minute, the rain began in earnest. I heard the drops hitting the outer branches and then their steady drips inside, but still I waited. Only after I had begun to shiver from the cold wetness did I silently sit up, wary and alert. I looked around. I knew this place. Johnny and I would hide here years ago. We called it the Cathedral. It was our sanctuary, a place where our imaginations ruled, and anything could happen. We made up stories here. I must have sought out this place as a refuge, but from what and why were questions for which I had no answers. I looked at my legs. I was still in my pajamas. They were soaked, and I was freezing. My feet were bare. This wasn't any make-believe.

I turned to look behind me. The entrance to the grove was as I remembered. I scraped my way through, feeling the twigs and undergrowth dig into my legs, feet, and hands, scratching my skin. With difficulty, I crawled out and onto the lawn. I stood, and the cold rain soaked me completely. The house, dark and still, was still there, and as I walked toward it, my feet were numb as water squished up between my toes from the soggy grass. I wondered how I could get back inside without disturbing Stanley or one of the staff. Logically, I thought that I must have unlocked at least one entrance in my flight from the house. The closest was one of the French doors to the drawing room. I saw that it was slightly ajar.

Relieved, I entered and almost cried out. The drawing room was bare. No furniture. No paintings, no tapestries—just the parquet floor with a thin covering of dust. I looked around bewildered in the silent tomblike room. Several of the other French doors had broken panes, and the shattered glass lay scattered about them. The house felt cold, sad, and abandoned. What had happened here? Where was everyone? Where had they gone? All that remained were random hints of its former occupants where an indentation in the wood floor told of the weight of a sofa leg or where a table had stood. I felt a strange mixture of sadness and a growing sense of panic.

I was so cold. I needed a blanket—anything to warm myself. I had to search the house for whatever I could find. It was that or freeze to death.

I passed through the drawing room and into the foyer. The same state of neglect lay all about. The table and the clock were gone. Dried leaves were piled against the inside of the front door. Down the hallway to my left, I saw that the door to Alice's apartment was open. I padded in that direction with only the echoing slap of my wet bare feet to keep me company. Entering, I saw that the door to the hidden library was gone and odd pieces of paper were strewn about inside. The shelves were bare. As I moved toward the room where Alice had slept, I heard something scrape along the floor behind the closed door—her bedroom, my bedroom. I froze. Fear gripped me. I quickly turned and ran back the way I'd come. I was suddenly terrified. I was a stranger here—a trespasser. How could I possibly explain myself?

I ran toward the servants' quarters and the stairway that led to the rooms above. I must be dreaming, I thought, only I can't seem to wake up. I had to hide. I passed the trunk room to my right and saw the door was open. I stopped. A little light from the window in the hallway leaked into the space. I took a step over the threshold. Piles of broken luggage lay everywhere. The giant trunk lay along the far wall. As I slid some of the broken bits out of the way to see more clearly, something sharp poked my left foot.

I reached down for what pricked me and felt rather than saw that whatever I had stepped on was caught in a kind of grating. I worked the metal object loose and carried it to the

81

light by the doorway. It was the key, the intricate one for the black trunk by the wall.

I began to shiver uncontrollably, not from fear but from deadly cold. I knew that in a few minutes I would stop shivering and be hypothermic. Not long after, I would die. I had to get warm. Perhaps there was something I could use inside the trunk? It had almost killed me once, and I thought it strangely ironic that maybe this time it would be my salvation.

I was shaking so hard by then, that I could barely put the key in the lock. On the third try I succeeded. I turned it. The lid opened smoothly as it had before. The stench that assailed me was horrendous. In the moment before I could cover my nose with my hand and turn away, I saw what vaguely looked like a small, mummified corpse. I looked away to breathe and back again. It was lying on its side in a fetal position with one hand to its mouth, like it was sucking its thumb. I stepped back toward the door to take a breath and looked at the trunk. The pristine white satin that lined the lid looked gray in the dim light. Some of it hung down in shredded strips, while other parts were streaked with dark, claw-like stains.

I knew in a dreamlike way what had happened here all those many years ago. I must have dropped the key rather than placed it in the lock in my hurry to hide before Johnny could find me. I held one hand to my face to cover my nose as I approached the trunk and looked inside again. The figure wore shorts, like the ones I had worn that day.

What prevented me from simply screaming in my panic were three things that happened almost simultaneously. The first was that my shivering stopped. The second was the awareness of a dim, slightly luminescent figure behind me and to my left. It said in a calm voice, "You must get in the trunk.

If you don't, you will die from cold. Get in the trunk." The last, shortly thereafter, was a scraping sound of something moving in the hallway outside the room.

"HIDE!" the voice cried out. *"HIDE! GET IN NOW! NOW! NOW! NOW!"*

I got in the trunk. I felt the bones of the corpse next to me dig into my calves, thighs, and buttocks. I lay down anyway. Before I closed the lid, I pulled the key out of the lock. The lid of the trunk slid down smoothly, followed by a click. Whatever was outside could not get in. Vaguely I thought I could also not get out. I knew that when dying from cold, everything made sense, but with a peculiar logic that only the desperate can manage. My decision to lock myself inside made sense to me. Of course, it did.

It was very dark and stank awfully, and I began to lose consciousness. I was exhausted beyond anything I had ever experienced. I was finished, and my life was finally over. I was so very tired, even breathing was an effort. Before I surrendered altogether, I heard someone calling, *"Help me! HELP ME!"* The cry sounded like that of a woman. I wondered who it was as something very large and very strong pounded and clawed on the trunk lid. My hiding place gave a terrific lurch, and I passed out.

16

I awoke, kicking at the covers as if they were ropes that held me to the bed and sat up in a rush. I was in Alice's room, but I could barely make out my surroundings in the dark. I breathed in great, convulsive gasps. I could barely catch my breath. I disentangled myself from the sheets, got up, and leaned over the bed, supporting myself with my arms. I willed myself to be calm. I was so horribly cold. I staggered to the bathroom and turned on the shower, hoping it would heat up quickly—anything to get warm. I stepped inside, pajamas and all, feeling the heat build and almost screamed from the pain as the hot water thawed my frozen limbs and fingers. The pain was so intense, I lay down at the bottom of the shower, and all I could do was cry.

After a time, I could stand, and I took my pajamas off. I left them in a soggy pile in a corner of the shower. Once I had dried myself, I considered the pajamas once again. I picked them up and hung them over the shower door. If anything, I felt heartily glad to be alive, but that was all. I couldn't process what had happened to me. I took what clothes I had from the night before and put them on—everything but the tie. I shook occasionally, but my convulsive trembling had at least subsided. I stepped over to the window near the table to peek at the weather and pulled the drapes apart. The light was feeble, and mist blanketed the grounds. The grass near the window was wet and gray. It had rained not long ago. I closed

84

the drapes, turned on a light. and picked up my watch. I saw that it was just past six. I then noted the empty crystal glass. My neck and shoulders ached, and my feet hurt, but my mind was oddly clear and sharp. If my ordeal had been a dream, or merely the result of some hallucinogenic cocktail, the memory was as real as any I had ever experienced. The details of that abandoned house and my terror were frozen permanently in my mind.

I stood, wondering what to do, and picked up the picture of Alice. I looked at it carefully before asking her image, "Was that you?" I put the picture down. She hadn't answered, but then I knew she wouldn't. I hadn't lost my mind, at least not yet. My benefactor had traveled down many paths searching for answers as to what haunted her, but whether she found them in the end, I didn't know. For now, it was far too early to consider such grim circumstances. The one thing of which I was certain was that I was in need of coffee, very hot and very strong. Everything else was not so clear. I decided to make my way to the kitchen.

I had never walked through the house at this time of the morning. The smell of polish was the same, but the light was subdued, and the colors muted. I passed through the drawing room and the dining room to the pantry and the kitchen. All was as it should be. The contrast between the two houses was distressing. I found Dagmar and Stanley sitting at the kitchen table, drinking tea.

"May I have some coffee?" I asked. Remembering my manners, I added, "Please."

They rose and offered me a chair. Their eyes, at first bright and questioning, grew troubled as I sat down.

Dagmar went briskly to the stove and poured me coffee in a mug. She returned to the table and gave it to me. I drank, holding the cup in both hands. It was wonderfully hot. Compared to the numbing cold that seemed to leach away all hope, I doubted I would curse anything hot ever again.

"Something has occurred," said Stanley, looking at me.

"Tell us," said Dagmar, watching me as well.

I looked at both of them, still clutching my coffee. What was I to say? What could I say? I shook my head, put the cup down on the table but still held onto it, and told my story. They didn't interrupt.

When I had finished, Dagmar folded her hands and looked down at them. After a long pause, she said, "The effects of that which you drank can take strange turns."

She looked up at me. "You must be careful now. Look at ordinary things, examine them closely, until you are more here than there. You have a gift, I think. Perhaps even a great one, although you may not think so. Unfortunately, not all gifts are happy. I could tell you to learn to use it well, but you would think me cruel, when I am not. You must give it time. Lastly, I suggest you remain here, at least for the next few days. Stanley, why don't you two go to your study? I must think on what has happened, and I must do so by myself."

Dismissed, Stanley and I rose and went to his office. Once seated, Stanley produced a cut crystal glass with a double splash of his reserve.

"Drink this," he said. "I'm sure you could use it."

The whiskey helped to steady me, and after a minute I asked, "What do you think happened, Stanley?"

He looked at me. "I don't rightly know, but let's start with the facts. You consumed a powerful tincture that Dagmar had prepared. You experienced something as a result. All else is speculation. Events and our interpretations of them are two different classes of things that are but loosely connected. I

86

could make the case that unconsciously you are certain that this house, and everything connected to it, will land in ruin. It is a possibility and would make some sense."

"Unfortunately, it would."

"It is the worst possible interpretation. There is another. What you experienced could be about the past and a possible future—specifically, what might have happened had her ladyship not found you in the trunk that day."

Stanley turned and poured himself a splash of his reserve in a glass as well. He sipped it before continuing.

"I do recall that day. You and Johnny were playing hide and seek, and you managed to lock yourself in *that* trunk. Had her ladyship not become intuitively aware that something was amiss and then acted on her fears, what you saw might very well have come to pass. I remember clearly the fright you gave her that day—not only her, but all of us."

"You too?"

"Oh, yes. The incident spoke loudly to me of the transitory and impermanent nature of existence—how quickly life can turn on a mere whim—yours—in choosing that particular place to hide; and hers—in deciding to seek you out. All our lives swayed precariously that day, first one way and then the other. We never knew how close disaster had come until afterward, when knowing made no difference. The precariousness of the outcome and the potential repercussions had you not been found disturbed me greatly at the time. It still does. It became clear to me that random events can affect all our lives and often in underappreciated ways. It was a significant moment."

"Good God. I had absolutely no idea. I should think you would have been pleased, given who my father is."

"It was because I knew him that the incident affected me the way it did. I will tell you how. Not long before, I had confronted her ladyship with my suspicions about your father. When she confirmed what I'd suspected, I decided to leave her employ. She convinced me to stay on, and we reached an uneasy agreement. Both of us would withhold any outward indications of our inner feelings about you. I adopted a detached indifference, and she did the same.

"I hated your father. I still do. By hating him, I hated you, but no one gets to choose their parents or the circumstances of their birth. Over time, I recognized the unfairness of my attitude and discovered that it wasn't my dislike of you that I had to keep in check but rather the opposite. You were a peculiar child, intelligent but strangely tentative. Johnny was your opposite number, but together you formed a cohesive unit that was quite unassailable. Dagmar and I would laugh out loud, often to tears, relaying your escapades to each other. The expression, 'what *will* they think of next?' became a standing joke between us.

"You and Johnny gave us hints of what it was like to be alive and free, unbridled by the constraints that adults must assume. Had you died, the effect on all of us would have been monumental. Her ladyship saw in you a kind of legacy. Had you succumbed, she would have been heartbroken. Johnny would have developed an impenetrable shell beneath which he would have destroyed himself. Mrs. Dodge would have become inconsolable, weighed down by guilt. Mr. Dodge, too, would have pined as his wife grew unapproachable and then unreachable. Many relationships would have sundered, and this house become a tomb of broken dreams."

We were silent for a time.

I said, "It seems unreal, given that I was of such little consequence."

Stanley looked at me. "It's not so hard to understand. Children are our promise of a future. When a child dies, a light goes out in the world. All that future goes with it, and someone *must* pay."

He took a sip of his drink. "For me, it is a law of human conduct. Parents or guardians will inevitably blame themselves or each other for a child's death, even when they are not at fault. Sometimes they are. Few marriages can withstand the heartache and emotional strain that recovery from such a loss requires. One either turns inward and kills oneself emotionally or saddles the other with a sin that can lessen over time but never be wholly forgiven."

I sensed a deep hurt within his past. I could say nothing. After a time, I said, "I never considered that."

"That, too, is a law, I think. We rarely understand the downstream effects of our interactions and relationships— how they cascade through the world. It is humankind's greatest blindness. Everything that we do matters. Everything."

Neither of us spoke but sipped our drinks, lost in thought.

I broke the silence. "What you said is true. We rarely appreciate the consequences of simply living. It certainly makes me wonder. One thing I do know, and which this experience has made clear to me once again, is that I owe Alice my life."

Stanley nodded. "You do, and more besides, if that is possible, which leads me to my next point."

Stanley took another sip and asked, "Do you recall that letter from Sir Henry, the one about sleeping in her ladyship's room?"

"I do very well."

"Both you and Sir Henry had similar experiences with two points in common: the intense cold and her ladyship's apparent cry for help; that is, if it was her ladyship you heard."

"Do you think the cry for help was hers?"

"Much of what occurred in your experience points in that direction."

"It does."

"If it was her ladyship, then yours is now the second indication that she fell into a dark place. It is not confirmation by any means, but still, it is deeply disturbing to me."

"I feel similarly. I don't know what can be done about it, if anything."

"For now, nothing. We must await further developments. I would also suggest that you remain here through this weekend. You and I have the preparations to attend to for a start. Secondly, you might consider convincing your fiancée to come up earlier than Friday. There are matters which you must discuss with her and tonight would be better than tomorrow, when your guests will be arriving. You also have a dinner scheduled with your future father-in-law tonight, and cancelling that would be ill-advised. Perhaps Johnny can take your place? Such a decision is up to you of course, but as Dagmar counsels, staying would be better for now. She has a feel for such things that I have learned to appreciate. I suggest we talk again later this morning when we will have more time."

"Thank you, Stanley, for everything you've said. If I might trouble you for a thermos, I'll wake Johnny upstairs with some coffee. Having Johnny take my place is a good idea, and as you said, there is a great deal to be done. I should stay."

"I quite agree. Allow me to get you a thermos and two cups."

While I waited for Stanley to return, I thought about what he had said. I was more inclined to take the darker view. It's what I had thought from the start, but what Stanley had expressed resonated with me as well. As usual, more than one interpretation was possible. I had traveled to a foreign land, even if only in my mind. I felt at once overwhelmed, and yet invigorated by the vision's intensity. My personal problems were small in comparison, and by acknowledging their true measure, I had acquired a better grip upon the future. I now felt wonderfully alive. I saw everything with new eyes. I would have to talk to Johnny.

17

S tanley returned with a thermos and two mugs. "This should hold you both until breakfast. Should you forego the city, please stop by my office around eleven. We can go over the details of this weekend."

I thanked Stanley and told him that I would confer with Johnny and let him know. I left him to complete the start of his day and climbed the stairs to the top of the house.

Johnny's bedroom door was open. He must have heard me, because he sat up.

Seeing who it was, he lay back down. "Breakfast in bed? You spoil me."

"Hardly," I answered, "but if you get up now, I'll supply you with some hot coffee when you're ready."

"That works," said Johnny, getting up. He stood and looked at me more closely. "You look different. You have news, I'm sure. You wouldn't be up here so early if you didn't. I'll be with you in five minutes."

I went over to the couch, put my feet up on the coffee table, and waited. Johnny was quick. He had put on some jeans and a polo shirt and plopped himself in the chair opposite.

"Seeing you in a suit and without a tie first thing in the morning is disconcerting," he commented. "You definitely need some clothes. I'll make my wardrobe available if you wish to get more comfortable, but tell me your news first and spare no details. You also mentioned coffee."

I poured him a cup, and as he sat back and sipped, I told him about my initial conversation with Dagmar, my decision, and the dream.

"Have you spoken to Dagmar and Stanley about this?"

I told him that I had and repeated what they both had said.

Johnny looked perturbed. "Thank you for bringing me up to date. As a news flash first thing in the morning, it's like waking up to an alien invasion from outer space. I mean good heavens, Percy, now what? But before we go there, are *you* all right? You look strangely calm, and I'm not sure if that is good or bad. Which is it?"

"Truthfully I don't know, but I think I'd lean toward the good."

"Well, that's something. If it was me, I'd be a gibbering idiot, so I think I will side with you on that. I need a smoke and a drink, and it's not even eight in the morning. I'll be right back."

He returned from his room with a splash of Stanley's reserve in a plain glass and a fresh pack of cigarettes. He sat back down, opened the pack, and offered me one. After we had both lit up, he raised his glass and said, "Now take it from the top if you can. I want to hear it all again."

"Very well," I said and repeated my story while Johnny smoked, listened, and sipped his drink.

When I had finished, he remained silent, thinking. I could tell that his brain was working a mile a minute.

He lit another cigarette and said, "Thank you for the repeat. Having heard your story for the second time, I can give you some initial thoughts, although as Dagmar mentioned, it's worthy of some serious and sustained analysis. For now, I believe Stanley's interpretation is closer to the mark as opposed to 'let's abandon ship because it's all about to go to hell,' which I'm sure you considered. His version at least has some hope, but with complications, such as the possibility that it was Alice who called out."

I nodded. "I'm inclined in that direction as well—the alternative being too distressing."

"It is. I'll never forget that day for a start. It altered our lives in so many ways, not the least of which was our giving up hide-and-seek as a daily occupation. More profoundly, it put front and center the reality that death can visit us at any time, even in the sheltered world we grew up in. It was the casualness and the nearness of it that terrified me. This Alice thing at the end is also most disturbing, and as to what clobbered your hiding place, I wouldn't even know where to begin. Without speculating as to the why and what exactly, it would follow that she may not be in a happy place, and that thought makes me anguished. Besides, what can we do?"

"Nothing for now, I think."

"I agree, nothing for now. Your story sounds like an excerpt from one of those horror movies that we were forced to sit through every Saturday night at that camp in Maine. They would scare the shit out of us—you more than me, as was the usual with that type of thing. Still, I could never understand how scaring the daylights out of a bunch of prepubescent boys could possibly be a benefit, but such is life under adult supervision. The reason I bring that up is because intense fear, the certainty of imminent demise, followed by an unlooked-for deliverance, can have a profound effect on the mind."

"It's like getting a second chance at life."

"Exactly. I do recall that the mystery religions of ancient Greece and Rome were reported to have done something similar. If that's the case, then you, Cicero, Plato, and maybe

94

Caesar now have something in common. I also think your wish may have been granted."

"My wish?"

"Those who underwent the mysteries, particularly the Elysian ones, and drank the *kukeon* experienced a transformation. Death no longer held a primal fear, and that change in perspective may have allowed those ancients to act in more courageous ways—something I believe you've always aspired to."

I thought about that. I had always wished to be less fearful and maybe even courageous given time. My fears and anxiousness were things I had struggled with and had worked on all my life but with only modest success. That I felt changed on some deep level was certainly true, but in what direction I had no indication. Johnny's take was so different from Stanley's and my own, but not to be dismissed by any means. What he had said resonated in ways I had yet to comprehend. He might even be correct.

I nodded. "You may be right, although I'll have to live with myself a while to see if that is the case."

"Please do." He paused and added, "I mean that. Lastly, you tend to favor the more dire predictions, and I think doing so in this case would be premature and ill-considered. Besides such an outlook violates my first law of prognostications. Do you remember it?"

"All omens are good."

"I see you do. So, for now, no more grim thoughts from you, Percy. Banish them from your mind. Yes, there is that point about Alice and yes, that does trouble me, but for now, I would do as Stanley suggests. We must await further developments. We are all free to interpret our lives in any way

95

we wish. The more empowering one is the preferred, I think. Given all that, how are you feeling?"

"Better, actually."

"Excellent. I'm sure we will discuss all of this some more, but for now, let's move on to happier things, like the pending dinner at 21 with your future father-in-law. That establishment has some outstanding vintages in their cellar, and I might be willing to sample one or two."

"I'm sure you would. Well, anyway, my thanks. I feel more optimistic, which is a marked improvement from earlier this morning. Now moving on as you suggested, I'm glad to see you feeling positive as well, particularly after last night's revelations about your mom. I'm sorry about that."

"Not to worry on that score," said Johnny. "Father and I had a good chat. I see my mother differently now. She's no longer just my mother, but a real person. I know that's a bit strange, but I feel I can speak to her now more realistically, and that can only be good."

I nodded and smiled. "Yes, it is a good thing. I was worried about you, but not any longer."

"See? Things are looking up. Now back to this evening. If I show up instead of you, Hugo will likely be a bit put out. My thought is to tell him I'm picking up the tab on your behalf."

I laughed, but inwardly cringed at the potential size of the bill. "I suppose that might work, since it is our only option. All I ask is that you control the wine list. I can picture you two breaking open a bottle of Lafite."

"Unfortunately for you, that might become necessary to convince him to stay. I'll use it only as a last resort, of course. Besides, they might have something better. I've heard they have some serious brews in their cellar, and tonight might be the chance to uncork one or two."

96

Johnny laughed at my expression. "We'll get through this," he said. "You'll see."

Johnny's enthusiasm was as infectious as ever, and I did feel better. He had made some sense of what had been impossible to understand. I sensed a change in myself. Rather than feeling tentative, I was filled with an eagerness to live that was altogether new and different. It would take some time to understand what had happened to me.

———— ◆ ————

18

Despite the night's events, mundane tasks took center stage once again. Anne and I sat down at the desk in the library and wrote out the invitations for Johnny to deliver, while he prepared to return to the city and have dinner with the baron. Anne also seemed in better spirits after a long sleep and a hearty breakfast. I let her do most of the work. Her handwriting was a work of art.

"Percy," she said after the last invitation was completed and sealed, "would you like some help with the table seating? I'm quite skilled in that department."

"Yes, of course. I was hoping you'd volunteer."

"How could I not? I'll make the necessary arrangements with Stanley."

"Thank you," I said.

Anne stacked the pile of invitations and handed them to me. "Now that these are going out, I suppose we're committed to whatever happens this weekend."

"We are," I said. "It's one of those things that must be endured. I can't say I'm looking forward to it."

"I can't say that I am, either. On another matter, have you told your mother about your engagement? I've not been able to reach her."

"Not as yet."

"Would it be all right if I told her?"

"Of course. Please do."

"I'm sure she'll be thrilled. I would also like to apologize about last night. I was not myself."

"There's no need. If anything, I should be the one to apologize for having caused you any upset. It was never my intention."

"I know. It was the news of your father's coming to this house that set me on edge. I met him long ago during a bad time in my life, and if it hadn't been for your mother, I'm not sure I would be here now. It is the reason I mentioned her. His pending arrival brought back memories that I thought were long since buried. It will be hard for me. Meeting him for the first time may be as difficult for you. Likely it won't be easy for either of us, but somehow, we'll get through it. It's what we do. Anyway, I've said what I wanted to say, and I will call your mother. She might even decide to come herself. What would you say to that?"

"Well, it would certainly ramp the tension up another notch and put my father in an interesting position. Nonetheless, having her here might make things easier for you, and for that reason I would allow it. Anything I can do for you, I will. Anyway, Anne, thank you for your help, as always. We'll both have to be brave."

"That we will. I'll speak with Stanley now, but before I go, thank you for saying what you did. I appreciate it more than I can say."

We stood and hugged each other. She needed that as much as I did. After Anne left, I wrote a hasty note to the baron. I explained that with so much to do in preparation for the coming weekend, Johnny was there in my place, and that I would cover all expenses. I was quite sure that Hugo would see this alteration of his plans as a golden opportunity to sample the cellar at 21 on my account.

99

I collected all the envelopes and met Johnny on the front steps. The chauffeur and the limo for the trip back to the city waited below.

"Should I call you?" asked Johnny.

"No need, unless it's urgent. Be back here tomorrow early and well before the crowd shows up. All you need to do is give the baron my letter and the invitations. Try to have a good time."

"Oh, I will, I can assure you."

"That's what I'm afraid of."

Johnny and I walked down the front steps. At the bottom, I said, "Thank you for your thoughts earlier, by the way. They really helped."

"I'm glad. It was an eye opener for both of us, and first thing in the morning, too, but it's how we do things. Anyway, I'm off. I can't wait to hear what happens should *both* of you sleep in that room."

I was wondering that myself.

We shook hands before I saw him into the car and watched it roll up the driveway. It felt strange not going with him. I had also been looking forward to that dinner. As a consolation, I wondered if Dagmar might offer me a better sole than 21. I considered the question as I went back into the house and chanced upon Stanley in the hallway.

"Stanley, I have a request."

"How can I help?"

"I was looking forward to a sole and a fine wine tonight. Do you think Dagmar could serve a sole that would put 21 to shame?"

"That has already been arranged. I told her that by forgoing your outing to that establishment, you might be feeling a little low. Dagmar assured me that although 21 serves a fine sole, hers is by far superior. I will even debone it for you at the table. As to the wine, I have something special that will suit—a very rare Clos Blanc de Vougeot that you should find quite surpasses anything to be found in the 21 Club cellar."

I smiled. "Thank you, Stanley. That should do quite admirably. John Sr. and Anne will be suitably impressed. One of these days we will have to figure out how to continue to keep our cellar stocked with gems like that. I'll be in the library making some calls and see you after."

"Very good, sir."

Stanley ghosted away to continue his rounds, and I made my way to the library. Rhinebeck had three telephone lines and three newly acquired fax machines that John Sr. had insisted be installed. There was a fax and telephone in Stanley's office, a pair in Alice's west wing sitting room, and another in the library. The fax machine was set up beside the desk, while the telephone, with a long extension cord, sat on a tiny table that could be wheeled to serve the caller anywhere in the room.

I wheeled the phone so that it was next to one of the comfortable chairs in front of the fireplace and sat down. I picked up the receiver and dialed Maw. She was in a suite at the St. Regis.

"Mary? Percy here, how are you?"

"Very well. I've been expecting your call. Are we on for this weekend?"

"Yes, absolutely. I was calling to invite you."

"Bonnie, Robert the Bruce, and I will certainly be there. Robert is invited?"

"Of course."

"That will do. John briefed me. This should be quite a weekend. I can hardly wait. We'll be there around four. I understand your father is invited."

"He is."

"Well, that should send the fox amongst the chickens. Lucky for you and lucky for me, I hunt foxes."

"One of the many reasons I wanted to invite you."

Maw cackled. "I'm looking forward to it. Hold on ... Yes, in a minute. That was Bonnie. She wants to say something. Well, I'll pass the phone to her, but have a care with that man, even if he is your father. I'll be available to give him a good smacking if he should become unruly. I've started taking classes in self-defense."

"Good God."

"Good God, indeed. I can't wait to use it in a real situation. I might have the opportunity this weekend. See you tomorrow. Here's Bonnie."

A few seconds later Bonnie came on the line.

"Hey Percy!"

"Hey Bonnie!"

"Lost the girlfriend yet?"

"Not yet."

"I have a surprise for you."

"You do?"

"I do. See you tomorrow. Prepare to be impressed."

"I'm sure I will be. You wish to complicate my life, as if it isn't complicated enough already."

Bonnie giggled. "My life's purpose. Ciao!"

She hung up. I shuddered. Bonnie was like a shark that scented blood in the water. I didn't want to imagine what she meant by her last comment.

I had considered ringing the baron, but John Sr. had advised against it. He had chuckled when I informed him that Johnny would be my proxy for dinner.

John Sr. had said, "It's about time Hugo and Johnny get to know each other. An excellent dinner with some serious drinking will do them a world of good. They'll surprise each other. What do you say we split the bill, since it's for all intents and purposes a business expense?"

"John, thank you. I've been dreading what those two will uncork with me not there. I can at least breathe a little easier."

"Johnny deserves it. He may not think that I appreciate him, but I do. He told me he wants to strike off on his own, with you as his partner. I didn't object, but I told him that I have an interesting counter-offer for both of you in that regard, but only after we all manage to get through this weekend in one piece. Can you hold off until then?"

"Of course."

"We'll talk about it on Monday."

John Sr. and Anne left the house for a walk while I made my way to the library. Thinking about that conversation with John Sr. had allowed me to put off calling Bruni a few minutes longer. It was not that I didn't want to speak with her. I did, but Bruni had a knack for knowing what I was thinking, and Stanley's revelations about her past were heavily on my mind.

19

I dialed Bruni's office, and the receptionist put me through directly.

"There you are, Percy. I've missed you."

"Me, too. Some news. Our seeing each other will have to wait until Friday."

"Elaborate on that."

Bruni, I noticed, tended to shorten her sentences when she wasn't pleased.

"It's a bit of a long story."

"Give me the short version."

"Very well. John Sr. told me yesterday afternoon that my father wants to physically see the treasures before he pays. In response, *your* father has postponed his contribution until mine does. The delay means that the maintenance trust is short 1.5 million dollars. To hammer out the kinks and complete the transactions, you and I have the honor of hosting a formal weekend party for both of them and at least six other houseguests starting tomorrow. I'm still at Rhinebeck working on that, hence the change in plan."

"Am I correct in understanding that your father is coming to Rhinebeck?"

"You are correct."

"We're hosting him?"

"Right again."

"I must say that's unexpected. Who are the other guests?"

"The same crew as the other weekend with the exception of the tall man, Malcolm Ault, but that is subject to change, as is usual in his case, and perhaps my mother."

There was a pause. I could almost hear her mind turning over.

"Your mother might be arriving?"

"Yes, it's only a possibility for now, but she might. Would you like to meet her?"

"Absolutely I would, but I have a question. Are your father and mother even on speaking terms?"

"They haven't spoken in years, as far as I know, so probably not. Then again, she and I haven't seen each other for a number as well, so I can't really say."

"Well, that should be an interesting meeting—almost as interesting as the one between your mother, my mother, and my father."

"Good heavens! I didn't even think of that. That could be cataclysmic. What should I do?"

"Nothing for now. You did say it was only a possibility, so it may not be an issue. I much prefer solving problems that do exist, rather than ones that might. It saves a great deal of unnecessary wear and tear. Besides, whether your mother arrives or not, this weekend is bound to be contentious, as is often the case when there are divergent interests and large sums of money involved."

"I think that's true. If she should show up, we'll handle it then. So, are you up for hosting a contentious bash?"

"One last question, will there be black-tie and white-tie dinners?"

"Yes, that's the idea. Both, in fact."

"Then I'm most definitely up for it. I have a new formal dress that I'm dying to wear. It's a little risqué, but you're going to love it."

"Hopefully, not too risqué," I said.

"Don't be a prude. You're concerned about my seeing your father again?"

"That did cross my mind."

"I bet it did. What about you? Are you prepared?"

"I'm working on it," I said.

"That's good. Having heard who else will be there, I feel better about meeting him again. Any potential awkwardness should be overshadowed by the reactions from others. Still, seeing him will require some courage on both our parts. Let's discuss what to do in more detail when we're together. All in all, I'd say it should be quite the weekend, and that's without Papa wanting to boil you in oil for standing him up. How are you planning to handle that?"

"Johnny is going to see him in my stead. I gave him carte blanche to explore the wine cellar."

Bruni paused. "That might actually work. I like it. Ready for a surprise?"

"In your case, always."

"Music to my ears. Now, I've been highly productive over the last twenty-four hours and managed to clear my desk for the next several days. I have that meeting later this morning, but other than that I'm free. I can drive up this afternoon, and we can spend all of tonight whispering sweet nothings in each other's ears. How does that sound?"

"That sounds wonderful."

"Wonderful?"

"Stupendous."

"Stupendous sounds about right. See you this afternoon. I have to run to this meeting. Love you. 'Bye."

Bruni hung up, and as she did, I realized that I'd forgotten to tell her to bring my suitcases. I called back to leave a message at reception to not only bring my suitcases, but to pack a few herself. We had a lot to discuss, but simply talking to her had my heart beating faster.

20

P leased that Bruni was coming up tonight rather than tomorrow, I went looking for Stanley. I found him in his office.

"Is now a good time to talk?" I asked.

"It is. Please sit down and tell me how I can be of service."

"There are several matters on my mind, not the least of which is that we have numerous guests arriving tomorrow, but before I forget, Brunhilde will be arriving this afternoon rather than tomorrow. There will be four for dinner tonight."

"I will inform Dagmar. Dinner will be at nine, and if I may be so bold, having your fiancée present will add that extra sparkle that will more than compensate for missing an evening at the 21 Club. It will also allow you the opportunity to discuss those other matters."

"The death of the second nanny being one of them."

"Considering that you are engaged to be married, I should think that a frank discussion about that would be more than prudent, don't you?"

"Yes, of course, but I'm not looking forward to it."

Stanley nodded. "Beginnings are often difficult. Every pair of newlyweds brings into their marriage their histories, their assumptions, and their flaws. Those who can untangle the knots they've made as individuals and use the loosened strands to weave something new together have a chance. Those who can't, find themselves eventually untethered and alone. It is something you will need to think on. Her ladyship was competent in many things but ineffectual in this respect, and it cost her dearly. Dagmar and I had a rough start as well, but we managed in the end. What happened and why might be instructive, should you wish to hear it."

"I would, very much."

"I married Dagmar as a solution to my loneliness when her ladyship was absent. Her ladyship may not have been overjoyed that I was marrying Dagmar in the first place, but over time she saw the wisdom of it and grew to appreciate the excellence of Dagmar's many arts. Working in her kitchen, my wife thrived in ways that astounded me. Shortly after our marriage, she transformed from a simple, wonderful, and talented cook into something much more. I, of course, asked about the changes I observed. She told me that she had found her place in the world at last and was free to be herself. And it was true. Everything Dagmar did, everything she learned, and everything she experienced formed a pattern that, when observed as a whole, was far greater and more powerful than anything I had anticipated. The changes took some getting used to, and I was ill-prepared mentally to accept her, not just as an equal, but in many ways as my superior. She was far more intelligent and perceptive than I'd first thought, and I grew resentful.

"The reasons for my resentment at the time might be laid partly at the doorstep of the masculine culture in which I grew up. It tended to view women as subservient and inferior to men. Her ladyship rather quickly disabused me of any such notion, but that was more in the general sense than in the specific. Living with Dagmar as my wife on a daily basis was something altogether different. I have come to accept that neither sex is the superior. Apart, male and female are less;

together they are more, but such a harmonious view was mine in the future, not then.

"To be frank, Dagmar baffled me. It was as if I had married a royal personage masquerading as a scullery maid, while I remained a mere servant, even if a senior one. It was a bitter pill for me to swallow. The teacher, if that is what I was, had become the student, and I grew jealous. Even her ladyship would comment that there was greatness and a genius in Dagmar that was truly something to behold.

"Along with my jealousy, there grew a further friction in our marriage. As I mentioned previously, I was enchanted by her ladyship from my first meeting. This affection I held hidden in my heart. It is difficult to play second fiddle to another when it comes to marriage. I loved Dagmar, and would do anything for her, but the status that her ladyship held in my eyes, and the image I had constructed of her in my mind, were ones that none could surpass. Dagmar perhaps sensed this initially, but over time, its presence grew and affected our relationship as if a ripening corpse had been stashed in our bedroom closet. Eventually, the incongruity of my feelings could no longer be ignored.

"One evening at the end of our day, I had put her ladyship to bed and entered the kitchen. I took one look at my wife and knew that there were matters to be discussed. I also suspected what was foremost in her mind, and in this I was correct. Dagmar waited until I was seated and didn't mince words.

" 'There can be only one' she said after I had seated myself. The silence following this announcement stretched to an almost unbearable length. She added quietly, 'You must choose.'

" 'I replied, 'Between whom?'

" 'Don't act the fool with me,' she said. 'You're better than that. It may be hard, but it is necessary, if we are to continue together.'

"I stared at her. I didn't know what to say. After some moments I blurted out resentfully, 'How am I to do that? Do not ask me to do what I cannot. I brought you here. I married you. It was *I* who did these things, and I was able to because her ladyship supported my decision and allowed it. I have done nothing untoward, and you should believe that. You owe me that much, at least.' "

" 'So you say, and it is true as far as it goes, but not entirely. In addition, you are jealous of who and what I am. For my part, her ladyship holds your heart in ways that I cannot, and I am jealous of that. My resentment toward you is growing. As things stand there can only be tragedy before us. If you cannot see that outcome, then you are blind, and that is something you are not. I must cease to be jealous of her ladyship, and you must cease to be jealous of me, or we are finished.'

"In a few words Dagmar had spelled out the situation before us, and in such a way that it left me no doubt that we were almost on the rocks, if not there already. It was a shock, and as I examined my culpability, I saw in myself a selfishness that was patently obvious, even to me. I had married Dagmar as a solution to the problem of *my* loneliness. Logically, this had merit, but only in one direction. I had not factored my wife's point of view into my solution, only my own. Such behavior was shameful. But what should I have done instead? It had not been my intention to hurt my wife, yet I had, and I had fooled myself into thinking that how I felt about her didn't matter, when it did. On the other hand, I couldn't simply stop loving her ladyship. That I could never do, but I considered that perhaps I could love Dagmar in such a way that she might be satisfied sufficiently to put aside her jealousy. It was a possible solution, only I didn't know how that might come about.

"Dagmar saw the impact of her words and my remorse but made no move to reconcile with me. I knew I had to be the one to acknowledge my error and tell her so. I took her hand in mine and said, 'I have made a grave mistake—not in marrying you, but in being unable to take our relationship to a level where rivalry can no longer be an issue. I would do that if I knew how, but I do not. I can only promise to find out. I, too, am jealous. You are so different from what I had expected. I feel hopelessly outclassed by you. I have tried to keep up, but it's as if I'm standing still. If there is a remedy that I could apply, or one that you could suggest, I would take it, only I don't know that, either. I feel ignorant and unwise. I am heartily, heartily sorry.'

"Dagmar took her other hand and placed it on my own. She thanked me for acknowledging the truth in what she'd said and added the following: 'You're not entirely the one at fault. I, too have made a grave mistake, and I am uncertain which of ours is worse. I have withheld from you some aspects of my past. I have also deliberately made you feel small and insignificant out of spite and resentment for what you couldn't give, and for what I couldn't have. I, too, am heartily sorry for it. Now is the time to let our errors go and begin anew. I have a possible remedy for both our issues that I will share with you. Are you willing to attempt it?'

"I told her that I was. She got up from the table and came back with two small glasses of dark liquid. She said, 'Drink this, and I will do the same.'

" 'What is it?' I asked, examining it with some distaste.

112

" 'It won't kill you, if that's what you're thinking,' she said.

"I wasn't thinking that specifically, but whatever it was it looked particularly unappetizing, like prune juice or some such variant. I answered her by saying, 'I should hope not, but I sense it is more than a drink.'

" 'It is. You wish to take our relationship to a level where rivalry can no longer be an issue. I would like to do that as much as you, but before I get to more specifics about what it is, you should know some things about me.'

" 'Such as?' I answered.

" 'Before I decided to become a cook, I studied biochemistry as it applied to plants, pharmacology, and food. I did research. I never told you, when perhaps I should have. Most people, looking at me, see only what they choose to, and that is a plain and simple woman, a cook. It is what I prefer. I could have remained in that other field and done well. The lab I worked for wanted me to stay and offered me all kinds of inducements, even heading my own team, but I refused. Working there was not my idea of where I wished to end up. I love to cook. It is my passion, and I much preferred my own workspace where I could accomplish almost as much. Besides, the results would be my own, not some corporation's. It was the choice I made.'

" 'You're not just a cook then?' I asked.

" 'I am a cook, and much more,' she said.

"Her revelation surprised me, but then it didn't. It just made sense. Dagmar continued, 'Getting a job as a cook wasn't difficult, and I was very good to begin with. Employers don't ask about your past. They only require references from previous employers, and those are easy to obtain, if you know what you're doing. Cooks are considered lesser souls in houses

113

like this. They do necessary yet menial tasks. No one looks twice at them, is this not so?'

" 'It is to some degree, but why didn't you tell me?'

" 'Would you have hired me, knowing I had been a research scientist? Would you have married me if you had thought that I was smarter than you?'

"Dagmar had put her finger on it exactly. She was correct, and I admitted it.

"Dagmar nodded then and took my hand in both of hers. She told me that my honest answer was why she had married me in the first place. She also said that her ladyship had lent her and then allowed her access to various books in her libraries that specialized in plants, fungi, mushrooms, and other unusual substances. Her ladyship also needed help in titration, distillation, fermentation, and the preparation of various complex organic compounds, Dagmar knew exactly what to do. It was her field after all."

"Good heavens, I said. "So, Dagmar helped Alice with her research?"

"Yes, she did, and her ladyship provided Dagmar with physical specimens and exotic knowledge from the field in the form of the exact procedures various indigenous people used, such as what was mixed together with what, and how various medicines, potions, and compresses were prepared. Much of Dagmar's research is stored within the special library with a blue tag."

"You know, that does make sense, Stanley, and explains a few things for me as well."

"How so?"

"I remember when Johnny and I had to wrestle with algebra. Dagmar would be able to show us how to answer certain problems, and how they worked, with only a glance.

We tried to get her to do some of our homework, but she refused and would throw us out of the kitchen. She told us she was only to be used as a last resort. After several ejections, we got the message. She even helped us with solutions to a few perplexing differential equations in later years but swore us to secrecy."

"That would be typical of her. She helped me arrange the library and pointed me in the right direction when I had questions, but anything more, she insisted I discover for myself. She is a firm believer in personal study. After she told me about her past in more detail, she said that she had discovered a very old grimoire which belonged to her ladyship's mother that made reference to a much older source that described a particular marriage ceremony. The couple would share a specially prepared drink, whose purpose was to create an unshakeable bond between them. Dagmar indicated that the drink before us was only an approximation of that ancient recipe, since some of the ingredients were unknown and had become lost along the way. Still, she had sufficient expertise to assure me that it would produce a similar result. It was to be taken before the marriage was consummated."

"Really? Did it work?"

Stanley smiled. "It did indeed, and I will spare you any details."

"I suppose that's just as well. I might ask Dagmar for a drop, should I need it."

"I would use it only as a last resort. Like the potion you consumed last night, such remedies can have unanticipated results. In our case, it was a calculated risk. Both of us wished to preserve our marriage at any cost, and so we drank the drinks that she prepared.

"Afterward, Dagmar confided to me that the essence of the male is to vanquish through action, and that it is the essence of the female to defend by not losing. The trick is to find the proper balance between the two, something that every individual, every couple, and perhaps all things must discover for themselves. Dagmar and I found that center, and after that evening, I never looked at her the same way. I saw not only a splendid being but a powerful and sensual woman of extraordinary intelligence and understanding whom I'd overlooked and underappreciated. She needed my love to sustain her as much as I needed hers. It was a revelation, and my life shifted irreversibly in a better direction from that moment. The love between us has continued to grow since then to previously unimagined heights, and the trust between us with it. Like a ring, it has no end. It is what happened to us. I hope my words have been helpful and that you might learn from my experience."

"Stanley, I don't know what to say other than to offer my thanks. I will speak with Bruni and go from there."

"Please do. Once that's settled, and settled it must be, keeping your guests entertained after they arrive, and resolving the pending financial transactions, are all you should have your attention on. A sumptuous series of meals, including a black-tie dinner on Friday, followed by a white-tie feast on Saturday night, have been planned and scheduled. The required bedrooms have been allocated and prepared. Dagmar is putting the finishing touches on the menus, and I have arranged for the extra staff needed. In addition, Mrs. Dodge has informed me that she will have the seating chart available later today. All is well in hand."

"I'm certainly glad to hear that."

"It is our intention to provide you with a suitable and diverting backdrop that will ease some of the tensions that this weekend will generate given the current guest list, which includes your father."

Stanley looked at me. He knew that my father was what we really needed to talk about. It couldn't be put off any longer.

I sighed. "That meeting has certainly been on my mind, and I'm not looking forward to it. Thinking about him in this house fills me with dread, and for now, all I have are questions. I don't understand why he's arriving, why he wants the treasures when he arrives, and why he's coming here now when he's not even invited."

21

Stanley looked at me. "I understand your disquiet. One might infer from what you've said that he doesn't want to risk you saying no to his being here."

"That would make sense, because he definitely wants to be here. I suppose it's possible that he also wants to see me, but given his history, it's not likely that shaking my hand and saying what a fine lad I've grown into is the reason. He could have invited me to visit him in England, and that would have been far easier for him, considering his age. Seeing me is not his primary motivation. It can't be."

Stanley considered my answer. "If he was an ordinary soul, I should think that seeing a child for the first time, even if an adult, would be high on that list, but he is not an ordinary soul. He might also be interested in a legacy of sorts, but then paying in the needed funds as he agreed to would have allowed that, and he has not done so. Regardless, I think that you are involved in some way, and seeing you is part of it."

"Maybe, but I think that my owning Rhinebeck created a plausible reason for his insisting that he come himself and in addition, has activated whatever plan he had in mind. My first thought was that he wanted to exact revenge on you. You said he swore he would, and he can only accomplish that if he is here in person. He, too, is one to hold a grudge and take the time to plan a suitable vengeance. He certainly did that in Alice's case. Still, doing away with you, I decided, would likely be an added bonus rather than the real reason. Revenge is an expensive luxury, and money has always been an issue with him from what I've heard. It must make economic sense and simply killing you doesn't. Would you agree?"

"I do. Money has always had an attraction for him. Exacting a revenge on me would merely be a collateral benefit—not that he wouldn't take advantage of the opportunity if it presented itself. I will be careful nonetheless, if that will ease your mind."

"Good. I was concerned for you. I also considered the possibility that he wants the estate for himself. It would be the final touch on taking revenge on Alice, since she refused to relinquish it in the first place. Owning Rhinebeck would be like spitting on her grave, although he is aware that the estate is in need of funds, which lessens that as a possibility."

Stanley nodded. "I don't think he wants to acquire Rhinebeck. You would have to be eliminated in some way, and I don't see how that could be done without raising suspicions. He is cunning, not crazy. Of course, that might be the subject of some debate. Are there other reasons that you've considered?"

"You mentioned that group of collectors. They wish to gather power to themselves. This location has an element of that."

"Perhaps. If he wants access to the power that resides here, then he must be here. If he lays his hands on the treasures, there is the power they inherently possess, in addition to his own. I think that is a possibility. It could also mean that the von Hofmanstals have a stake in that outcome. That thought makes me uneasy. For now, there is nothing concrete. Whatever he wants and whatever his intentions, he will make them known, and then we will be able to respond. Until then, we must wait."

"That's the conclusion I came to as well. I'm going to ask John Sr. if he could make Raymond available this weekend."

Stanley nodded in agreement. "That would be entirely appropriate. He has the necessary street-smarts and an intimidating presence. Anything else?"

"You mentioned *xenia* and that there would be consequences, if there was a violation. Can you explain that?"

Stanley said, "*Xenia* involves the deportment of guests and hosts. It means that this house is a kind of sanctuary with all implied by that word. The host is responsible for the safety, protection, and welfare of the guest. The guest has the obligation to behave in an appropriate manner. I mentioned it to reaffirm to myself that I must act to preserve your father's safety and well-being while he's here, lest I forget myself. I can keep my loathing of the man in check, but only up to a point. Given that, I think it would be wise for you to explain to him that as a guest in this house, inciting discord and disharmony would be woefully ill-advised given the nature of this estate, and that for his safety, which you as host are obligated to ensure, he should have a care and exercise some caution."

"Well, Stanley, I don't think I've ever looked at being a guest or a host in quite that way. I'll be sure to pass that message along. I suppose that might be called an offensive defense."

"Exactly. It's how I worked out how to behave in his presence."

"I see. Do I have cause to worry, Stanley?"

"From me? No."

"I'm happy to hear that. Do tell me if you feel yourself slipping."

"Rest assured, I will."

"Well, thank you, Stanley. It's been enlightening on many levels. I'm looking forward to dinner. I'll leave you to it."

"My pleasure."

22

As I passed through the kitchen, I thought about what Stanley had said. I doubted Stanley would fly off the handle, but then I had never met my father, so I was uncertain as to how abrasive he could be. For now, I had to let the matter drop.

I passed through the house and out the front door, intent on a stroll to work out how to broach the matter of the nannies with Bruni as well as settle my thoughts about all that had happened in the last twenty-four hours. I found myself by the tennis court and sat.

A line of crows perched on the fence surrounding it. What did that mean? It was part of an endless game I played inside my head. When my future looked bleak, which was often in my opinion, I'd look for signs to let me know that all was not as dark as I'd envisaged. There were seven of them there, a good number. Wait. One flew off. Was six as good as seven? I shut down that line of thinking as quickly as it arose.

What would Bruni think of such craziness? More importantly, would she be able to stand living with me? On the other hand, given Stanley's revelations, should I really be contemplating marriage to such a woman? I had managed to suppress the question until now.

I had seen what love had done to Johnny. He would forget all reason. Was I not doing the same? Losing Bruni would surely break my heart, but losing my wits would break much more, and Stanley had raised legitimate concerns about Bruni's past. I felt torn apart. Logically, I knew that I had yet to hear her side, but the possibility of not having a future with her caused my heart to ache. Beyond that, there was the bigger question of whether I was up to the task of being her husband. She required a gentle strength. I understood the gentle. It was the strength part I doubted.

I was mid the thought when I heard a car. I stood and saw a long, black limousine turn from the access road and sweep down the driveway toward the entrance of the house. Any reflection would have to wait. I walked toward the entrance.

I joined Stanley and Simon as the chauffeur opened the car door, and out stepped the object of my anguish.

"I'm early," Bruni announced proudly to me. "I hope you don't mind."

I had forgotten how beautiful a woman she was until she stood before me in person. She radiated light. I stepped toward her. "Seeing you now is much better than later." I gave her a welcoming kiss.

"I should think so. By the way, as requested in your message, I brought an extraordinary amount of luggage, including yours."

"Excellent. Well done! I will make sure Simon and Harry lend a hand."

"Wonderful!" She beamed at me and then turned to Stanley. "So good to see you."

"Welcome back," said Stanley with a thin smile. "Would you care for some refreshment?"

"Always." She grabbed my arm, and we followed Stanley into the house.

After champagne and a warm welcome from Anne and John Sr., Bruni and I retreated to our new bedroom. As we unpacked, we were quickly surrounded by makeup cases, bottles of assorted lotions, bags of gowns, piles of undergarments, dresses, pants, suits, tops, shoes, and the many specialized items that Bruni had decided were absolutely necessary. I looked over the varied assortment and was amazed that so much had managed to fit into an oversize limousine without the use of a roof rack or a small trailer. Judging the amount Bruni had brought with her, I allocated myself what I thought was sufficient space in our sprawling walk-in closet. Bruni considered this arrangement. My portion was more than fair, she said, but perhaps overly generous considering what she had left of hers to put away. I told her that I would reconsider and after surveying what still remained in our bedroom, I offered to reduce my space once again. Bruni looked pleased.

While we unpacked some more, I pondered how to broach the matter of the nannies, or even if I should. The mere sight of her was enough for me to postpone bringing it up indefinitely, but as Stanley had said: beginnings can be hard, and both of us had threads from our respective pasts that needed to be untangled and rewoven, provided we could do that. The question was, could we? Doubts swirled about me like a cloud.

"You're awfully quiet. Having second thoughts?" Bruni asked.

"Perhaps we should move to the sitting room, where there is a bit more order, and we can sit down in comfort."

"You *are* having second thoughts about marrying me."

I sighed. "Let's go sit down."

"You are."

"And you have none?"

We passed to the sitting room in silence and sat down on the couch. Bruni leaned back at one end and draped her arm over the back, gazing at me with eyes of cobalt blue set off by a blue-gray blouse and a cream-colored skirt. Her beauty left me searching for words. I sat down at the other end— spellbound once again.

"What?" blurted Bruni.

I took a deep breath and said, "I want to know about that second nanny, the one that slipped out the window, after the first one tumbled down the stairs."

Bruni looked at me steadily and said nothing. She did not react but allowed the silence to build. Finally, she said, "I will tell you, but I have questions first. Do you recall the first time we took a walk and kissed?"

"Of course I do."

"I said at the time that talking truth is hard and comes in layers. I then asked what you had done to me to make me so besotted, and how you had managed that. I want you to answer those questions now."

Like her father, she wanted her questions answered first, yet nothing I could offer would adequately answer them, since I didn't understand those things myself. She, too, had doubts, else she wouldn't have brought them up.

This wasn't going quite the way I expected, but I continued. "I will tell you about that weekend, but I want some answers first."

"No, not until you answer me. What happened between us that night is on you, and because it is, I have that right. Now, answer me."

What seemed like ages ago, I had held her in my arms and knew that I would have to tell her what happened that night, and that time was now.

125

"Very well. I'll go first, then you. Agreed?"

Bruni gave me a nod. Her silences were as effective as her words.

"The night before we met, Stanley told Johnny and me the story of Alice. When my father was married to Johnny's aunt, he locked her in a trunk to make her more compliant. During her captivity, she felt she was visited by some spiritual entities whom she called 'the people.' Being held in the dark in a box was oddly coincidental with a recurring nightmare she'd had since a child. Putting these two events together, Alice concluded that she was cursed. She experimented with many drugs to try to reconnect with 'the people,' hoping that they might tell her how to lift the curse she carried. Alice's mother was also heavily into the occult, and Alice, once she had extricated herself from my father with Stanley's help, followed in her footsteps. Alice felt she was the reincarnation of a priestess from Ancient Egypt and collected many artifacts from the period to aid her in her search for expiation. You saw several of them after the lunch, when we became engaged."

Bruni nodded again but said nothing.

I continued, "The night of your dream, Johnny decided to summon a demon. He wanted to see for himself if the occult was real or simply a figment of the imagination. He followed the procedures that Alice used and slipped me one of her tinctures. Alice had written that the concoctions made her visible to other entities so they could interact with her. Whether the summoning was successful or not, I found myself in your bed. In truth, I wanted you from the moment I first saw you, and I got my wish and then some. Whether the dream was physically real, I don't know. I don't have full recollection of that night. We also dreamt similar dreams, which you must admit is highly unusual. The experience with you was frighteningly intense and almost realer than real. You felt it."

"It was coincidental, and the explanation seems farfetched. I don't know how to explain it other than that I felt overwhelmed and overpowered. Now, answer me this: did you slip me something in my food or in my drink? Tell me."

"Good heavens, no! How could you even think that?"

She continued to look at me steadily before nodding.

"I'm sorry if I shocked you. We all have a history, Percy. Me included. I believe you, but I had to ask. It's a possible explanation which leads me to my next question: do you doubt me because you fear I won't accept the peculiar things that have happened here with you, or do you have doubts about me because of what you've heard about me?"

"Both may be true, but what about your doubts? Can you tell me that you have none?"

She stood and looked down at me.

"Then let's get to it. We both have doubts, and that's a fact. But here we are *engaged*. I must know once and for all if you're backing out, or whether you are cowardly enough to want me to do it for you. Because if either of those is true," she pointed to the bedroom, "then I've absolutely no idea how I'm going to pack up what's in that room and get it back to my apartment!"

I stood as well and said, "And I must know once and for all about your past. You must tell me."

"Unbelievable! Well, if that's the case, I want a cigarette and a walk. I won't tell you in this room!"

"Bruni, I don't wish to upset you, but—"

Bruni interrupted. "Upset me? *You* have a lot to learn about what upsets me. What you said, doesn't. What you will say, won't. Your feeble attempt to allow me the option of backing out of our upcoming marriage, rather than making that decision yourself—now *that* upsets me. If that's the case, then maybe I *should* reconsider. I don't want some simpering idiot, too afraid to say what's needed or do what must be done. I want someone to *stand by me!* Now, *listen*, because I'm only going to say this once. If you try to give me one more reason why *I* shouldn't marry you, I'm going to start screaming. Then you really *will* see me upset. So, Percy, for the very last time, what do *you* want to do? Not me! *You!*"

I reached over and held her shoulders in my hands. I looked into those flashing eyes and said firmly, "Bruni, I can't help myself when it comes to you. I want to marry you very much. I really do. I love you, and that is all I know for certain, but you *must* talk to me. *You must!* For god's sake just *tell me what happened!* There, you have my answer." I pulled her close and said in a softer voice, "Now, how about that walk? You can tell me all about that nanny while we look at the trees and enjoy the view. Sound good?"

23

B runi said into my shoulder, "So you really want to go through with this?"

"I do."

"Very well. Now, I'll tell you what you wish to know."

She pulled away and said, "Let's walk. Bring some cigarettes and something to drink."

I looked down at her high heels., "I'd put on some comfortable shoes and a coat. It can get chilly here. While you change, I'll gather up some smokes. Would you prefer vodka or whiskey?"

"You choose. I'll have some, but the liquor is mostly for you. You're going to need it."

She gave me a peculiar smile as I left her for Johnny's room and his secret stash. As I walked down from the top of the house well supplied, I concluded that life with her would likely be far more interesting than I had anticipated. Then again, life with me at Rhinebeck might not lack in excitement either. Bruni met me at the bottom of the stairs in a light windbreaker, jeans, and sneakers. I had borrowed one of Johnny's several flasks, a pack of his cigarettes, a jacket, a pair of his pants, and some casual shoes. I was thankful that he and I could exchange clothes. While I was changing upstairs, I realized that I could use my old closet for anything that didn't fit downstairs. That discovery alone had been worth the trip.

"Ready?' I asked as I made my way to the front door.

"Yes. Are you?" she answered.

"Absolutely. I was thinking that our lives together will always be exciting, so we might as well get started. I have just the spot. It isn't far."

Bruni took my arm but didn't tell me her story right away. We walked in silence up the driveway and then toward the river. The wind blew the sporadic clouds before the sun at odd moments as we walked westward under the leafy trees that lined the road. The asphalt turned to gravel and then narrowed to a dirt path that eventually emptied into a clearing. At its center was a granite rock that looked like the back of a breaching whale upon a lush green sea. We climbed to its top, several feet above the ground, and sat. I could see the river in flashes through the foliage. I lit both of us a cigarette, passing one to Bruni. I poured a measure of Johnny's brew into the cup that functioned as a lid and handed it to her.

"You first," she said.

"Don't you trust me?"

"You know I do, and after what I have to say, you'll know that for sure."

I took a sip and handed her the cup. Bruni took a gulp. As she did, my thoughts flew back to Johnny and that night when we had done the summoning. I had the horrible realization that maybe this flask contained the remnants of Alice's tincture. Johnny had said that he had added a few drops to my drink that night, but knowing him the way I did, he would have mixed a small batch in case it proved effective. If he had, then I had no idea what was about to happen. Bruni was still holding the cup, but before she could take another sip, I took it and poured what remained onto the rock beside me. The flask was now three quarters full, about the right amount if my suspicions were correct. With an uneasy feeling, I put it back in my jacket pocket. Bruni didn't notice but continued to stare in the direction of the silver speckled flashes of the Hudson through the trees. She took a long drag of her cigarette and blew it out.

"Kiss me first," she said and turned toward me. I did.

"Thank you," she said afterward and rearranged herself to sit cross-legged. "I've thought about this moment many times. About telling someone the story of my childhood, the way it really happened. No one knows it but me."

She sat in silence gazing into nothing. She looked at me again and said, "Every day, I manage one crisis after another in an endless parade, not because I want to, but because I must. I owe, you see, and that weight never seems to diminish. That burden and my fears for the future wake me every morning and keep me up at night. The truth is, I need you far more than you need me. I want so badly for it all to stop. I want to be safe and most importantly ..."—She turned to me with tears in her eyes—"...I *need* to know I'm loved without reservation in spite of who I am. I would have gladly given my life at one point or another for even the slimmest possibility of that happening. Being loved unconditionally and being safe are the two things that I've dreamed of since I was a little girl. I need a home, Percy. I really do."

Bruni turned away as a tear dropped onto the front of her jacket and smoked some more. She stubbed her cigarette out and spoke again after a minute. She turned and looked at me.

"I told you not to worry about your darkness, and that I welcomed it. I see you, Percy. I also see in you myself, and I have darkness enough for both of us. God knows what will happen if we should have children. My parents must have felt

131

the same, but I'm sliding away from what I need to say, and what you need to hear."

She paused again and whispered, "I killed them both, you see. I had to. The first was bad enough, but the second ... If you thought Alice was cursed, think again. She had her people and her spirits to guide her. I had no one, and I was very small."

24

Bruni began to cry. I held her and tried to imagine what could have possibly driven her to do what she said she did. I wondered if it was even true. Children see things differently. With limited experience how can they view the world as it really is? Perhaps she had it wrong? All I could do was wait, comfort her as best I could, and say nothing.

After her tears wound down, she pulled out a handkerchief and blew her nose. She sniffed and said, "You want to know what happened, and I suppose I have to tell you. It's almost impossible for me to talk about it. I don't want to, but I must."

After a pause, she said, "When I look at myself objectively, I think I've always been a little crazy. It's also possible that I was made crazier. When you're completely in someone's power, and they want to drive you insane, what can possibly be the result other than to become crazy enough to do something about it? Madness and courage are hard to differentiate."

Bruni looked toward the Hudson through the trees. "I should have felt guilty after Nana died, but I didn't. That fact might raise a red flag in some, but it didn't bother me. Rather it was the suspicions that came after that caused me to doubt my state of mind and to question my sanity. The staff at the castle began to have concerns about my version of events. I saw skepticism in their furtive glances. I wanted to scream out loud what I knew to be true, but I kept my mouth shut. Confession would have served no useful purpose other than to put me in a funny farm for the rest of my life, and *that* was not a path I had envisaged for myself. I contributed to the gossip by not shedding any tears. In fact, I was the happiest I'd ever been, and it showed. My joy made them wonder."

Bruni looked away and then back again.

"Suspicion is hard to pin down, but when it's present, it's as real as anything else. It also never stops. I think that people around me, those that watched me growing up, sensed that I wasn't quite right from the beginning. After Nana died, I puzzled them even more. If I'd killed her, I was playing by no rules that they could imagine. Perhaps they thought they were next? I became an outcast in my own house, and that either strengthens you or breaks you. The unfairness and injustice made me very angry. I suppose I still am."

She lit another cigarette.

"I don't blame my parents for my early life. They were away much of the time when I was young. They loved and helped me as much as they could, which was a great deal, but they had each other and their mutual interests. I think I surprised them when I was born. I was a girl. Neither knew what to make of me when they wanted a son instead. Rather than alter their lifestyles, I was given a nanny, and not any nanny. Her name was Olga Horst. I called her Nana. It sounds like such a sweet name, something you would give a goat, or a cuddly farm animal. She was neither. I don't recall when she became my nanny, exactly. I have no memory of a time before. I don't know where those memories went, and yet she was not always there. For me, there was only the time when she was. Perhaps I was five or six. It is uncharacteristically vague."

Bruni smoked in silence. I watched her consider what to say.

"Pain is a useful commodity. It focuses the mind. It surely focused mine but doesn't make for a happy childhood. And yet if it weren't for the pain and Nana's iron discipline, I doubt I would have developed the intensity of will that has allowed me to survive and accomplish what I have. Being mentally strong and disciplined can be an asset, but it comes with liabilities. One can't be that way forever, and I found it difficult to know when it was safe to let my guard down. That flaw has been my undoing in many instances—like with my ex-husband, and with Lord Bromley. That includes you—but with you, I'm hoping it will be different. You accept me for who I am, no more, no less. I've staked my future on that belief; nonetheless, I'm worried about your reaction. We'll just have to see, won't we?"

"We will."

"It is my hope. To love in spite of reasons not to, is to love indeed. I was that way at the beginning. A child will do whatever an adult says, expecting little in return. A smile, a look, anything is enough. Then there are those who find any display of affection abhorrent. Yet a child will try and get a response. Nana loved God but hated the devil more. One morning she discovered that I had peed in my sleep. Do you know how many bones there are in the human foot?"

"No," I answered.

"There are twenty-six bones, thirty-three joints, and countless nerves. The soles of the feet can be struck leaving little evidence, and a switch of springy wood swung fast and hard upon them can instill a surprising amount of agony. Nana believed that God showed his goodness in the head and heart, while the devil inhabited the feet. One blessed the former and beat the latter. And so, my world was made. She was very strict. Any wrong, any error in a lesson or deportment was punishable by striking one of my feet. She let me choose which one. The perversity in that was ever so subtle. She let me decide. I had a choice, and as insignificant as that may seem, it was mine, and I chose which one each time.

"Nana was a Calvinist. She believed that those who were predestined to salvation showed it in their thoughts and deeds. Those fated for damnation did the same. She said that I was clever but wicked, and that my wickedness could be found in my eyes. I hated my eyes. They were so blue. Adults would be hypnotized by them, but Nana saw only an evil that had to be laid low. Unchecked, their influence might lead even her astray, which is what they did—that and other things.

"My upbringing was strict, but I knew of no alternative. A child can grow accustomed to anything. At some point, when I was nine, or maybe ten, I complained to my parents. It was a moment of weakness on my part. I told them that Nana beat me without mercy. Neither took it seriously. Why should they? Both my parents had endured severe upbringings, perhaps as strict as mine. How else was self-discipline to be taught, they asked. And they were right. How indeed? I realized then that what they said was true. My parents, in spite of their seeming indifference, spoke to Nana about what I'd said. Since I rarely complained, and was quiet and well mannered, my mentioning it at all must have impressed them.

"All was well until my parents went away again. Nana waited until then. I couldn't walk for two days after that, but in my bed, I decided that I would never again be betrayed and humiliated by my own weakness. I made a decision, the first big one of my life. I decided that I would never allow Nana another opportunity to beat me, if I could prevent it by hard work. It was a victory of sorts. Over time, I learned several languages and mastered so many subjects that even Nana could barely find a fault. We assumed an uneasy truce up until I reached puberty. When I reached that point, evidence of my sex exploded, and that caused to grow in her a persistent question.

"Give me another cigarette and some more of that drink."

I lit Bruni's and gave it to her. I lit one for myself and said, "Perhaps we should spare the drink."

"I want a swallow."

"Only a swallow, then." I poured a small amount from the flask and gave it to her.

"I said this was for you, but I do believe I lied. Fancy that, but this amount is meager, Percy. I want more than that, and you should drink as well. We will do things together since together we will be."

Bruni seemed strangely animated. I poured. We drank. She smoked while looking into a far distance before she said, "I'd learned to ride horses. It was proper for me to do so, and it was the only time I could be away from her. Nana hated animals and wouldn't go near them. I rode as often as I could. Because my body developed so early for my age, Nana decided to find out if I was chaste. I will spare you the specifics, but the result surprised us both.

"Up until then, I had lived among facts, figures, and abstractions. That was my world. When Nana physically confirmed that I wasn't a virgin, I discovered my sexuality. I wasn't completely ignorant of the possibility. I'd certainly read enough about the subject and was familiar with the theory, but reality is often very different from the theoretical.

137

"Nana knew nothing of girls and horses, and that hard riding can tear that part of a girl's anatomy. I didn't, either. I professed my innocence and told her truthfully that I'd had no chance to interact with others of my age, let alone a boy. How could she not know this? But the evidence was undeniable. From then on, she kept a close and careful eye on me, and in her zeal to do so, she was immensely strong.

"Looking back, it was *her* lust, not mine, that cast the die and sealed her fate. It was a grim year up until that moment when she toppled down those stairs. She wouldn't leave me alone. I couldn't speak to my parents about what she was doing because of what Nana had done to me before. There would be reprisals, and in what form I didn't want to know. Besides, who would believe me? In the end, I knew that I had no one to protect me other than myself. That is an unwholesome truth to get one's wits around at any age, let alone at twelve or thirteen.

"The Greeks called it *ate*, that moment when reckless impulse takes control. That deity laid waste to prideful men as she skipped above their heads. It was her gift. But what happens if she should touch a girl? The poets never said. Perhaps the opposite was granted, like Dionysius and his maenads. Maybe. I don't believe in gods and goddesses, but something happened at the top of those stairs. I experienced a sudden burst of courage, or of madness, and from where it came, I cannot say. Whichever it was, it was my deliverance, and I am most thankful for it."

Bruni stopped speaking and looked about her as if to orient herself before she went on.

"Nana took a step. We were arm in arm, but my foot came down on hers. Being clumsy isn't murder, but letting go is something else, and I most certainly let go. I could have saved her, but I chose not to. Let her break her neck, I thought, and then she fell, end over end. When I saw her lying, sprawled, unmoving on the stone below, I felt ecstatic. I flew down those stairs as if on wings to be sure that she was dead, and she was. I was free of her.

"So was that murder, Percy?"

She looked at me, searching my face for whether I thought less of her. I said what I believed.

"Perhaps it was simply justice."

Bruni sighed and nodded. "I thought so, too ... at least at first, but then Lina became my governess, and I found myself hard-pressed once again. It made me wonder if perhaps I'd acted wrongly. The first incident might have been bad luck, but the second? That was difficult to account for. Nana was twisted, but Lina was insane."

———————————◆———————————

25

"**A**fter Nana's death, I floated the idea of no chaperone or supervision to my parents, but they said it was out of the question for a girl my age. Shortly thereafter, they hired Lina as my governess. Lina was a small, blond woman in her mid-twenties. Had my attitude toward her been different, I think we might have become friends. Instead, I protested my parents' decision and made it clear to Lina from the start that I hated her because of what they had decided. Lina took my initial tirade with hardly a raised eyebrow. When I ran out of steam, she informed me that she didn't give a damn about what I thought. I wasn't her employer. I was merely a means to be closer to her boyfriend, who was one of the grooms. I could do whatever I liked. True to her word, whether I studied, misbehaved, or sulked, Lina didn't show the least concern or lift a finger.

"Looking back from her point of view, it must have been difficult. I wanted her to quit and acted like a stuck-up little princess to ensure she did. I had reasoned that my parents would find hiring another governess near impossible since suspicions about Nana's death had begun to circulate, but my plan backfired. I should have realized shortly after she arrived that Lina was unusual. She may have been almost twice my age, but she and I had a similar twisted tendency for one-upmanship. Whenever I insulted her, which I admit I did frequently, she would retaliate. After several of my bitter outbursts, Lina began to plop herself in a chair in my library where I would study, and stare at me until I couldn't stand it. I would yell at her to stop. When I removed the chair, she simply stood. It was a juvenile game that little by little spun out of control.

"It did not take me long to learn to control my temper and simply ignore her. Stymied, Lina resorted to theft. A ring or a pair of undergarments would go missing. Lina denied taking them, but after several more of my things disappeared, I lost my temper once again. Unintimidated, Lina slyly confessed and told me there was nothing I could do about it. I was known as a liar, and my accusations would be dismissed as fabrications. In truth, she said, I was a stuck-up, impotent little bitch and her thieving was a necessary supplement for having to put up with me.

"I was outraged, although what she said was not untrue. I had been supremely difficult and deliberately so. On the other hand, she was stealing and had called me impotent, while daring me to do something about it. Well, I thought to myself, if she could steal from me, then I could steal from her. I would take her boyfriend.

"My plan was simple but effective. I made sure to smile, flutter my eyes, and lean against him when he hoisted me into the saddle. My tactics worked and as he came more and more under my spell, Lina grew jealous. She told me to leave him alone. I told her that if she quit, I most certainly would. This she agreed to. I had won. Unfortunately for both of us, the boyfriend's attentions were not so easily decided. He started to avoid her.

Lina was at first dejected but then became enraged. She accused me of not holding up my end of the deal and threatened to make my life a misery. I thought she was all talk, but I was wrong. The next morning, I awoke to find Lina sitting by my bed staring at me with a large pair of shears in one hand and a large chunk of my hair in the other. I was so shocked. I didn't know what to do or say. Lina smiled and said in a soft voice that if I didn't convince her boyfriend to treat her like he used to, she would do far worse to me. Everyone must sleep eventually, she said, and she was right. I realized that I was vulnerable, and that Lina was crazier than me. I decided to surrender.

"After breakfast that day, I went down to the stables to convince her boyfriend. On the way, I thought about my predicament. I knew that I was the one at fault, but I questioned what the aftereffects might be of simply rolling over and surrendering. I had lived my life in constant fear, and thinking about it made me sick. I threw up breakfast, and when I'd finished vomiting and had cleaned and refreshed my mouth, I knew with certainty that I would never choose to experience such abasement again. I'd rather die. I resolved to fight and damn the consequences. I, too had power. I had power over men.

"I marched up to her boyfriend as he held my horse and kissed him soundly. I looked into his eyes when I was done and saw that he would do whatever I asked. I told him to dump Lina if he wanted more of me. He readily agreed but expressed his nervousness about doing that. He said that Lina had permanently scarred a former rival by scalding her with boiling oil. The girl was permanently disfigured. Lina would do the same to me, or worse. I didn't care. Instead, I was elated. I'd fought back in the only way I could.

"When I returned from my ride, Lina was waiting. She attacked as I dismounted. She may have been older, but I was taller and as strong. We fought like feral cats. After what seemed like forever, Lina stopped. We stood leaned over, gasping for breath, unable to continue. Lina croaked that I was as good as dead before she staggered away. I hadn't won, but it was a victory nonetheless. I watched Lina as she retreated and knew that war had been declared. To survive at all, I had to act quickly, decisively, and with force. There'd be no second chance.

"I arranged for two things to happen simultaneously: negotiations for a truce with Lina in my library at noon and for her boyfriend to call up to her from beneath the window at that time and then leave. He did as I requested, and when Lina leaned out to see what he wanted, I pushed her. I make no defense other than to say that she would have killed or maimed me at the least. I knew that then. I know that now."

Bruni considered what she had said before continuing.

"Under most legal systems, I could've made a case for self-defense and won. Lina, it turned out, had a long history of violence. I was also a minor, and courts tend to be more lenient where children are concerned. In the end, resorting to the law proved unnecessary. My parents made sure it never became an option. They were correct in their assessment. Proving my innocence in a court of law when weighed against the destruction of the family's reputation and my future infamy made the choice obvious. Guilt or innocence are immaterial in the arena of public opinion. From the first and ever since I've said that both deaths were unfortunate accidents, but now you know the truth. Did I commit murder? Was I justified in how I acted? I thought about these questions over and over."

Bruni paused for a few moments before continuing.

"I became an attorney for no other reason than to evaluate the extent of my culpability. I discovered in my studies that there is no law against stupidity. My crime, because I did commit one, is not a crime in law, but in fact. I started and then escalated a conflict to the point when deadly force became necessary, even if interpreted as self-defense. I behaved like a spoiled little brat, and Lina's death resulted. As to Nana's death, I have no such clear-cut answer. If there is one, it still eludes me.

"From that time on, I vowed never to act with such a blatant disregard for consequences. It is ironic that as I grew into a beauty, I set similar events in motion wherever I went. Men would swoon, and women would break out knives. Knowing the tragedy that can result, I quickly learned to defuse such potential conflicts before they could begin. Men are far more easily manipulated and intimidated than women, and I made a point of learning how. Over time, I earned and developed a reputation that made any man who knew of me think twice before making an advance.

"I've answered your question, and I had one of my own, only I can't seem to remember what it was. Hold me, nonetheless. I'm feeling singularly strange."

I, too felt strange. The world was spinning, and I felt myself falling once again. I held onto Bruni for dear life.

26

I awoke alone, lying on the rock looking at a full moon suspended far above in a midnight sky. The orb's cold brilliance outshone the stars. Nothing moved, and all was silent. I felt the coldness of the night through my jacket. It reminded me of late October, that time of the year when life moves underground, autumn turns to winter, and the boundaries that separate life and death are tenuous and frail. Where those thoughts came from, I didn't know. I clambered down from the rock, as much to see if I could move as to get a grip on where I was.

Moonlight bathed the surrounding meadow in frosty white. The shadowed spaces beneath the trees lay black and hidden. I didn't see the path that led back to the house, but the rock was the same. At least I knew where I was in relation to the access road and started in that direction. There was no sign of Bruni. Perhaps she had awakened and returned to the house before me?

I passed through woods of milky light and inky dark, listening to the crunch of my footsteps on the dead leaves and the occasional scrape of bare branches as I pushed past them. The absence of any other sound added to the mystery of my surroundings. I felt uneasy.

When I came to where the access road should have been, there was only a broad expanse of creamy meadow dotted with isolated clumps of dark, denuded trees. The monochrome land before me rose gradually to a small hill. Beyond it, a thin line of white smoke rose straight up, stretching toward the moon. I walked toward it. At the top of the modest hill, I saw a smooth circular depression. In the center was a small round structure of gray and black. White smoke rose from a hole in the roof.

I walked down the gentle slope and found an entrance to the hut on the far side covered by a dark material on which were strange white markings. I was about to ask if I could enter when a voice called out from inside.

"Do not enter, *Demon*! I know you're there. You may sit at the entrance, but no closer."

Whether the voice was male or female I couldn't tell. It was muffled by the covering. It spoke in a language I'd never heard before, but nonetheless I understood. I sat down upon the freezing ground by the door.

The voice called out again, "I didn't summon you, *Demon!* Why are you here?"

"I don't know. I saw the smoke from your fire," I answered in what I thought was English, but the words came out differently.

"Are you lost?"

"Yes. No. I don't know."

"Where is your guide, *Demon*?"

"Guide? I have no guide," I said.

"Then you *are* lost. I cannot help you."

"What should I do?"

"Go back to where you came from."

"And what then?" I asked.

"Don't wander here again."

"I'm not a demon."

"How do you know?"

"Because I'm human."

"Are you sure of that?"

"Yes."

"Do you see colors?"

"No, only the light of the moon."

"Then you are *not* human, *Demon.* Go back to where you awoke and do so quickly.... Did you hear that?"

"Did I hear what?"

"Go, *Demon!* Even spirits die on nights like this."

"Where am I?" I asked.

"Goodbye, *Demon.* I would run, if I were you, but then I'm not a demon. Now go! *I COMMAND YOU! LEAVE!"*

Far away I heard a howl. The sound rose and fell and rose again before it faded away. I felt a chill other than the cold.

Perhaps the voice from inside the hut was right. I rose and walked back the way I had come. I heard the howl again. It was closer, and I began to run.

Base! I thought in a dreamlike way. *I must touch base before it catches me.*

I began to run and then sprinted toward the distant line of trees and the river beyond the meadow. The landscape moved in slow motion like in a dream, yet I was running as fast as I could.

I reached the dark shadows beneath the trees and started barreling through the brush. The branches clawed at me, but I kept scrambling forward. For a moment, I slowed to catch my breath, only to hear a terrific crash behind me. Whatever hunted me had hit the tree line with a ferocious impact. It was catching up impossibly fast. I looked behind but only for an instant. I saw trees swaying. I turned, and my mind dissolved in panic. I tore through the underbrush, leaping over rocks, and dodging tree trunks in a frenzied desperation. I caught sight of the whalelike rock in the middle of the meadow through a tunnel-vision haze. I raced toward it, in a wild, all-out sprint that expended all my strength. I heard a roar impossibly close and crashed into the side of the rock full tilt. I felt rather than saw a brilliant flash of light. The collision spun me around, and in my last moment of consciousness, illuminated by the blazing moon, I saw something black, grotesque, and huge scrambling on all fours, stretching out to eat me.

27

I couldn't breathe. I writhed on the ground beside the rock, desperate for air that wouldn't come. I heard Bruni above me. "Percy, what time is it?" And then louder, "Percy? Percy!"

I must have made a sound because I saw her head appear above me. She scrambled down beside me.

"Percy! Are you all right?"

I tried to breathe and looked up at her in a desperate plea for help, but no words came.

"You must have fallen off. I'm going to extend your arms above your head like you're diving. Breathe in through your nose and out through your mouth."

She extended my arms and after a moment I could breathe a little.

"It's working. Jesus, Percy! You scared the shit out of me. Don't do that again, please."

After a minute more of lying on the ground, I could sit up.

"Rest for a bit," Bruni said, "You had the wind knocked out of you. I've done that more than once falling off a horse. It's awful."

She sat next to me and enfolded me in her arms. After a minute she asked, "How are you feeling? Better?"

I nodded. "I can breathe again. Thank you. That was unexpected."

"It most certainly was. Whatever was in that drink?"

"I think it was a leftover portion of Alice's tincture. Johnny must have made a larger batch."

"Well, that explains a few things. Can you stand? Here, let me help you."

We got up together.

"Lean against the rock," Bruni said.

I did and took a deep, expanded breath at last. "I'm fine, I think."

"You're still very pale. Will you be all right?"

"I think so."

"Let's head back then. Do you know what time it is?"

"Late, but we should be able to make it back in time to change for dinner."

"Come on then. Hold onto my arm."

Hanging on to each other, we walked along the path toward the access road. The leafy canopy cast the ground in darkness, and the trail extended before us in different shades of shadow. I wanted to see the house to be certain of what was real and what was not. My head hurt. Whether it was from crashing into the rock, or because I had fallen off and hit the ground, I didn't know. The tree trunks in the dimness showed elongated faces shouting silent words.

Bruni broke in upon my thoughts. "Thank you for listening to me. It means a lot. Now that you've heard it … "

I remembered Bruni's story then. It seemed a long way away and in the distant past. At some point, I would have to tell her about my waking dreams, but with the approaching darkness, I couldn't. And Bruni was waiting for my answer.

Finally, I said, "Thank you for telling me about your childhood. That must have been extremely difficult. I still love you. You needn't worry about that. Not now, not ever. Of course, if there's anything else that I should know about …

150

telling me later would be better. It's getting dark, and I'm in need of light. I'm very cold."

Bruni reached over and felt my face.

"You're freezing." She held onto me tighter. "What happened on that rock?"

"I don't rightly know. I went somewhere, and it wasn't nice. I hope you had a better time."

"I did. I'll tell you later, but thank you for what you said. I feel closer to you now than ever before. Something new has happened between us. I can feel it, but right now, I need to get you home. All else can wait."

We reached the access road, and a few minutes later we could make out the roof of Rhinebeck and its four chimneys silhouetted against the sky. I was almost home and never happier to see a house in my life. I felt stretched, and hanging onto Bruni was all that prevented me from simply drifting away.

Bruni looked at me. "It will be fine, Percy. I'm here. We're here. We'll be okay."

I nodded. I hoped she was right. For now, I hardly knew what to think.

28

Bruni stood before our full-length mirror in a slim, black cocktail dress with matching patent leather high heels. A large, blue star sapphire on a platinum chain rested above her cleavage. Both her face and the stone glowed with an inward luminescence. I stood behind her.

She adjusted the pendant a fraction and looked at me in the mirror. "My earring case is somewhere in the bedroom."

"What does it look like?" I asked.

"It's a medium-size leather box. I think it's black, but then it again might be midnight blue... How do I look?"

"Like a divinity."

When we had returned from our walk, I had taken a long, hot shower and felt warmer. Afterward, she had looked me over and said, "You're not so pale. Food and drink will help. We need to get ready for dinner."

While she had busied herself in the bathroom, I had decided I needed to feel some physical objects, as Dagmar had suggested. I had gathered up the clothes I wanted to transfer to my closet upstairs. They weighed more than I had expected, and as I laboriously climbed the many stairs to my old room, I counted each of the steps, one by one. Counting had always helped me shift my attention away from things I didn't want to feel or imagine, and once again, it had worked.

I had returned to our bedroom feeling better, dressed in a dark blue suit. I had also borrowed one of Johnny's bright

Hermès ties, the ones he kept hidden. Having found them at last, I had noted that a splash of color was definitely something I had underappreciated. I would have to reconsider that.

When I had opened our bedroom door, Bruni was in her underwear, rifling through various garment bags searching for a dress. In truth, I could have remained watching Bruni in her underwear for the rest of the evening. Looking at her, I could barely think of anything else, which was fine by me. I had noted as I looked around that there was also the task of putting some order into our bedroom. It was a disaster. I hoped that neatness was a quality that Bruni and I had in common. Living together would certainly make that clear. My visions did have one positive effect. I appreciated the little things, like picking up the room or choosing a tie. They were trivial, but wonderfully grounding. On top of that, I was alive, and Bruni and I would be living together. That thought had made my heart sing.

Standing behind her now, I watched her study her reflection in the mirror. She turned her head one way and then other and said, "I keep looking at my ears. I really must wear earrings; some diamond studs, I think, the big ones. You'll have to help me. I've no idea where that case is."

"I could also ask one of the maids to help put everything away while we're at dinner?"

Bruni looked thoughtful.

"Would you?" she asked at last. "That would be splendid, but two might be better. If you could send them in this direction, I can tell them what to do, while I look for the case and finish getting ready."

She smiled at me.

"Excellent idea," I said. "I'll do that now."

I kissed the back of her neck, right where soft little hairs grew, before making my way in the direction of the kitchen to find Stanley and get some help. Bruni having a personal maid might work. As I passed the library, I wondered what she had experienced. I would also have to consult with Dagmar and Stanley about what had happened on the rock, but I had no idea when. For now, I was quite content to simply be here. Everything, including my father's visit, seemed far away. I thought it quite liberating.

The kitchen and servants' areas were bustling. I managed to spy Stanley coming up from the cellar carrying a couple of bottles of wine as if they were infants.

"Stanley, I hate to interrupt, but our bedroom is an unmitigated disaster. Can you spare a maid or two for an hour at least?"

Stanley paused. "I do happen to have some extra staff. Three should put it right. On another matter, did you manage to resolve the pending issues between you and your fiancée?"

"We did, and then some. I don't know how, but we seem to be closer than ever. Much has happened since we last spoke."

"That is excellent news. I sense there is more to be said, and I would like to hear it, but tomorrow would be better, tonight being out of the question. That you resolved the matter to both of your satisfactions is no small thing. In keeping with that, there is some rather outstanding champagne on ice in the drawing room. Simon is there to serve you. I will put these bottles aside and send the maids along."

"Excellent, Stanley. Thank you. I'll leave you to it."

I entered the drawing room. Compared to the kitchen and the bedroom, order reigned. Simon stood by the bar. When he saw me, he uncorked a bottle of Cristal, poured a flute for me, and placed it on a silver tray. He proffered it in my direction and commented, "This is a very special vintage. Stanley said I should mention that."

"Really? I didn't know. Thank you, Simon."

"You're welcome, sir."

I sipped the champagne, and it was good. In fact, it was positively brilliant. I looked around me. The light falling throughout the room was a wonderful orange yellow. I raised my flute to watch the tiny bubbles rise from the bottom. They streamed to the surface through an effervescent golden nectar. I'd never seen such an extraordinary color.

Anne and John Sr. came in and headed toward me. Anne wore a black cocktail dress and John Sr. was in a dark suit. While John Sr. collected two glasses, Anne approached me. "Is Bruni staying on after this weekend, Percy? She brought a remarkable amount of luggage. I would hate to see what she might bring on a real vacation."

I smiled. "She did, indeed. She and I might stay on for a time, but for how long, I don't know."

"Really? That is good news." She looked at me more closely. "I must say, darling, you look positively lovestruck. What have you been doing?"

John Sr. handed a flute to Anne. He had heard the last of Anne's comment. "Lovestruck? Well, before you expand on that, a toast … to love and happiness."

"To love and happiness," Anne and I said in unison.

We clinked our glasses and drank. Anne continued. "Look at him, John. I see a man hopelessly in love. Don't you? He reminds me of someone years ago." She looked at her husband over the rim of her flute and smiled in a knowing way.

John looked back at her and smiled as well. Years seemed to drop away from him, and I could see the two gazing into each other's eyes as the world receded into the background, leaving only them.

"Champagne," said John, interrupting my thoughts, "is truly a nectar of the gods. There are happy brews, and there are those that make us sad. Cristal is the happiest of spirits in my opinion, and this one is ... well beyond the ordinary. Exceptional, in fact. I trust that we will resolve all the matters before us this weekend so we can drink champagne of this quality more often. Spectacular."

"Truly it is," I said. "Now John, speaking of this weekend, I'd forgotten to ask, could you allow Raymond to remain here over the next few days?"

"Already done. I thought it prudent."

John Sr. was about to say more, when Bruni entered. She gave us all a dazzling smile and joined us as an awestruck Simon offered her a flute on a silver tray. Bruni thanked him and said to the three of us, "Thank heavens for extra staff! I'm going to love living here."

John Sr. smiled. "I think it's a marvelous idea, but what about work? It always seems to get in our way."

Bruni nodded and took a sip. She looked at her glass critically. "My God, this is good. In fact, this might be the very best champagne I've ever tasted!" She looked at the three of us and asked, "Is it me, or is this something special?"

"Both," I said. Bruni's brilliant blue eyes looked into mine for a long moment.

Anne laughed. "It's not only Percy, John. *Look* at them. We'd best get through dinner quickly."

John laughed as Bruni turned to her and said, "Absolutely not. I intend to savor every last drop of this champagne, and more if I can get it, but really, Anne, I think this is a case of you looking in a mirror and seeing yourself reflected back.

You two look mighty happy. Don't think I didn't notice. And as to work getting in the way, John, it's always open to discussion and negotiation. Should Percy and I decide to spend more time here, my father will have to visit. Besides, there's always the library. I'm quite sure he'll want to go through it in minute detail. He might even want to stay for an extended visit."

"Really?" Anne, John, and I asked at the same time.

Stanley interrupted by announcing that dinner was served, and that we should bring our flutes. It was just as well. None of us were willing to relinquish them without a fight. It was that good. I looked back to make sure that Simon had brought the bottle.

We took our places. The leaves that extended the normal size of the table had been removed, creating a smaller more intimate setting for four. The table was covered with a white delicately embroidered tablecloth. The plate settings were white with pale green lips and sparkling gold rims. Simon served more champagne.

Dagmar's first course was a lobster bisque with a hint of sherry. The centerpiece of tonight's dinner, the sole, was wheeled out by Stanley on a trolley, and as promised, he deboned it at the table. Simon served creamy mashed potatoes followed by broccoli with hollandaise sauce. The result was impressive. The fish had an exquisite balance of butter, lemon, parsley, and toasted slivers of almonds. As Stanley came around with the Clos Blanc de Vougeot, the meal settled into absolute silence as if we were at church. Dagmar had outdone herself once again.

It was only after we had finished every last crumb, speck, and morsel that Anne said, "I doubt I've tasted a better sole. That was absolutely superb. On another subject, one I hesitate to bring up given this wonderful dinner, but what's the plan for this weekend, Percy? Do you have one?"

"Yes and no," I answered. She had a point. I had been lost in the present. I contemplated what to say. "The overall objective is relatively simple: One point five million dollars in the bank with the future of Rhinebeck secured. How we get there is unclear. I will have to sit down with my father and get his agreement to do what he said he would do. What he has in mind, and why he chose to come here specifically, I don't know. I imagine he'll get around to telling me, and then it's a question of working out a solution. It is possible that he simply wants to see me, but I doubt it. Everyone seems to have an issue with my father, and even speaking to him might be difficult. The man has a bad reputation. My only thought is that we can't get hooked by our reactions to him, even if he does have more lures than a fisherman. Meeting him will be trying, at least for me. Perhaps we'll all learn something by the time this weekend's done."

"Well put," said John. "He's not exactly Jack the Ripper. From my experience, the most dangerous opponents are those whose charming personality hides a deviousness that's hard to detect, let alone decipher. I don't doubt that we'll all be charmed before he yanks the rug out. What do you think, Bruni?"

Bruni picked up a spoon and toyed with it. "He's charming, but he'll be playing before a rough crowd. Perhaps he'll win us over, so we had best discover his plans lest he take us unawares. Once revealed, the real games begin." Bruni raised her spoon. "Frankly, I'm far more interested in dessert. The sole was extraordinary, the wine superb, and the champagne beyond description. Stanley, please tell Dagmar we were all enchanted, and know that your wine choices were pure magic." She flashed him a smile.

He bowed in return. He said that he would convey our compliments and return with dessert, soft homemade vanilla ice cream with Dagmar's signature pound cake.

The dessert arrived and once again the table was silent. I savored every creamy bite until there was no more to be had, no matter what I did with my spoon. I suggested we move to the other room before we started licking the plates. Everyone laughed but paused a moment to consider that possibility.

We arose. John and I left the ladies with their coffee in the drawing room before we made our way to the library. John poured me some brandy in a snifter while I lit a cigar. We sat down in front of the fire.

John, after he had lit one himself, broke the silence. "That was one of the finest meals I think I've ever had."

"It was," I said. "Sitting down to dinner with only the four of us was something I've always wanted to do, and the smaller table made it all the more intimate."

"The table is rarely set up in that way, but it makes for a wonderful change," said John. "By the way, Bruni looked exceptional tonight, absolutely stunning. Coming up here seems to agree with her. Hugo tells me that she works incessantly, and although he may enjoy that as an employer, both he and Elsa would like to see her take a more balanced approach to life."

I nodded and said, "Bruni is extremely focused, but coming here more often should give her some of that. At the very least, it will get her away from the office."

"It should. Have you thought about your wedding?"

"Not specifically. We're more into learning how to live together right now."

John puffed at his cigar and then relit it. "It is the acid test. There are the expectations, and then there is the reality. My advice is to agree with Bruni far more often than not. It's called cooperation, and marriage, in the end, is a corporate and cooperative endeavor. Anne and I meshed rather easily for that reason, and I now have peace in my life. Many have strived for that and not succeeded."

"It is an underappreciated achievement. Now, if I can settle the financial matters with my father and Hugo, I might be able to have the same."

John nodded and then brought up the subject that was obviously most on our minds. "Have you thought about what to do?"

"More often than I'd care to mention. My father has a plan, I'm sure. I have to find out what it is."

"Whatever it is will be revealed in its own time, probably when least expected. One thing you should know, Hugo came to me with a business proposal about a year ago. It's likely that Hugo ran it by your father when I declined to participate. The proposal was a big deal, and as is the case with many of that size, it's possible that it didn't go as planned. I say that, because there may be some additional friction between Hugo and your father."

"Will I have to intercede in some way?"

"Quite possibly. I wish I could be more specific, but confidentiality requires that I speak in only the most general terms. I would simply be aware of that possibility and know that the funding delay may have little to do with you, but everything to do with what is happening between them."

"I see. Expect complications, in other words."

"Yes."

160

"Well, thank you for the heads-up. I was hoping it could all be taken care of rather simply but from what you say, that may not be the case."

"When money is involved, particularly large sums, it's rarely simple. I've said all I can. Shall we rejoin the ladies?"

"Yes, but before we do, thank you, John, for that information. I'll keep it in mind."

John and I arose and returned to the drawing room. Once there, I thanked both Anne and John for their company and a spectacular evening. Bruni and I said good night and wandered back to our apartment hand in hand. When we passed through the sitting room, I opened the door to our bedroom. Splendid order reigned—the floor was clear, every last item had been put away, and the bed was turned down invitingly. Bruni stood next to me. "What a wonderful room. I think it's time we sample this bed in earnest, now that we can see it."

"Absolutely," I said. "I wonder when it was last used for the purpose we have in mind?"

Bruni hugged me. "Perhaps never. We may be the first. We should christen it properly. Can you help me with my hook?"

She turned her back to me so I could unfasten her dress.

"I will, but I should warn you, sleeping in this room might be eventful, because ..."

Bruni turned and placed a finger on my lips. "My love, I have absolutely no intention of sleeping in this room anytime soon."

29

I awoke from a dreamless sleep. It was still dark, and I could hear the wind sloughing outside the window, even through the drapes. I reached out to my left, but Bruni wasn't there. I slipped on a bathrobe and went into the sitting room in search of her. The fire had burned down to almost nothing, and Bruni in a white silk kimono sat cross-legged on the sofa, staring at the subdued light of the coals.

"Are you all right?" I asked.

"Yes and no," she said, not looking at me.

"Tell me. Perhaps I can help." I sat down beside her.

"I doubt it. Feeling happy makes me wary, and being supremely happy scares me witless. Such pleasurable moments are too often followed by disaster. Percy, I am wonderfully happy here with you, and that scares the daylights out of me. Last night was truly glorious. Thank you."

I held her in my arms.

"My love, what can I do?"

"Nothing."

"For what it's worth, the Greeks thought similarly, but I'm not sure they were correct. Being happy doesn't mean that sorrow follows, and I know of no law that states that for every joy there must be an equal measure of sadness."

"You may be right, but you should know that it's rare for me not to get up in the middle of the night and ponder. I hope that won't bother you?"

"It won't, but I'm hoping you might find that you need to less and less."

"I'd like that, if it's possible. It may not be. I worry a lot."

"You don't show it."

"I'm good at hiding what I think and feel. I'm secretive, and that may not make for a happy marriage. I don't know if I can change who I am."

"I'm like you, but I've improved, I think. You will, too, given time. We'll work on it together."

"But what if we have children? Won't they be equally as dark? Wouldn't that be bad?"

"If you would rather be alive than dead, then wouldn't they feel the same?"

"Yes, but it will be hard for them."

"It's hard for everyone. What else?"

"I'm messy."

"I wondered about that. I'm not. I can help, and then there's room service here. It comes with the place."

"But can we afford it? We're living large, and that concerns me, too."

"You and me both. We'll have to see. At least it gives us an incentive to work like crazy when we must, and then relax like mad."

"How exactly do you relax like mad?" Bruni asked.

"I don't, really."

"I didn't think you did. Neither do I. I think too much, and there's always something that needs to be done."

"Me, too. What woke you?"

"I had one of my nightmares."

"You have nightmares?"

"Off and on. They vary, but they have a similarity. Typically, I dream I murdered someone and left the body in a

163

closet, only I can't remember how I did it. This time I went downstairs, where people whom I've never met asked me if I'd seen a man I didn't know. They told me that they saw him walking up the stairs. I said I hadn't seen him, but I knew it was the man in the closet. Usually, I wake up terrified that I'll be found out and put to death. Sometimes, when I realize it was a dream, and none of it is true, I cry with relief."

I held her. "That's horrible."

"Do you have nightmares?"

"No. Yes. Recently I've had living nightmares, and I don't know what to do."

Bruni sat up and looked at me. "Really? Are they scary?"

"Very."

"I'm all ears. I love a good scary ghost story. I really do! Of course, I don't believe in ghosts, but stories about them are usually worse than my nightmares, so they make me feel better."

"That's weird."

"Isn't it?" Bruni brightened up like she'd turned on a light. She seemed happy to have something other than herself to talk about. "You must tell me about them. I have a perverse streak, and I love things like that. Tell me you like horror movies!"

"I don't want to disappoint you, but I hate them. Johnny and I were subjected to many at a camp we went to. I actually screamed in one or two, most of them really, other than the ones I was too petrified to even do that. Most of the time I put my hands over my eyes and peeked through my fingers. My friends thought I was such a wimp, except Johnny. Johnny thought that subjecting us to such barbaric torture was another example of the perils of adult supervision. He told me to carry on what I was doing as a form of protest. The next year, the unending parade of Saturday night horror films stopped.

164

Several influential parents had complained. Apparently quite a number of children at the camp felt the same way after Johnny had spoken with them about it. Johnny was a bit of a closet revolutionary growing up."

Bruni giggled. "So, Johnny Dodge was really Che Dodge in his youth?"

"Not really. He rebelled as a matter of course. Since the people and the institutions that he rebelled against were pretty smart, he felt he had some worthy adversaries. He gave it all up when he discovered women."

"Really? Who knew? Thank you for telling me about that. Talking about your nightmares might help. It would certainly help me. I might be able to get back to sleep."

"Okay, Bruni. That's really weird."

"Weird it may be, but you love me, right? I can be a little weird."

"You can."

"Now let's hear your story, Percy. Please tell me."

"Okay."

And so, I did. She snuggled against me, and I told her about the absence of my intuitive gift, Dagmar and the potion, the abandoned house, Stanley and Johnny's comments, and then about the incident on the rock. I don't know how long it took, but the fire had died completely by the time I had finished. Bruni listened. She was very good at that.

When I had run out of words, she squeezed my arm and said in a sleepy voice, "What do we do?"

"Speak to Dagmar tomorrow, and early, if we can."

"Yes, I think that's wise. I'm glad you told me. Your dreams are definitely scarier than mine. I'd hug you, only I'm too sleepy to move."

"Would you like me to carry you to the bed?"

"Would you?"

I put my arms underneath her. "Put your arms around my neck and hang on." I managed to lift her and stagger to the bedroom before placing her as gently as I could underneath the sheets. She was remarkably heavy. By the time I got around to my half, Bruni was purring in her sleep. I doubted that I would ever tire of that sound.

30

W e awoke to the braying of my alarm.

"What in God's name is that?" asked Bruni from underneath the covers.

"My Big Ben."

"It's hideous. Make it stop!"

I reached over and turned it off.

"Thank God!" Bruni peeked her head out and then sat up. She looked like a sleepy goddess. "That will have to go."

"How else are we to wake up?" I asked.

"I have a telephone service, but I'm sure someone can knock on the door with a tray of tea or coffee in the future."

"Oh." I hadn't thought of that. Bruni raised her arms above her head and stretched. If I was half asleep before, I was now fully awake.

Bruni looked over at me. "Don't get any ideas. I haven't even brushed my teeth."

"Breakfast isn't until nine."

"Tough luck. You should have set it earlier, but … I suppose we could shower together."

"That's a good idea. We can save water."

After dressing, Bruni and I wandered into the dining room hand in hand. Anne and John were already down, looking refreshed. Bruni squeezed my hand and motioned in their direction with a slight nod of her head. They did look happy. I was, too, and I had breakfast to look forward to.

Breakfast at Rhinebeck was my favorite time of the day. The familiar smells of coffee, bacon, and toast would assail me, and I would feel happy. Today, there were even breakfast sausages. I was in heaven.

Bruni and I said hello as Anne and John looked up from their papers. Anne nodded her head and went back to reading with a smile on her face. John was smiling, too. Bruni and I sat down and started in. I would catch her looking at me from time to time. I suppose I did the same.

When there was no more left, and we had finished the last of our coffee, Bruni and I excused ourselves and went in search of Dagmar in her kitchen. A quick look told us that speaking with her would be impossible. She had three assistants doing different tasks while she moved rapidly from one to the other to make sure they were following her instructions. Bruni and I hastily retreated to the foyer.

We stood by the clock as Bruni said, "Dagmar's certainly very busy. She makes even me feel lazy. Shall we take a walk? We would then be doing something, and I can tell you what happened to me on the rock."

"Good idea," I said. "Why don't we swing left past the tennis court, say hello to the crows if they're there, and walk among the trees to the south?"

"Why not."

We passed out of the front of the house and to the left. The day was bright and sunny with a band of high clouds in wispy streaks to the west. The crows were high up in the trees at the edge of the south lawn, chuckling and cawing among themselves.

"I wonder what they're talking about?" I asked Bruni.

"Food."

"You think so?"

"With the occasional snippet of gossip thrown in."

"I've often wondered. So, what happened to you? You said it was very different from my experience."

"Completely different."

"Tell me."

"Okay, here goes," she began. "I was in a pretty odd place to begin with. I had finished my story, and the relief I felt at having finally said what I'd thought impossible to say was indescribable. It was its own euphoria, and then another feeling came along, a kind of contented bliss. I felt so relaxed, I laid down and awoke in the middle of the day, not the late afternoon. The sun was shining down from above, and I was hot. It felt like late spring. The surrounding woods were quiet and still. I looked about and saw a large doe at the edge of the meadow standing underneath the trees. She was like a statue watching me with her ears alert. After a time, she began to make her way toward me. Her belly was large and round. I watched her as she approached. She moved slowly and deliberately. She would bend down and nibble at some blades of grass and then take a few steps in my direction. I was fascinated and sat as still as I could. She ended up quite close.

"She raised her neck and stared at me. Her eyes were liquid pools in which I could lose myself. They held no fear. They simply looked at me as if to say that we were the same. I've never felt so calm as I was in that moment. I can't possibly describe it. There we were, the two of us, together.

"I've looked into the eyes of horses and seen them looking back at me. You can sense that they know who you are and have an intelligence, but this was different. There was not merely a recognition, but a knowing.

"The doe then turned and walked slowly, step by step, back into the trees. I watched her until she disappeared. I think I lay back down and went to sleep again. I awoke and asked you what time it was, but you weren't there. I called your name and heard something move next to the rock. I knew then that you'd fallen off. I found you on your back looking up at me. I jumped down to help you. I was back in the world. My dream was thankfully very different from yours, powerful yet filled with peace."

"It sounds it."

"It really was. I'm not religious, or even spiritual, but that vision, if that is what it was, has made me reconsider. The doe had a presence. It was sacred. I use that word because I know of no other that comes close. Like you, I don't know what to make of it."

"If it strengthens you, then it is good."

"Yes. It was distinctly female. Perhaps your dreams were distinctly male?"

"Being filled with terror is not so male, I think."

"Maybe it is."

"How so?"

"Overcoming fear is what a man must do. How that is to be done is a mystery. It is part of the hero's journey, Percy."

I looked at Bruni. I hadn't considered that. "Perhaps it is. But in the end the hero must defeat his nemesis or be destroyed."

"It's how the story goes."

"Then we'll have to see."

"We will, but now we must shift our focus away from such things. Guests will be showing up, and we must deal with that. I must also make some calls. I want to know when Papa is arriving, and any news on your father. While I'm doing that, why don't you speak with Stanley about the schedule for today? We must return to the house, but before we do, kiss me. We won't be able to be alone for much longer."

We kissed by the trees at the edge of the south lawn.

"Thank you, Bruni."

"No, thank you, Percy. That will have to hold us. I'll join you when I'm finished. I won't be long."

We walked back to the house, she to the library and me to Stanley's office. I thought about what Bruni had said and wondered if because I was afraid, I was less of a man. Or was I more, given the magnitude of that fear? A case could be made for either, but fear or no fear, I would do what I had to do. How I felt was immaterial. I'd learned that much at least.

31

S tanley was at his desk and offered me a chair.

"How can I be of service?" he asked.

"I just wanted to know how it's going. Bruni is finding out when her parents and my father will be arriving."

"All is prepared on this end. How about you? Are you prepared?"

"About as much as I can be, I think."

"Good, I'm glad to hear it. On another matter, have you spoken to your fiancée about the secret library?"

"Not as yet. It hasn't come up."

"Good. I recommend that you keep its whereabouts and access strictly to yourself until after this weekend. I might even suggest until after you both are married."

"Any particular reason?"

"Just a hunch, but I've learned to trust such things."

"I see. I'll follow your advice, although I'm curious as to why you say that."

"I know no more than what I've told you, but what I suggest will do no harm and could prove helpful in discovering what others are planning. Should anyone make such a request to visit or look over the library, I would be interested in knowing."

"You don't trust Bruni?"

"The more important question is, do you?"

"I do, but there are likely earlier threads that have yet to be unraveled, particularly having to do with her family and their business. I'm sure both come with obligations. Untangling those will likely take some time."

"I would agree. Being open is not easy if one habitually hides what one thinks. Such a behavioral change is difficult, even if she should want to change."

"Quite true. Still, we're making progress. You mentioned the library; do you think that's the reason behind my father's coming here?"

"I think it highly likely, although I have no evidence. It's a guess at this point. On another matter, how are your new quarters? Are they acceptable?"

"Very acceptable. By the way, I didn't have any dreams last night, so I think I can sleep there with no further issues."

There was a knock at the door, and Bruni entered.

She greeted Stanley, who offered her a chair. She thanked him and sat down. "I've spoken with my father. Lord Bromley will be arriving with my parents early this afternoon. Malcolm Ault is coming. He may not be invited specifically, but he will arrive late this evening as well. By the way, Stanley, where have you decided to put Lord Bromley?"

"In the room you stayed in when you were here last," Stanley replied.

We were interrupted by the sound of a car crunching around the roundabout. I hoped it was Johnny and not one of our guests.

32

S tanley had opened the front door for Bruni and me when Johnny stepped out of a black limo. He wore dark aviator sunglasses and looked a little worse for wear.

He waved halfheartedly at Bruni and Stanley, gave me a pat on the shoulder, and said, "Meet me in the common room with a thermos of coffee in about fifteen minutes. While you do that, I'll attempt to scale the stairs one at a time, keeping my head absolutely still. Should it somehow detach itself en route, please pick it up gingerly and bring it with you. We're probably going to need it. I have news."

Bruni and I watched Johnny slowly mount the stairs. Bruni whispered, "I can't imagine how much they drank. Papa was not exactly bubbly when I spoke with him. Other than telling me that he would be giving Bromley a lift, he didn't have a lot to say. He told me to call him back when he was more recovered. I think I'll do that now while you speak with Johnny. Later we can compare notes. We need a plan."

"Good idea. Give your father my best, if you think it will help. I'll speak with Johnny. See you in a bit."

I went to the kitchen where Stanley was already preparing a thermos, two mugs, and a small glass of greenish-brown liquid that had been placed on a small tray.

"One of Dagmar's concoctions?" I asked, examining the contents of the glass.

"Hardly. I don't prepare it often, but it is an excellent palliative for those moments when we have gone too far but have an active day ahead. Have him drink it first, with a coffee chaser. It should do the trick."

"What's in it?"

"Never ask a question if you aren't prepared to receive the answer."

"I withdraw the question."

"Would you like me to bring this up to him?"

"No, I'll do it."

Stanley smiled. "Always a good idea."

I thanked Stanley and made my way upstairs balancing the tray. I found Johnny sprawled on the couch with his eyes closed and a damp washcloth on his forehead. He was making odd gurgling sounds.

"Good heavens, Johnny, how much did you drink? Don't answer that. Lucky for you, Stanley has sent up a concoction that can wake the dead."

"It's not one of Dagmar's little treats, is it? If it's all the same, I'd rather not. I don't think I could survive it."

"No such luck. It's a Stanley original. He said to drink it all at once and then chase it with some coffee. You'll feel better rather quickly."

"I'm game. Put it down and then help me sit up. I will open my mouth, and you can pour it in."

"I'll help you up, but you drink it."

"A worthy compromise. Help me."

I took the damp cloth from his forehead and placed it on the coffee table. I helped him sit up and handed him the drink. He looked at it and said, "Well, anything is better than the way I feel. Here goes."

175

He tossed it back and swallowed. His eyes seemed to bug out slightly as he reached for the coffee, spilling some in his haste. He drank eagerly. I thought the coffee a little hot, but that didn't seem to deter Johnny in the slightest.

"My God, I'll never drink that again. Just the same, I think it's working. Although what it's doing exactly, I have no idea. I'll be right back." He headed for the bathroom.

Five minutes later, Johnny opened the door. Some color had returned to his face, and his eyes looked clear.

"Good morning," I said.

"It is, compared to how I felt earlier. Everything looks up from here. I'm not well, but I'm alive. I suppose you want to know my news."

"Yes."

"And I suppose you have some of your own."

"Yes but tell me yours first."

"Very well. Hugo was surprised to see me, as you can imagine. He was sitting in a back corner on the first floor. I was escorted to his table, said hello, and sat down. I handed him the invitations and duly informed him that I was treating him to dinner. He put the invites unopened in his breast pocket and looked at me steadily, saying nothing. I felt like an insect looking at a toad right before it decides to have dinner. Realizing at that moment that he and I were at a critical juncture, I went all in. I picked up the wine list and pointed to a section with some very large numbers next to them. I couldn't see what they said exactly, as they were upside down. After a few seconds of looking at me while I held the proffered list, he looked down, and seemed to smile. 'Three of these might be worth drinking. We'll give them our attention. Do you know how your father and I met?' And we were off. What followed was the most extraordinary meal I've ever had, only

I can't recall how it ended exactly, other than with a great deal of applause and lot of waiters herding us out the door into a waiting limo as we staggered in each other's arms. I do believe Hugo drooled on my suit."

Johnny picked up his suit jacket and pointed to a stain on the lapel. "See? There it is. Proof. It was one hell of a night. I've never experienced such debauchery. I don't know where I slept, or even if I did. I don't know how I got here. I don't even know if I paid the tab, although I must have. I came to when the chauffer opened the door, and I stepped out. You were all staring at me with some concern. That's it. That's all I can remember."

"Surely you remember more. You said you had news."

"I do. The details are slowly coming back to me. It was after we opened that bottle of Napoleon's brandy. It created quite a sensation apparently. Any more coffee?"

"What?"

"I wish it wasn't true, but there it is. Can you please pour me another cup? It might help me remember more."

"Johnny, you're scaring me."

"And with good reason, but there is some good news. Hugo is definitely on our side, or at least on mine. He told me I was the finest fellow he'd ever met, other than my father. It could have been the drink talking, but maybe not."

"Johnny, I think I'm going to kill you if you don't start from the beginning. Did you say napoleon brandy or Napoleon's brandy?"

"Napoleon's. We even have proof, although I can't recall what happened to that letter. It came with the bottle. I think I'll pour that coffee myself if you don't mind. I see you're a bit preoccupied."

"Preoccupied?"

Johnny poured some more coffee. "Yes, preoccupied."

"Stunned is more accurate. You drank Napoleon's brandy, his personal brandy? You have seconds to start telling me all of it from the beginning or, so help me God, I'll strangle you right now."

"Steady. There's no cause for violence, at least not at this point. It's coming back to me. What a night."

"Johnny!"

"Okay, okay. Keep your shirt on. We started off with Hugo telling me about my father and their adventures together. They met at a fencing school in Spain, of all places, when they were lads. I never knew my dad fenced, but apparently he was rather good. Both of them were. They were bitter rivals until one night they were jumped after practice by five very tough fellows.

"Together, they managed to kill one before the others were driven off. They dumped the body in a river and fled the city. By the time they arrived at Hugo's castle all the way in Austria, they were friends for life. They never could figure out who did the deed exactly, so they agreed to split it. I never knew any of this."

"Your dad killed a man?"

"Apparently. It was self-defense, but still, it was a revelation. No wonder they're such pals. At least you and I didn't have to go to those lengths to form a friendship. It was after that story that we ordered the Chateaubriand and a rather exceptional Margaux. Bottle followed bottle in the course of the meal, the next one better than the last. After each was emptied to the last drop, Hugo and the sommelier would huddle together and discuss what they should open next. A selection would be made, and the sommelier would almost burst into tears of admiration. He would repeat over and over 'outstanding choice! Simply outstanding!' and literally run to do the man's bidding. New glasses would be put down. The entire service would be removed and replaced. By the end of the evening, there must have been at least eight waiters seeing to our every need. It was extraordinary. Hugo told me story after story of he and my father going here, going there, and getting into all kinds of trouble. If even half of it is true, they both deserve our admiration and respect. I was completely captivated. The baron and I matched glass for glass. By the time dessert was served, we were pretty far gone. During a pause, he told me that my father was his one true friend, and that he saw a lot of him in me. It was a joy. I think he even cried at that point. He then announced in a sober voice that we needed to commemorate this moment with something truly extraordinary. He called out in a commanding tone to the sommelier who was hovering nearby. 'I want the bottle. It is time.' Well, there was a hush. The sommelier began to quake and then stumbled to do his bidding. After a minute or two, a team of waiters, assistant sommeliers, maître d', kitchen staff, chefs—the whole shebang came out in a somber procession with an ancient bottle resting on dark blue velvet in a leather case. I may have been seeing double at that point. I don't know. It was quite a parade. A table with various surgical tools was laid out, and the opening began. Both bottle and cork were carefully assessed by various members of the staff. They could have been attempting open-heart surgery from the way they were carrying on. The entire process took several minutes, with several intervening urgent discussions before the cork was finally drawn, the brandy carefully poured and presented, along with the letter signed by the esteemed emperor himself, proving its authenticity. You could have

179

heard a pin drop as we both raised our snifters and toasted each other before inhaling deeply and taking a sip."

"What did it taste like?"

"Like brandy, of course, only exceptionally smooth. The house applauded. In fact, we got a standing ovation. Hugo was in fine spirits and even allowed the sommelier a taste, which caused the poor man to blubber uncontrollably. He had to be led away. That was the moment Lord B. decided to make his appearance."

"Wait a second! You actually met my father?"

"Yes, Lord Bromley in the flesh, him and a man named Cobb. Hugo told me his name later. Formidable fellow, that. He looked like someone had worked him over from an early age and kept at it for some years thereafter. I never understood the term 'cauliflower ears' until I saw his. He's bald, has a nose that's been pushed sideways, and never said a word. Frankly, I think we're all in a whole lot of trouble. Stanley, especially."

"How did you know the man was my father?"

"He was an older version of yourself. His hair was black, his eyes dark, and he stood ramrod straight with that Cobb creature beside him. He looked very fit and well turned out. He may well be ancient, but his looks and bearing were that of a late-middle-aged man. It was disconcerting. Hugo and I made the effort to rise, but that proved impossible. Lord Bromley looked down at me and asked, 'Are you my son?' I told him 'No.' He turned immediately to Hugo and said, 'You said he would be here.' Hugo shrugged. Lord Bromley looked rather annoyed and snapped, 'This is not what we agreed.' He started to walk away, only to reverse course. He picked up my glass, lifted it, took in the color, swirled it, and drank. He paused for a moment before putting it down. 'The emperor always had good taste.' He left with that Cobb fellow parting the crowd like Moses and the Red Sea. One moment he was there; the next, he was gone."

"You really met him?"

"I did. Talk about breaking the mood. I asked the waiters to change the entire service and bring me a clean snifter. I looked at Hugo, who simply shrugged again and said, 'Plans change, and sometimes for the better. Forget him. Let me pour you some more of this brandy, and I'll tell you about my dungeon. It has quite a history.' Before we began again, I asked Hugo why Lord B. was coming to Rhinebeck in the first place and he said, 'He wants to see his son, among other things, but that subject right now is verboten. Tomorrow is tomorrow. Tonight, we enjoy. Drink with me.' We finished the bottle, and by the time we did, neither of us could do much of anything. It was quite cathartic."

"Cathartic?"

"Yes, cathartic. We told each other many secrets, knowing that neither of us would be able to remember what the other had said. It was the listening to each other speak words we would not normally say and then watching the other nodding and accepting that made the evening."

"Then I suppose it was time well spent. I do have one question, however."

"Which is?"

"How much did you spend?"

"I can't remember. I used my Dodge Capital card, I think. I vaguely remember a telephone being brought to the table, and a Mr. Something from American Express attempting to say a word or two, but what transpired exactly I don't recall. The establishment was very kind. They half-carried us to the limo, which means it must have turned out well. I'll give them a call, if you wish."

"I wish."

"Perhaps this afternoon."

"Very well. I will have to inform your father of the amount, since we're splitting the bill."

"What?" Johnny sat upright. "When was that decided?"

"After you left."

"Why didn't you tell me?"

"I didn't think it important."

"Not important? My God!" said Johnny, paling visibly. "How could you? Remember that bar bill at the Southampton Bathing Corp? He really blew a gasket then, and that was for a mere pittance. This one is several orders of magnitude larger. You should have called and told me, Percy. You really should have."

"Well, don't try and make it my fault. I wasn't even there. Right now, you need to pull yourself together. People are going to start showing up soon. For now, I've no idea what to do about your tab. Perhaps that will have to wait until we're through this weekend."

"I most certainly agree," said Johnny.

I stood and resolved to try and put the cost out of my mind.

"Not so fast," said Johnny. "You almost got away with it, but not quite. You were about to leave and not mention what happened while I was gone. I know your methods. Sit back down and tell me. I'll even pour you some coffee, which in my condition is nothing short of heroic. Speak."

I sighed and sat. "You're correct, but I'm stuck on that brandy thing. How much do you think that bottle cost?"

"A pretty penny I'm sure. Think about it. You're paying retail with a likely five- or ten-times markup on top of that, since it was served in a restaurant, and please note that doesn't include the tip or the tax. I'm pretty sure we made their year."

"You're not helping."

"We'll see about that. Now, to more pressing matters. You need to put aside your concerns about last night and move on. Spare no details. I'm ready to listen."

As I spoke, I realized that much had transpired since he was away. When I had finished, he looked thoughtful.

Finally, he said, "The Bruni story is extraordinary. I don't know what to say. We cannot judge her, at least I can't. I'll

183

keep it to myself of course, and that whole demon thing. Terrifying. One thing is certain, that flask and any such potions are off limits to you for now. Where is it, by the way?"

"Back where I found it."

"Good. And then there's Dagmar history. Of course, that makes sense. She's always been far smarter than any of us. Well, most of us. Frankly, with your father showing up with that Cobb fellow, this is all getting a bit out of hand. Allow me to get my yellow pad to see if I can make some sense of it. There are so many diverse disturbing bits. In the meanwhile, do something useful, like get us some more coffee. I need to think."

I grabbed the thermos and rose to do his bidding. Johnny was in his element, and I wanted to talk to Bruni. It would be my last chance before being the host made doing so problematic.

I ran into Stanley in the second-floor hallway checking the guest bedrooms.

"Stanley, I have some news. Johnny ran into my father at 21. He was accompanied by a man named Cobb. He looked like an ex-prize fighter apparently. You should find out what you can about him. If my father is trouble, then that man appears doubly so."

Stanley nodded. "Was he bald with a nose pushed to the side and pummeled ears?"

"That is pretty much how Johnny described him."

"We met years and years ago. Interesting that he should be arriving at this time. He has many underworld connections."

"Should I be worried?"

Stanley smiled. "Leave him to me. You have enough to worry about. My past, it seems, is coming back to haunt me. I trust you have secured Raymond for this weekend?"

"John Sr. has made him available."

"Well, that should suffice. I will make adequate preparations. Will there be anything else?"

"No, just thought you should be informed."

"I appreciate it. Your father will be arriving shortly. Consult me should you feel a need."

"Thank you, Stanley. I will."

I left him to his duties but thought I heard him whistling as he walked away. I'd never heard Stanley whistle. Whether that was a good sign or a very bad one, I wasn't sure. With Stanley, it was hard to say.

———◆———

34

I passed through the kitchen and asked one of the staff to refill the thermos and bring it up to Johnny on the top floor. In the library, I found Bruni staring out the window.

"Penny for your thoughts?" I asked.

She turned and smiled. "You'll have to offer me more than that. You have no idea how high my billing rates are. I made some calls. My parents and Lord Bromley are well on their way and should arrive fairly soon. Are you prepared?"

"Not really. If you hold me for a minute, maybe I will be."

Bruni hugged me. "Feel better, now?"

"Yes."

"Me, too. I do have a concern, however. We will likely be drawn apart this weekend as we attend to everyone else's needs. We'll have to make time for us."

"Yes, I quite agree," I said. "We should retire as soon as propriety permits this evening and plan on taking walks during the mornings. I have a concern as well."

"Which is?" Bruni pulled away to look at me.

"Negotiating with my father may get complicated. Any advice you can give me would be helpful."

Bruni nodded. "Let's sit down for a moment."

We sat next to each other before the fireplace. Her professional mode was much in evidence as she started in.

"I've had some experience with negotiations. Most clients, as well as opposing counsels, rarely say what the crucial issue or issues are at the beginning of a discussion. It is usually the third or fourth item on the list. The simplest way to find out is to keep asking what their best outcome might be. When it finally comes out, the key point will have little emphasis."

"I am aware of that. Johnny does it all the time."

"It's not uncommon. Some lay everything out at once to hide what's important among those things that are not. It's a variation; the trick is to listen and ask sufficient questions. As a general rule, if it's in the best interests of both parties to come up with an agreement, then negotiations are usually a matter of finding common ground and collaborating on solutions."

"That makes sense."

"The present case is far less straightforward. When a deal negotiated in good faith falls apart at the last minute, there are three possible reasons. The first is that what was agreed upon is not able to be delivered by one or both parties. The second is that a better offer has come forward and is being reviewed by the delayer. The last is that by reneging, the offender believes they can force a better deal."

"You think that's the case here?"

"It might be."

"That is troubling. Is there anything you think I should do?"

"Be patient. If the last scenario is correct, then the key negotiating point won't come up until the last minute, when you are desperate and more amenable to agree to terms that are unfavorable."

"That would be typical."

"And not easily handled. Your father can be charming one moment and tyrannical the next. Lastly, he is charismatic. Be charmed, of course, but don't be blinded. I say that because I was. It could happen to you."

187

"I'll keep that in mind. Now, how about yourself?"

"I was thinking about that as I looked out the window. The best I could come up with was to be gracious and attentive while keeping my ears and eyes open. That sounds trivial, but for now that's the best I can do."

"That sounds reasonable and likely the best. Thank you for being in my corner and looking after me."

"We're in this together, Percy."

"For better or for worse, it seems."

"Yes, for better or worse. Did I hear a car?"

"I think so."

Although Bruni's advice had helped settle me, the moment that I had dreaded was at hand. I shivered, but whether from fear or something else, I wasn't sure.

35

A long black limo circled the roundabout like some monstrous raptor descending to land. We were all out front in a long line, even Anne. The staff, with Raymond looking suitably intimidating, stood not far away. Johnny whispered, "Showtime" and gave my shoulder a pat before he went to the end of the line. Bruni stood beside me.

The car halted, and a chauffeur stepped out to open the rear door as a bald man exited on the far side carrying a black doctor's bag. He did look like a prize fighter. The man gazed at us, covered his head with a black bowler hat, and stood by the car door as the baron exited. Hugo looked a little tired, but other than that, I could discern no ill effects from the excesses of the night before. He nodded at me and reached in to hand out Elsa, who dazzled with a smile. As they stood to one side, I waited for my father to disembark. I had been dreading this moment, and now that it was upon me, I felt an anxious curiosity.

Lord Bromley stepped out and looked about. He was smaller in size than I imagined, and Johnny's description of him was accurate. He was an older and better-dressed version of myself. He wore a tailored dark blue chalk-striped suit, white shirt, and gray silk tie with tiny blue dots that matched his handkerchief. His black eyes took us all in before ignoring everyone and focusing on me. Hugo stepped forward and made the introduction. "Percy, may I introduce your father, Lord Bromley."

"Welcome to Rhinebeck," I said. "Allow me to greet my future in-laws, and then I will introduce you to my guests."

Lord Bromley smiled. "Thank you for the invitation. I don't wish to stand on ceremony; however, it might be best if we all moved inside where introductions can be made at leisure. I also want to apologize in advance for any inconvenience my unanticipated visit may have caused. I have brought a friend to look after my needs, should that be a help. I am delighted to finally meet you. Perhaps your fiancée would be kind enough to take my arm and accompany me inside?"

I nodded. He was very smooth, I had to admit, and I noted that he liked to take control. I glanced at Bruni, who stepped forward and said, "It would be my pleasure. Lord Bromley, come this way, and I must say, you look remarkably well preserved considering your years. You may take my arm."

Her tone was warm and reassuring. My father hesitated, unsure whether he was being complimented, but finally acquiesced. I glanced at Stanley, who was staring at Cobb with a peculiar smile. Cobb didn't return the look.

As the guests filed in, I took the opportunity to welcome my future in-laws. The baron nodded in my father's direction and said, "You have met him at last. You may not have wanted to, but he is your father after all, yes?"

"Yes, he is, but what that means I cannot say."

"Then you will find out. On another matter, I noted your absence last night at 21, but there were compensations. You are forgiven. Shall we go in?"

"Yes, let's. According to Johnny, last night was quite an experience."

The baron chuckled as Elsa grabbed my arm, gave me a kiss, and said, "It is good to see you, *Liebchen*. Now, enough chit-chat and on to important matters. I expect to be seated next to you tonight at dinner. Let us move along. I don't want to miss a minute. The tension here is already thick. My daughter handled that man well, yes? You should thank me."

"I do. Every day."

She beamed and patted my hand. "You are as I remembered. We'll have fun tonight."

Stanley stood by the front door as we entered. He still had that peculiar expression on his face. He murmured that champagne was being served in the drawing room. I thanked him and fell behind to say, "You seem pleased, Stanley."

"I am. With Cobb present, events have taken an interesting turn."

"So it would seem. I would like to hear what you have to say about that, but for now let's try and accommodate him. You might have to attend to my father otherwise, and I doubt either of you would enjoy that."

"My thoughts exactly. Lunch will be at one."

I followed the last of my guests. My father was by the bar drinking champagne, chatting with Bruni. I went up to him. "I do believe you know everyone here other than myself?"

"You are correct, other than yourself. One thing you should know: I dislike wasting time. At my age, there is a limited amount—a fact you will appreciate should you be lucky enough to live as long as me. Where can we talk and remain undisturbed for a few hours? I want to do that now."

"I would like that, but after lunch. Dagmar's cooking is not to be missed. Ask Hugo. He will say the same."

He scowled. "Is such idle luxury so important to you?"

"Sometimes."

191

"Provided you can afford it, which I believe is the point of my being here." And then added, "At least from your perspective."

"True. And from yours? What is the point?"

"Well, we'll have to see about that, won't we?"

"I do believe so. Simon, standing over there, can show you to your room. Lunch will be served shortly."

He nodded. "My friend is a medical man and will be staying with me in my room. Please make the necessary arrangements."

"It will be as you wish. Please speak with Simon about what you require. He will see to it. We will speak after lunch."

He drifted away and out the door, led by Simon. Bruni stood beside me. "Prickly," she said.

"Very. Has he changed much from what you remember?"

"Older, of course, and more on edge it would seem."

"Coming back here must feel strange I should think. I'll be speaking with him after lunch. His intentions remain unclear."

"He is hard to discern let alone manage. One moment he is cantankerous, the next, all smiles. It's one or the other. Let's talk to Mama and get her opinion."

Elsa was speaking to Anne over a glass of champagne. They stopped talking as we approached. Elsa asked me, "Is he what you expected?"

"I'm not sure."

"One is never sure with such a man. Tread carefully and question all he says. Still, he is worth listening to. He has done many things and seen much. Most of all, enjoy the fact that you have a real father. Many do not."

I nodded. I wondered how I was to do that. I hadn't even known he was my father until Alice had informed me in her letter. I felt no sense of connection between us. He could have been anyone as far as I was concerned.

Bruni chatted with her mother and Anne. I looked about as Johnny came up beside me with an extra glass of champagne. We moved away. "Take this," he said. "Abstinence won't prepare you for what's next, but a glass of very good champagne might. Drink up."

I accepted the glass and drank. "You're probably correct. By the way, my father wants to sit down with me for an extended talk after lunch."

"Excellent. He's not wasting any time, and you might glean an inkling of what he's after."

"Possibly, but I'm not sure I can stand being alone with him for that long."

"Oh, I think you can. It's business, remember? You and I've sat through countless unpleasant meetings, and we even smiled once or twice, if I recall. We all do what we must, Percy. You included. Besides, it's almost lunch, and I'm eager to see what Dagmar has prepared. I heard it was pea soup with peanut butter and jelly sandwiches."

"Really? That can't be right."

"I heard it on good authority."

"Well, if it is, there's little I can do about it at this point. That being said, I do like peanut butter and jelly, but I'm not sure everyone else will. Do you use a knife and fork when they're served formally?"

"I believe it depends on the size. If they're rather large and likely to ooze, I'd go with the knife and fork. If they're tiny, then why bother. Didn't you approve the menu?"

"No. Dagmar said she'd handle everything."

"Then there's little you can do. Perhaps Dagmar's using the peanut butter to disguise the taste of one of her potions?

193

Peanut butter worked like a charm on old Robert the Bruce. You wouldn't believe the ghastly things I'd get him to eat using a simple dab of peanut butter as a ruse. I put some on a tennis ball once. It was quite electrifying. The combination almost drove the creature mad. He'd lick it for over an hour, whimpering away in canine ecstasy before finally chewing the thing to pieces and savoring every last morsel as he swallowed it down. It was a great way to keep him busy."

"That couldn't have been very good for him."

"Probably not. The experiment was short-lived and therefore inconclusive. I stopped only because I heard the doorman complaining about all the rubber pieces that began springing up around the trees at the front of the entrance on Fifth Avenue, particularly after a good rain."

"Disgusting, Johnny."

"It was, and the doorman was growing suspicious as to the cause."

"Well, lunch, like most everything these days, is out of my hands. If peanut butter and jelly sandwiches are on the menu, then they will likely be the best peanut butter and jelly sandwiches that anyone has ever tasted."

"Absolutely, hence my interest," said Johnny.

My father reentered the drawing room with Cobb, and Stanley announced that lunch was served.

Bruni and I waited by the doors as our guests filed past and searched the table for place cards with their names on them. Bruni whispered, "What's for lunch?"

"Peanut butter and jelly sandwiches, according to Johnny. I left the menu completely in Dagmar's hands, so I don't really know."

"Interesting choice, if it is. Peanut butter is great way to disguise a taste. My dogs go wild for it, even if it contains an awful tasting pill."

"Johnny was telling me the same thing."

"Well, I'm excited, then. Looks like your father is sitting to your left. If he gets unruly, kick him, and then say it was an accident. Good luck."

I cringed at the idea as I walked Bruni to her place at the far end of the table and pulled out the chair to seat her. I walked back to mine at the end closest to the drawing room. My father was indeed to my left, with Cobb next to him and Hugo to my right. Next to Hugo sat John Sr. and then Anne, whom I noted was as far away from his lordship as possible. Johnny sat opposite his mother on Bruni's right and next to Elsa. I figured she would give him plenty to think about. I seated myself and wondered what would happen next.

True to Johnny's prediction, pea soup was served with small, triangular sandwich quarters on small plates beside each bowl. The wine was a German Riesling that I tasted immediately to cover my nervousness. Hugo did the same and said, "This *trocken* Riesling is surprisingly well-balanced. Now, what do we have here?"

Hugo tasted the soup and bit into a corner of one of the sandwiches. He closed his eyes and said, "Ah, I'm in heaven." He opened them, picked up his spoon and pointed it at my father. He said in a loud voice. "You know, Bromley, you really missed out by leaving before your ex-wife hired this cook. Had you sampled her fare even once, you would have done about anything to return."

My father sniffed. "Perhaps I did, and you don't know it. That being said, I doubt I would make the effort for pea soup and small sandwiches. Economy usually starts in the kitchen and is obviously much in evidence. The place is falling apart."

"Appearances can be deceiving," I said as I sampled the soup. I thought about kicking him, but only for a moment. The color of the soup was a bright, almost fluorescent green, reminding me of freshly picked peas. The color alone was irresistible. The taste was even better. The image of a hidden garden came to mind. There were hints of mint and other herbs, in a blend I couldn't quite identify. I found myself having another spoonful to make sure it really tasted as good as it did and then another. I was determined to forgo the sandwiches based on what Johnny and Bruni had said, but after a few more spoons of soup, I gave it up as a lost cause. Each of the little triangles, I discovered, was different in subtle ways, either through various combinations of jams and jellies or because of a hint of bacon or some other addition. I looked around and noticed that no one was speaking.

Hugo finished first, sat back, and began to clap his hands. "Bring out the cook!" he roared. "I must see this woman!"

Stanley looked at me, and I nodded. He ghosted away. A few seconds later, out stepped Dagmar from behind the Chinese screen. The baron stood and clapped some more. Others followed. He stopped, put his hands to his sides, and gave her a formal bow from the waist before sitting back down. It was, I realized, his highest compliment. Dagmar gave him a nod. She looked around at the applauding guests and then at me. She gave me a slow wink and disappeared back to her kitchen.

The baron got my attention and asked, "Is there more? Tell me there is more."

"Hugo, patience. We'll have to see," I answered.

There was more, but in tiny amounts. As each guest finished, the first course was whisked away, replaced by silver bowls filled with crushed ice. Laid on top of each were white porcelain shells containing crab salad. The baron dug right in. I noted that although there was little talk, everyone seemed animated, concentrating on the task of eating as small a bite as possible to prolong the experience. Wine was consumed as if it was water, and all my guests looked slightly flushed by the time the course was done.

I heard Bruni, Elsa, and Anne shriek at something Johnny said. At my end, it was more subdued. The meal progressed in a dreamy way. John Sr. and Hugo chatted off and on while myself, my father, and Cobb said not a word. Both seemed transfixed by what they were eating. Dessert followed, consisting of pale-yellow Meyer lemon sherbet. Bruni and I looked at each other along the length of the table. She grinned at me. I gave her a nod, after which she announced that we would pass through.

As we rose, I noticed that all of us seemed slightly dazed. My guests gripped the backs of their chairs to hold themselves erect. In that anchoring pause, a thought came unbidden into my mind. "Immortal Circe, she of braided hair, sat her loom within her hall of polished stones and waited for unwelcomed guests." An image of the raven-haired enchantress flared in my mind only to fade away like the chime of a temple bell. Was that normal? I wondered. I decided it was not. Nonetheless, the lunch had settled some of the hard edges of my dread and allowed a space for something different to begin. I turned and saw my father standing near, watching me. Had that thought about Circe been his? But if not his, whose?

"You dislike me, that much is clear, and why shouldn't you?"

My father paused and looked about. We were walking along the access road in the direction of the river.

He continued looking straight ahead. "I can hardly blame you. You know only what you've heard, and that is nothing good, I'm sure. The absence of information generates its own erroneous opinion as much as any falsehood."

After lunch, while the ladies had retired to the drawing room and the men to the library, my father had pulled me aside by the arm and had said, "Walk with me outside." I had reluctantly agreed. At the front door, Cobb had asked him if he should follow at a discreet distance, but my father had shaken his head.

We had walked in silence when he stopped at the end of the road where the asphalt turned to gravel and dirt. Out of politeness, I did too.

"I have a question to ask you," he said. "It requires a simple yes or no, so nothing too difficult. However, unlike many such queries, your answer will determine our future going forward."

"What is your question?"

He raised his hand. "Allow me to finish."

I nodded.

"Should you answer *no*, I have a check in my breast pocket I will give you, and that will be the end of it. I've left my bags packed, and by now my friend has arranged a car to take me to the city, should that be required. I don't wish to force my presence on anyone, let alone my son. Is that acceptable?"

"You haven't asked the question, but that would be fine by me."

He seemed amused. "If your answer is a *yes*, then the future is less defined, and my departure will be delayed. All I ask is that you consider carefully before you respond, and that you give me your reply only after we return to the house. Can you agree to that?"

"I think so, but should I have further questions, I will ask them."

He chuckled. "Very well. You've heard much about me and have drawn your own conclusions. With no alternative, you were free to believe what you've been told, but that portrait, as I mentioned, is likely to be inaccurate and incomplete. Do you have the courage to listen to what really happened between me and my former spouse, or do you wish to cling to a sanitized version? That is my question. We will walk back while you consider your answer."

I thought about his request, but it didn't take me long to come to a conclusion. If I refused, then he would leave immediately, and I would have the funds. That was a good choice. Although much would be solved, not all. On the other hand, I was quite sure that he wanted me to agree. That I would refuse was a calculated risk he took. I sensed there was more happening here than a simple question. He had a wily reputation and from what others had told me, it was best to sift his words. In the back of my mind, I wondered if the check even existed. I decided to find out.

By the time we reached the front door, the broken gray clouds had coalesced into a low dark ceiling. A limo stood parked in the drive out front, but there was no sign of Cobb or any of my father's bags.

"What is your answer?" my father asked as we mounted the front steps to the house.

I paused halfway up. "You were invited here because I heard you were on your way and would arrive regardless of how I felt about the matter. I will take the check immediately in compensation, and in addition, I will hear what you have to say. You owe me the truth at least, but lie to me, and you will go at the first opportunity."

He looked at me with amusement. "Allow me first to—"

I cut him off. "The check now, or we are done."

He smiled broadly, "Excellent! You don't believe I have it, and why should you?" he reached into his pocket and took out two envelopes. He handed me the thinner one. "No matter. Here is your check. Given my reputation, I forgive your skepticism. Are you satisfied now?"

"I am."

With those words whatever goodwill my father had shown toward me evaporated. His face hardened, and I saw disgust written there. He slowly shook his head. "Wouldn't it have been wiser to have cashed that check before agreeing that you're satisfied?"

"Is that necessary with you?"

"Considering my reputation, absolutely. You should have verified that the amount was correct and checked whether the draft was even signed. For God's sake, Percy, we're talking about three quarters of a million dollars. I could have simply given you an envelope, and you would have been none the wiser!"

He was angry now, slipping rapidly down the slope toward rage, and for what reason, I had no inkling.

His face reddened with each word that he spat in my direction. "There are two types of people in this world: the deceiver and the deceived. You are clearly of the latter class and are therefore stupid, naïve, unsophisticated, and untrustworthy. I see it plainly now. I cannot trust you!"

"Me?" I asked. I knew he had a hair trigger and was given to fits of rage that could appear at any moment, but his outburst seemed irrational and disturbed.

"Yes, you! You didn't even *look* inside the envelope I gave you!"

"I didn't have to. The check is there, or it is not. It is valid, or it is not. I can't believe you came all this way to fool me, but it seems that was what you had in mind all along."

"Fool you? Don't be dense. I came to test you! I had to see with my own eyes whether you were worthy of my time. You were skeptical and mistrustful when we met. I liked that. You suspected a trick while we were walking. You even called my bluff. Such behavior was worthy of my approbation, but such delightful skepticism was the result of fraud. I was about to give you everything. Everything! But like your stupid mother, and that thieving bitch who lived here, you betrayed me!"

He struck me violently with the thick envelope on my chest.

"I would have trusted you with this," he wheezed, spittle flecking his mouth while he shook the envelope in front of my face, "but no! I've seen and heard enough. I must be leaving!"

Folding it in half, he jammed the thick envelope into the side pocket of his suit and reached for the door. There, he paused, turned and hissed at me with scathing contempt, "You are such a disappointment!" He pulled the door open and froze. A shadowy figure that looked like Alice stood inside the dark interior of the house, blocking his entrance. Stunned, my father's face turned gray as he stared at the figure with his mouth open. He seemed paralyzed before he coughed, raised his hands toward his throat, stumbled, and fell backward down the steps. He lay motionless, staring at the sky with eyes that saw nothing. I rushed down to see if he was dead.

———◇———

38

"Stand aside, Percy!" commanded Bonnie as she bolted down the steps toward him. "Call an ambulance!"

Bonnie was feeling for a pulse as Cobb, alert to my father's anticipated entrance, scrambled down beside her, assessed the situation, and said to me. "Get my black bag! It's in his lordship's room at the foot of the bed!"

"Right away," I said and turned. In doing so, I noticed that the thick envelope my father had struck me with, lay half folded, leaning against the vertical riser of the bottom step. I picked it up as I scrambled into the house, almost colliding with Stanley, who held the needed bag.

"Here!" he said.

I slipped the envelope into my breast pocket with one hand, while I passed the bag to Cobb with the other. Cobb grabbed it, placed it on the ground, and snapped it open. He took out a syringe, stuck a long needle on it, and pulled a vial of clear liquid from one of its pockets. He filled it and quickly injected the contents into my father's thigh through his clothes while Bonnie began CPR.

After a few seconds Bonnie said, "He's breathing and has a pulse."

"Good," said Cobb. "Help me carry him upstairs. I have a defibrillator and IV equipment there. Let's be quick." Turning to me, he said, "Leave off on the ambulance. I have all I need for his lordship in his room."

Bonnie picked up one leg and I, the other. Cobb took hold of the arms, while Stanley took hold of his midsection. At the top of the main staircase, Stanley let go, causing Bonnie and I to stagger as he moved ahead to open the door to the bedroom. We placed him on one of the beds, and Cobb ordered us out. "I know what I'm doing," he snapped. "Close the door behind you."

Stanley, Bonnie, and I looked at each other and did as we were told.

"Fuck me!" said Bonnie when we were in the hallway and had closed the door. "That kind of greeting could give a girl a complex. I take it that was your father, Percy. Sorry about that. Anyway, what do you think of my new 'do?"

"Surprising," I said. Her hair was now shorter and black. In the light of the hallway, her eyes appeared more gray than blue. They sparkled when set against her raven-colored hair. Bonnie had upped her appearance, perhaps not yet to the sensational level, but definitely enough to turn more than a few heads. I noted the resemblance to Alice. If my father was vain enough to not wear glasses, her unanticipated appearance must have been a shocking reminder that the dead don't always lie still.

"I'll say," she continued. "He took one look at me, had a fit, and rolled down the stairs. Wow! Thank you for your help, Stanley. You were awfully quick with that black bag."

"The highest form of service is anticipation," said Stanley.

"Well, you get the blue ribbon in that department. Lucky for him you were around."

Stanley looked amused but said nothing.

205

"Yes, it was. Like old times, if I'm not mistaken," I said, looking at him as well.

Stanley chuckled at my comment. "Indeed, sir. His lordship has always led a charmed existence, but I doubt he's out of the woods yet. Cobb may be a doctor, among other things, but even he will be hard-pressed to keep him around much longer."

"Cobb certainly doesn't look like one," I said.

"No, he doesn't, but he is a doctor nonetheless, even if his practice is limited to a single patient. I suggest we make our way downstairs. You have guests to attend to, while I have my duties."

"Quite right," I said, "but thank you just the same."

"Of course, sir."

Stanley turned and took the back way down to the kitchen as Bonnie grabbed my arm and walked me toward the main staircase. "Glad to see me?"

"Always."

"Well kiss me hello and mean it."

I leaned in to kiss her on the cheek, but she turned, slipped her arms around me, and put her mouth firmly on mine. After a long second, she released me. I stepped back, somewhat shocked. Seeing my discomfiture, she said, "Take it easy. The wedding bells haven't rung yet, so you're technically fair game. Well, maybe not completely, but a girl can dream, can't she? Now, let's move along. Mom will be waiting, and when she hears what happened, she'll be gnashing her teeth at the lost opportunity to get in a couple of digs of her own. I can't wait to tell her."

I recovered my poise. "You two are still on friendly terms?"

"More than ever. It's been a trip. We're not all buddy-buddy, but we like and respect each other, which is a giant leap forward. How's your world rockin' these days?"

"Rocking describes my world quite well. You and I should talk more at length, but for now duty calls."

When we were at the bottom of the stairs, I said, "By the way, Bonnie, you have the timing of a saint."

"Anytime, cowboy. There's a great deal unsaid there, if I'm not mistaken. Make sure you tell me everything. Well, all that you're willing to. Who knows, I might be able to help. You'd be surprised what I can do, so think about it. That's what pals are for. Mom is eager to see you."

We crossed the hall arm in arm to the drawing room. Although I was hesitant to let her get too close, she was a good person to have in my corner. The envelope I picked up would have to wait, and come to think of it, I had yet to examine the envelope with the supposed check. Those matters had to be put aside for now. It was time to officially welcome Maw.

39

"Percy! There you are. I expected you to greet me. Where were you?"

Maw's voice boomed across the drawing room from her seat in the middle of the couch surrounded by the three Von Hofmanstals, John Sr., Anne, and Johnny. She and Bonnie had arrived earlier than expected, and it must have been their car I saw out front. Although fast approaching eighty, she was a powerful and vibrant woman. Blessed with a steely resolve and a cunning mind worthy of a Medici duke, she personally controlled the economic resources of a small country and was, in every respect, the matriarch of the Dodge family. Proud, physically strong, and weathered from years of equestrian pursuits, she had a voice with a singular biting quality, honed by years of training horses, riders, and dogs. When she commanded, all obeyed, including me.

"Mary, I do apologize. Please forgive me," I said, striding toward her. "I was walking with my father."

"Well, where is he?"

"Upstairs," I replied.

"Incapacitated," added Bonnie at my side. "In fact, I may have killed him not five minutes ago."

"What!" said everyone in unison before crowding around Bonnie and me to get the details.

"I'm afraid so," continued Bonnie. "He saw me and keeled over. Bam! Down he toppled and hit the driveway like a ton of bricks. Lucky for him the bald guy's a doctor, at least according to Stanley. The four of us carried the body upstairs to his room. The man had a pulse and was breathing to some extent, but that's it as far as I know. The doctor kicked us out. Heart attack, I think, but maybe a stroke. He won't be traipsing down the stairs anytime soon, that's for sure."

"Shouldn't we call an ambulance?" asked the baron.

"Nope. The doc nixed the idea, saying he had it under control. I suspect that kind of episode has happened before. It sure added some drama to my day."

"Well," said Maw, "I suppose allowances must be made. Still, he could have chosen a better time. Sit beside me, Percy. You'll want to say hello to Robert. He's underneath the couch."

At the mention of his name, Robert wiggled out from underneath, gave me a snort, and sat on his haunches. His black eyes fixed on Maw before he turned his head and looking at Johnny. He ignored me completely, as was usual with him. Everyone else backed away and clustered around Bonnie as she described in more exacting detail the latest news.

"Has he put on a little weight?" I asked as I sat beside Maw.

"Pff!" she said. "He's in great shape."

I wondered about that as I watched him. In his prior existence, Robert routinely took advantage of Johnny's prodigious lack of canine skill, to trick his master into grueling bouts of "capture the dog." Such games lasted several hours until Robert, having decided that he had had enough exercise for the day, submitted to the leash once more. I doubted he could get away with any such juvenile antics with his current

209

owner. Robert looked at me and panted as if to agree. He flopped down in front of Maw and stretched his hind legs behind him while obscenely itching himself on the carpet. He stopped, turned his head, gave Johnny a wistful look before shifting his focus back on Maw, and turned into a sphinx.

"Well, he does look good, I must say, and so do you. Welcome back to Rhinebeck," I said.

"My pleasure. Now give me a kiss and then you and Johnny can take him for a walk."

I gave Maw a kiss but before I could respond, I saw Cobb at the drawing room door, giving me a nod.

"Maybe later. The doctor is at the door. Perhaps he has some news."

40

"Is there somewhere we might talk in private?" Cobb asked in the accent of an Oxford don. When he had spoken upstairs, he hadn't sounded quite so refined. I closed the door to the drawing room before I answered.

"Of course. The library. It's to the left down the hall."

As we walked, I glanced at him out of the corner of my eye. He certainly didn't look like a doctor, but his superbly tailored suit and well-polished shoes said otherwise. He was shorter than me, but what he lacked in height, he made up for in muscled width. Cobb looked like a thug, but judging from his accent, a frightening intellect might yet lurk beneath the surface.

Once we were seated in the leather chairs in front of the fireplace, he leaned forward, resting his elbows on his knees, and started in.

"Your father is not in the best of health, as you can well imagine. I counselled him to forego this visit, but he was insistent, and once his mind is made up, there is little that can be done other than to make the best of it. I agreed to accompany him, hoping my presence and my skill as a physician might alleviate some of the strain on his system. What do you suppose happened to cause this latest episode, if you don't mind my asking?"

"I will tell you, but I have a couple of questions first, if that's okay."

"By all means."

"Will he live?"

"Nothing is ever certain when it comes to medicine. For now, he is sedated and resting comfortably. He's had two similar episodes under my care, and in both instances, he recovered faster than expected. That may, or may not, be the case on this occasion. Likely, he will want to be up and about tomorrow evening. He has a remarkably robust constitution and delights in proving medical science wrong. Nothing deters him. Nonetheless, a human body has its limits, and I doubt he can survive many more such incidents. I will argue for him to remain in bed upstairs, but he is a difficult patient at the best of times and will do what he wants. For now, we'll have to see how he is when he awakens."

"Thank you, Doctor. It is Doctor, isn't it?"

"It is. I had a practice in Harley Street, before his lordship convinced me to confine my practice solely to himself."

"Does my father wear corrective lenses?"

"He doesn't, but that's not to say that he shouldn't. Why do you ask?"

"It would explain what happened. He opened the door, and I think he mistook Miss Leland for his former spouse. There is a likeness, and since his former wife has been dead many years, it must have been quite a shock to see her standing there."

"That might explain it. He mentioned that this house was filled with ghosts. I pooh-poohed the idea, but he countered that I was ignorant and had seen little of the world other than the insides of my patients. On another matter, I noted when I undressed him that he had neither of the envelopes on his

212

person. The dialogue between you both must have gone well, and that is good news from a medical point of view. He was much concerned with them. I would read the contents of the larger one at your earliest convenience. Now, I must leave you. I need to get back to my patient."

"Of course. Please continue to update me as to how he's doing, or if there's anything further that you or he require."

I hoped he wouldn't ask me more about the second letter and hustled him to the hallway, where he assured me that I would be kept informed. He was about to say something more, but I saw Johnny slip out of the drawing room. I cut him off before he could begin and said, "Johnny, there you are. Please excuse me, Doctor. We'll speak again, but now I have other matters to attend to." Dismissed, he nodded thoughtfully and moved off to see to his charge.

"That was close," I said once we were inside the library with the door closed.

"You're up to something, I can tell. Perhaps we can take a few minutes and catch up."

"Good idea. Here's where things stand so far."

I briefed Johnny on events since we last spoke, including the conversation with my father, the two envelopes, and what the doctor had to say.

"You have both?"

"I do."

"Well there's a letter opener. Have at it! No, wait a moment. They're sealed?"

"They are, and I'm happy to see that great minds think alike. We need Stanley to steam them open and reseal them. We'll know what my father's up to, but he won't know that we know. We might even get a step ahead for once."

"That would be refreshing and unusual. Even handing back the first envelope unopened might allow events to play out to a better conclusion, given that we'll know far more about what he has in mind. You can use it to restart the conversation. Who knows where that might lead?"

"Interesting idea, but that man has a temper, and I hate being yelled at. Can you take care of all this?" I handed Johnny the envelopes. "I've been away from my guests too long. Hopefully, I'll be able to join you shortly."

"Of course. Now, to be clear you want me to open both, examine the contents with Stanley, and reseal them."

"Yes. But you need to be quick. I can well imagine my father waking up and having another conniption when he finds the second letter missing."

"That might depend on what we discover. Leave the decision to us. If it's warranted, we'll see it's returned to him in its original condition. After all, the larger envelope really did fall out of his pocket and should it be found and turned in, one might be suspicious but not overly so, provided the time frame was reasonable. I'll keep the one he gave you."

"That works."

"Count on it then. This is far more fun than I expected."

"Lucky you," I said. I gave him a pat on the back as he made his way to the kitchen to find Stanley. I closed the library door and went back to the drawing room.

41

I was immediately surrounded by guests eager to get the latest news on my father's condition.

I repeated most of what the doctor had told me. The baron nodded and summed up the information loudly to John Sr. "Bromley will be out of the picture until at least tomorrow. That will allow some peace to prevail and a more relaxed dinner this evening."

"We should all be thankful," said Anne.

"Fiddlesticks," said Maw. "I wanted to give him a poke or two to find out if he's really as bad as they say. I suppose that will have to wait. Percy, what's next?"

"Drinks at seven, followed by dinner at nine. Black tie. Until then, make yourselves at home. Bruni and I have some household matters to discuss, so we will see you by seven at the latest."

Bonnie said, "On that note, I think it's time for a nap. Lugging that body up those stairs has worn me out." The others murmured their agreement.

Bruni looked at me curiously as I eased us out the door. Her father followed and stopped us before we could get away.

"I'd like to see the library, if you don't mind."

"Of course. It's right down the hall," I answered.

"You know the one I mean."

I paused. Both father and daughter looked at me expectantly.

"What library might that be?"

"Don't play coy with me," countered the baron. "Those treasures of yours aren't kept in plain view, nor should they be. They're tucked away, along with the hundreds of volumes Alice had collected over the years. I know that for a fact."

"You are correct, but that part of the house is off limits for the time being. Of course, once all the financial affairs are put in order, I would be more than happy to show you."

"What? Bromley didn't give you his check? He said he would. I have mine right here." The baron patted his breast pocket.

"My father mentioned something about verification of funds, so the matter is still pending. Of course, I'll happily accept yours."

The baron chuckled. "I think I'll wait. Good for you on insisting on verification. I always do. Not to worry, we can sort it out tomorrow when he's up and about."

"The doctor wasn't so certain about that."

"Doctors. What do they know? Your father has more lives than a cat. He'll be up tomorrow. Count on it. Now, have fun, you two, and don't do anything I wouldn't."

The baron chuckled again as he returned to the drawing room.

Bruni took my arm. "I take it not everything with your father went as planned."

"No, it didn't."

"Perhaps we can walk, and you can tell me."

I sighed. I had my attention on the envelopes but decided to let Stanley and Johnny work it out. Bruni might be able to help me get my wits around my father. He seemed a thoroughly awful man, and I needed some fresh air to put my conversation with him behind me.

"Good idea," I said. "Let's head toward the tennis courts."

Once outside and away from the possible intrusions of others, Bruni and I held each other.

"I think I needed that," she said.

"Me, too." I told her all that had happened since lunch. When I finished, we sat in silence on the steps that led down to the court and looked out at the leafy trees along the edge of the enclosure. The sky was overcast and brooding, yet I felt content being alone with her. I thought to myself that having houseguests was diverting but seriously overrated.

Bruni interrupted my thoughts. "From what you've said, your father was testing you, and you failed."

"I'd say that pretty much sums it up. I do need to get with Johnny and Stanley and find out what is in the envelopes. I'm hoping that what they reveal might open a door of some sort."

"They might, but I have two things to tell you that might help. The first is based on what just happened and might sound counterintuitive."

"I could use some counter-intuitive. What is it?"

"You need to talk to your father, despite his upset. Only the two of you with no agendas. My mother and I were never close until we managed to bridge that gap, and that happened, strangely enough, because of him. Such a conversation won't be easy, but I do know that you have to make peace with him, and he must make peace with you. I'm not talking friendship, rather seeing the other person and having some compassion and understanding. That's all."

"Given the circumstances, that in itself would be a miracle."

"Perhaps, but you have time. He doesn't. His window is closing faster than he thinks. You are in the more powerful position, so the overture must come from you."

217

I sighed. "That's true enough, but how do I even get there with him? Frankly, he scares me, and from what I've seen, he will simply hammer away at any vulnerability I might care to show until any chance of a reconciliation becomes impossible."

"Maybe. Ask him about Alice."

I looked at her. "Alice?"

"Yes. His life began and ended with her."

I wasn't so sure about that. Alice seemed a radioactive topic when it came to my father.

I shuddered and asked instead, "What's the second thing?"

"I think I know why your father is here."

"Really?"

"He wants to recover items that Alice had in her possession. He thinks they're his, and I can't be more specific."

"How do you know that?"

"My father told me."

"And he thinks they're in the other library?"

"Yes."

"Tell me more."

"I can't. Likely I've overstepped the limits of what I can say. It's part of a legal matter that took place before you and I met. I couldn't comment about the firm that caused your partnership with Johnny to implode. This is the same. I love you and want to tell you everything, but there are many things I cannot speak about. I'm hoping that what I mentioned will come up in that letter your father decided not to give you."

"You could have told me earlier."

"You didn't have the letter."

"And now I do."

"And now you do. I know you're not happy with me for not saying all I know."

"I'm not. I feel … betrayed. Here I am searching for answers, only to find out that the person next to me knew all along but never bothered to say. I know that's not fair, but that doesn't keep me from feeling that way. I also understand your position. If our roles were reversed, I would constantly be tempted to say more than I should, and that would be equally difficult." I sighed and murmured, "I wish this weekend would end, and everyone would go away."

I looked out at the trees. Bruni hugged my arm.

"I'm sorry," I said after a pause. "You're not the reason I'm out of sorts."

"Not entirely, but I realize now that passing on bits and pieces only makes it worse. I will have to think about that. Know that I'm sorry for causing you any upset."

I nodded and patted the arm that intertwined my own. "The first part you mentioned has me quaking inside. All I want to do is avoid him, yet I get the feeling that a positive outcome for all of us may hinge on my being able to put aside my dislike, look him in the eyes, and see someone other than the peevish, terrifying old man he is. When I look at him, I wonder whether I'll turn out like that. I hope not, yet the same lineage that produced him runs in my blood. It's a troubling thought."

"I've had similar, I can assure you. For now, the best we can manage is one thing at a time. Between us, we'll find a way. We have each other now, and that fact counts for more than a little. It's time to return to the house. I have to figure out what I'm wearing tonight, and you have those letters to examine."

42

"What have you discovered?" I asked.

Stanley and Johnny were in Stanley's office, sipping whiskey. They looked troubled.

"Sit down and have a drop," said Johnny.

"What is it?"

"First the drink, then the news," Johnny answered as I was handed a measure of amber liquid in a crystal glass.

"Thank you, Stanley. That bad?"

"I suppose it could be worse," said Johnny, "but not likely. I won't prolong the suspense. In envelope number one is a demand draft in the amount of $750,000 drawn on Morgan Guaranty's London branch in Berkeley Square to the main office in New York as drawee. The draft is valid, I'm sure, and requires no verification of funds. The difficulty lies in the payee section. Your name is there, but so is your father's. Both of you will need to sign it before it can be cashed. It has been resealed in the event that you wish to return it unopened."

Johnny handed me the first envelope.

"Of course there's a catch. That would be so typical of the man," I said.

"And that's not the half of it. The choice bit is found in envelope number two, but before we get to that, you must thank Stanley for his skill in opening and sealing both in a way that left no traces. Stanley will explain."

"Stanley," I said, "my thanks as always."

He nodded. "I took the liberty per your instructions of returning the missive to the sender after I made a copy of both documents in the fax machine. Johnny told me about your earlier conversation with the doctor, and I am happy to say that he was noticeably shaken when I handed it to him. Whether that was due to his embarrassment at having assumed that your father had given it to you, or because he had avoided another medical crisis when your father found it missing was unclear. My returning it personally may have added to his troubles. In the end, he will conclude that the best course is not to mention the temporary absence to his employer. We will need to discuss the implications of what your father wrote after you have absorbed its contents. Here it is."

Stanley handed me a folder with several fax pages inside.

43

------◆------

Percy,

What kind of man are you?

I wonder if you have the necessary skepticism and certainty of self to not be governed by the constraints that "civilized" society demands. Most people are pawns destined to be leashed at birth, indoctrinated by what passes for education, and cemented in place within a system that holds wealth attainment and material consumption as the best and only measure of value. I disagree. To place economic survival as the be-all and the end-all of existence is idiocy.

I take a dim view of humanity in general. Progress, if such a thing exists, is factually up to a few 'bad' men, the rebels, and supposed misfits—those who have the courage and the genius to lift the remainder to a higher place despite the bulk of humanity's cries of protest. The majority thirsts for individuality and personal recognition yet crave security and convenience more and thus are trapped in lives of quotidian desperation and little meaning. If there is one thing I have learned, it's this: The best is always a minority and always will be. To this height you must aspire. Only the best can be truly great, and that requires courage as well as the use of all our gifts, including those of a darker nature.

Society despises our faults and demands purity and goodness from its members, yet none are truly pure or good. We are who we are, weaknesses and strengths combined, and yet we're scolded from an early age to mend our ways—to be good. In other words, obey, or suffer the consequences. It is an evil thing. More men, women, and children have been killed or tortured in the name of what is "good" than have ever been victimized by "evil," or for any other reason for that matter. The majority can keep their "goodness" and be damned. Nature makes no such distinctions and nor should you. The above is the only advice I think worthy of passing on.

I doubt I will do myself justice in a letter. I would rather speak in person and say what really happened with my former spouse. Regardless, there was too much violence between us—too much pain and too much hurt. I played my part, and she did too. I doubt you will have heard that, but for us to have connected so often and so horribly, there must have been great fault on both sides, and a bond above all else. I only married once for good reason. She more than that. In the lexicon of those that knew us, I am a bad man, an evil man, but she and I are more than similar. She is my opposite number and no less my equal. There, I've said it.

You have your money now, or almost. With it, I've bought what cannot be taken away, and because the items can't be moved, I must move to where they are. That is why I'm here—but more on that later. I will keep my word. I will remove nothing. Instead, I will adapt to the constraints I've structured for myself. In truth, many of those items locked away belong to me, and now I will have paid not once, but twice for the privilege of owning them. The first time was for the joy of having, and the power they possessed. The second, now, is because of personal need and the coexisting chance of finding out who you are— to plumb our similarities. Allow me to elaborate as to how these peculiar circumstances came about.

Years ago, your benefactor required a certain piece of ancient pottery. What hands made it, I wish I knew. The shape was exquisite, but its purpose was much more refined and not easily understood. The sound produced when blown correctly created a chill that moved up the spine to the hairs at the back of the neck. From there the vibrations tickled the inside of the skull until the note resonated deep within, *reminding the hearer of something lost, like a word caught on the tip of the tongue, or a whisper heard in the dead of night. I have felt it. The thrumming tone stirred things deep inside me, but what they were I could not remember. I felt the memory, or perhaps the vague perception of a door opening onto paths no modern can imagine.*

It was her minion who contacted me to structure a deal so that she might have it. Hers was lost. I don't know how. I don't know why, other than fate touched us once again, our physical separation notwithstanding. We made an agreement. She needed for a time that piece of ancient crockery and an idol that we had mutually discovered. This I understood and agreed to, but when her use of them was done, they were to be returned to me. This she promised! God knows I paid for both, but then she did too, but that wasn't all that she agreed to.

She hadn't realized I knew about the jeweled forearm bracelet. I did. My knowing shocked her, but how did she think she got the piece in the first place? Not even her simpering slave knew or knows to this day. She and I called it by an Arabic name, <u>ayn al-qalb</u>, the eye of the heart, after that place in the mind that facilitates direct spiritual knowledge. It was a fitting name. She was obsessed with such knowledge and by means of her fixation, the stone bound her. I thought her impossibly foolish. Sometimes we latch onto things that drag us down. It would have been far better for both of us if she had let it be.

As I've said, there's darkness in us all and not all of it is focused on others. More often it is directed at ourselves. I pitied her, poor thing. Her fixation ruined her. It ruined everything.

I have my own reasons for wanting to have that bracelet now—for removing it, the little pot, and the idol from whatever vault they lie in fast asleep and taking them to the room you choose for me. Above all else, I want what is <u>rightfully</u> mine. There are more items that she took. I will look through her collection and have them back as well. This you must agree to. Suitable documentation will be drawn up to *acknowledge my full ownership, and thus my right to remove them, should it be my wish. I have my solicitor handy and should you refuse outright, I will tender a document with your benefactor's signature confirming they are mine and mine alone. I will either take with me all that I own when I leave, or they will remain here and me with them. Choose which suits your fancy.*

But let us not go down that road. All I have will be yours should you agree to let me stay, and what I have that you don't know about will make you gape. You have <u>no</u> idea!

Be strong. Be proud. Be true but choose ... choose because you must or choose because you wish it, whichever, it makes no difference.

— YOUR FATHER

PS: There is much that I can teach you—so very much, and you have much to learn.

PPS: Have you seen her books? There is one in particular that is mine. I want it back.

44

I passed the folder to Stanley and took a sip of whiskey.

"Impressions?" Stanley asked as Johnny looked on.

"I don't know what to say. I'm stunned but not altogether surprised. We expected something dire, and now we know to some degree. There may be more that we don't. For now, I have no doubt that he has all the necessary legal documentation to prove that a portion of the treasures is his. I could say take them and go. It's a choice that solves the problem, provided he signs the check. On the other hand, the letter from Alice stated that if I were to accept her bequest, which I did, then I was responsible for the house and *all* its contents both physical and otherwise, including the libraries and artifacts. Ownership was not mentioned, only that failure to care for both carried heavy penalties and unknown consequences. She further warned that what was intended as a gift may not be. I took that in the general sense, but the sentence takes on an additional meaning with this new information. I won't have him staying here, that I do know."

"It is a hard choice," said Stanley. "What do you intend to do?"

"That *is* the question isn't it. For now, I've no idea. Johnny?"

"Offhand, I'd say you may have to agree to him staying despite how you may feel about that. He would have to sign over the check, of course, but once you secure the funds, you can begin to renegotiate more favorable terms. Likely there's a better solution, but the good news is he hasn't had a chance to deliver his ultimatum yet. We have some time to come up with a counter-move before he does."

"Not much time. He will be up and about tomorrow, according to the baron. Since my father refused to give the ultimatum to me, I expect that he will simply drop the documents that Alice signed in my lap and demand I hand the items over."

"That he will," said Johnny, "but he'll give you the ultimatum, nonetheless. He'll expect you to lawyer up, and then he'll apologize and say there might be another way to avoid any unpleasantness as he slips you the letter. He wants to stay here. I'm sure of it."

I considered that. "I could agree to have him stay, but he will delay signing the check for as long as possible, and that will likely be a very long time. Likely that has been his plan all along."

"I agree," said Johnny. "Well, we've some time at least to come up with a suitable plan, although not a lot. I will think on it."

"Please do. Stanley, any ideas?"

Stanley shifted in his chair. I could see from his face that the letter troubled him deeply.

"He has plans for the items he mentioned. For what purpose, I have no idea. The letter also reveals that there was contact between him and her ladyship of which I was unaware. That possibility surprised me, but then why should it? She was away much of the time, and the chances of connecting with him were many. Perhaps he held her in his sway more firmly than I had considered. His name was hardly ever mentioned, but that doesn't mean he wasn't thought

227

about. I did initiate the arrangements for the little pot. The terms to obtain it were finalized through a written contract. A notarized signature of her ladyship was required, and once completed, the duly prepared documents were sent off. Her ladyship did receive the requested item in return. I was unaware of what was spelled out specifically. It was a legal matter and not my place to advise her, or so I thought. That, with hindsight, was an error. I recall being puzzled by the need for so much legal maneuvering at the time. There may be more that I can remember after I mull it over. One point I noted was his mention of a book. It might hold a clue as to what exactly he has planned regarding the artifacts, although I don't know which one he refers to. There are numerous possibilities. I think I will slip away during the dinner and take several likely candidates from the repository this evening and look them over."

"Good idea," I said. "There is more going on here, and this ultimatum is merely the opening skirmish. The real battle will come later. For now, we must gather as much information as possible. Do you think you could speak to Cobb? I'm sure he knows something."

"He does, but I doubt I'm the one to do it. Raymond might be useful, in that regard."

"Bonnie would be better," said Johnny. "Think about it. They're both medical people. It would be unusual, but Bonnie is unusual. She might also get a more realistic picture as to your father's life expectancy."

"You may be right," I said. "But regardless, my father is both the problem and the solution. In the end, I will have to speak with him. No one else is willing to, I'm sure, and the letter is addressed to me."

"There's also the Bruni matter," said Johnny. "I don't mean to bring up a painful observation, but you did note the part that said he had his attorney handy?"

"I did. She and I will be speaking about that. In the meanwhile, we need to discover whatever else we can in the time we have available. We'll sit down again tomorrow morning. Stanley, research the library. Speak to Raymond, if you think it useful. Johnny, I need some serious brilliance."

"Not to worry. I have my yellow pad. I'll be on it all night if need be until I come up with something."

"Well, that's it then. I'm off to change."

As I made my way to my quarters, I remembered that I needed to look at the seating arrangements for tonight. It was time I spoke with Elsa. Elsa was no fool, nor was she bound by any attorney-client privilege. I also noted that my father stated with uncharacteristic honesty that Alice was his equal. I had no idea what that meant exactly, but I could sense a dark thread there.

It was only when I got to the door to my bedroom and heard Bruni moving about that I realized the clothes I needed were on the top floor. Bruni and I had much to discuss, and that included our closet space. Enough was enough.

45

I reversed course and made my way up to the top of the house. Johnny was putting the finishing touches on his black silk bowtie in front of the bathroom mirror.

"There you are. I've been expecting you," he said, turning toward me and then back to the mirror.

I grunted in acknowledgement as I went to the closet in my room to get out my dinner clothes.

"I would be rather quick if I were you," yelled Johnny. "We haven't much time."

"I know," I yelled back. I wrestled with my clothes. I said in a normal voice, more to myself, "All this running around is getting to be a royal pain in the ass."

"It is, of course, but it's what we do here."

Johnny had finished adjusting his tie and stood leaning against the doorframe of my room as he looked at me.

"I suppose," I answered.

"Your feathers do seem a bit ruffled," he said. "And I noticed you were agitated even before you read that letter. You and Bruni must have had a disagreement of some sort. Tell me."

"It's complicated."

"Tell me anyway."

"Okay," I said, putting on pants and adjusting suspenders. "Bruni and I spoke before I saw you and Stanley in his office. She had a couple of thoughts about my father. The first was to suggest I simply speak with him, one person to another. She advised that I use Alice as a starting point."

"Easy to say but hard to do, I should think."

"My thoughts exactly," I said, looking for my tie. "She's right, but I seriously wonder whether getting to know him will be worth the emotional cost of finding out. Even more daunting is that I see no other solution to resolving his demands than doing exactly what she suggests. I don't like him at all. That man has a nasty way with people and seems to take pleasure in creating pain and upset. I once thought Maw was scary. I had no idea what scary was until I met him."

Johnny looked at me.

"So, you're basically *afraid* of him."

"Yes. Very much," I said. I stopped what I was doing and looked at him.

"He's plenty scary, but his scariness has a falseness to it, I think. He bullies and boasts. *Really* scary people—Raymond, for instance—don't say much. They never do. Anyway, I've been thinking about all this for a while, and then it came to me. Fear has many guises. It can look like anger on the surface. Intolerance and an inability to forgive are often its companions, and all those character traits describe Bromley rather well. Down deep, your father is afraid. I don't know what of, but I watched him rather carefully from my end of the table, and I do believe I'm correct. Which means you two might have much more in common than you think."

"Really? That's surprising."

"Not at all. You handle your fear in a different way. You suppress it. He, on the other hand, channels it into a perpetual individuation and a raging intolerance. He wants everyone around him to be as scared as he is. Maybe he fears death? That specter is dogging his steps, although his fear is likely a long-term affair. Alice may not be a bad starting point, but talking about his fear is how you'll really reach him. It's where he lives."

"Jesus, Johnny! You do have your moments. I will have to digest that."

I continued dressing as Johnny said, "I know, and you should. I'm brilliant, and that's a fact. Now, you need to make sure that Elsa is sitting next to you at dinner. You also said Bruni had a couple of thoughts. So far you've only mentioned one."

"Bruni said she knew why my father's here."

"Really? What did she say?"

"That he's here to take back what is rightfully his, but she only told me that after she knew I had the letter in my possession."

"In other words, she's known all along."

"Yes, and I'm not happy about that. I may understand it intellectually, but it gnaws at me."

"Attorney-client privilege, you think?"

"Yes, although not stated specifically. 'I can't talk about it' falls under that category."

"And so does a nondisclosure agreement. Either way there's more to be revealed. I can understand your upset. It comes down to a question of trust. Do you trust her?"

"When there are professional matters involved, I'm not sure who takes precedence, me or her clients? It's a hard choice, and we need to discuss it. I must know where I stand. I'll do that tonight. How's my tie?"

"Your tie looks fine. Bruni told you that your father wanted to get back what was rightly his?"

"That's what she said."

"In other words, he'll get what's coming to him."

"Very funny," I said.

"I doubt that."

"No, it isn't funny. You're right, but for now, let's have some champagne while I mull over what you said."

46

Everyone else was down, the men in tuxedos, the ladies in long evening dresses that ranged from black to blue and silver. Champagne was flowing and staff passed trays of caviar and smoked salmon. Bruni saw me as I slipped in from the dining room and quickly rustled over in a gown of shimmering silver satin. The fabric glistened like water, emphasizing her blue eyes and jet-black hair. Diamonds flashed on fingers and ears. She didn't wear a necklace. Her cleavage was more than adequate. Johnny moved toward the bar, where one of the staff was handing out Cristal.

"There you are," Bruni said in a soft voice. "I couldn't figure out where you'd gone to until I remembered your clothes are upstairs. That's obviously ridiculous. I'll shift some of mine so you can bring what you need downstairs. I really do apologize. Will you forgive me?"

"That was one of the issues we needed to discuss. I'm glad that's settled."

"But not all, I gather. Let's step into the hall for a moment."

"Now is not the time."

"It is. I won't go through this evening watching you glower at me from the far end of the table. You'd look like your father. Now, come on."

Her comment about whom I might look like overcame any possible resistance. I also thought that if this was one of the few times that I could dine without him, I was going to enjoy myself, and banishing my growing anger was a prerequisite.

We stepped out of the drawing room. "Tell me what's bothering you," Bruni said.

"Put plainly, I don't know where your loyalties lie. When your professional persona is involved, who takes precedence? Me, us, or your profession?"

"I thought that might be the case. To be clear, you and I take precedence, but that choice is not strictly between you and my profession. It is work set against everything else. Mine has taken on a life of its own, and I must disentangle myself or be consumed. Our last conversation left me feeling rather awful, if you must know. That can't happen again, so I thought about what to do. I've decided to make us the priority and tell you what's involved when we're alone tonight. Will that suffice for now?"

"Yes, it will. We need to work together on this. Will there be trouble if you tell me?"

"That depends."

"As if we don't have enough going on already. That being said, I'm relieved to hear you say that we take precedence. Without that elevated status, you and I are lost. And yes, I forgive you. I'd kiss you, but I'd ruin your makeup."

"And I'd let you, if I didn't have to run to our room to fix it. You can always kiss the back of my neck instead."

"Really?"

"It will give me goose bumps."

"Oh."

I had lifted Bruni's hair and was about to kiss the back of her neck, when the front door opened and in stepped a tall man in a crumpled gray business suit. Malcolm Ault had arrived.

235

"Sorry to interrupt. I do apologize for being late, but I'm here now. Bruni, you look smashing, by the way."

I felt like a teenager caught in the act as I stepped back, and Bruni said, "Thank you, Malcolm, and welcome. Here are Stanley and Simon to give you a hand. Change and join us as quick as you can."

"I will. I will." Malcolm nodded to me. "Percy."

"Welcome and glad you could make it," I said. "Cristal awaits in the drawing room if you hurry."

"I won't be long at all. You two looked divine together. Must dash."

Simon had stepped outside to retrieve the bags as Stanley led Malcolm up the stairs to his room.

"That was close. Well, I think all our guests have now arrived—at least I hope," I said.

"What about your mother?"

"I'm not sure."

"Percy, you have a lot to learn about women. She'll be here, and like my mother, nothing could possibly prevent her. She'll move Heaven and Earth."

"Likely you're correct. I have been thinking about her."

"And well you should. I may have my issues with work, Percy, but you really do have some things to sort out with your parents. From where I stand, it looks like we both have more than a few. Now, are you ready to enjoy yourself?"

"Yes. I'm much better. Thank you."

Bruni and I returned to our guests. Now, I needed some champagne. After both of us were supplied with glasses of Cristal, Bruni said, "Why don't you mingle with my parents? I'm going to speak with Mrs. Leland and her daughter. It's about time I get to know them better."

"Interesting choice," I said.

"I'm always one to check up on the competition," she said as she glided away in their direction. Maw was in a black gown with a necklace of large emeralds, as was her preference in formal gatherings, while Bonnie sported dark blue satin with a sprinkle of diamonds around her neck to offset her new hairstyle. I was quite sure theirs would be an interesting conversation, but one I should likely avoid. I moved over to speak with the baron and Elsa, who were talking with Johnny's parents.

During a pause, I said, "The tall man has finally made his appearance. He'll be with us shortly."

"Then there must be something exciting about to happen. I can hardly wait," said Elsa. She was wearing a close-fitting evening gown of black and white raw silk cut low, with a diamond necklace that must have weighed at least a pound, and that didn't include the platinum setting. The many gems sparkled beneath her elfin features.

"Oh, Elsa," said Anne, wearing a more sedate evening attire of crimson and black. "You always want something to happen."

"I do. It's so entertaining, and Malcolm's always around when something does. Haven't you noticed?"

"Yes, unfortunately, but at least one possible source has left the field. He and that doctor will be absent from dinner tonight, and I am thrilled about that."

"And me too if it calms you," said Elsa. "Percy, any more news on your father?"

"None, although your husband tells me to expect him up and about tomorrow."

We all looked at the baron expectantly.

"He won't remain bedridden for long. It's not his way. For now, peace reigns. I can't wait for dinner. That cook is

237

sensational. Where did she come from again? I heard she has more potions than a witch."

Anne shifted while John Sr. drank from his flute.

"Where did you hear that?" I asked.

"I have my sources. Do you suppose she'll try one out on us?"

"Who says she hasn't already?" I answered.

He beamed. "No wonder I feel so good. Ah, there's Stanley. Soon, I'll feel even better."

Malcolm entered, grabbed a flute, and made his way into the dining room with the rest of us. He was just in time, as usual.

47

I was at the head of the table with Elsa to my right and Johnny to my left. Bruni sat at the far end between Bonnie and Maw. If she wanted to find out more about them, this was the time. Next to Maw was the baron and then Anne. On the other side next to Bonnie was John Sr. and the tall man. I wondered if sitting next to Elsa would make him feel as uncomfortable as the last time he had visited. I looked over the white and silver of the table. Plates with silver pinstripes were set on a starched white tablecloth, picking up and accenting the gleam of the heavy silver cutlery. The guests seemed in good spirits and talked animatedly as they anticipated Dagmar's first course. Johnny and his mother were speaking with their heads together.

Elsa interrupted my thoughts. "Percy, I'm happy to be sitting next to you. How are you and my daughter getting along?"

"We're learning to live together. I'm glad you're seated beside me. I can pepper you with questions."

She nodded. "I am just as happy. I can do the same."

"Ladies first then," I said.

"You are always the gentleman, but I can be a lady for only so long. You may not like what I have to say. It is only fair I warn you, yes?"

"I expect that from you, Elsa. It's part of your charm, and I should warn you in return. You may not like what I have to say either." Her laughter was like music, and her eyes sparkled with pleasure. I'd forgotten how captivating she was. I looked up at Bruni, who was fixated on what Bonnie was saying.

Simon poured Cristal while a plate containing three sushi pieces was placed before each of us along with a pair of jet-black chopsticks. Elsa looked at her plate.

"Can we use our fingers?" she asked.

"Of course, but I'm going to use these." I picked up the chopsticks. Their weight surprised me. I wondered if they were made of onyx. I had never seen them before.

Elsa popped one in her mouth, and her eyes widened. After she swallowed, she said, "Well, that was extraordinary. What do you suppose it was?"

"I've no idea. I gave Dagmar free rein with the menu."

"How daring, but I must admit, well worth the risk. Now, to business. I understand that you and Bruni might be here for an extended stay. Is this true?"

"To some extent. Bruni's decided to balance her work with some time away. What that means exactly, I'm not altogether sure. She'll have to discuss it with her father, of course. Anne told you."

Elsa finished her second piece.

"Marvelous! And yes, Anne did. Why do you think Brunhilde has decided that?"

"You will have to ask her, but I think she wants to reappraise where she is in life to be happier. Work can be a means to avoid one's own well-being, particularly if work is all one ever does."

"It is true what you say. Work can be all-consuming and distasteful besides. We're often required to interact with unpleasant people and perform tasks we'd rather not."

"You can name names and give me details. You have my permission."

"Perhaps I will, but first, what you offered as her justification is not the reason Brunhilde wants to remain here for a time. This I know."

"What is it then?"

"Men conjure complicated reasons when the truth is often simpler. She is pregnant."

"What?" I almost dropped my chopsticks. "Are you sure?"

"I'm her mother. See how she glows? Her skin is like white fire with a hint of pastel rose."

I looked at Bruni. She must have felt our gaze because she looked up and smiled in our direction before turning back to Bonnie. There was no doubt that something about her had changed. Bruni always glowed, but now she appeared radiant.

"She hasn't mentioned it," I said, feeling light-headed and short of breath.

Elsa offered me a sly smile. "She may not know herself. Sometimes we act unconsciously in ways that are surprising in their genius. Living with her, you must expect to be surprised."

Both mother and daughter were full of surprises, in my opinion, and neither acted impulsively from what I'd seen. Perhaps they both had plans of which I was unaware.

"Elsa, do you think I'm being played a little?" The question escaped as I finished my last piece of sushi and put down my chopsticks. It seemed my paranoia was once again sadly in evidence.

Elsa laughed. "Of course you're being played! We're all being played! It is a question of degrees and mutual benefit. Everyone here has an agenda. Look around you. Take me, for example, I want to know what you know. You want to know what I know. John Sr. wants to know what my husband knows. Anne wants to know what Malcolm knows, particularly about her past. Bonnie wants to know about a possible future with you. Bruni wants to know the same. Mrs. Leland wants to know whether Bonnie can handle her fortune. Johnny wants to protect you. Malcolm is here as an alternate should your father become incapacitated. He wants to know where things stand. And what does Lord Bromley want? Everything. Do you see now?"

"I do. What do you think your daughter wants?"

"She wants what her father and I could not provide."

"And what is that?"

"Herself, only she doesn't realize that she follows wherever she goes, and with her comes her darkness and her light. Even if she should step into another world, it will be the same."

"Another world?"

"It's an expression, yes?" Elsa looked at me carefully. "My daughter had a troubled childhood. To our sorrow, she was faced with adult situations far too early. She is strong. But learning vulnerability can be difficult when strength is all one knows."

"Bruni told me about her past."

"Then she must love and trust you a great deal. You are lucky. It is a wonderful thing to build a universe of two. To let another in and find shelter with each other. Look around you. This is a magnificent house. Who wouldn't want to live here undisturbed? But such an ideal is impossible over the long term. In this universe, no closed system, let alone an economic one, is able to survive indefinitely and remain unaffected by larger forces. The greater and the more complex will always dictate terms to the smaller and the simpler. You should know that even if you are lucky enough to solve the pending issues between my husband and your father, the result will be the same. More money will be needed. It is the way of the world. I hope that is fully understood, not only in an economic sense, but on many levels."

Elsa sipped her champagne. She obviously felt that Bruni was running away. I considered that. Perhaps she was a little—maybe more than a little. If God, according to Napoleon, was on the side of the heaviest battalions, then God was also on the side of those with the most economic clout. Escape for either Bruni or myself would never be allowed.

I answered after a moment of reflection. "Whether here, or in New York, I'm sure Bruni and I will be seeing a great deal of you. After all, both you and Hugo are very much part of our lives and will be for a very long time."

Elsa looked at me over her glass of wine. "As I said before, you're not just a pretty face."

"And neither are you, Elsa."

"That is far truer than you know."

"At least you know how to threaten politely."

"I'm Bruni's mother and your future mother-in-law. How could I not be polite?"

48

The next course was chilled cucumber and watermelon soup served in thin glass bowls to showcase the pale green of its color. A new wine was served, an unusual, golden-green Chardonnay. It was a perfect complement to the soup, which lived up to expectations. There was no conversation.

When I had finished, I thought that I might give Dagmar a freer rein in the future. Whatever she served was extraordinary. How far she would push the boundary of the culinary arts, I had no idea, but wherever she went, I would happily follow.

I turned to my right and said, "Elsa, would you care to elaborate on what you said before?"

She smiled and took a sip of wine. After a pause, she said, "Why belabor a point, when we already understand each other? Let us proceed on a different tack, *Liebchen*."

"By all means," I said.

"What do you know about Johnny's aunt?"

"Some things, but not everything. I knew her personally, although I was quite young when she was alive. Of course, I've heard much about her."

"I'm sure you have. Do you know what she did when she was away?"

"I've heard that expeditions were a big part of her life."

"They were, but that wasn't all she did. Much of her time was spent seeking out sources of arcane knowledge as well as unusual artifacts. She had the necessary funds, and many dealers in such items were happy to supply her, including your father."

"He sold her one or two."

"More than one or two. Your father ultimately supplied her with a large number of the items she acquired, although indirectly, through intermediaries. It was a good business for him. I think she realized that he was behind many of the pieces that were offered for sale, but she chose to overlook that fact."

"Why would she do that?"

Elsa shrugged. "He had what she wanted. Besides, transactions need not always be positive, in the sense that there is a material gain or favorable benefit for buying or selling. There can also be more important negative elements, such as when each party feels that they have gotten the better of the other. That creates a type of negative feedback loop that can be self-sustaining."

"Tell me."

"Let's examine the parts. Take secret knowledge and the occult. Is there really such a thing? Some would say it is delusion. Your father thought so. Alice, on the other hand, was willing to pay for what she believed, and he was more than willing to feed her beliefs for monetary gain. I'm sure he overcharged her."

"He wasn't a believer himself?"

"No, but his being here now might say differently."

"What changed his mind, do you think?"

"You would have to ask him."

I paused. "Perhaps I will. Coming back to what you were saying, do you think Alice was taking advantage of my father?"

"Now that is what I find so interesting. He wanted a second chance, and she strung him along."

"Really? Given their history, that wasn't ever going to happen."

"Exactly, but she held out the possibility. It was an odd relationship. Each wanted what the other thought impossible, and each gained by knowing that they had taken advantage of the other's misguided fascinations. Every acquisition kept the other's dream alive, and so they strung each other along, one transaction at a time."

"That has a perverse sort of logic. How do you know it's true?"

"Alice, as I said, was rarely discreet. What she thought, she told the world. As for your father, I found out in a most peculiar way."

"He told you?"

"Not in so many words. Your father is a slippery man in conversation. He dissembles. You never know who or what he is by the end, or even in the middle. Perhaps he doesn't know himself. Even I have trouble assessing him. I saw Bromley truly only once, and that but briefly. He whispered to himself with his back to me as he looked out the window in our library one late afternoon. He held a whiskey glass in his hand and toasted to something I couldn't see. It could have been the pines that surrounded our castle. It could have been an imaginary figure. 'Another chance for pity's sake. It's all I've ever asked for. It's all I've ever wanted.' Although said in a whisper, there was such vulnerability and sincerity in the tone, I thought another man had said it, but it was him. He never knew I heard him. No one did, and that is why I know he spoke the truth."

"Could he have meant someone else?"

"Possibly, but I doubt many others have moved him the way she did. In addition, Alice may have resided in this house, but she was away for most of that time. Who knows what she really got up to when she wasn't here? Who knows what he did, either?"

"Do you think they met secretly?"

"That I cannot tell you."

"Can't or won't?"

Elsa paused again. "In this instance, I would rather not say."

"I see."

"Do you? Men play games and women, too. Your father loves to play games. To what lengths did he and Alice go to in their game? I sometimes wonder. Your father will likely play games with you, if he hasn't already started. He can't restrain himself. He and Hugo are playing games right now. It is a question of how far either will go. What is delightful about you and me, Percy, is that we can play and have all of the fun with none of the consequences. That is not the case with them. It is possible to go too far, and then there will be consequences for everyone."

"That is somewhat disturbing, Elsa."

She smiled. "It is, and now you see everything more clearly, and I see we have another course! Hugo is not the only one who loves this cook."

The next course of grilled sea bass with tiny asparagus drizzled with hollandaise was served before I could reply. The wine was unchanged. I ate and marveled at the food while contemplating what Elsa had said, when Johnny leaned over and whispered, "You were oblivious. I tried to interrupt twice."

"Sorry about that," I said.

"No need, but I thought you'd like to know. Others might be aware of that as well." Johnny motioned with a nod toward the other end of the table. I looked up and saw Bruni observing me. It might have been a glower, but it was gone when Maw asked her a question and she turned to answer. I tried to catch Bruni's eye, but she didn't turn my way again. I would have to handle later whatever upset I may have inadvertently caused. Right now, I needed information, even though I wanted peace. It was then I noticed the baron staring at me. He didn't look away, and when I smiled, he didn't smile back. Perhaps he thought the baroness had been speaking out of school? There were many secrets held between them, and both he and I knew that his wife had a mind of her own. I decided to ignore his stare and have a talk with him in private.

In any case, Elsa was right about one thing: the best that Bruni and I could do was carve out a temporary sanctuary from time to time. Hiding would be impossible. We came with too many threads. For Bruni, there were, in addition to her work, the obligations to her family that likely needed further clarification.

Growing up, I always considered the Dodges my family, but now I had another. There was my father, and much of what was happening here was his doing. Someone had to rein him in, or as Elsa said, there would be consequences for all of us. She was very clear about that. The oddity was that I had two families. My father and my mother were my real family, even if I didn't think they were.

Stanley entered from the drawing room door behind me. He walked quickly to Anne's side, and whispered in her ear.

"Heavens!" she said. "Tell Percy."

We all looked up as Anne excused herself and went out the way Stanley had entered. He came up next to me, leaned down, and whispered, "Your mother is in the foyer. I alerted Mrs. Dodge so she might be the first to greet her."

"You did the right thing, Stanley. I will follow in a minute. Any thoughts?'

"Only one. Invite her to sit at the table and take part in the last course. This she must do. We'll improvise as to where she will sleep."

"Very well."

I rose and murmured to Johnny and Elsa that I would return shortly. They both looked suitably puzzled. Instead of walking out the door, I went around to Bruni, leaned over, and said, "My mother seems to have arrived, as you predicted. This could get awkward. I'll smile. You'll smile. We'll get through this. Please forgive me if I seemed preoccupied by your mother. It's an occupational hazard with her."

I squeezed her shoulder, and I felt her tension ease. She smiled up at me. I was forgiven.

One down, for now, with the baron still to go. Unfortunately for him, his composure would likely be strained further. My mother had thrown him over many years ago, and since then, both had avoided each other like the plague. As I walked through the drawing room, I thought that once again I had no idea what was going on. *My* house? That was a joke. And Bruni *pregnant*? I didn't know whether to laugh, cry, or be scared to death.

49

"**M**other?"

"Percy, darling. It's so good to see you. My, my, but you do look handsome and well turned out."

She smiled and offered a cheek for me to kiss.

I did and said, "Thank you for the compliment. I'm delighted to see you. Please join us for dinner."

"Impossible. I'm not dressed for the occasion. Just the same, I'd love something to eat. I must also speak with Cobb."

"Cobb?" Recovering from my surprise, I said, "That can be arranged, but you are now my guest. Come to dinner anyway. It's been far too long."

"I don't wish to impose."

"Surprises can be blessings, and all are welcome here. It's an ancient tradition." I turned and asked, "Anne? Am I not correct?"

"Absolutely," she said. "Come, Mary. Stanley and Simon will see to your bags. Off with the coat. The wine tonight is delightful, and I have something for you to wear, although I must say, you do look presentable just the way you are."

"If you insist, but I must use the ladies' first."

"Of course," I said. "It's on the right down the hallway where the light is. We'll wait for you here."

As I was speaking, Anne quickly mentioned to Stanley to move John Sr. to her place at the table. She would take John's and he should prepare a new place setting next to her. On no account was my mother to be seated next to the baron. Stanley nodded and left.

I watched my mother click her way to the bathroom. She was dressed in a dark business suit but with a flare that Italian designers seemed to capture instinctively. It would more than do and looked like it cost a fortune. Her bobbed hair was blondish gray or a grayish blonde. I could never remember which. The color struck a fine balance between middle age and what the well-to-do thought of as "later years," a period of time always left suitably undefined. It had been ten years since I saw her last. She had aged, but the years had added refinement rather than weight. She was slim and fit. She had always been naturally elegant, and I supposed that she always would be. It was a knack she had.

Anne interrupted my thoughts. "When your mother and I spoke on the telephone, I told her about your father's pending arrival and your engagement to Hugo's daughter. I said that you wished to extend an invitation for a visit this weekend, and that you apologized for such short notice. She said that she would pretty much have to drop everything and take the next flight out, but she would see what she could do. Obviously, she did just that, because here she is."

"I'm happy she made it. I'm also glad that she and Bruni will be able to meet, although Hugo won't likely be amused."

"No, he won't be, and speaking of not being amused, your father may find himself on oxygen after he catches sight of her. I mean this house is simply strewn with ex-lovers of his. He'll be lucky to leave in one piece. I did make a point of requesting that your stepfather not make an appearance. I love your mother dearly, but the two together, at a gathering such as this one, would be like hosting a black-tie rumble with spoons and

251

forks for weapons instead of stilettos and flick-knives. By the end of the weekend, only a smoking crater would remain to mark where the house once stood. It's all quite beyond the imagination. Still, I'm very happy she's arrived."

"I'm very glad that you arranged it. It's a pleasant surprise for once, this weekend being quite another. Up until a few days ago, I had my heart set on a nice quiet stay in the country, where we might have had a chance to sit down and talk at leisure. That hasn't happened, and I'm sorry for it."

"Don't be. We had last night's dinner, and that was lovely. It really was. You also needn't worry about me. I'll be fine now. This weekend is all quite exciting in an unnatural sort of way—like surviving a hurricane, provided you do. Do you have any idea why she wants to speak with that man, Cobb?"

"Not a clue."

"Well, there's obviously been a great deal going on of which none of us have been aware, at least those in the immediate family, and I include you in that—a surprising amount in fact. Leave it to me. I will know the reason before the night is done, even if I have to shackle her to a chair and beat it out of her." Anne giggled. "I'm sorry. I shouldn't have put it in those terms. Let's say the wine is very good and leave it at that. Ah, here she is at last."

I smiled as I followed the ladies. They walked ahead arm in arm, chatting and basking in each other's company. They reminded me of Johnny and myself.

I slipped ahead and opened the dining room doors.

50

Rather than announce my mother's presence, I simply accompanied her to one of the two empty places to the right of the table and seated her and Anne together. In spite of the lack of ceremony, my mother's arrival was acknowledged. The gentlemen rose as she was seated, the women looked her over and nodded. Dinner resumed as I sat back down and tried to gauge the reaction to my mother's sudden appearance.

Johnny looked a little wide-eyed and unsure if what had occurred had actually taken place. He looked at me and said, "Well, that is unexpected. Do you think your stepfather will follow?"

"He shouldn't, but I've no idea. My only thought is to eat while we have the opportunity. What will happen next is anyone's guess."

Elsa asked, "Is that your mother?"

"It is."

"Was she invited?"

"Not directly, but then again, she is my mother. How could I possibly say no?"

"Just so."

I continued in a low voice. "How is Hugo taking this? I haven't dared look."

"Like a stoic," Elsa replied.

I looked up. The baron was speaking with John. He acted as if he hardly noticed. I knew I would hear about this, but since I didn't know what to do about it anyway, I decided I would sample the wine. What else was there to do?

"So far so good," Johnny said. "Nobody's pulled a knife. We may make it through the evening yet. How's Maw doing? I can't see."

"She's drinking more wine."

"Well, it's a Lafite, after all. You do remember what I prescribed for you a while back?"

"Drink heavily and many times a day."

"There was wisdom in my words. I suggest we both have at it."

I drank a sip and then some more. I started in on the lamb, that had been served in my absence, and before I knew it, most of what was on my plate had disappeared. Fortified, I turned to Elsa and asked, "So, what do you think Alice was doing all that time she was away from Rhinebeck?"

"I don't know in detail, but apropos of what we were saying, she and Bromley crossed paths on numerous occasions. You will have to ask him to get the specifics."

"I doubt I'll have to ask him. He said he wanted to tell me his version of their relationship before he collapsed."

"That is good. I think it important that you speak with him. On another matter, why do you suppose your mother is here?"

"She wishes to see Anne, meet Bruni, and have a word with Cobb."

"It must be a financial or legal matter. Cobb does a great deal more for your father than simply take his pulse and write it down. I would ask Brunhilde. I said earlier that one often has to interact with unpleasant characters. That man is one. Your father is, of course, another."

"I thought as much."

"Then you are correct, but enough. Let us turn to something much more pleasant and far more relevant. Do you think my grandchild will be a boy or a girl?"

It was at that moment that Stanley announced to the table that Dagmar had created a very special ending for the dinner. As he spoke, the previous course was whisked away, and plates of sweet biscuits with a small red crystal glass in the middle were placed at each setting. The baron called out to Stanley, "Is this a potion?"

"It is an old Nordic recipe created and distilled for very special occasions. The tradition calls for locating another person with whom to drink, raising your glass high while calling out in a loud voice the person's name. Once eye contact is made, you say '*Skaal*' and repeat the name, such as '*Skaal, Johnny.*' Johnny will respond by lifting his glass high, and then both must keep looking into each other's eyes as the drinks are sipped. Once done, both raise their glasses in a final salute, still looking at each other. The *skaal* ends the moment the glass is back on the table. Only then can another *skaal* begin. In this ceremony, you will *skaal* everyone at the table and they will *skaal* you. This translates into twenty *skaals* each. I suggest small sips. Your glasses will be replenished as needed. Please know that this is an ancient and solemn ceremony that few have had the honor to partake in. Dagmar and I will demonstrate."

Dagmar came out of the kitchen holding a glass for Stanley and one for herself. Everyone applauded when she appeared. Once the applause had died down, Stanley cried out "Dagmar" in a loud voice and raised his glass. "*Skaal, Dagmar!*" Keeping his glass raised, Dagmar raised hers. They stared at each other and sipped. Still not looking away, they

255

raised their glasses to each other one last time before lowering them. Dagmar then called out "Stanley!" and they continued the ritual until both had lowered their glasses.

"That completes the demonstration," announced Stanley. "Know that failure to s*kaal* with everyone at the table will have repercussions. Long ago, the fates would note those who didn't comply and punish them, and lest you believe this is all in jest, remember where you are. Now, please enjoy yourselves. This is a gift."

While others looked around, unsure of how to begin, I raised my glass and shouted out, "Bruni!" She looked at me. I shouted, "S*kaal*, Bruni!" She lifted her glass, and we both sipped. Her eyes widened, and I'm sure mine did as well. The liquid was fiery but smooth as silk. It started with a hint of juniper and had a finish that tasted of strawberries and maybe even chocolate. I was quite sure that nineteen more of these would see me drunk as a lord and looking up at the underside of the table. Bruni shouted out my name, and so it began.

By the end of my first five *skaals*, the noise level at the table had notably increased. By the tenth, shouting was the only means of being heard. Maw's equestrian trainer's voice cut through the babble like a buzz saw. "Percy!" She commanded, and I complied by raising my glass. Only eight more to go, I thought, but who they were was uncertain. I had tried going in a clockwise direction, but with my name being called out from random points of the compass, it proved impossible to keep track. Faces seemed to blur, and voices rose and fell like the sound of gusts through pine trees. I noted that others were having similar difficulties. The baron and Johnny had s*kaaled* at least three times with each other, and by the third were laughing like idiots. By the eighteenth, I noted that my ability to count had substantially deteriorated. Starting back at ten

256

seemed a sensible alternative. Having arrived at twenty *skaals* by several alternate counting methods, I was grinning foolishly along with the rest.

Elsa called out, "Percy!" and another round began, followed by another from Johnny.

In the back of my mind, I noted that whatever preexisting hostilities between the various guests had submerged beneath an ocean of goodwill and bonhomie. A feeling of peace and tranquility took hold. The manic laughter and hysteria ceased like wind subsiding after the sun had set. We sat in silent inner contemplation.

I imagined I was looking at a fire on a clear dark evening in a forest. I could hear the snap of bubbling sap and smell the wood smoke. A figure spoke from the other side of the fire. The flames obscured my view of who it was.

The voice said, "Long ago we spoke with the Earth, and the Earth sang back. We sang what we heard. Others came from far away and took our places. They played a different music and sang of the deeds of men. We were forgotten, but in the still of the night, it is possible to hear us. Our songs never stopped, only the listeners."

51

E arly the next morning, I walked the silent house in my socks, wearing last night's clothes, before climbing the stairs to the top floor to change. A new day was starting, and I felt better than I had any right to expect, given the revelries of the prior evening.

How long I had sat at the table in tranquil stupor, lost in dreams, I didn't know. It could have been ten minutes or several hours. Time had warped in strange ways and deposited me at the other end, calmed by the peace and warmth of my vision, but filled with a certainty that I would not forget the evening any time soon. I doubted anyone else would either.

I recalled Elsa giving me a kiss that had seemed unusually long. She had patted my hand and murmured that she was going to collect her husband lest we find him in the same place at breakfast. Johnny, his father, and the baron had sat swaying with their arms around each other's shoulders. Bruni, Maw, and Bonnie had been doing pretty much the same. Malcolm had slept. His head would droop and then spring up at odd moments while Anne and Mary had held hands with their eyes closed, dreaming as one.

I remembered standing up, sitting down, and trying again. Gradually, my reverie had subsided. I had watched bodies disentangle, as my guests had looked around them. They had seemed puzzled, but in a dreamy way, content to let the world be, the rough edges of their dislikes filed down to smooth surfaces.

The baron had called out to question if moving to the library was next, but had remained seated, swaying slightly. His wife came round to collect him, and once she had him standing, they had made for the door and the long staircase to follow. Observing their progress, I had thought that such an undertaking might take some time. Bruni in her silver gown had floated toward me from the far end of the table like a wraith—beauty sculpted in icy silver. Her eyes were closed, but when I touched her, they had opened as she slipped into my arms.

"Take me to bed," she had murmured.

Her accent had been strange. I looked at her and then around us. Stanley and his crew had everything in hand.

"Go," Bruni had said as she laid a hand upon my shoulder. She had glided beside me as we passed from the dining room through the drawing room and down the hall, her eyes stayed mostly closed, as if walking in a dream.

After, as she lay in my arms, she whispered into my bare shoulder, "So much to say, so much to hear. I'm so happy and too content to begin. Let us sleep while we can. Dawn will wake us in its time. Sleep, my love." She had given a sigh and out she went like a light.

The room had been gray as dawn broke. We had gazed into each other's eyes and started to laugh.

"Last night was ... indescribable!" Bruni had exclaimed. "That drink was more than a simple alcoholic beverage."

"Without a doubt," I had said.

"Well, whatever it was, I feel calmer now and oddly reassured."

"I'm happy for that. By the way, you were speaking strangely before we slept."

"I did? Well, I'd returned from an odd place, so it's more than likely."

"Where did you go?"

"Somewhere I've never been. I sat in a heavy, high-backed chair on a dark green, velvet cushion, in front of a roaring fire in the main hall of a castle. A singer with a lute sang of long dead heroes, unrequited love, and places far away. It may have been France. I felt comfort in the words and safe where I was. I still feel that way. I might even sleep better going forward. I don't know why I know that, other than that I do."

"I went someplace different. I found myself in a dark forest sitting on a blanket in front of a fire. A man on the opposite side of the flames spoke of the distant past."

"Definitely different. Papa will be thrilled no matter what happened to him. He was eager to try one of Dagmar's concoctions."

"He can now check that off his list, and speaking of things to do, we were going to talk last night but doing so proved wonderfully impossible."

"Planning is often overrated. I suggest we get up and get dressed. We can talk now. Perhaps you might find us some coffee? Today might get a little weird. What I have to say will likely contribute to that, but I'm feeling optimistic despite my trepidations."

"Sounds good. I must go upstairs to get some clothes, but I'll be back soon."

"Sorry about that. We'll fix it. For now, I can take my time in the shower. You see? Things *are* looking up. Kiss me first and come back to me."

I had been so lost in my thoughts that I gave a start when I finally arrived at the top of the house. I opened the door and noticed the door to my room was shut. Stanley must have put my mother in my room, likely over Johnny's objections. I would have to wake him to get any clothes at all. Having been subjected to years of annoyance due to his methods first thing in the morning, I thought it only fair to return the favor.

I banged on his door with his same rapid, irritating knock.

There was a squawk followed by "Who is it?"

"Your landlord," I answered.

Johnny opened the door a crack to be sure of who it was. "Oh, it's you," he said as he opened it wider. "I suppose you're here for my rent. Will jeans and a shirt suffice in lieu of payment? By the way, we must get the formula of that drink from Dagmar. We don't need anyone else's money. That stuff is pure gold. We'll make a killing. On top of that, one hundred thousand people screamed my name in ecstasy last night! Me! It was marvelous. I went to heaven, if only for a moment. Of course, that little fellow behind me kept repeating over and over that victory was fleeting. That quickly got old, but then it would, wouldn't it? I simply ignored him and basked in the approbations of thousands and thousands of cheering fans. I feel fit as a fiddle. No sign of a hangover. Your mother's in your room, by the way. I must say I was surprised to see her at dinner, and even more when she thought my door led to the bathroom. She wasn't wearing a stitch. It must be a European thing. You know she actually looks quite good for someone her age. You're awfully quiet."

"You're awfully talkative for so early in the morning. I can't get a word in edgewise."

"It must be a side effect of the concoction. We'll have to note that somewhere on the labeling: unrestrained babble before breakfast, or something similar. I'm still doing it, aren't I?"

"Yes."

"Oh well. I hope it wears off, but then again, maybe it won't. I suppose I'll have to live with it—no matter. Now speaking of 'supposed to,' I was going to come up with a brilliant plan last night, only my deification before an adoring populace put a kink in that. Not to worry, I will get to it. Perhaps you could send up some coffee, and I can get started right away? What do you think?"

I showered and changed as fast as I could. That amount of self-adoration was almost sinful. The drink had hit him exactly where he lived. At one point I think I shushed him only to have him respond with, "Did you shush me? Really? Me?" I left hurriedly, promising to send up coffee. What had looked like certain payback had turned into a rout. I laughed as I descended the stairs. How he managed to always turn the tables on me, I never could fathom.

52

T he house was stirring, and I was able to ask Jane to send some coffee up to the top floor, while grabbing two cups and a thermos for myself. Back in our apartment, Bruni was in the bathroom drying her hair with a towel. I placed a full cup on the table by the sink and retreated to the sitting room.

Bruni joined me on the couch with her coffee.

"Thank you for this. How is Johnny feeling?"

"Very well—too well, in fact. While you and I had more subdued visions, he experienced being a Roman emperor. You can imagine how he's feeling. Besides thinking up a plan to conquer the world, he's working on a means to counter my father's soon-to-be delivered ultimatum."

"Ultimatum?"

"It was in the second letter. I either hand over the treasures that my father has documentation to prove are his, and he departs with them, or I allow him to live here indefinitely, so he can play with the artifacts upstairs in his room. On top of that, the check he gave me requires his signature. He can delay signing it for as long as he wishes."

"I see. That is a hard choice, yet he didn't deliver the second letter. How come?"

"He was angry with me and considered me unworthy. Besides, my father would rather dictate terms than negotiate them. Johnny thinks he will deliver the legal documentation to me this morning, and then follow up with the ultimatum letter as a kind of peace offering."

"That letter's likely not to be his final demand."

"I'm sure it's not. He's obsessed with playing games. He is also rather heavy-handed, which got me thinking. If he uses threats with family, how does he handle friends? Your father seems troubled, and your mother hinted that there is something going on between those two. Is there?"

Bruni paused and sipped her coffee before she replied. "The short answer is yes, most definitely, and that brings us to what I wanted to talk to you about last night. The abridged version is that your father and mine are at odds over a business deal that I helped structure. For now, your father holds the upper hand. It's messy, and the conflict between them is getting out of hand. The only good things about the entire affair have been my pending divorce, and that you and I met. Strangely, you have your father to thank for that."

"Really? This I would like to hear."

"I'll tell you, but you won't think highly of me by the time I'm done. The whole sordid business is why I want to stop working for my father, at least in the acquisition area. It's one of several changes I need to make."

"That all sounds rather ominous."

"Because it is." Bruni sighed.

"Tell me."

"It's complicated, but I'll try and be brief. Several months ago, while I was working on a transaction for my father and Bernard, my briefcase was stolen from our hotel room. In it were the acquisition terms and conditions to purchase a large, family-owned business. A great deal of money was involved, and the theft put the transaction in jeopardy."

"I imagine it would have."

"After the theft, Bernard and I knew no peace. He thought an unknown bidder, privy to what was in the briefcase, would come forward with a better offer. That possibility drove him crazy. He blamed me for the theft, and he was right to do that, since I was responsible for it."

"Responsible?"

"I suggested it at a planning meeting with my father. So yes, I was responsible."

"I see."

"Bernard had questions about the missing briefcase and grew suspicious. His behavior changed. He began blaming me for any delays in the negotiations. Since holdups are inevitable with a deal of that size, he grew more and more antagonistic and aggressive."

Bruni sipped her coffee and considered what to say next.

"Tolerating Bernard's tantrums was my way of making up for the part I played. It was a flawed concept. Several unpleasant incidents followed, until one day, I couldn't endure another minute. I exploded, and afterward, rapprochement became impossible."

Bruni paused again. I waited for her to continue.

"The blowup happened in an underground parking garage beneath our office in Geneva. It had been a difficult day. I had started the car and was about to drive back to the hotel, when Bernard called out for me to stop. He walked up and leaned his head through the driver's window. I didn't realize how mad he was until he yelled, 'You're really stupid! Do you know that?'

"Granted, it had been a bad day. The sellers had added a last-minute condition. They wanted a seat on the board, to which I had agreed. To me, this was a throwaway. It made no material difference. I was the lead negotiator and had the authority to make decisions without further consultation with my team, but adding this stipulation delayed the signing in order to amend the mountains of paperwork. To Bernard, this was inexcusable. He thought that the holdup was deliberate. I had previously explained to him that by allowing the family a board seat, the chances of closing were significantly increased, but he disagreed. Besides, I'd suggested the addition to the family in private, a fact I didn't tell him, for reasons that will also become clear."

"Yikes!" I said.

"That day, the stink of his breath mingled with his cologne, and as I backed away from the open window to avoid it, his head moved farther inside the car. I'd left the ignition on, and the electric windows were quick. The rising window caught him by the neck. He tried to break free, but I threatened to press the 'Up' button again. He stopped struggling, and I was able to speak without interruption. I made sure to lock the door.

"I told him calmly that the deal was proceeding as planned and would close. All he had to do was shut his mouth, leave me alone, and let me get on with my work. The deal would make him very rich, but without me. He and I were through. To make sure he understood the finality of my decision, I turned off the car, left the keys in the ignition, and got out by the passenger door. I'd had enough of him. I took a cab to the hotel, packed my things, and moved out. After that, we saw each other only at business meetings. No competing offer materialized, and the acquisition went through as I said it would, a fact I was happy to point out to him."

"I can understand why Bernard has harsh feelings toward you."

"The feelings are mutual, but what followed once the deal completed heightened them even more. Part of the acquisition package was a convertible bond offering to the family. The bonds paid a generous income but could be exchanged for shares of common stock in the new company. It was a feature that the family was not expected to exercise because the income would cease when the conversion was made. Second, the number of shares that the family would receive, although significant, would be insufficient to take back control of the company. With me so far?"

"I think so. The family had the choice of a nice stable income or partial ownership but not both. I take it the family wanted income."

"The founder wanted to retire, and acquiring a regular income for the family was the reason the business was being sold in the first place."

"That makes sense. Who controlled the new company?"

"Bernard. My father took only a forty-five percent stake, since Bernard had come up with the idea and knew the family personally. Bernard owned the other fifty-five percent and had controlling interest."

"Who came up with that arrangement?"

"I'll get to that. Papa's long-term plan was to complete the acquisition, merge with another privately held company that had tentatively agreed in concept, and then take the new conglomerate public. The plan, once the conglomerate is taken public, will reap many millions, but my father was concerned that if Bernard knew about the long-term objectives, he might refuse to take part. Bernard had been previously sanctioned by certain regulatory agencies and is banned from holding a management position in a publicly traded company. A public offering would require that Bernard step down, a course of action that he would likely not agree to willingly. Since Bernard owned over fifty percent of the company, he had the power to refuse any future mergers and keep the company the way it was. To counter those possibilities, Papa and I put in place a contingency plan."

"In other words, Bernard's days were numbered from the beginning."

"Yes, and that contingency plan involved your father. At the next board meeting, your father walked in having purchased all the bonds from the family and having already converted them to company shares in his name. How exactly he arranged this, he didn't say. With Lord Bromley on the board, the ownership picture changed dramatically. There were now three owners who controlled roughly a third apiece. Voting together, my father and yours had the majority and overruled Bernard. There was nothing he could do."

"Nothing at all."

"It was not a pleasant meeting. The merger with the new company is now in progress."

"I see. My father had the swing vote. Giving Bernard fifty-five percent initially was brilliant. He stepped right into the trap. Who thought of that?"

"I did."

"And the stolen briefcase?"

"In one of the planning sessions with my father I mentioned that if such a theft took place, Bernard would be so concerned with the possibility of a competing bid that he would push for the fastest closing possible. He would sign off on the convertible bond offering, rather than allow weeks of negotiations to come up with a better arrangement. Papa must have considered the idea worthwhile, because the briefcase was stolen shortly after."

"Who did it, do you think?"

"Cobb, or one of his people. For what it's worth, I thought that the contingency plan would prove unnecessary. Bernard stood to make a fortune if all he did was go along, but I was wrong about Bernard from the beginning. To Bernard, it was never about money. It was always about power and control. Unfortunately, I learned that too late."

"I suppose he will have to be content with only moderate riches. Thank you for telling me. I have a few questions."

"I'll answer them if I can."

"For the briefcase to be stolen, someone must have signaled the thief that the briefcase was available. Who did?"

"The night of the theft, Bernard, myself, and my parents had dinner at a restaurant on the other side of town. I was going to work in the hotel room, something I did regularly, but Papa invited us out and insisted we join them. He even picked up the tab himself, rather than have the company pay for it."

"I see, and speaking of picking up the tab, he probably put up most, if not all, of the money that my father used to purchase the bonds from the prior owners."

"I was too engrossed in the negotiations and too distracted by the issues with Bernard to pay much attention to anything else, but I would say that is a distinct possibility."

"Unfortunately for Hugo, if he did, that didn't prevent my father from turning the tables and betraying him. I imagine that by owning the shares, my father could vote whichever way he wanted. I'll wager that he threatened to side with Bernard if Hugo didn't agree to certain conditions of his own. Am I not correct?"

"You are in a clever mood this morning," said Bruni. "But that isn't the half of it. Your father has refused to sign over the shares to Papa now that Bernard is no longer in control. That was a critical part of the arrangement between them, and there is little my father can do."

"Isn't that illegal?"

"Maybe. I don't know the details to be able to determine that. I had made it clear at the beginning what could be done, and what couldn't. Whatever was decided between them and arranged was done without my knowledge. Right now, the shares are in your father's name, and to get his hands on them, my father must do whatever your father wants."

—•—

53

"A nd Hugo has no recourse?"

"It's called coercion, but proving coercion depends on the circumstances and the jurisdiction. There is also the clean hands factor, and that hinges on whose money was used to buy the bonds from the family. If it was Bromley's, then the transaction could be legal. If it was my family's money, it's a different story. So far, Papa has not said one way or the other, and I have not asked the question. At some point, it will be necessary that I do, and I may have an ethical dilemma that I don't want. For now, I'm out of the office. If I'm not there, I can't ask and can't be told."

"I see. I suppose the best course would be to resolve the dispute between them."

"Absolutely. It's imperative."

"Given that, what do you think my father wants?"

"I don't know, other than that the library and the artifacts are key. Papa has never said specifically, and once again I haven't asked. The auction the other week was meant to resolve the matter between them. Strangely, all would have been fine, and the matter dispensed with, only you showed up."

"Me?"

"Yes, you. The ownership picture changed, like it did when you father converted the shares. One moment Bernard was in control, and the next he wasn't. You did the same. You became the new owner and stipulated that the artifacts remain here. Given that constraint, of course your father was going to arrive. What else could he do? Disposing of the library and the artifacts was the reason we were all here then, and likely why we're all here now."

"I see. Who would have won the auction had I not been present?"

"That is difficult to know. The end result would have been that my father recovered the shares, and your father owned the artifacts. What price each would have had to pay the other is not easily answered. It is that conflict that must be resolved, and how that is to be done is still on the table. I can guarantee that there is more to follow along those lines."

"Each will take his pound of flesh."

"Oh yes. My father, because he hates being compelled to do what he doesn't want to, and yours, because my father failed to deliver the artifacts into his hands when he said he would."

"What do you suggest we do?"

"At some point both men must sit down in a room together and hammer out a solution. Only you can arrange and oversee that. I have to remain outside those proceedings for obvious reasons."

"That would make sense. I will try and arrange that. One thing you could do is speak with your mother. She might give you some insight. I'm sure she is aware of what is going on, and how far Hugo is willing to go to resolve the matter."

"I'll speak with her. Perhaps she can come up with an idea as well. The difficulty I see is in creating sufficient trust between you and my father such that he would willingly agree to sit down with you and yours. The expression 'like father

272

like son' comes to mind, and he will wonder whether you might betray him and use the information I have given you against him. It's how Papa thinks. On the other hand, if we managed to nullify the coercion factor, he would be indebted to you, and that could come in handy in the future."

"What if my father dies before it's resolved?"

"I'm sure both have considered that. Papa looks at everything, which means he has also considered the possibility that if your father dies, for whatever reason, you may *not* be the one who inherits. What happens to the shares then? You may look like the obvious choice, but it is more than likely that your father has made other arrangements and for that reason. Nothing is ever certain with him, least of all his will."

"That thought never crossed my mind. It would also take my father's death off the table as a workable solution to the issues between them. I'm sure my father made a point of mentioning that to yours. It would be like taking out an insurance policy."

"Exactly."

"Well, I'm certainly glad you mentioned that. On a much more positive note, your mother said that there is another reason you might wish to remain here for a while."

"What was that?"

"She thinks you're pregnant."

"Really?" Bruni looked stunned. She took a long moment. "I've wondered about that," she said finally. "Dagmar hinted and Mama is very perceptive, so I would take that as a confirmation. Wow! Who would have thought? We're going to have a baby! That changes everything!"

"Happy?"

"You have no idea!" Bruni beamed. "Of course, growing as large as a refrigerator and getting stretch marks are not to my liking, but such discomforts are a small price to pay. I wonder if it will be a boy or a girl? We'll have to find out. Whichever it is, our child will be absolutely gorgeous, and that thought makes me giddy. Now that I think about it, I'm sure I am, and that is a perfect reason for reducing my work obligations. It smooths out any potential friction with my father. The downside is that we may have two semi-permanent houseguests in the form of my parents. Still, I'm so excited!"

Bruni slid over to my side of the couch, and we held each other tightly.

"Will you still love me when I'm huge?" Bruni whispered.

"How could I not, when I always will?"

"That's good. This makes everything different, you know."

"How so?"

Bruni sat up and switched to her professional mode. She looked at me steadily as she said, "We need to resolve this mess and get your father out of this house. I'm sorry, but I want him gone."

"I feel the same."

"Good."

A second later she smiled and looked the happiest I'd ever seen her.

"I can't believe I'm pregnant. After this weekend, we really should plan our wedding, but on to more immediate matters. Do you have any more questions?"

"Only two. Your mother mentioned that I should ask you about Cobb. What do you know about him?"

"If your father wants something done, Cobb is the one who either does it or makes it happen. He goes too."

"For sure. Last question, my father also mentioned that he has his attorney available. Is that you?"

"I work exclusively for my father. He has asked me in the past to help with a few of Bromley's transactions with Cobb acting as intermediary. I reviewed the paperwork involved. My father also mentioned a couple of weeks ago that there were legal matters between this estate and your father. I'm not Lord Bromley's attorney, nor would I ever be."

"That answers the question. I apologize. I had to ask."

"That man likes to seed discord whenever and wherever he can. It's time to do something about him. Why don't you have an audience with the emperor upstairs? He might have an idea or two. I'll find out if Mama is up. Kiss me, and let's get started. That man and his flunky will be leaving soon—both of them, face up or face down. It makes no difference to me."

54

I found Johnny upstairs in the common room, scribbling on his yellow pad. The door to my room was still closed, but I was quite sure my mother would be up and about soon. I suggested that we take a walk outside so we could confer without interruption. He handed me a windbreaker.

The sun had barely risen as we stepped out the front door and walked around the house to the bench behind the stately cypress trees. There was no wind, and the sky was clear. I filled him in on all that Bruni had told me.

"Well, that explains several things and adds more complications," said Johnny as we sat down on the bench.

"It does. How's the plan?"

"Planning is only as good as the data to hand, and this last bit changes things once again." He sighed. "At least we know what's been driving events here. I suppose that's something. I must integrate this latest information into my overall thinking. It might help if I expound a little and go from there."

"Fair enough. Fire away," I said, lighting a smoke.

"I'll take one of those," said Johnny. Once he lit it, he continued. "Based on what we know so far, Lord B. wants a number of pieces that Alice had in her possession for unknown reasons and has coerced Hugo into helping him get his hands on them. For what purpose remains a mystery. So far, so good?"

"For the most part. The questions I have are why involve Hugo at all? If my father has the documentation necessary to prove the artifacts are his, why not simply go to court?"

"I've considered that. To begin with, we know he specifically wants the figurine. He mentioned that in the letter. I'm sure Aunt Alice told him that she hadn't received it when they were negotiating over the little pot. Likely, she'd had to repeat that a thousand times before he believed her. Legal was pointless until now."

"That would make some sense. The only question Hugo asked me when he and I spoke was about the idol and the jewel. I told him that we'd found it, and that it had shattered."

"Which is how Lord B. knows it's here. I'm guessing the breakage was never brought up. That's not something I'd want to mention when Lord B. has you under his thumb."

I grunted.

"No grunting. That it's broken has some serious potential and will cause a stir at the least. I'm not sure how to take advantage of that, but to return to your question, any legal threat Lord B. has conjured up is a lot of hot air no matter what documentation he says he has."

"Why do you think so?"

"Your father's life expectancy. He has a year or two at the outside, while you can string any proceedings along for many more, and that's with only moderately competent legal counsel. Secondly, there are laws now about pilfering national treasures. He would have to specify the item, and that could lead to complications."

"Interesting point. I agree. It's an empty threat."

"It is." Johnny paused and smoked.

He continued, "I wish I had a more concrete plan but that's not possible yet. For now, the best I can come up with are some educated guesses as to what went on. Still, they may prove useful. Would you like to hear them?"

"Please."

"The first is that it's likely that Hugo failed to mention the potential value of those shares to your father when the scheme was originally put forward. The second is that Bernard found out after he was booted from the management side and got in touch with Lord B. and told him. Bernard might also have told Cobb. After all, why would a Harley Street physician, with underworld connections per Stanley, hang around your father in the first place?"

"I've wondered about that," I said.

"Perhaps Cobb stands to benefit from the shares in some way?"

"It's possible. It is an odd relationship. I must speak with Stanley about Cobb."

"I would. My last is that Hugo *must* have those shares back or risk a major financial setback. I mean, if he put up the money to buy the bonds from the family using Lord B. as an intermediary, that must have been quite a sum. He must be feeling some heat. I wonder if Elsa even knows how extended he is?"

"Bruni is speaking to her. If Elsa doesn't know, she soon will."

"Ouch. That could be painful and first thing in the morning, too. In addition, there are the odd extraneous bits that puzzle me—like your mother wanting to speak with Cobb. I don't know what to make of that. What is really needed is for everyone to lay their cards on the table. The question is, how are we to make that happen?"

"Perhaps I'll have to announce that there is to be a meeting in the library to resolve all the pending issues?"

"Use it only as a last resort. There are too many secrets between the parties involved. I would start with something unexpected, like telling your father that you've decided to do nothing for now and handing him back the envelope with the check. He'll go ballistic, but he might let slip what he really has in mind. After the explosion, you can modify your position by suggesting that you and he sit down with Hugo to work out an incentive as to why you should do anything at all. It will mean that the two will have to work together to convince you, which is an interesting twist. Anyway, that's the best I can come up with for now."

"That isn't bad. I'll think on it."

"Don't take too long. Time is running out."

"And patience," I said.

"Patience?" asked Johnny.

"A less stressful and contentious atmosphere is necessary. We must get rid of Cobb and my father before Bruni gets involved. She may be pregnant, and she's beginning to get a little ferocious."

"Really? Pregnant? Congratulations! The news never stops. That means I'll be an uncle of sorts! You know, I've always wanted to have a nephew or niece. Won't that be something! Well, if you want your father and Cobb gone, then we must get busy. I think I'll chat up Malcolm. He's always in the background and might know something."

"Do that. I'll get with Stanley now."

55

I n the front hall, Stanley was checking the flower arrangements, and I asked him if he had a moment. On our way through the kitchen, I told Dagmar that last night's dinner was unparalleled and never to be forgotten. She beamed and assured me there was more to come.

Once Stanley and I were seated in his office, I repeated what I had learned from Elsa, Bruni, and Johnny, and announced that Bruni was pregnant. Stanley folded his hands and considered what I had revealed.

At last he said, "Well, let us begin with my hearty congratulations to you both. Having a child in this house will be an unprecedented blessing. Dagmar, of course, informed me of that possibility some time ago; nonetheless, hearing it from you is a most welcome confirmation. Normally, I would offer a glass to honor such an occasion, but the hour is still early. On the other hand, a moment such as this can only happen once, and it is significant. Shall we?"

"Let's."

Stanley produced two glasses of whiskey. I noted that this brew had a different color than the previous ones. I was about to comment, when he said, "To begin, I wish to drink with you not as your servant but as your friend. May I do that?"

"You may indeed, Stanley."

"May I also address you as Percy?"

"Please do."

Stanley grinned. I had never seen him grin. He looked like a young man.

"Thank you, Percy. That means a lot to me. In the future, when we sit down in this office and only the two of us are present, I would like to address you by that name. In those moments, you can call me Stan. I have allowed only a few to call me that. Outside this room, we must have our formal relationship, which I will maintain as a matter of course. In my life, I have had so few real friends. You have achieved that status with me. I don't know how that happened. Anyway, there it is."

"Stan, it would be my honor."

"Thank you, Percy. Now, we have two reasons to celebrate: a friendship and the beginning of new life. In your glass is an exceptionally rare and in my opinion, the finest whiskey that you will ever drink. The man who created it is long dead, having taken the secrets of its manufacture to his grave. He was a legendary figure where I grew up. It was said that he did a favor for a sorceress, who in return asked him what he wanted most in all the world. He told her that he wished to create the finest of whiskies—one that had no equal in either Heaven or Earth. The sorceress agreed but had two conditions of her own. He could make but one barrel a year, and the secret must never be written down or revealed to another, even in death. The deal was struck, and he kept his word. Rumor of this brew grew to legendary proportions. I had forgotten all about it until my previous employer bequeathed me two bottles in his will. As part of the bequest, my former employer asked that I enjoy them only on special occasions. Specifically, he wrote: 'Share this gift with another. Drink slowly, savoring every drop, and do so only in those moments of deep satisfaction, or in commemoration of an outstanding happening. All I ask is that when you drink, think of me and speak my name.' "

"This is very special then."

"Of all the wonders in the cellar here, this is the crown jewel. Dagmar and I drank a glass when we were reconciled long ago. I've had no occasion since. We will drink to Hamish and to our good fortune—specifically to having a friend, and that friend expecting a child."

Stanley raised his glass. "To Hamish, to friendship, and to new life."

"To Hamish, to friendship, and to new life," I repeated.

We looked at each other and drank. It was smooth, smoky, and then not. The taste seemed to change in so many subtle ways that I had to restrain myself from taking another sip as I tried to clarify what I had just experienced. The smell reminded me of honey, but that, too, transformed in impossible directions. Neither of us spoke until we had emptied our glasses to the last drop and even then, the intoxicating smell lingered like some magical bouquet.

I looked at him. "Wow, Stan. That was impressive. We must have another draft when the issues before us are resolved. That possibility will give me all the incentive I need, even if I have to confront the devil himself."

"My thoughts exactly," replied Stanley. "And along those lines, I did some further research late last night. I have come up with a couple of possible explanations as to why your father wants access to certain objects, why he is here specifically, and what he intends to accomplish."

"Tell me."

"I will, but first a question: are you familiar with spiritualism?"

"I've heard of it. I believe it was popular during the late 1800s and had to do with contacting the dead through a medium."

"That is correct. Of course, with that subject we are touching on points that are at the edges of reality as is it is commonly known, but my conjectures are not without some foundation. My first supposition is that your father wants to speak to the dead."

"To Alice?"

"I believe so. From what the baroness told you and from the letter he wrote, your father may hold her ladyship in his heart as highly as I have. To me, it is a distressing thought but no less true. In addition, I have long suspected that whatever copy of the Book of the Dead your father supplied, and her ladyship used, was purposely flawed or incomplete. The question I have asked myself is did your father know of the imperfections at the time? More relevant in this case, what if he did not? I had never considered that possibility until yesterday. It is one thing to harm another deliberately, but quite another to do so unintentionally, particularly if you loved them to begin with. That he would wish to make amends for committing such an unintentional error would follow."

"I agree," I said.

"The second is that he wishes to be healed."

"That, too, would be logical. He does seem remarkably youthful, but Cobb said that he's had similar episodes and all together would indicate deeper health issues."

"I will have more to say about your father's youthful appearance when we discuss Cobb. In any event, my conjectures on these two points have some foundation. This area and the surrounding Hudson River Valley have a long history of occult activity. The list of prophets, trance-induced

283

writers, and spiritualists that inhabited and sprang up in this extended valley is long and exceptional. Is that mere coincidence? As I mentioned before, some locations are more conducive to the mystical than others. We also have this particular property and the power it contains to consider. Is it any wonder that he's here?"

"No. So his coming has little to do with me directly," I said.

"I'm not convinced of that in its entirety. For now, it appears to be the case."

"I agree. Anyway, please continue."

"Living in this area, her ladyship studied spiritualism as a matter of course. Its weaknesses, she told me, were twofold. The first was the need for a medium who might not be a medium at all, and the second was the assumption that the dead still lived. With the first, the results could be manipulated, but more important to her was the second: the tacit assumption that death was not the end.

"To her ladyship, being dead with nothing more to follow was the best possible ending. She would be free. She thought at first that science would ultimately succeed, but over time, she felt she had to reject its view that death was simply the passage to nonexistence. What changed her mind were her studies of Siberian shamans, their practices, and subsequent influences. Ancient Shamans were said to be able to mediate with the spirit world and were able to travel outside themselves. This technique differed from spiritualism in that spiritualism required a medium, a psychic individual, who became possessed of an alien spirit. With shamanism there were no such intermediaries. The shaman, himself, traveled to another world and, once there, often received supernormal wisdom.

"We would speak about her research in this area from time to time. She would tell me about the healing ceremonies that involved ecstatic experiences that separated self from body. Such procedures, she thought, must have been grounded in some form of reality, because the concept of a separate body and self not only survived but expanded in its influence. Shamanic practices and beliefs spread throughout the Asian continent to points as far away as Indonesia and into what is now modern Turkey, well before the Homeric era. There they found acceptance and new adherents in the form of the Pythagoreans, the Orphic and the Elysian Mysteries, the followers of Dionysius, Cybele, Bendis, and Sabazius. Still later, Christianity took much from these pagan practices, including the concept of a soul. To trace the movement and power of an idea was one thing, she told me, but what she wanted most of all was proof.

"One particular conversation has relevance to what confronts us now and explains why her research went in that direction. Her ladyship told me plainly, 'It's the drugs, Stanley.' She said that true ecstasy, spiritual quests, as well as visits to other worlds are not easily achieved in a normal state. Saints and monks with years of ascetic training, and those who have been touched, have been able to accomplish such feats, but they were the exceptions. She said further that for the concept of a spirit being separate from the body to become so widespread and almost universally accepted must have required extraordinary proof of some kind. She said that we find that proof in the special substances that were prepared and taken with food or drink as part of ancient ceremonies like those of the Elysian Mysteries and early Christians. She said specifically, 'In the end, what is experienced for oneself cannot be disputed.' Later, she talked about how certain substances were used to make real what are for the most part abstract concepts to many religious followers today."

"Fascinating. What does Dagmar think about that?"

"I told her what her ladyship had said, and her comment was that even a carrot can act as an ecstatic substance, if you know what you're doing."

"Really?"

Stanley chuckled. "Her exact words were, 'What do you think I do in this kitchen?' That was a revelation to me."

56

I looked at Stanley and said, "It's true. Dagmar's meals are almost holy. Would Cobb be able to supply the necessary substances that my father might need, assuming that is what he wanted to do?"

"Perhaps. It would be one more reason for his presence."

"On another, not necessarily unrelated, subject: my mother's arrival is a further complication. She said she wanted to speak to Cobb. Can you tell me about him?"

"I can. From personal experience, Cobb is a highly intelligent individual whose thuggish appearance has fooled many. He was my sparring partner. We met years ago for the same reasons. I was thin and somewhat weak, while he, on the other hand, was round. Neither of us were athletes in the Greek model, far from it, and both of us had decided that being beaten by those who had the inclination to do so and the time to spare was no longer our preference. Cobb looked like a potato, but that did not mean that he was weak. There are many of that peculiar Gallic lineage who have a similar physique but are endowed with stamina and inner reserves that are not apparent at first glance.

"By the end of our acquaintance no one called him fat. He became Cobb, another person entirely. I suppose I had something to do with that. I grew up with horses, and one equine version is a powerful animal with short legs known as a cob. I called him by that name, and it stuck. He added a 'b' at the end. His real name is Angus Maxwell-Hughes. He had an aristocratic upbringing, but high society held little appeal. He preferred the streets, but they held different and more physical perils. Cobb learned to take a beating and eventually turned that capacity to advantage. In the ring, stronger and larger men would grow exhausted as they pummeled away at him. It was when they were spent and exasperated that Cobb would take them apart methodically, scientifically, cruelly. It was a sight to behold. He grew skilled and learned to take the long view, to endure whatever punishment was necessary before he chose to act. And act he would. The punters loved him. So did certain criminal elements.

"He was studying to be a doctor of medicine, and whether through his knowledge of anatomy or instinct, he knew how to hurt. He also knew how to heal. He saved the life of the son of a powerful man, and over time acquired the reputation as a doctor of great discretion as well as skill."

"He sounds formidable," I said. "I take it you and he parted on less than good terms?"

"We did. His connections were suspect, and I chose to distance myself. I had also decided that boxing, although invigorating, was not at all where my talents lay. After a particularly painful thrashing at his hands, I told him that I would spar with him no longer.

"Sometime later, he approached me to smooth the way in contacting a distinguished gentleman. Knowing his underworld connections, I refused. He tried to exert what pressure he could, and when he threatened me one evening, I hit him upside the head with a full bottle of a nice Bordeaux. I was quite lucky in that I happened to have just purchased it. Once he regained consciousness, I told him that I was aware of some of the surgical procedures he was performing and that if he troubled me any further, he would find himself without

288

the possibility of becoming a surgeon, a status that he eventually achieved. I made it clear that I harbored no ill will toward him—in fact quite the opposite—but that could change if he bothered me again. From then on we've had no contact."

"Do you think he wants to get even?"

"We established a live-and-let-live policy that has held for a long time. I see no reason to change it, but should he interfere, then I will make a reassessment."

"Hopefully, it won't come to that. Thank you for that information. Before we end, you mentioned my father's youthful appearance in relation to Cobb."

"Cobb has always been keen on the subject of the preservation of the body. Hormone therapies are an interest of his. I know that because a friend of mine, also in service, asked me about them. His employer was eager to try it. I answered that I had no opinion other than the fact that Cobb's skill as a medical man has never been in doubt. In fact, I considered him rather exceptional, having watched him attend to various fighters."

"My father is on such a regimen?"

"Quite possibly. Such a therapy requires certain dieting restrictions, and such courses of treatment can have the side effect of the aggressive behavior which your father displays. I doubt it means anything, other than that he might not always be as rational as you might wish.

"Breakfast is next on my agenda, and to close out our conversation, I would suggest the following: find out why you mother is here. Speak to you father, and above all, make sure that he and Cobb attend the dinner tonight. It is a white-tie affair, and I'm quite sure they've brought suitable attire. If not, it can be provided. Everyone must be at the table tonight. No exceptions. I, too, have my orders."

57

I stopped by our bedroom, but Bruni wasn't there. I was happy to see that the bed had been made and everything put away. I figured Bruni was talking to her mother. I thought that might be an interesting conversation if Johnny's surmises were correct. I looked in at the library and saw Bonnie in jeans and a crisp white Western shirt sitting in one of the easy chairs reading.

"Hi there," I said. "I'm glad someone is taking advantage of this room. It's wonderful in the morning."

"Hey, Percy." Bonnie put down her book. "This room is perfect. Pull up a chair and sit. We have some time before breakfast."

I sat, and Bonnie shifted closer.

She continued, "By the way, last night was a trip. I mean literally. I think I ended up in Delphi, of all places. I met this woman who could have been the Pythia for all I know. It was as if ancient Greece came to life before my eyes. Whatever was in that drink?"

"It was an old Nordic recipe, so I have no idea. What did the lady look like?"

"Like your typical oracle—indeterminant age, long robe, blindfolded, willowy assistant attending, small fire on a tripod with vapors coming up from the ground, that kind of thing. I was already high as a kite, but after I sat down at her knees and started to inhale the green stuff that was swirling about, I really streaked across the sky. I mean kaboom! It was like I was attached to a rocket. I thought I might have died for a moment. After I grooved on that possibility for a while, I achieved some kind of stable orbit. Since I really seemed to be where I was, and so was she, I asked her how Apollo was doing these days, and she said he was the same as ever and found it amusing that I should ask about him. Of course, she didn't say it exactly that way. Her Greek was as precise as only a Greek can get. She also tended to use a lot of fancy endings. Our dialogue was on the whole much more formal. My Greek may have been a tad rusty, but we had as lucid a conversation as any I've ever had. Of course, she asked what I wished for, and I said you, of course. She counseled that I look elsewhere, specifically in the direction of a healer. Again, this was parsed much more formally, but I followed right along. She also wanted to know if I had a question that I wanted answered. I told her nope—being with her was good enough for me, but I asked for a rain check anyway. She said she didn't do that sort of thing but would consider it. Again, this was all said politely and rather formally. I murmured to her that I loved the dress—hers had those fabulous pleats—and that the visit was a dream come true. She said it was that way for many, and that she enjoyed speaking to someone so very different for once. Sensing our time was at an end, I arose and gave a half bow and curtsy. I'm not sure that was appropriate, but it seemed to work. The next thing I know I'm back, swaying arm and arm with Mom and Bruni, like a bunch of sailors on an extended shore leave. By the way, you'll be happy to hear that Bruni and I are pals. She's quite charming. Of all the dinners I've ever had, that one was by far the best! Extraordinary finish. Anyway, I think I'm babbling, and it's not even breakfast. How are you feeling this morning?"

291

"Good, actually. I still must sit down with my father, which adds a grim prospect to an otherwise splendid day. Who knows how that will turn out? I certainly don't. Last night's dinner was a delight, and Dagmar told me in the kitchen that there was more to come tonight."

"Well, based on last night's performance, I'm certainly looking forward to it. What do you think she'll give us?"

"I have absolutely no idea. On another matter, I find it interesting that the Pythia pointed you toward a healer. I think you should speak with the doctor."

"You need my help?"

"I do. I'd like you to find out why Cobb and my father are working together and what the story is between them. Stanley confirmed that he is a doctor and quite a good one. He's also really smart, so have a care."

"You need information. Well, espionage is my middle name. I'd be happy to do that, only he seems to be permanently upstairs."

"He'll be at the dinner tonight."

"Really? That ought to be interesting. Make sure I sit next to him. Perhaps he'll need help with the cutlery. That's always a good opening."

"His real name is Angus Maxwell-Hughes, so I doubt that will be particularly new for him."

"A blue blood then?"

"Apparently ... with underworld connections."

"That will add some spice. I could always do with some underworld connections I suppose, although their rules tend to be rather severe. I might wander up there this morning and look in on him. I'll let you know what I find out."

"That ought to work. I think it's time for breakfast."

"Lead the way," Bonnie said, standing up and putting her book on a side table. It looked like Xenophon's *Anabasis*.

"Light reading?"

"I've read it before, of course. I love it. My edition has the Greek on one side and English on the other. Anyway, to breakfast. I could eat a horse. I love saying that but not around Mom. She gets irritated, and the whole day goes to hell in a heartbeat."

onnie and I wandered into the dining room. Johnny was there along with Malcolm, my mother, Anne, and John Sr. To my surprise, notably present were my father and Cobb. My father in a tweed jacket and button-down shirt without a tie looked unaffected by yesterday's episode, but Cobb sitting beside him seemed to indicate that he needed watching. Seeing both of them was unexpected, and first thing in the morning, too. Regardless, I wasn't about to object. Breakfast was the one meal that I liked to eat in peace. If Atilla the Hun had wandered in and seated himself, I would have nodded and passed the coffee. I noted that I had missed seeing my father's reaction when he saw my mother at the breakfast table. Perhaps it was just as well.

Since the first meal of the day was informal, there was no assigned seating for guests. There were empty places on either side of my father and Cobb. Bonnie chose the one next to Cobb. I sat in my chair, said good morning to my mother who was on my right, and nodded to Johnny on my left. He looked like he was expecting trouble. His eyes were flicking back and forth, a sure sign that he was nervous. As I poured some coffee, Maw, in faded jeans and an ancient denim work shirt, strolled in with Robert the Bruce. She gave the table a once-over and sat down next to my father. Robert scooted under her chair. She wasn't wasting any time finding out whether my father was really as bad as his reputation. All the von Hofmanstals were conspicuously absent.

I drank some coffee and, keeping my voice low, asked my mother how she had slept. "Remarkably well," she said and suggested that we have a chat later. Before she could continue, the von Hofmanstals arrived in a somber procession. Both Hugo and Elsa, he in flannel pants and a dark cashmere sweater and she in the female equivalent, looked grim and took places on opposite sides of the table. Elsa had taken the chair next to Johnny, forcing Hugo to sit next to my mother. Judging from her expression, that was deliberate. Bruni looked at me as she seated herself and raised her eyes toward the ceiling as if to say her father and mother were having a bad day. This observation was interrupted by a loud cackle from Maw as she responded to something my father said. He was obviously turning on the charm. Sitting next to one of the richest women in the world, I thought, tended to do that.

Eggs and bacon along with triangles of white toast with no crusts were served in silver racks. John Sr. eyed Hugo, and Anne whispered something to Elsa, who sat next to her. Elsa said nothing and glanced in my direction. She looked like a queen trying to decide whether to fry someone in oil or have them broken on the wheel. For a moment I thought I was the target, until she looked across at her husband. The day was getting started, and already the softness of the night before was turning brittle.

I whispered to Johnny if there was something I should know.

He whispered back. "It's as we suspected. Hugo's definitely in the doghouse."

I nodded. After having a chat with her daughter, Elsa had likely stormed into their bedroom and kicked her husband

295

awake to confirm how bad the situation was. Judging from the volume of Elsa's upset, it was close to a worst-case scenario. I wondered vaguely whether I might have to prepare the governess's quarters upstairs, so Hugo would have a place to sleep tonight.

Johnny whispered, "Are you ready?"

I sighed. "Let's finish breakfast first. I'll speak to him after."

"Best of luck, then. Hopefully you can pull Hugo's chestnuts out of the fire before Elsa starts chewing on them."

"He's on my list. I'll see what I can do. Anyway, speak to Malcolm this morning, if you can, but definitely have a word with your mom—and soon."

Johnny got the message. He needed to find out from Anne why my mother wished to speak to Cobb.

As I ate, I wondered how feasible it would be to have everyone present sit down and hammer out a solution that satisfied one and all. It would be like attending an economic conference to work out a coherent policy, and likely just as impossible.

With that thought, breakfast came to a close, and it was time I got to work. As we all rose, I reached behind me and confirmed once again that the sealed envelope my father had given me was still sticking out of the back pocket of my jeans.

As my guests began to file out, I walked up to my father, who was standing beside Maw. I heard him say, "Let's speak again at lunch."

Maw seemed to like the idea. As I waited for them to finish, I thought it strange that no one spoke openly about my father's recovery. I supposed it was another peculiar trait of the people here. Each of them abhorred weakness, and by acknowledging a recovery, one acknowledged the sickness, something to be avoided. I was quite sure his resurrection would be discussed among themselves in private and speculated about in minute detail.

Maw finally said goodbye and left, with Robert following close behind. He stopped and looked back at me for a second. I wondered what that meant. I was nervous. Even the thought of speaking with my father had me thinking twice about having eaten that last piece of bacon.

With no possibility of putting off what was inevitable, I said, "Father, I believe we have matters to discuss. I, too, dislike wasting time. Perhaps we might discuss them over coffee in the library?"

59

"The coffee is very good."

That was the first positive opinion I had heard my father express. We were sitting side by side in the library in front of the fireplace. Simon and another member of the staff had quickly set up a small table covered by white linen with a coffee service. I had thanked them and said that my father and I would pour our own.

While I had been arranging for the coffee to be brought to the library, I had noted that Cobb and Bonnie were deep in conversation, and judging from Cobb's expression, Bonnie held more than a passing interest. Perhaps the Pythia knew something after all.

My father brought me back to the present. "I judge the competence of a kitchen by the quality of the coffee that is served. I drink it black, so there is nothing to disguise the taste. If such a simple thing is well managed, then competence must follow in everything else."

I answered, "I must admit, I do the same. It can make or break a meal."

"Quite right."

As we savored the taste, I noted that the coffee we were drinking *was* outstanding.

My father sighed in enjoyment. "So ... I wish to begin again. Can we?"

"I'm amenable to that."

"Thank you. Now, before we continue, there are some preliminaries I would like to dispose of first. Would that suit?"

"By all means."

"To begin, I must apologize for my earlier behavior. Returning here has been difficult, and seeing you for the first time has made it doubly so. I have no patience with people in general, let alone dealing with a child of my own whom I've never met. I'm quite aware of your age, of course. You are an adult, but I am cantankerous by nature, and old age has likely worsened that propensity. The time left to me is short, you see, and the paucity of it makes me resentful of those whose life will likely extend beyond my own."

He looked at me and chuckled. "Actually, my being crotchety has little to do with that. At my age, one cannot hear well, see well, move, or remember details that were once easy. Sometimes even the simple act of conversing, requires performing unfamiliar mental gymnastics to say what one wishes without always remembering what one was referring to in the first place. There is also a mental blankness that can descend at any time. It is a constant threat. Halting midsentence is like an actor forgetting his lines. Such unexpected lapses cast a spotlight on what the elderly fear most—senility, dementia, and the losing of one's mind."

My father sipped his coffee and continued.

"It is also a predicament for the listener. What are they to do? Must they ignore the mishap or consider placing the speaker in a rest home with 'round-the-clock care lest he or she run naked through the streets?

"For the aged, the solution requires either ceasing to speak altogether or snarling at those in one's vicinity, lest they think to take advantage. Old men are like the injured leaders of a pack of wolves. Old women are like the matriarchs of cackles of hyenas. Both must dominate or die. To do any less is to risk being eaten. That is what old age is like, and why I get bad-tempered. Will you forgive me my prior rudeness?"

"We are beginning anew. Old age is a daunting future we all must face, and allowances should be made. Apology accepted."

"I thank you for putting aside what went before, but there are limits to what can be forgiven. That you can choose to overlook my tantrums says much about you. But in case I gave you the wrong impression by exaggerating the disability of my condition, old age is not all bad. One can also find oneself thrown into the past and stunned by the brightness of a memory—one more luminous than the present, and fantastically alive. The heart swells with the certainty that one might have been supremely happy then. Such random experiences are so vivid, they can bring on tears. Is life worth living, given the fallibilities of one's memory and the shuffling of time? Oh yes. Oh yes, it is, and that is what I wish to talk to you about, but to do that we need to make a peace, of sorts."

"What kind of peace?"

"Before I tell you, I wish to make you a wager. You do make wagers on occasion, yes?"

"I tend to be on the losing end, so I usually don't."

"That is wise, but this wager is a simple yes or no answer to a question once again, but different from before—less contentious. I wish to wager that your answer to what I will ask will be a 'yes.' If it is, then all I require is that you listen to what I have to say. In addition, the funds from the check in your back pocket will be used toward the purchase of the items as per the original arrangement, again with the understanding that no item will be removed from this estate as you requested.

If it is a 'no,' then I will leave now, and the money will be my gift to you. As a gesture of good faith, I will sign the check immediately, and you will have the funds I promised."

My father took out a pen from his breast pocket as I hesitated.

"Come, come. What do you have to lose? If you think I'll trick you and refuse to give it back, the check requires both our signatures. Please, I'm serious. Lay the check on the table so that I can endorse it. I won't even touch it, if that is your wish. My purpose for the wager is to demonstrate to you that I know you better than you think, and maybe better than you think you know yourself. We are related by blood after all, and that matters. You may be aware of that fact intellectually but not in your heart. There is a difference. Also, by taking the money element off the table, in that you will have it regardless of the outcome, I am decreasing the stakes to a more acceptable level. Should you lose, all you risk is your time. Should you win, then there will be my departure to look forward to, should you wish it. Will that suffice? Are you willing to play?"

I paused for a moment to consider the question and asked one of my own instead.

"Before I answer, I must ask about your health. Are you recovered? Should I be concerned?"

A flash of irritation crossed his face before he answered. "In other words, should my life expectancy be a matter of a few days or hours, am I worth your time? I can understand your concern. Relationships of any kind require time and effort. Perhaps you meant it differently, but from my perspective, weakness is not something I dwell on or wish to draw attention to. With advanced years, people in one's vicinity act strangely. They question everything you do. How are you feeling? Should you really be doing what you're doing? I ask them in return why should they care? Life is a disease that is terminal in every case, and death its only indication. Without death, how are we to know that we are alive? The old are not fragile, just more easily bruised. I count myself even now as one of the living, and contrary to what passes for geriatric care in the current milieu, being alive is not the same as running about in a diaper under medical supervision. It is my mantra that he who dares wins, and he who doesn't, loses every time, if only incrementally. So, to answer your question. I am living my life, whatever that may be, in the way I wish. Should that be a concern of yours? I don't think so. The more pertinent question is: are you living yours? Are you alive, Percy? Do you dare to exist on your own terms and not on someone else's? Will you take up my wager?"

I paused once again. The similarity to one of those bar tricks that Johnny occasionally pulled off when we were penniless teenagers came to mind. Johnny would offer to cut a lime in half with a Marlboro cigarette. It was a stupid trick that involved burning the filter with a match and shaping it into a hard, cutting edge. It would win us a drink or two. Sometimes the stakes grew quite large, and I recalled running for my life after one particularly lucrative haul. This was the same, only from the opposite perspective. Was I the potential mark? I couldn't imagine how, but from experience, that usually meant I was. The plus was that half the money I needed would be handled. There was still Hugo's portion to secure. Perhaps it was the baron who was bluffing? There was also the matter of the shares. I delayed my answer.

"And yet you're under a doctor's care," I said.

"Cobb and I have a relationship that covers a wider brief. It is not unlike you and Stanley. Once again, mark the similarities. Now, no more quibbling. Your answer, please."

"Very well. I am willing to accept your wager with the understanding that I wish to make another wager with you in return."

"Oh? You have my interest. What are the stakes?"

"The shares."

"The shares?" My father smiled.

"You know the ones I mean."

My father grinned broadly. "You've been busy, I see. My compliments. I am willing to listen to what you have in mind. I must say you surprise me, and for that I thank you. You are more than I expected. Now, I have a question for you in return: should we close out the bet that is currently on the table, or would you like to up the stakes by adding those shares to the pot?"

"I think a separate wager would be better."

"I'm fine either way, but a separate wager would be quite outstanding. There is nothing like a high-stakes gamble to get the heart racing and confirm that we still exist. I look forward to hearing your terms, but first, take out that check, and I will sign it. Once that is done, I will ask my question."

"What if I lie?"

"You won't, and you will understand why you won't, when you hear the question."

"Interesting. That must be some question."

"Oh, it is."

I looked at my father for a long moment. Was I smart enough to go toe to toe with him and win? It was possible, but only if I set it up so that I could. This bet was one I would surely lose, but would losing really matter? Like Bruni said: this wager was likely a throwaway, and he and I had to start somewhere. That was a difference between us. My father liked to gamble, I didn't. The reason for my dislike was obvious, even to me: I usually lost. I had to speak to Johnny. He would be in his element with what I had in mind. For now, I would have to rely on my own wits. Did I dare do that?

My hand shook as I ripped open the envelope and laid the check on the table face down so he could endorse the back.

60

—

"There, the money is yours. Satisfied?"

"I recall the last time I answered that question. Forgive me if I give the answer a pass."

"Yes, I quite understand. I was disappointed then, but I have since changed my mind about you."

"And why is that?"

"It is because the answer to my question, the one we are wagering on, and the reason for my change of heart are the same. Are you ready?"

"I am."

"Very well. You read my letter in the second envelope, yes or no?"

I said nothing as my father looked me in the eye. "I know you did. So, you might as well admit it. Am I right?"

"Yes," I said.

"Then I have won the bet. As far as bets go, it is a small thing but nonetheless instructive. I'll tell you why I know you read it. You've read Sun Tzu. How many times, do you think?"

"Probably a dozen."

"And well you should have. That part about knowing the enemy's plans comes to mind. Who do you think put that book in the library upstairs for you to read? I did, along with dozens of others. I made sure that your benefactor kept you

305

and your compatriot well supplied with suitable reading material. I played no direct part in your upbringing, but that doesn't mean I didn't indirectly. I had my reasons for acting in that manner. Coming into your life other than now when you are mature would have sowed confusion, and I know what that is like. You deserved peace. Any child does. Does that surprise you?"

"It does."

"I suppose it should. There is more, of course. I also paid for all your education and upbringing. Let's put it this way: a sum was transferred and found its way for your benefit. Alice was accommodating in that regard. She could have done that herself, and she did in her own way, but by allowing me to play a part that was significant but hidden, I tacitly agreed to keep my distance and thus secured her household from the wreck that would surely follow had I not done so."

Once again, what I thought I knew was not necessarily the truth, or was it? I had no idea.

I said, "Who did what, as regards my upbringing, was never made clear to me. I thank you for having done that, if that is what you did. I have a question. You speak of your former wife as Alice in one sentence with some affection, and as my benefactor in another, having none. You seem conflicted. Why is that?"

My father looked at me for a long moment.

"I could tell you, but I'm not sure I will. Love between two people is a private matter. An observer can witness love in a glance, but what that love is exactly will always be an abstraction. Relationships are defined by different things, and none but the two involved can know their significance. These shared moments form a special bond. Should there be betrayal, all is changed. Contempt follows eventually, and what was once lovely turns into a hateful reminder of what was once sublime. Walking back from such extremes is near impossible, but sometimes the gods intervene, and what was out of the question is impossible no longer. It is what happened. We hated each other and loved each other, but not at the same time."

"I'm not sure I understand."

My father shrugged and said, "I can't say that I do, either. We are talking about love after all, and it is a mystery unto itself. There is also hate, and I can assure you that is as mysterious. Hatred may seem the easier to grasp, but it is not. Both upend the normal flow of human interaction, and what marks their presence is a turbulence. With hatred, that turbulence can extend for generations. With love, its presence is less conspicuous, and perhaps its passage is marked by quiet spaces for the lineage that follows. Add in economics, capricious fortune, religion, and the subtle ministrations of what we don't know, and here we are. Love and hate play their part."

He looked at me with amusement before continuing.

"Coming back to my letter, I knew you read it because *I* would have read it. We may be the result of genetic mixing, but that doesn't mean that certain familial traits are diminished. We all have a heritage. All those somebodies stretching back to the beginning of time have one thing in common: they will not be silenced. They speak and act through us in odd ways. That is also what I wish to talk to you about. We are cursed, you see—both the Bromley line and Alice's, but in different ways. Those afflictions are what brought us together at the beginning—before we broke, and she became your benefactor, followed by Alice once again.

Such things are surpassing strange. Are you interested in stories from my life?"

"I am, but I don't understand where this is going," I said.

"I can tell you more. You may see things differently when we're done, not that it will give you any comfort. We are all tied to the past as much as to the future. After you hear what I have to say, we will discuss the items I mentioned in my letter, and then your wager, but perhaps not all at once. More coffee?"

61

My father was a liar and a thief. I knew this, but that didn't mean I wasn't enthralled. I found myself fascinated and captivated by what he said. All great storytellers do that. It's their words, and how they use them. The sounds flow and ebb, while the facts they present march back and forth in bewitching patterns as if by magic. I drank my coffee and listened.

My father put down his cup and said, "You've heard much about me. Do you think I'm mad?"

"Do you mean mad as in demented, or mad because you're angry?"

"Mad as in demented."

I paused again. The answer was as difficult as the question. I answered, "There might be some of that, if what I've heard is true."

He nodded. "It is an honest answer, and I agree. There is a madness in me, perhaps more before than now. Of that, I have no doubt. I was certainly mad before. I know that, and because I do, I'm not. It is a paradox with no easy resolution. At one time I thought I was the sanest man alive. That should have been a warning to me. Since I *was* truly mad, I didn't give such a possibility another thought. It was only when my life lay in ruins that I began to understand that my mind was broken. I could see it. That was an awakening. The question I have asked myself ever since is: are we born that way, or do we do it to ourselves? Do you know the answer?"

"I don't. Perhaps we're driven mad by others or by the circumstances in which we find ourselves."

He nodded. "That is possible. There is another."

"And what's that?"

"The gods touch us."

"I didn't think that was even remotely possible before living here. Now, I'm not so sure."

He chuckled. "It is not acceptable as a hypothesis in this day and age. I'll tell you why. If that were true, then the gods can make us sane, and then where would we be? The pharmaceutical people would have a fit. Science and the medicos would revolt. Of course, such an impossibility wasn't always so. Thoughts along those lines make no sense in a modern world, and yet that is what I think happened to me. I can understand if you are doubtful, but judging from your reaction, you're not overly shocked. Welcome to the club. Now, I will tell you a story. Afterward, you tell me which of the theories we mentioned is correct. None are mutually exclusive, of course. It's possible all of them are valid—or some of them—or even none. You be the judge."

My father poured more coffee into his cup and offered me some. I accepted.

Once he had finished pouring and had sipped, he said, "I awoke to my current life staring at a tree trunk in an Ecuadorian jungle. I didn't know that I had been changed then. I simply stared at what was there before me. What was it like to be a tree? I wondered. The patches of different-colored bark created a pleasing mosaic that soothed me, and yet I'm sure it was quite ordinary as far as tree trunks go. It was, after all, only a tree, but I felt its aliveness. I felt my own. We were not so very different. I heard someone call my name. It was Arthur, Arthur Blaine. I mistook him and attacked him.

310

Lucky for both of us I was weak. I could barely raise my arms. Perhaps he was in a similar state. We pawed at each other before we collapsed on the ground. I lay there breathing hard, capable of nothing. I remember his face looming over me. He told me to sit tight. He had found some food and water. How long it took him to nurse me back to a semblance of health, I do not know. A while, I suspect. He lit a fire, and all I could do was look at it, lost in the little flames. I ate. I don't remember what. I drank water. My thoughts were simple. All of what I was before seemed to have sloughed off, like the pieces of bark that lay about the camp. I existed, and that is all. The simplicity of that state was so profound. Then it began to rain.

"The river rose, and we had to flee. Arthur said we must follow the water, and so we did. It wasn't easy in my condition, and I slipped into a walking daze. How long we stumbled along I do not know, but we came across a village, where we collapsed. They put us in a hut. We lay upon a mat, and they fed us. We slept and slowly recovered; at least I did. Arthur was not so lucky. He grew weaker and weaker—with what sickness, I didn't know. They moved him to a different place, or perhaps it was me they moved.

"When I was alone again, my dwarflike tormentor returned. I haven't mentioned him, but he showed up when I awoke in front of that tree. Now, he sat beside me and poked me with a piece of reed. It was sharp but not sharp enough to draw blood, just pointy and annoying. He liked doing that. He and I knew each other quite well by then. He wouldn't stop unless I begged him to, and then he would nod as if to acknowledge that he heard me before he began again.

"I suppose my pleadings and my screams disturbed the village. They sent for someone. The villagers spoke some

Spanish, and so did I. They told me to be patient and left me. Food would be placed outside. I would crawl to the entrance, eat what I could, and go back to my mat. My tormentor would wait patiently, sitting in a corner playing with his reed.

"After a time, a man came. Again, I have no recollection of how long before he arrived. Time moved in strange ways—taking forever and then not so. He was quite old, I think. With indigenous people, it's hard to say. He could have been thirty. He could have been sixty, or even older. He was a most peculiar man. He said hello to me and said hello to my tormentor. Both the man and my tormentor were not dissimilar in that they possessed a peculiar feel—a blankness and yet behind their eyes they watched and saw everything. The man asked if he could ask me questions. He asked the same of my tormentor. My tormentor looked at him and raised his reed as if to ask permission to continue poking me. The other answered that it would be more helpful if he ceased. My tormentor nodded, moved to a corner, chewed on his reed, and waited. He looked curious, but then so was I.

"The man introduced himself. He had a most peculiar name, one impossible to remember, let alone pronounce. He spoke in Spanish. I answered in the same. It was odd in that he was quite eloquent, but then so was I, something I was not before. We shared a drink that he took great pains to prepare. He added all sorts of dried plants and herbs that he kept in little pouches. He offered some to my tormentor in the corner, but my tormentor continued to chew his reed and didn't answer. The man told me to ignore the creature and to drink. Once we had finished the bowl, my inquisitor asked me where I'd been? What had I seen? What had I done? And so, I told him everything. I told him of my life, all that I could remember. I spoke eventually of the idol, of Alice—what I'd done to her, and what she'd done to me. I spoke of experiencing days of madness, and the sudden appearance of my tormentor. I had no idea how he came to be there, or even if he was real. In my daze, I had once asked Arthur if he saw him, but Arthur had simply shaken his head. As I spoke to the man, I wondered if perhaps the creature had been there all my life. Maybe I had been so locked in the world of my own infallibility that I'd never noticed. I told that man with the peculiar name everything, you see. I couldn't help it. I spoke until there was nothing left to say.

"The man asked if I wished to rid myself of my tormentor. I took some time to answer. It seemed such a shocking question, like imagining sight when one was blind from birth, but in my case it was worse. He was asking if I wished for sanity when I thought myself as sane as sane could be. I didn't see the need other than that my tormentor liked to hurt me, and I was tired of the pain. I nodded and agreed.

"What followed was not what I expected. He made another drink for me and had me inhale smoke from the fire after he had laid some plants upon it. When I had finished, the walls of the hut began to move, and then the whole forest that surrounded us. The world danced in a way I understood but couldn't follow. A woman, if that was what she was, came to me then. She was covered in short, tawny fur with dark spots. She seemed half human and half animal. She sat in front of me like a cat. Her eyes were a mustard yellow as she looked into mine. All I had ever wanted to see lay inside her eyes, and then she spoke. Do you know what she said to me?"

"I have no idea."

" 'Madness is a gift you don't deserve.' Then faster than I could follow, she turned and began to eat that creature with the reed."

313

62

M y father sipped his coffee.

"She ate him?" I asked.

"Reed and all. I was too shocked to move at first, not only by the intensity of her presence, but by the violence of her eating. I quickly turned away, but I could still hear the crunching of tissues, bones, and god knows what. If it takes some minutes to eat a steak, you can well imagine how long she took to consume a thing so much larger.

"While I waited for her to finish, sickened by the sounds, the man with the peculiar name watched me. At length, there was a protracted silence. I waited some more before I turned to look at what remained. A dark stain that seemed familiar lay in the corner. Had it been there all along? When I turned back to speak with the man with the peculiar name, I found myself alone in the hut.

"Over the years, I've asked myself, was *any* of it real? Had that woman even spoken to me? Was the man with the peculiar name imaginary? Did I become so lost in the dancing walls of the hut and pulsing jungle that surrounded it that I failed to notice their leaving? Where had they gone? Where had my tormentor gone? I felt confused at the time, and so I slept. I awoke the next day with my head clear but feeling oddly fatigued, like I had traveled a great distance. I took some joy in little things—the way light played on the ground, the smell of the earth, and the sounds of the village. It was good

SHADOW OF THE SON

to be alive. It came to me then that I had been quite mad in my prior existence, and yet my madness had a benefit that I had failed to recognize as such. I had a certainty before, a sense of my own rightness and infallibility, but that was no longer the case. I now had doubts.

"In earlier ages, those who were touched by the gods could act in any way they wished. What they did or said was not simply dismissed as crazy nor were they necessarily held to account. Their madness in a sense protected them. I realized then that mine, too, had been a shield. Behind it nothing could harm me, and I was free from the consequences of my actions. Without it, I was defenseless. Madness, like anything else, can be either a blessing or a curse. For me, at that moment, I had the wreck my life had become to contend with, as well as the many disasters I had managed to avoid thus far, but no longer could. What was I to do?"

My father sipped again.

"And?" I asked.

"I simply did the best I could. I've wondered ever since. Had I created my own madness, or had my circumstances required it? Was I born that way or had the gods touched me twice? Once to bestow it, and the second to take it? Having heard my story, do you think I was always mad and never noticed, or do you think I was driven that way?"

"It's a most unusual story. I don't know which answer is correct. From what you say, you were mad before, but the madness left you. My question is, did being rid of it make you sane?"

My father chuckled. "Being free of disability does not automatically make one able. The capacity to act merely allows for the possibility. There is also the matter of quality. Little Jimmy's scribbles are not the line drawings of Picasso.

Sanity is its own path and requires its own craft. For myself, the world had been a backdrop upon which I fancied that I played a leading role. After my experience in the jungle, I understood that I was merely an extra, someone with a walk-on part—like everybody else. To answer your question, was I made sane? No, just more realistic."

"I see. I don't wish to appear unsympathetic, but what I think you're trying to convey to me is that you're different now, and that you're not the same man who locked Alice in that trunk so many years ago. Does the one forgive the other?"

My father looked at me for a long moment. "Your question might be considered indelicate, although it is not without merit. You are prejudiced against me based on what you believe to be true. I accept that. Perhaps I've waited too long to reveal myself. That was always the weakness in my version of this moment. Whether fortunate or not, circumstances have not permitted us to meet until now, and this time is all we have together. The question is, what are we to make of it? Nonetheless, I will do you the courtesy of an answer.

"I am the same man, but not the same. We all have reasons for having done the things we did. I will tell you this, and you should take it to heart. There may come a time when your actions will be interpreted wrongly and yet to reveal the truth, no matter the rightness of it or the desire to set the record straight, will only make matters worse and be more harmful. Only Alice and I know the true reasons and circumstances of what happened between us, and we are the only ones who know why she did what she did.

"All opinion is, in essence, judgmental. The facts in my case lead easily to the darkest possible interpretation, but reality is not so easily explained. One can simplify in order to understand, but that simplification is not the thing. Life, real life, isn't simple. I could tell you more, but you and I, Percy, have some distance to travel before I feel I can. It requires a certain compassion, and you and I have yet to come that far. Do you see that?"

I nodded. Perhaps I shouldn't have said what I had said, but in my question lay the essence of the conflict that bubbled inside me. He had committed a great wrong, but weighed against his obvious fault were my own feelings of a righteousness that I distrusted in myself. Taking the moral high ground was all too easy, and usually in error, not in the sense that I was incorrect in my assessment as to right and wrong, but in the magnitude of my certainty and the severity of my censure and condemnation. What really happened between them I didn't know, nor could I ever. More relevant to me was the question of whether a tiger could change its stripes? Closer still, given that he and I were related, could I change mine? My mind would do flip-flops whenever I would think of him. Was he like me, or was I like him? Could I avoid the consequences of either?

My father continued, "On top of that, I sense that you are conflicted, and perhaps even disgusted by me. Given what you've heard, that's neither illogical nor undeserved. In spite of your feelings, I wish to say what I've wanted to tell you for some time: I wish you no harm, Percy. I really don't. Nor have I ever, but how *are* you to know that? How can I make that clear? I am not your enemy. Conversely, can I say the same of you? Do you wish me no harm, and as importantly, how can you assure me that you feel the same way? It is where things stand between us, and we must cross this bridge together very soon, or we never will."

317

He paused a moment and leaned forward, speaking in a softer voice. "I might add that it's not a question of whether we might wish to, but rather, whether we should?"

He thought for a moment. "*My* father and I came to this same juncture ... exactly where we are now ... *He* decided that we shouldn't cross. For myself, I'm not sure that was the best choice, but at least my father was consistent. It is the Bromley motto, you see: *se nesciunt*, they will know *not* each other. Don't think for a moment that curses don't exist. They weave throughout our lives. Our relationship is stunted and deformed, but that is the rule for our line, not the exception. Will it change? I don't know if it can. It has been that way generation to generation since the beginning of recorded history, and that, Percy, is a long time indeed."

I thought about what he said. "Given that, what should we do?"

"Perhaps we should end this conversation now while all is well between us and reconvene after lunch. Would that be acceptable?"

"It would. I apologize if I've been disturbing. Meeting you has not been easy for me, and allowances should be made on both our parts. Thank you for the check and for telling me all you have. It has been enlightening and instructive."

"It has been on both sides. I would like to make a further suggestion, if I may?"

"What is it?"

"First, let's put aside my letter, the one you read and returned to me. As individuals we decide what is best, but the bridge that lies ahead for you and me can only be traveled jointly. Either of us can decide our relationship is not worth the effort and with that decision, neither will cross. To make matters worse, there is no guarantee as to what we'll find on the other side once we get there. Given that, all I ask is that you consider carefully what happens next and make a decision as to what you wish to do. There is no clear path before us and no right answer. I will do the same.

"Now, I think I will search out Cobb, lest I find him in the bushes with Mrs. Leland's daughter. I truly enjoyed the coffee and our time together. Allow me to shake your hand, if you would care to."

He stretched out his hand toward me, and I did the same. We shook. It could have been in greeting, but it could as easily have been goodbye.

63

I remained in the library after my father had left. The conversation had been very different from what I'd expected. The signed check was in my pocket, and that was as much a relief as it was perplexing. Granted, that had been the agreement, but the aftertaste was strange, almost anticlimactic, and secondary to what he had wanted to talk about. I noted that there was a disarming vulnerability about him that I hadn't anticipated. He hadn't asked about me—not even a "how are you?"—and that seemed odd. I needed to speak with Johnny. I left the library and chanced upon him coming down the main staircase.

He looked around to see if anyone else was present and asked, "Well? How did it go?"

I showed him my father's signature on the check.

"Well, what do you know? Perhaps we should talk outside, where we won't be overheard."

We made our way to the bench behind the cypress trees and sat down.

Johnny pulled out a smoke. "Your father did come through with the funds, and that is worthy of some sort of celebration. Congratulations. Tell me about your talk and let me see that check again."

I handed him the check and told him what my father had said.

When I had finished, Johnny said, "I can't believe it was that easy." He looked at the check more closely but could find no fault with it. "I'm sure there's a catch somewhere. I just don't know what it is."

"Perhaps we're being overly paranoid?"

"With him? Not a chance. It's almost an operational imperative. Still, you've moved from opposite corners toward a middle ground where some form of collaboration might be possible."

Johnny handed me back the check. I folded it into my pocket. "I'm quite sure the coffee had something to do with it. It really perked him up."

"Well, some say that the coffee house was where our modern market economy actually started. I noted one thing of importance that your father emphasized: trust. Have you decided whether you wish to go beyond a superficial level with him?"

I thought about that. "It's hard to say. When he shook my hand, it could have been an ending as much as a beginning. Still, he is interested in the wager idea, and that will spur further interaction."

"I'm sure it will, but that course of action comes with complications. Your father will be putting up the shares. You will have to put up something comparable."

"The artifacts, I think."

"At the very least. He will likely ask for more than that."

"He might. The good news is we now have a chance to win it all."

Johnny looked at me in surprise. "Good heavens, Percy. What's gotten into you? I'm the one who usually embraces that attitude. In this instance, I'm not so enthusiastic. Not at all, in fact. Do you actually think he'll sign over those shares if you manage to win?"

"It's the losing part that concerns me. You must be the one to formulate the wager and the terms. I'm utterly hopeless when it comes to that."

Johnny smiled. "That's true. Still, to beat him at his own game will require some serious brilliance and an unusual amount of cunning, even for me. He can be persuasive as well as eloquent, and that combination is a formidable weapon by any measure. I shudder to think what he will talk you into."

"I'll be careful."

"Extremely careful. In the old con game, you have to give the mark a taste of victory. Please note that taste is in your pocket."

"You think that's why he signed the check?"

"I may be overly suspicious, but if you hadn't offered up the idea of a wager, I'm quite sure he would have gotten around to proposing one. As it stands, he didn't have to. You did it for him."

"I hadn't considered that. Nonetheless, he did come through with the money. The baron certainly hasn't."

"Yes, and that bothers me, too. I'm quite sure Hugo is waiting for the share business to be resolved before he does a thing. It puts the pressure on you to handle your father, for a start, and Hugo doesn't have to raise a finger. Elsa might be able to help, but from a practical point of view, Hugo's play is the best for now. Elsa won't interfere. What I would do is get an update from Bruni. She should be able to tell you what is financially possible or not, given the current circumstances."

"I'll speak with Bruni. On another matter, how did it go with your mother?"

"Before we go there, I have more to say." Johnny sighed and took out another cigarette. He offered me one. We lit up.

Finally, he said, "Percy, I want you to do a mental exercise with me. Will you?"

"Sure, but time is short."

"It won't take long. All you have to do is listen for a few minutes. When I'm done, you can disagree all you want. Fair enough?"

"This doesn't sound good, but I'll go along."

"Okay. I want you to note a number of oddities while drawing no conclusions about them at this time. Okay?"

"Go ahead, I'm listening."

"First oddity: I overheard something Elsa said at last night's dinner. 'What does Lord Bromley want?' she asked rhetorically. 'Everything' was her answer. I mention that because of what you said just now: 'we can win it all.' Second oddity, you hate to gamble, and yet here you are contemplating a wager of epic proportions that you want me to structure. Third, before your father collapsed, he told you that there were two types of people in the world, the deceiver and the deceived. He said you were in the latter category, and that you were not only a disappointment but not worth his time. A day later, he goes out of his way to give you his undivided attention, almost rips the check out of your hands to sign it, and then leaves it up to you as to whether you and he should get to know each other a bit better. Fourth, you've had two visions in which you were being hunted. Perhaps you are. One interpretation we didn't consider is that you're being warned, simple as that. Lastly, family has always been an issue with you, and now not only is your father here, but your mother as well. Bruni may also be pregnant. You are in what I would call a psychologically vulnerable position, and that is beginning to concern me greatly. In fact, it is freaking me out. With me so far?"

"I'm following right along."

"Good. Now, grant you, all this reeks of paranoia and distrust, so here is what I propose. Imagine a scale with two pans. In each pan is a hypothesis. Hypothesis One is that your father wants to finally have a good relationship with you and has decided to play nice. Let us call that one the Nice Hypothesis. Hypothesis Two, on the other hand, is that he wants it all, like Elsa said. He wants the artifacts, the library, and perhaps something tucked away that not even Stanley knows about. Perhaps it was kept as a secret between him and Alice. Something far more valuable than the check in your pocket. This is the Not Nice Hypothesis.

"At the moment either could be true, and the scales are balanced. Each has a probability of fifty percent. All I want you to do, and this you *must* promise me, is to update the probabilities in your mind as to which is most likely correct. At some point the preponderance of the evidence will go in one direction or the other. Do I have your most solemn promise that you will not risk anything until you know which one is correct?"

"Fair enough," I answered.

"Then shake on it."

I shook his hand. "This really is like old times. Shouldn't we have spat on our hands first?"

"Too messy. It reminds me of that whole blood oath thing we tried at one point. If I remember correctly, you needed stitches to stem the bleeding."

"Only two, and I can't recall why we decided to do that in the first place. Still, I want to say that I'm not completely brain-dead. There is a game being played here, and the warning interpretation is not only possible, but likely. Taken altogether, the Not Nice Hypothesis carries more weight than the alternative. I get it."

"Do you really? You're neither stupid nor brain-dead. I know that. It's just that you can be a bit ... naïve, is all. All I ask is that you be aware of that tendency and agree to nothing unless Bruni or I concur."

"You trust Bruni now?"

"Don't you?"

"Well, yes."

"Then I do, too. Now, one last point. You needed his signature on the check. You have that. What does he *need* specifically? We don't know, and that is what you must find out. Now, moving on. According to Mother, there's a pending transaction between your mom and Cobb, and likely your father. Your mom's here to collect now that she knows where he is. Both Cobb and Lord B. can be rather slippery as to their location, according to your mom. Please note the addition of another little weight to the Not Nice Hypothesis. Yes?"

"Noted. What else did she say?"

"Your mom thinks Bruni isn't a good choice for you. She's heard things. and judging from what Mother told me, bad things."

"Did she give you specifics?"

"No, since she was told in confidence. Mother's message was to get on it and soon."

"I'll speak to my mom next. While I'm doing that, you might pop in on Bonnie and find out what she's discovered. She's working on Cobb, or Cobb is working on her. I'm not sure which it is. Something sparked between them."

"Bonnie and Cobb? Are you serious? I should think he's a little out of her league."

325

"His real name is Angus Maxwell-Hughes."

"I didn't know that. Who told you?"

"Stanley."

"Stanley? When?"

"I'm sorry, Johnny. I forgot to tell you about my conversations with Stanley and then Bonnie this morning before breakfast."

"You've been busy. Tell me, but be quick."

I filled him in on Stanley's thoughts, Cobb's history, and Dagmar's request for everyone to be present for tonight's dinner.

Johnny considered what I had said for a moment and said, "That is news. Dagmar definitely has something in mind, and it will likely be spectacular."

"We'll find out soon enough. At this point, I've enough to worry about. You'll get with Bonnie?"

"I will. You should talk to your mom and then Bruni. Hugo will come after that. Our schedule is getting a bit cramped, and lunch will be upon us before we know it."

"Such is life in the country. The good news is we're coming around the far turn and into the home stretch."

"We are, and judging from past experience, that's usually when things start getting out of hand, so let's get cracking while we can."

I sighed. Having spoken with my father, it was time to speak with my mother. Johnny and Bruni were certainly right about one thing. I definitely had issues with my parents.

64

I found my mother in the common room library on the top floor. She stood looking at the many books that lined the walls with her hands in the back pockets of her jeans. From behind, she looked like a young woman.

She turned toward me. "Percy, there you are. I thought you'd find me eventually. It's been ages since we've actually talked. Come, let's sit, and you can tell me what you've been up to."

We both sat down in the comfortable easy chairs and looked each other over. I noted once again the physical changes from when I had last seen her, ten years ago. She appeared older, but her aura of easy grace coupled with an elegant glamor was the same. When I would walk with her in New York City, I would watch people appear to recognize her. She would leave them wondering which famous film star they had seen. Whomever she spoke to had her complete attention, and that alone would melt their hearts. She could dissipate my sorrow with a glance, like she was doing now. She was always like that. I loved her, missed her, and resented her prolonged absences from my life.

She looked at me steadily. "How are you're doing, Percy? Really."

"Fine, I think. My life and circumstances have changed in many ways. Alice bequeathed me this estate and told me about my lineage."

She said nothing and looked perplexed. I waited.

"Anne said as much," she murmured. "I suppose I should apologize for not telling you … about your father. I do so now."

She fidgeted and looked away for a moment and then back again. It was an awkward moment.

"The time to do that never materialized quite the way I wished," she said in a low voice, "and so I never said. I didn't know how."

It was likely true. I didn't blame her. Down deep, far below the surface, in the hidden and often opaque center of my being, I think I wanted to. I wanted her to feel my hurt, to experience the countless nights I had lain awake wondering where she was. Did she care that I existed? In the end, I simply felt sad, but I would never give anyone the satisfaction of knowing that, not even her. Not ever.

I said instead, "I figured that was the reason. We are similar. If I don't know how to do something in a good way, I put it off."

She looked at me carefully.

"Do you think that made a difference?" she asked.

"A difference?"

"You know what I mean. Would your life have turned out differently had you known much earlier?"

"I'm not sure. I grew up as part of the Dodge household, and I'm very thankful that I did. Would those circumstances have changed had everyone, myself included, known that Lord Bromley was my father? I think so, but not necessarily for the better. To put your mind at rest, the result speaks for itself. I am happy now, and that is as rare as it is good."

She nodded. Her eyes looked inordinately bright. I thought she might pull out a handkerchief, but she reached for a pack of cigarettes lying on the table. She took her time lighting up. "I'm glad. My silence has worried me. Do you blame me for not telling you?"

"Do you mean was it better that I didn't know until now, or are you asking if I think less of you for having handled it in the fashion that you did?"

She paused. "Both, I think."

I considered her answer. "I don't blame you. I can't. Should you have told me sooner? I don't know that, either. For myself, I would have liked to have seen more of you, but having learned some of our family history, I doubt that was much of an option. You did what you thought best. We all do that. You never forgot my birthday or missed a Christmas. The truth is we lived in different worlds that rarely intersected. We do so still."

She nodded again and looked down. "I wish it had been different for you ... and for me." She looked up and into my eyes. "I really do."

I nodded in agreement. "I know. I say to myself often enough that if wishes were horses, I'd be in the ranching business. Neither of us are, but that doesn't mean we never wanted things to be different. Dreams hardly ever come true, but sometimes we can substitute them with a good approximation."

"You sounded like your father when you said that."

I lifted a hand and dropped it back onto the arm of the chair. "I hardly know him."

"That makes two of us." She smiled. A comfortable silence arose between us.

"Tell me about him."

"That is harder than you think, but I'll tell you what I can."

329

She looked down and seemed to gather herself, thankful to speak of something other than the many paths she never took and where they might have led. "At the time I met your father, I hated him. Anne's life was a wreck. Do you know about that?"

"I do."

"I blamed him for what she had become, not realizing that I was as much at fault. Some people must be nurtured and supported. They're like flowers. Without water and the sunlight of our attentions they grow sad. Neglected further, they wither and die. Back then, I had left Anne alone, more often than not. Hugo was the center of my world. I trust you know about that."

"I do."

She continued. "I had neglected Anne and only realized my error when I saw something quite by accident. What I saw shocked me. I will not tell you any more about that."

"I know the story. John told me."

"He did? Don't tell Anne you found out. She would feel less in your eyes, and she holds your affection for her most highly."

"It hasn't affected how I feel about her."

"I'm glad of that. You know more than I expected."

"Never enough. Please continue."

"When I saw the marks on her body, I wondered how this could have happened. How could she have allowed it? How could I have let it? She told me everything, and I was shocked again. I could not possibly report it. The repercussions for doing so would have been far worse than keeping silent. It was up to me to do what I could. I contacted this man who was responsible, but I was utterly ill-prepared for what I found. It was like being struck by lightning. Everything I had learned, but never believed possible, was true, and my world upended. I pray it never happens to you, but I fear it has already. It's the reason I am here, but once again I've gotten ahead of myself."

She looked at me as if to confirm what in her heart she already knew.

I said, "We've never had the chance to speak of these things until now. We may not have this chance again. Please continue."

She smiled, and as she did, the smile moved to her eyes. I saw for a moment what she must have looked like when she was young. If my father had struck her with lightning, she must have done the same to him.

"I've always wanted to tell you. We're both old enough to appreciate that life can take unexpected turns—that love and fortune can sneak up and assault us from behind when least expected. I was in control of my life when I rang that peculiar bell to his flat, but in the brief span of time it took for him to let me in and me to step inside, everything changed. The man who stood there before me was all a man could be. I suppose it was my imagination, what *I* put there, that carried me off. Some people can tease out of us our dreams, and when we look at them, that is what we see. He did that to me, and I was filled with the heat of anticipation and possibility. I didn't see the danger then, only the blessing. Looking back, it is hard to imagine I would ever be so struck, but the world was a brighter place back then. The future lay in the far distance, and anything was possible. I'm speaking like a girl, but that is who I was back then. I could talk anyone into anything and loved all that was beautiful. He was beautiful, and we were beautiful together. In that second, I willingly and knowingly surrendered to his enchantment and my fate, but then, after a time of the most exquisite bliss, I missed my period. From that

331

moment, the dreams I'd built began to crash down in slow motion like the breaking of a giant stained-glass window as it falls upon the marble steps of a cathedral. What was left after the fall was a gaping hole through which I could hear the screams of those inside, one of whom was me."

She seemed to come back to the present. "Am I saying too much, Percy? I'm sorry if I am. I talk this way sometimes. It's not becoming, but then the story and what I was doing isn't either."

This was a side of my mother I had never seen or ever imagined possible. I realized then that it wasn't my father I took after, but my mother. In an instant I understood her. She was just like me.

I said, "Maybe it wasn't becoming, but I'm glad you're telling me."

She nodded. "I thought my pregnancy was a curse back then, brought about by all the joy I felt, and all the suffering I'd let happen. I didn't see it coming, but that doesn't mean I wasn't warned. The future will always find us. It's why a curse will live there. It's another name for the price that we must pay. In the end, there's nothing to be done but to pay it, but what do we pay it with? Do you know the answer?"

65

"I'm not sure I do."

"There are only two types of coins in our pockets, Percy—joy and sorrow. Either one is legal tender. We have a choice as to which we use to pay what is demanded—perhaps it is the only choice we have."

She paused.

"Always pay with joy, Percy. It's what I decided in the end, after I let you go. Had I continued to pay with sorrow, I would have drowned in the ocean of my tears."

She looked at me as if to see if I believed her. "Your father refused to marry me. I was devastated—ruined. I really was. He wouldn't, or he couldn't. I would have done so gladly. He had his own curses to deal with, I suppose. We call them issues now. They weren't mine. They may be yours. He will tell you about them, or he won't, but that's his story, not mine.

"After his refusal and the ensuing wreck that was my life, it was Anne who picked up the pieces of what little of me was left. By doing so, I think she healed herself. My affair with your father had lasted for some time. I had been careful but obviously not careful enough. After a while, my situation could not be avoided. I told Anne everything, and by doing that, Anne realized that what had happened to her was not entirely of her making; and by seeing that, she recognized that I wasn't completely to blame either. It strengthened the bond between us, and so she went to work.

"Hugo, although I was engaged to him, would not suffice. It was a matter of timing, and what the child might look like— you being that child. It would have raised too many questions followed by too many answers that might be nearer to the truth. That would have been disastrous, knowing Hugo's temperament. Anne is quick. She doesn't always look it, nor is it her desire to appear that way. She remembers everything, and she recalled a man who at a distance looked like he could pass for your father. She saw the look in his eyes when he stared in my direction and unbeknownst to me, arranged to meet him at a café. There, she told him that if he should want me, he had but one chance and one chance only. He had to travel to Austria and be at the train station at a specific time and place. This he promised to do. On that train, there was a spark of sorts between us, but I was lost within myself. We were in the dining car when Thomas went off to grab the three of us a table. Anne whipped me around to face her and hissed. 'Don't fool with him. Set the hook and be done. This is business, not pleasure. Do it now, or I will slap you right where you stand, so help me God!'

"Coming from Anne, who was always so polite, this was a shock, but had she not done that, I would have come up with some excuse to avoid what I had to do. Left to my own devices, I would have wallowed in my hurt while grasping the weight that grew inside me. I knew that without her, I would have held it all the way down into the cold and dark, until the possibility of reaching the surface far above was no longer possible."

My mother looked down at her hands and said nothing. I waited. I noted that without Anne I would likely not be sitting here.

I said, "We have much to thank Anne for, for being in our lives."

She looked up. "Oh, yes. I thanked her in the only way I could, but that was later, not then. Now, I see my life more clearly. Hugo was the dream, your father the reality. Thomas was the compromise. He was and is more than that word might indicate. You do not know him as well as perhaps you should. Never underestimate a good compromise, Percy. A good one can be far more useful and life-sustaining than settling only for one's dreams. Over time I grew to appreciate him. He learned the truth about me. I told him everything on that train. It was my last chance to sabotage my life and continue my descent. I spared no detail of my many faults. To my surprise, he accepted all with open arms and tender kisses. Then he told me about himself.

"Shining knights in armor are only men underneath, and Thomas was a man. I was amused by the tales of his many escapades and conquests. Then Anne met John. I saw what flashed between them and knew at once that my troubles were far from over. In fact, they seemed to breed unchecked at every turn. Motivated by a thirst for vengeance, John's mother had singled out Thomas for what he'd done to her, and by my marrying him, you and I were added to that list. The three of us became fugitives, hunted and harassed by a woman with almost unlimited resources at her disposal. We should have been extinguished, but we weren't. Someone intervened."

She stopped and fished out another cigarette from the pack on the table.

In the pause to light it, I asked, "Who was that?"

She blew out smoke and said, "Fortuna."

66

"F ortuna?"

"The Roman goddess of Fortune. She is often depicted at a wheel, and as Ovid said, she always has its apex beneath her swaying foot. Those in power fear her, but those less fortunate can sometimes find themselves revolving upward to a better place."

She smoked and looked at me again as if deciding what to say or how.

She continued. "Life after you were born was hard. We fled the United States to Europe. We moved about a lot. For five long years, we struggled. My parents, your grandparents, had died, and what money I had inherited was gone. Thomas couldn't seem to hold a job. He always ended up dismissed. It may not have been his fault. He blamed John's mother. He continued to search for a position while I cared for you. We settled for a time in London with what little cash was left, since Thomas thought that he could get work there. Do you remember that?"

"I remember little of my early life, other than that we moved around a lot. London was a dark city. We lived in a single room. There were no curtains."

"London was singularly bleak. I was at my wit's end. Everything hopeful would fall to pieces. On those few days that I could escape to be by myself and recover, I would wander the aisles of Fortnum & Mason and do some window shopping. I couldn't afford to buy, but at least I knew where to shop, and I could dream. Dreams cost nothing, even now.

"One such afternoon, I failed to look where I was going and ran smack into Hugo, and Hugo, not looking where he was going, ran smack into me. So surprised were we at seeing each other that we both jumped back. I bumped into the shelf behind me, and a bottle of olive oil wobbled and fell. Feeling so much emotion and adrenaline at seeing Hugo, I bent down quickly to catch it before it broke. Hugo did the same. Our heads collided. The violence of it caused me to see stars. We staggered into each other's arms—me to keep from falling down, and he to catch me. We could say nothing other than look at each other and gape. At last, Hugo said it was his fault and invited me to tea. I accepted. He asked where I might wish to go. I told him the Ritz. 'Why not,' I thought, and off we went.

"In the taxi I almost vomited. My head throbbed. I had lost a glove. I barely knew where I was when I began to cry. Hugo told the driver to head to the Connaught instead. By the time I was in his room, I was sobbing like something out of a Greek tragedy. All that came out of my mouth was how sorry I was. How very sorry. How very, very sorry. I could not stop. He laid me on his bed and sat on the edge looking at me. I cried like I have never cried before, like I've never cried since. I cried for the lost love, the lost dreams, the grim poverty that threatened all of us, but most of all, for the pity that was me. All those backlogged tears came out at once. In time, I cried myself to sleep. When I awoke, it was dark, and I was alone. I got up and went to the bathroom to make myself look like someone other than a madwoman. Afterward, opening the bedroom door, I entered the living portion of his suite, and there he was, sitting in a chair with hands clasped together looking at the carpet, waiting for me.

"He looked up and bade me sit. He arose, made two drinks, and handed me one. He sat down across from me while I sipped and cupped the glass with both hands. 'Tell me,' he said. 'I want to hear everything.'

"And so I told him everything, except who your father was. What prevented me I do not know, but that piece of information I refused to say. I couldn't. Hugo insisted I tell him, but I told him that his knowing would not change my circumstances. When I had finished, he asked how he might contact me and noted it down. He told me that he would see what he could do and said that it was time that I get home. He arose and picked up my purse, slipped in some bank notes, gathered my coat, and walked me to the door.

"Before he opened it, he turned and said, 'It is well that you did not tell me his name. I would have had to hunt him down and kill him, and then where would we be? There was a time when I would have done anything to have prevented those tears, but now that they've been shed, leave them here with me.... Among them you will likely find my own. It's time for us to go our separate ways. I have a family of my own now, just like you.'

"That was the last I saw of him until last night."

She looked away and said softly, "The brand of olive oil that dropped was called Fortuna, by the way. I still use it."

By the time she turned back, she was herself. I smiled to reassure her. "I'll remember that brand in the future. Seeing Hugo after all that time must have been difficult for you and for him."

She sighed. "Those rounds of drinking last night, and what followed, surely helped. I owe Hugo a great debt and would never do anything to cause him further pain, although I'm sorry to say that my presence at the table did that. Such meetings bring back memories, and from there, it is but a short step to wondering what might have been. In truth, I doubt I could have served him as well as Elsa has. I am smart, but she is as brilliant as the gems she wore last night. Hugo is a most decent man, and she is blessed for having married him, but that veneer can slip when he feels cornered."

"Does he feel cornered?"

"He does, I think. It is one of the reasons I am here."

"One among several, it seems."

"But no less important. It's time to settle accounts, and there are several that are in arrears, mine included."

"I see. Do you feel you owe him?"

"I know I do. He not only helped financially, but it was shortly after our unexpected meeting that I met Alice. She knocked on the door to our tiny flat one overcast morning. Thomas had taken you to the park. I opened the door, not expecting her. I looked like something the cat dragged in, only we didn't have a cat. The chain of events that had led to her standing there that morning is unclear. Hugo was the initial cause. He told John. Soon after, there she was, a picture of elegance and poise. I have never experienced such embarrassment and humiliation as when I opened that door and saw her standing there. I knew who she was. What prevented me from slamming it in her face and howling in my pain and protest at the picture I presented was a peculiar mix of pride and helplessness. I was beyond embarrassed. So much so that I felt myself beginning to reel. When she said that she knew who your father was, I dropped to the floor. My secret was out in the world for all to know, and because it was, I was undone.

"I came back to myself lying on the bed with a compress on my forehead. Alice had the kettle on. I must have made a sound, because she looked at me across the room. She said as if she knew the reason for my collapse, 'This place is a palace compared to some I've known. The world hasn't ended. Other than Anne, John, and the father, I'm the only one who knows. I have a proposal for you. My name is Alice, by the way, but I suppose you know that. May I call you Mary?' "

67

"Once I was somewhat recovered, she said, 'In war, you must be able to maneuver. You cannot do that looking after Percy.' She told me that Anne and John had wanted a brother or sister for Johnny ever since he was born, but there were issues at his birth. Anne could not have another, and she blamed herself. By doing what she proposed, I could help Anne, and she could help me. She told me that the choice she offered was a difficult one, but that I should consider it. She said that she would return tomorrow at the same time for my answer. I agreed and saw her to the door.

"Later, I sat at the little table, weighing which was the lesser evil. By giving you up, there might be peace, but in exchange I would always carry a guilt that only a mother can appreciate. By refusing, I would have a semblance of self-respect but nothing more."

She paused and looked at me as if to see if I understood.

"That was a hard choice. You did the best you could under the circumstances."

"It was a difficult decision. With hindsight, it may appear obvious which was the better choice, but at that time, given my mental state, it was anything but."

She smoked. "We eventually became good friends, Alice and I, but that took time. Giving you up was painful, and one sometimes blames the messenger. When Thomas and you returned, I told him about the visit. He was ecstatic and said, 'Mary, this is a gift. I cannot feel for your child in the way that you do. That's impossible, regardless of whether I am the father, which I'm not. I think this may be our opportunity. Please think on it. I will do and support whatever you think best.'

"His enthusiasm was all too much. All I felt was outrage at my circumstances. To give you up was to confess my own inadequacy, not only as a mother, but as a person. I told Thomas to mind you, grabbed my coat, and walked out the door. I had asked for none of this, least of all my squalor, and a reality that was killing me. I was born with a thousand advantages that apparently counted for nothing in this world. It was outrageous. Needing rescue was more so. It was insufferable. I stomped my way toward the river. I needed help, that was clear, but it was my desire for it and my need that I hated most. It shouted weakness. When all one has is pride, it's hard to surrender it, and I couldn't. I wouldn't. I told myself that over and over, such was my inner rage."

She smoked and blew it out toward the ceiling before she continued.

"Not a minute later, I watched a woman no older than I walk in front of a number ten bus. She closed her eyes before she took that fatal step. I saw her scrunch them shut. There's always a lower rung on the ladder of our lives, and that was hers. I was shocked by what she did and the pooling of her blood beneath her as she lay in a heap on the street. She was me, not then, but soon—perhaps very soon. That realization, and all that blood, shook me utterly. I decided in that instant that if I were to be anything other than her, I could at least keep my eyes from screwing shut. I could do that. It was the tiniest thing, the least possible, but once decided, I saw that ever since my pregnancy, and the subsequent erosion of my dreams, I'd been closing not only my eyes but everything about myself. To live, if that is what I really wanted, I had to let life in, and so I surrendered to my living. In that moment, I understood what life was telling me—begging me, in fact—to see the world as alive with possibility and, most of all, surprise, both good and bad. I had been surprised by Hugo, Alice, and this unknown woman—three times in as many weeks. I wondered what might happen next, and with that thought, I had a future.

"The very next day, I met Alice, not at the flat but on the street out front, and asked that we go somewhere to sit and talk. I suggested the Ritz, having not made it there with Hugo. She said that would be better. Once arrived and settled with some tea, I told her that I agreed in principle with her offer. You would grow up with Anne and John, provided John's mother would agree to leave us alone. Without that provision, there was no point. In addition, I had my own demands. I required that Thomas, you, and I travel to New York, first class, to ensure that you were suitably settled. After that, Thomas and I would return to Europe—Florence, specifically, where we would take up residence, out of sight and out of mind. I also required sufficient funds to move and start my own business of buying and selling works of art. I didn't need a lot, but enough, and with no additional obligation for having received it. Alice agreed to everything, and so it happened. I never paid with sorrow after that. I refused to, especially when it came to you."

There was a silence as she smoked and looked at me.

"I understand, at least more than I did before, and that's something. Thank you for telling me. Speaking of the future, Bruni's pregnant. You will be a grandmother."

"Really? That's also unexpected. I wish there was a nicer word than grandmother. It fairly reeks of age."

"It does. Perhaps we'll find another. I hear you might have some objections to my marrying Bruni to begin with. I'd like to hear them."

"Given that latest piece of information, whatever objections I may have are immaterial. Now that you know my story, how could I possibly object? You have my blessing and my best wishes for a lasting happiness."

"Thank you for that. Someone once described Bruni as a sharp knife, and she is that and more. I'm not blind to her faults, but comes a time, one must decide to love a person unconditionally, or not. To do any less is to be selective. Once begun, where will it end? I don't wish to change her, only to love her, because that's all I can and want to do."

"Thomas said something quite similar to me. She is lucky. Perhaps as lucky as I've been. I hope so. Now, there are other matters I should attend to. I must speak with Cobb and possibly your father. Cobb owes me, and because he's connected to your father, he will have to pay in cash."

"Not joy?" I said with a smile.

She smiled back. "For me, yes. For him, absolutely not."

"I see."

She smiled again. "I hope so. I've been dealing with reality for years. It's dealing with our dreams that I find much more difficult."

I understood that my mother was saying one thing while meaning another. She was indirectly referring to my father and Hugo.

I answered with that in mind, "Indeed. I do like Elsa a great deal."

"I do, too. That's why dreams are difficult. I've enjoyed speaking with you and seeing you. I wouldn't mind a hug, if you are willing."

"I'd like one, too."

We both stood and hugged each other.

"There," she said at the end. "I expect both Thomas and I to be invited to the wedding as well as the christening, should you do that sort of thing. Do you think you can handle seeing Thomas?"

"I'm sure I can. I'd love to see him. I'm glad we talked."

"I am, too. I also liked sleeping in your room. I did notice a particular bear."

"Yes, he's still here. Just don't tell anyone."

68

I stepped into the drawing room and saw Hugo standing
with his arms folded, staring out at the south lawn.

"Baron," I said, "care for some company?"

He turned to look at me. He pursed his lips and then
nodded.

"I know a spot where we can talk in private, should you
care to."

The baron looked at me for a long moment. Finally, he
gave another nod. I opened one of the French doors for him,
and we stepped outside. A cloudless sky of perfect blueness
stretched above a pale haze that marked the boundary where
the blue and the earth met. The breeze smelled of cut grass.
We said nothing to each other as I led him toward the bench
behind the cypress trees. I noted that for a simple bench it was
getting a remarkable amount of use.

The baron wiped it with a handkerchief, and we sat down.
He reached into his pants pocket and took out a gold cigarette
case that held a dozen small cigars. He offered me one. I took
it. He selected one for himself and pulled out a gold Dunhill
lighter from another pocket. He lit his cigar and handed the
lighter to me. I lit mine and handed it back. We both sat back,
smoked, and looked at the cypress trees in front of us.

Finally, I said, "I'm not my father."

"Oh?" The baron looked at me out of the corner of his eye.
"How can you be sure?"

"I spoke with my mother this morning. I'm more like her."

The baron said nothing for a time and then nodded. What conclusion he had come to, he didn't reveal. "How is she?" he asked.

"Good. She wants to help you."

"She told you this?"

"Yes. She said she owes you a debt she can never repay."

After another pause, the baron said, "She does. Your family has caused me a great deal of heartache and trouble over the years."

"Yes, and me, too."

The baron looked at me and smiled. "And you, too."

"What are we to do?"

"What do you wish to do?"

I paused. "Recover the shares and give them over to you, if I can."

"How do you intend to do that?"

"A wager."

The baron nodded. "What if you lose?"

"Then you and I will be in the same position."

"I wouldn't recommend it," the baron said.

"I have an alternative."

"And what is that?"

"The three of us sit down and work out a solution."

The baron smoked and considered that. "You're making the assumption that your father has sufficient motivation to want to attend such a meeting."

"I don't know what he wants specifically, but should it become part of the discussion, perhaps one can be traded for the other?"

"It is possible, but you would have to be able to provide what he wants, and that may be more difficult than you think."

"Perhaps, but that might square things between you and me."

"You owe me nothing," the baron said.

"There has been a lot of heartache and trouble."

"Too much, but such emotional costs can never be recovered. There are only the future costs to consider."

"How bad is your situation?" I asked.

"Bad enough."

"Elsa didn't look pleased this morning."

"She gets angry. She'll get over it. Living with her is not for the faint of heart."

"I think that applies to your daughter as well."

"She falls into that category. You and I must be attentive but with a hard shell. They are often right in their assessments, but putting their beliefs into practice is not always possible in the way that they envisioned. That your father would betray me was unexpected, and yet without him, neither of us would be here right now. It is the way life seems to work. Even the worst have parts to play, and out of them often comes great good but at great cost."

"You trusted him. Why?"

Hugo shrugged. "He seemed trustworthy. I was wrong."

"Is it money that he wants?"

"What he wants, money can't buy."

"And what is that?"

"Atonement."

We sat in silence for a time. Finally, I said, "That will be difficult to deliver. Did he plan this from the beginning?"

"The deal I offered him allowed an advantage over me that he had not expected. He capitalized on that and made me agree to obtain certain artifacts that are part of this estate. I knew that John needed funds. I suggested a sale, and all was arranged. You showed up, and that idea went out the window. Your father expects you to try and get your hands on his shares. It would allow you to curry favor with me. It is not a bad idea as far as ideas go. But you will fail, and then he will dictate terms."

"So I'm doing what my father expects?"

"Yes. You walking away from the whole business is the worst-case scenario for him."

"But that will leave you in a bad place."

"I've been in far worse," he said.

I considered that. "I suppose I could return his check."

"You could. What do you think will happen then?"

"He'd get very angry. He might have another episode. What happens to the shares if he should collapse?"

"He has made arrangements. How well do you know your mother?"

"Not well. Until this morning, not well at all. Is she planning something?"

"Everyone is planning something, even you."

"I suppose that's true."

"People never do nothing. What they are doing may be important, but more so is how they are connected. What are the obligations? What are the freedoms? What are the constraints? That is what you must examine. I appreciate your desire to help me, but helping can make matters worse as often as it can make things better. The best that you can do is look after yourself as your first order of business. Without a secure foundation, how can you expect to aid others without expiring in the process? You have two advantages that you have not considered. Do you know what they are?"

"No."

"I will tell you. The first is that the idol is broken. The second is that he and I will be grandparents. These things he doesn't know, and they will make all the difference. Why atone for something when it is the future that's important? Sunk costs are sunk costs. Past emotional expenditures, whether good ones or bad ones, can never be recovered. Any attempt to do so is foolishness. It is future costs that must be assessed and managed. Your father doesn't understand this, and so what he has set out to do is not only irrational but impossible to achieve. Ignoring him may not be easy, but it's the better choice. To engage with him is to risk being ensnared by his words and locked into his dreams. We all make mistakes, old men especially. They see only the past with their wrongs, errors, and mismanagements underscored in red. Life is always about the future. Death is something to be relegated to mausoleums, and his has already been made. In many cases, and in this one especially, it pays to walk away. You don't deserve his censure any more than he deserves your approval, even if he is your father, and you might feel obligated. Now, what do you suppose that cook of yours gave us in that drink last night? Can you tell me?"

"Hugo, I have no idea. Firstly, I thank you for your advice. I will consider it well. Lastly, you should know that all guests, including Cobb, are to be present at the feast tonight. Dagmar's orders."

"You take orders from your cook?"

"Absolutely."

"In that case, I'm excited. There is much to look forward to."

The baron and I rose. I said, "One of these days I would love to sit down with you for dinner, just you and me. I was looking forward to ours on Thursday. Perhaps in the future we could do that?"

"We will. I did enjoy my time with the son of my oldest friend. They are similar, and both are rare individuals. Whatever happens this weekend, Elsa and I are thrilled at the news of a grandchild. You will be seeing much of us, so the opportunities to sit down together for a long night of eating and drinking will present themselves in due time. Speaking of which, you and Brunhilde need to get cracking on your wedding. It will take place at our castle. Choose a date. Both of you need to get your acts together, in my opinion. What both of you consider important needs some serious adjustments—this business with your father being one of them. For the record, I will likely break even no matter what happens, and who knows, I might even come out ahead when all is said and done. I never bet the farm on anything, nor will I ever. Look to *your* house and take care of *my* daughter and *my* grandchild. Do that, and all will be well, in spite of what you may think. You are free to act in any way you choose. Just choose wisely. You will hear from me if you don't."

The baron chuckled. "Oh yes you will. And by the way, I do have that check, but I wish to see how you deal with your father. Impress me with your brilliance. It is a requirement with me. I already know my daughter is smart. You, I'm not so sure about—other than that you wish to marry her. The fact that you spoke with me now is a further indication, but not proof. Now, off you go. I wish to walk alone and smoke in peace."

69

I left Hugo to his walk and let myself into the drawing room. I passed through it, and as I opened the door to the foyer, I saw Johnny.

Johnny looked about. "How did it go with your mom?"

"Very well. Perhaps we should step outside for a moment?"

"Good idea."

We stood on the front steps.

"Well, what's the news?"

"I spoke with Mom and then Hugo. The Bruni objection evaporated when I mentioned that she would be a grandmother. I did ask about the reasons for her visit, and she said that she wants to settle a pending transaction with Cobb and possibly my father, as well as help Hugo since he had helped her in the past. How she intends to do that, she didn't say. We had a most agreeable conversation. I ran into Hugo shortly after. He said he would be fine financially no matter what happens to the shares, something I hadn't considered. He suggested that I walk away from anything my father proposes. He also mentioned that the idol's breakage may thwart whatever my father has in mind."

"Interesting. Did you ask him about *his* check?"

"He wants to see how I handle my father before he hands it over. Specifically, he said that he would like to see me demonstrate some brilliance. He's not convinced I have any, but is willing to hold the thought in abeyance, depending on what I do. He also thinks Bruni and I have our priorities out of whack. We should be planning our wedding and choosing a date rather than fooling around with the share business. All in all, he was his usual self, direct and to the point. At the end, I was given my orders and dismissed, which is a happy ending when it comes to him. He also mentioned that he thoroughly enjoyed his dinner with you the other night."

"I'm glad to hear that last bit. Hugo can be rather brusque, but that's the way he is. Given his advice, what are you planning to do?"

"I'm going to return my father's check for a start. That will likely be explosive, so it's a question of timing. Since Dagmar wants everyone in attendance tonight and given the potential for another episode, tomorrow might be better. I'll have to play it by ear."

"Well, I would certainly like a heads-up before you do. You said 'for a start.' What else do you have in mind?"

"I'll forgo any wager and gift him the idol, or what's left of it, as a kind of peace offering."

"Isn't that one of the legacies?"

"Technically it isn't. The idol arrived after Alice's death and isn't covered by her instructions. I suppose that could be argued either way, but it has a grim history. It might even be connected to the visions I've been having. The causal connection is rather remote, but we did use it to summon a demon, and demons are a thread that runs through these experiences of mine. I intend to run the idea by Stanley, to be sure. What do you think?"

"It's not a bad plan. It's like giving him a consolation prize. I certainly agree about returning your father's check and avoiding any wager. There's far too much risk there. As to

353

Hugo's portion, perhaps Bruni can talk him into gifting it to both of you as a wedding present, no strings attached. My only concern is that your father will likely refuse to accept his check back and then argue the point until he convinces you to keep it in exchange for whatever he wants. He's pretty good in the persuasion department, so we'll need to think up a suitable counter."

"I expect him to. I thought I might present the idol and the check to him in a gift box at dinner tonight. What could he possibly do? Should he explode, he'll make a public spectacle of himself."

"I doubt social conventions will restrain him. He'll go ballistic and make a mess at the table as he expires horribly in front of everyone. Nonetheless, the idea does have some potential. Let's speak with Stanley now and go from there."

"I think that would be wise."

We made our way to the kitchen. Preparations were in full swing for both lunch and dinner. We kept our heads down and dodged various staff before we made it to Stanley's office door.

I knocked and asked if we might have a moment.

Stanley invited us in. "I don't have much time, but I doubt you'd be here unless you have something of importance to discuss. How can I help?'

I reiterated what I told Johnny.

Stanley looked thoughtful. "Your idea has merit. As a suggestion, you might present him with the figurine today and return the check tomorrow. Whether the idol's power has diminished from the breakage or even had it in the first place, we cannot know. What we do know is that the figurine has a dark history and that your father covets it. In its current condition, the idol may be unusable, and that will most certainly put a crimp in his plans. I might also suggest that you explain that it was damaged in transit to avoid discussing how it came to be in that condition.

"Now, what I find most favorable is that you consider whatever he has in mind to be an unwelcome distraction going forward. That is a major step in lessening his influence. Of course, he will most certainly try and reverse that, but I have every confidence that you will hold to your decision. He might even reveal his true intentions as he tries to make his case, and that would be a benefit.

"As a last recommendation, I would speak with your father only in the library. Should you find yourself hard-pressed, you can always ring for me from there. I will arrive shortly after and inform you that you have some urgent decisions to make regarding this evening. Such a ruse will allow you a plausible exit. What is most important is that you remain confident and secure in your beliefs. As to the idol, I will have the shoe box with the pieces available to present to him after lunch. Will that suit?"

"It does indeed. Johnny, any thoughts?"

"I like it. In fact, I like it a lot. We've shifted from defense to offense, and that can only be good."

"I agree. Thank you, Stanley as always. You've been most helpful."

Stanley nodded. "With pleasure. Now I must get back to my duties."

70

Johnny and I took the back stairs up to the top floor, rather than pass through the kitchen, which was is a state of controlled pandemonium as the lunch hour approached. My room was empty and my closet available. I changed for lunch and met Johnny in the common room.

I asked, "Were you able to get with Bonnie?"

"No. Finding people in this house is like playing an endless game of hide and seek. They disappear, and then you have to look everywhere. The good thing about lunch and dinner is we know exactly where they'll be. I plan to speak with Malcolm before lunch, and Bonnie after. Hopefully, by the time you get through round two with your father I'll have some information, and you will have some, too. After that, we'll have to see."

"Speak with them, by all means. I'm going to stop by and say hello to Bruni. I'll meet you in the drawing room shortly."

"Very well."

I found Bruni in our apartment changing for lunch. I brought her up to date as she chose various items to wear and laid them on the bed. "I'm glad you spoke with your mom. I should sit down with her as well. On the home front, Mama is not pleased with Papa. In fact, she is more than a little cross, but from what you say, Papa will be fine, and that's good. I've decided not to worry about either of them. We do need to pick a date for the wedding. Let's start on that next week. I want to have it take place fairly soon. Oversize wedding dresses are not a preferred item with me. Lastly, I would love to be a fly on the wall when you hand your father that figurine. One quick piece of advice, should he start coming unglued: speak softly and quietly. When there are a lot of exclamation points, toning down the rhetoric and whispering will help keep things from spiraling completely out of control. Sometimes even that doesn't work, in which case I would ring for Stanley and bail as soon as possible."

Bruni stopped what she was doing and looked at me. "Do you feel up for it, Percy?"

"For the most part. At least I've decided to forgo his schemes and will be sending him on his way tomorrow, whether he likes it or not."

Bruni grinned. "Oh Percy, I love it when you get manly."

I wasn't quite sure if she was joking.

I answered, "In that case, give me a kiss before I go off to battle."

"Well, get over here then, and I'll see what I can do."

After a send-off that left me a little breathless, I made my way to the drawing room. John and Hugo were speaking with Malcolm by the bar. I helped myself to a flute of champagne and stood beside them. The baron was saying, "Do you think he'll continue to survive, then?"

"With Cobb's help, he should," Malcolm answered, "at least for the foreseeable future. Should he pass unexpectedly, I will be able to carry on in his stead. That is, should any further negotiations be required."

"He's covered all the bases then," said the baron.

"He has."

"Well, good to know. Ah, the ladies have arrived."

Anne and Elsa entered, followed by Maw and Bonnie. John and Hugo went off to greet them and I stood alone with Malcolm. "Does my father plan on staying here long?" I asked.

Malcolm looked down at me. "I think that depends on several factors."

"Such as?"

"I don't think I'm at liberty to say."

"He's fixated on Alice, isn't he?"

"Well, I don't know about fixated, but I believe he has a concern about her."

"Even if she passed on years ago?"

"Some people believe in a hereafter."

"Does he?"

"I should think he does. Haven't you agreed to let him proceed as planned?"

"I'm not sure what that means exactly. Perhaps you could give me some specifics?"

"I'm not sure I should."

"Why not? I'll know eventually."

"You will, but in general terms, I believe he wants what everyone wants."

"And what is that?"

"Peace."

"Really?"

"Oh, yes. He's quite firm about that. He doesn't like being thwarted. Then he gets unpeaceful."

"Unpeaceful?"

"He gets upset when things don't go his way."

We were interrupted by my father and Cobb. Both had flutes of champagne, and since I was feeling good, I asked my father, "Did my mother find you? She told me that you both have some unfinished business."

My father gave me a hard look. Perhaps he thought I was making a joke. "I believe Cobb is taking care of it," he said. "Not that it should be any concern of yours. Isn't that right, Cobb?"

Cobb nodded and said nothing.

"Well, I'm happy it's being sorted out. On another note, I have something you want. I'll give it to you after lunch in the library, when we resume our talk. Hopefully, you'll like it. Now, if you'll excuse me."

I saw my father's eyes light up when I mentioned that I had something he wanted. I noted that I still had only vague hints of my father's plans and that was beginning to annoy me. Anne stood by the door looking about. I grabbed an extra glass of champagne and handed it to her before asking, "Have you been able to find out what my mother and Cobb are up to?"

"No. Everyone is playing things a little too close to their chests for my liking, including Mary, and that's getting tiresome. By the way, your mother loved speaking with you. She even got a little teary-eyed when she told me. It made a huge difference to her. Now here's Stanley. We're ready to go in. Do you have any idea what we'll be eating?"

"Anne, we'll just have to see."

"Well, you really do need to start taking charge, Percy, but maybe not until after this weekend. Come along. At least I know where the two of us are sitting."

71

I seated Anne and then Bruni. Anne was at Bruni's right. I walked around to my place at the head of the table. With more table leaves having been added, it was a longer walk. Maw was on my right, with Johnny on my left. There were now six guests on one side and five on the other, with Bruni and me at the ends. My mother was on Bruni's left next to Malcolm followed by John Sr., Bonnie, Hugo, and Maw. Across from them were Anne, Cobb, my father, Elsa, and Johnny. Anne's placements of the guests were arranged to create as calm an atmosphere as possible, given the peculiar dynamics of former lovers, rivals, and my father. I was thankful that the table was large enough to accommodate thirteen. Thirteen was not the luckiest number to have for either lunch or dinner, but there was little I could do about that.

Maw turned to me and asked if we were having corn for lunch. I told her that I had no idea, which I realized was now a stock phrase with me.

"Corn, Mary? Why do you ask?"

She whispered, "Corn on the Cobb" and proceeded to cackle uncontrollably.

After a time, she said, "I apologize. I couldn't help myself. You do serve excellent champagne. Now, Percy, to business. When are you and Johnny planning on taking Robert for a walk?"

We were interrupted by cold vichyssoise served in small porcelain cups surrounded by beds of ice in larger silver bowls. The texture was smooth and thick as cream, while the taste was an exquisite amalgam of savory, tanginess, and texture. Once again there was a silent table.

After I saw that Maw had finished, I said, "To answer your question, I have my father scheduled after lunch, and have no idea how long that will take."

She looked at me. "Yes, I imagine there is a fair amount of catching up to do. Walking Robert isn't particularly important, other than it might help you relax. What do you think of your father so far?"

I considered that. "Neither talking to my father, nor walking Robert the Bruce could be classified as relaxing, but Robert does have one advantage. I seem to get an extraordinary amount of exercise when I'm out with him. With my father not so much. I find him very eloquent and persuasive."

"Isn't he now," she said. "I dislike too much eloquence and persuasion. Such talk usually hides a thorn or dresses up some request. Plain speech makes the point and is far more efficient. I say come out and say what you want to say. It makes things simple. Request made, answer given, and that's that. Next? Sloppy minds and beating around the bush tend to go together—that and underhandedness."

"Is he being underhanded?"

"He offered me a chance to make some money. Me? For the love of Pete, I have enough trouble keeping track of all that I have without him adding to it. My accounting looks like an encyclopedia, and that's only the quarterlies. The year-ends are another matter entirely. Rather than speaking with your father, your time would be much better spent taking Robert for a walk, and as you said, you would at least get some exercise. I don't trust him, Percy. I don't. Even Robert can't stand him, and he knows, believe you me."

She reached down under her chair and gave Robert a pat.

When she had returned to an upright position, I said, "Well, if Robert doesn't like him, then that's saying something."

"Don't be condescending, Percy. It's unbecoming. Not all dogs are clever in that way, but this one is. He even growled at him."

"Did he do the teeth thing?" I asked.

"What teeth thing?"

"His mouth opens, and it's like a great white shark. He also makes ghastly sounds that are truly frightening. I saw him do it once. He scared the hell out of me."

"He did that to you?"

"Oh, no. It was something lurking in the shadows of the wine cellar. Anyway, it was an experience, and unless I'd seen it, I wouldn't have believed it."

"That's it, exactly. Your father backed away rather quickly."

"I would have run."

"Well, you're smart, Percy—for the most part. Robert's reaction made me reconsider everything that Bromley had said. I can lend you Robert. He can lie underneath your chair and glower away. Your father won't dare do anything untoward. He might even lose a leg, and where would he be then?"

"I suppose he'd be without a leg to stand on."

Maw thought my quip hilarious. Her cackling laughter exploded across the table. "That's better than my 'corn on the Cobb'! I had no idea you could be so funny." She leaned closer and whispered, "I think he heard me, but then why should I care?" She said in a normal voice, "Frankly, I think it's a combination of the champagne and the soup."

We were sipping champagne with abandon. That might have had something to do with it. Still, a smiling, and laughing Maw was much better than an angry one.

"I do thank you for the offer, but Robert and I have a 'live and let live' policy that works for us."

"Well, all right then. Oh my! Is that lobster?"

"I believe it is."

"You do have a good cook, Percy, and good eating can make all the difference in gatherings such as this one. By the way, when is the baby due?"

"You are sharp-eyed, Mary."

"I am."

"Yes, you are. To answer your question, sometime after the wedding."

"Well, I'd get that done rather soon. Where will it take place?"

"Austria."

"I do love a good castle. Make sure I get invited."

"You're family. I'll insist on it."

"You are clever, Percy, but don't let it go to your head. Now, cold lobster with mayonnaise is exactly what I wanted, and here it is. Wake me when the dream is over."

Once again, conversation evaporated as cold Maine lobster was served with sides of Russian salad and chilled asparagus with lemon.

Johnny leaned over and said, "I don't think I've ever heard Maw laugh that loud at anything."

"I doubt it's me. It's the food and the drink. Dagmar has likely been busy."

We looked about and noted the many smiles, and that a hint of mischief was in the air.

Johnny chuckled and said, "More than likely. Still, it's good to see some high spirits for once."

Johnny's comment was punctuated by shrieks from Bruni, Anne, and my mother. Anne almost fell off her chair. Cobb was beaming away, red in the face. I noted it really wasn't much of an improvement. Even Elsa looked happy, her eyes, bright and flashing. John, Bonnie, and Hugo had their heads together, and Bonnie and Hugo were giggling madly at something John was saying. My father seemed isolated, lost among the revelry around him. Malcolm threw back his head and made a remarkable imitation of a donkey, sending the girls at the other end into fits.

Johnny leaned in and said, "My God! They'll start throwing lobster tails next."

"Only after they've been eaten," piped in Maw. "I also have very sharp ears, young man. Now you and Percy *will* be taking Robert for a walk this afternoon or else … *or else I'll cut you off without a cent.*" She sounded exactly like the wicked witch from *The Wizard of Oz*. She saw the look on Johnny's face and laughed uproariously. Once she was able to control herself, she said, "You're far too easy, Johnny, but luckily, I like you. Forgive my foolishness. Whatever will be served next?"

It was the question, and the answer was ice cream—and not any ice cream. It was homemade vanilla with swirls of orange sherbet served on a lake of warm chocolate. Thin butter cookies were placed on the side of each dish.

Maw said, "I can't possibly eat that! Just kidding. Watch me."

Johnny laughed. "This lunch is almost on par with that birthday party at the Sullivan's years ago. The one where the punch bowls got mixed up and forty pre-adolescents got plastered on a mixture of rum and that splendid Trader Vic's punch. You and I were blamed, but vindicated when Joyce yelled at her husband, 'The blue bowl! Not that one! Good God, Jim! The children have been downing a hundred proof rum punch for the last hour! You complete blockhead!' "

"It was madness. They made us drink a lot of coffee."

"Yes, they did, only we'd never been allowed to drink coffee, something about stunted growth. The Sullivans then had to contend with forty buzzed children hyped on alcohol *and* caffeine."

Johnny and I laughed at the memory of that day.

"Kevin Sullivan was never allowed another birthday party after that one," I said.

Johnny smiled. "Nonetheless, it was a high point of that summer. I can't wait to see what Dagmar has planned for tonight."

"Me, too. I wouldn't be surprised if guests start lining up at six. On another subject and to honor Maw's request, lest you be cut off without a cent, let's take Robert out after I speak with my father. He doesn't appear to be really taking part, does he?"

Johnny looked in his direction. "No, he doesn't. Perhaps he's worried?"

"I doubt it," I said.

"I'd let him settle before you spring that box with the busted idol on him. After that moment, he'll wish he'd gotten into the spirit of things here."

"More than likely. I'm not looking forward to our chat, but it's what I must do. Wish me luck."

"Piece of cake."

"There's cake?" interrupted Maw.

Her hearing was really quite good. Lunch wound down as successfully as it had begun, and I realized then that my father and I could talk only after my other guests had departed from the library. I gave a nod to Stanley. He glided over. I asked if coffee could be served for the two of us in about forty minutes. Stanley said it would be done, and that the box would be delivered along with the service. He would be standing by should he be needed.

My father liked the coffee and so did I. That would at least start our talk on good terms.

72

Once dessert was finished, Bruni rose and announced that we would move to the drawing room and the library. She added that drinks would be available at 7:30, with dinner at 9:00 sharp, white tie. The men made their way to the library, with Johnny and me behind them.

Before we went in, Johnny wished me luck. "Think Quintus Fabius Maximus pitted against Hannibal, and you'll do fine."

"Now that is a piece of advice that's actually useful. Thank you, Johnny."

He gave me a pat on the shoulder. It was good counsel. Fabius Maximus was a master of non-confrontation against a superior enemy and one of my heroes. Johnny and I moved over to the bar. I picked up a small brandy and a cigar. Johnny did the same. John Sr. and Hugo had sat down and were talking shop, while Cobb, my father, and Malcolm stood in front of the fireplace.

I walked over and asked them how they had enjoyed lunch. Cobb answered that he thought it wonderfully refreshing. Malcolm agreed with him and turned to my father, who said, "The cook has some talent. The Russian salad had a little too much mayonnaise, in my opinion. The best I ever had was in Romania."

I said, "Oh? What were you doing in Romania?"

"I was sounding out the government's feelings about loans from the International Monetary Fund. I did such things from time to time. It was quite lucrative."

"I see. I didn't know you were interested in international finance."

"I dabble here and there. Are you a dabbler, Percy?"

"In international finance? I have no such aspirations. There are usually too many strings attached."

"Oh, yes, but that's the point isn't it?"

"It is, which is why I'm not so interested. Now, other than too much mayonnaise, you found the lunch satisfactory?"

"As a rule, I don't eat lunch. I made an exception in this case."

"I see. I'll remember that. We'll speak more in a bit. Gentlemen."

I nodded to them and went over to talk with Johnny, who was standing by the bar. I was quite sure he'd been listening.

Johnny said, "Interesting exchange."

"Yes. As a Fabian, he's pretty good. He never answers a question he doesn't want to. I'll have my work cut out for me."

"Perhaps. He also mentioned international finance. Whenever I hear that term, I run for the hills. How's the Not Nice Hypothesis coming along?"

"It's getting weightier."

"It is. For his sake, he'd better hope that his comment doesn't get back to Dagmar. I doubt she would appreciate it. To me, the Russian salad was Russian magic, but to each his own. Do you think he's the jealous sort?"

"I have no idea. Maybe."

"Perhaps he's jealous of you."

"Of me? I doubt that entirely."

"You might be surprised."

I considered that. "He is *something*, but I can't say what that something is exactly."

"Then perhaps he's afraid."

"Of me?"

"It's possible."

"I doubt that, too."

"Then certainly afraid of something."

"You mentioned that before. I'll explore the subject when I speak with him, although I doubt that he'll come right out and tell me."

Johnny smiled. "Probably not, but if you should mention it, I think you'll have a most interesting conversation. Now, let's find a chair so we can smoke in peace."

"Good idea. We get to experience a brief calm before the coming of heavy weather."

The others departed, and my father and I remained in the library. The coffee and the box would arrive shortly. We were sitting in the same chairs.

My father began. "So, Percy, referencing our last conversation, have you made any decisions regarding you and me?"

"I thought I would reserve any judgment at this time, rather than make a firm decision. Our relationship will evolve, or it won't. We are talking, and that's what's required, regardless of which way it goes."

"Fair enough. We are not so different."

"We are, and we are not. You look at me and see a younger version of yourself, and having been that younger version, you think you know me. Having spoken with both you and my mother, I think I'm more like her. You told me that you wish me no harm, but I'm wary of you. I don't know why that is."

My father nodded. "Perhaps when I look at you, I'm making assumptions that are inaccurate and have envisioned a connection that doesn't exist in the way I think it does. Nonetheless, we are family, but what that means is hard to know. Perhaps the connection that I perceive manifests in ways we haven't considered, such as in our sense of humor, our mannerisms, or our interests. Why are you so wary of me, Percy?"

"You have a reputation that precedes you. Again, I wish to emphasize that I try to keep an open mind, but when I think of you, I think of breakage. You break things, and I'm wary of people who do that."

My father looked pained and was about to respond when there was a knock on the door, and Simon entered with the coffee service.

"Please forgive the interruption," I said, "but I thought that we could use some coffee."

My father nodded. We waited for the service to be set up and the coffee poured. When those tasks were completed, Simon reached beneath the tablecloth like a conjurer and handed me the shoebox. I thanked him, and he left.

"What is that?" my father asked.

I handed him the box. I watched his face fill with eager anticipation as he opened it, only to see his countenance turn grim and hard.

"Is this some kind of a joke?"

"No. It is the idol and the jewel you wanted. It is a gift."

"A gift? This is no gift. It's a travesty! How dare you speak to me of breaking things! It's ruined!"

"Is it?"

"How did this happen?"

"Is this not what you wanted?"

"Do you have any idea what you've done? You, stupid, stupid boy! Get out! I don't want to see you! This is unforgivable!"

My father stood, lifted up the box and its contents, and hurled them, crashing, into the fireplace. He then picked up the coffee service and hurled that in as well.

He turned, still raging, and looked down at me. His face was wild, misshapen, and grotesque. He raised both his fists

371

above his head and swung them down viciously until his both his index fingers pointed at me.

"I curse you! I curse this house! I curse the people in it. *I curse all that you wish for and everything you touch! You … you … bastard!*"

With that, he slumped back into his chair and began to weep. I watched his shoulders heave as he sobbed. I looked across at him in a detached way. I had no idea what to do. His upset was not unexpected, but the degree and the form it took surprised me. On top of that, I was tired of the whole father-son dynamic. It was time I treated him like a normal person, and it was time he acted like one as well. Enough was enough. He was my guest, and having to put up with his ill humor, his volatile nature, and his veiled condescension, was not only growing tiresome but intolerable. He was in my house—*my house*! On top of that, he had cursed me. Could he do that? Could anyone do that? How dare he!

Then I recalled that Dagmar was expecting him and everyone else to be at the dinner tonight. I had no idea why she insisted that everyone attend, but I sensed it was important. With that thought, a fog inside my head seemed to lift. I saw clearly that I could let the world collapse, or I could act to fix it. Rhinebeck could become a tomb of broken dreams at any time, but only if I let it. The choice was always mine to make.

I knelt down beside my father and spoke to him in a whisper. "I broke the idol. The power in it flowed to me … and to a demon."

"What?" My father stopped and looked at me, his face still anguished.

I continued to speak softly. "Perhaps you should hear the story before you decide that all is lost."

He took hold of my face in one hand and looked into my eyes.

"You broke it?"

I didn't pull away and said softly, "I fell, and it did too."

He continued to look at me. "Perhaps I should hear your story."

"Perhaps you should, but I want some coffee first." I stood, looked down at him, and said, "Don't you ever hurl a coffee service into the fireplace in *my* house again. The coffee here is too damn good for that. I would also suggest you pick those pieces of the idol and the jewel out of there while I make arrangements for more coffee. This discussion is far from over, so don't even think about wandering off!"

74

I opened the library door and stepped into the hallway. Both Simon and Stanley were standing a few feet away. I supposed they heard the crash and were wondering whether to intervene.

Stanley asked, "Is everything all right?"

"No, but we're in the middle of things," I said in a low voice. "At least he didn't drop dead when he saw the state of the figurine. Simon should bring a trash can and remove the coffee service from the fireplace. I doubt there is much that is salvageable, other than the silverware. My father is picking out the pieces of the idol. I suppose he might need some help. I'll get back in there in a moment. In the meantime, Stanley, could you provide another coffee service? A thermos and two cups would work, if necessary. I doubt he'll do it again, but you never know. Nothing got on the carpet, which is a plus, and the fire was out by the time he did that."

"I see. Are you getting anywhere with him?"

"I believe so, and strangely, I think his upset is what it took to get there."

"Very well. Simon and I will see to it. If you need me, ring. More coffee will be with you shortly."

"Excellent, Stanley, and thank you, Simon."

I reentered the library. It looked like my father had managed to extricate the box from the fireplace, along with the pieces. It lay at his feet.

I sat down. "More coffee will be with us shortly."

"I want an explanation," was all he said. At least it was said in a normal tone of voice.

"Which you shall have, but I will have my coffee. I would rather not be disturbed while I tell you, so we will wait."

Simon arrived with a large wooden box, a whisk broom, and a dustpan. He began to clear the fireplace. Stanley arrived with a thermos and two mugs on a silver tray. Given the robust nature of the service, Stanley wasn't taking any chances, and judging from the grimness of his expression, the previous service must have been a valuable one. He left as soon as it was placed on a side table. Simon quickly followed, and the door closed with a click. After a pause, I grabbed a mug and the thermos.

"Would you like some?" I asked.

"I suppose."

I poured him a cup, handed him the mug, and made one for myself. It was hot, delicious, and exactly what I needed.

"I will tell you the story. Are you ready?"

"Obviously."

I looked at him for a long moment. "Very well, but before we begin, I wish to speak with you simply as one person speaking with another. I will do so with the necessary respect that your age demands and with due regard to your status as a guest in my house. I wish for you to show me a similar courtesy, and that is all. Can you agree to that?"

"You wish to forgo the father-son relationship."

"Yes, for now."

"Very well. I agree."

"I will tell you the story. Robert the Bruce was the one who discovered the idol."

"Who?"

375

"Johnny's dog, the one who growled at you. Mrs. Leland owns him now. Robert discovered the box in the wine cellar, where it had sat unopened among a host of other items that had arrived and continued to accumulate after Alice died. Johnny and I wanted to know more about the circumstances of her death. We also wanted details about her life. During the examination of the many items, I found a letter to an M. Thoreau written by Alice shortly before she died. It had been returned unable to forward. In it, Alice described the idol, its discovery by Arthur Blaine, and her subsequent escape with it into the jungle. She wrote that she had made arrangements for the figurine to be delivered here, but for whatever reason, it showed up after she had already passed on. Nobody knows when the box arrived, exactly. We opened it, saw what it was, and Johnny decided to use it to summon a demon."

"Why would he want to do that?"

"He wished to find out whether the occult was real or not. The occult had been an important part of Alice's life, and by exploring that element, he thought he might understand her better."

"Was the summoning successful?"

"The results were inconclusive, and yet there were indications that he succeeded. Johnny found some notes in one of Alice's books that outlined the procedure to follow. He followed her instructions to the letter, including the use of a tincture that she created to facilitate the summoning. In addition, it required a specific item that had 'occult' properties. Alice normally used the forearm bracelet, but in this case, Johnny used the idol."

"You actually did this?"

"Yes. I consumed the tincture. My recollections after I did that are confused and unreliable. According to Johnny, I began to speak in a voice that was not my own. Johnny was supposed to have asked one question but asked two instead. Whatever was speaking through me became upset. Johnny said that I grabbed the idol and told him 'For me, for him.' Johnny agreed. The voice said that I had received much more than was agreed upon, something extra. A new bargain was struck between them, and I collapsed immediately after. The idol broke and the jewel sheared in two in the fall."

"There is a great deal missing from your narrative."

"There is, and those parts may or may not be relevant, I admit. I've related to you the facts without embellishment. If you have questions, I'll try and answer them."

"What was the extra you received?"

"An intuitive sense that disappeared when I left to go back to California. It has not returned."

"Describe it to me."

"I understood people, their motives, and what they felt."

"And you can no longer do that."

"Not in that way. It is a matter of degree, rather than the capability itself. It was far more profound."

"And you lost it?"

"Apparently."

"Do you want it back?"

"No. There is no pressing need for it. I feel I am fully capable without it."

"But you did need it then."

"I did. I was more fearful and needed that intuition to settle me. I'm still fearful, but less so. I now have something more useful."

"And what is that?"

"Balance. I see both sides."

"And what about my side?"

"Let me tell you about your side."

"Go on."

"You are not my only guest. I am responsible for all whom I invite into my house. I did not invite you. You invited yourself. However, by my accepting you, you became a guest, with all that implies. That being said, you have managed to create upset among most if not all of the others whom I invited specifically. I have yet to ask Cobb if you've upset him. He is my guest as well. In any event, I want no more upset from you in this house. We are very old-fashioned when it comes to how a guest and a host should behave. The ancient Greeks called it *xenia*. I'm sure you've heard of it. Given that, it is quite all right for you to be upset with me, although I will tell you now that I will do all I can to accommodate you. As host, it's my duty. It is also my duty to protect you—to give you sanctuary—and you're making my job extremely difficult. Now, what is it you wish to say to me about your side? Perhaps I can be of some assistance."

My father studied me carefully. "You wish to help me?"

"If it is within my power. I'm certainly willing to listen to your request, but unless you spell it out, I can do nothing. Perhaps we can begin by you telling me what specific problem you're trying to solve?"

"What if it's none of your business?"

"Then it's none of my business."

My father continued to look at me. I looked back.

He said, "You also have things that belong to me that must be returned."

"Such as?"

"The pot, the forearm bracelet, and this." He kicked the box with his foot. "There are more items she took."

"Very well. Suppose I agree to give them to you when you leave. Will that work?"

"No."

"Why not?"

"As I wrote in my letter, I want to take them to my room."

"And do what?"

"What I do there is *my* business."

"And yet whatever that is must happen upstairs in *my* house, and you won't tell me anything about it. From my perspective, we've traveled as far as we can go. As to the several items that you claim are yours, you may be right. I'm willing to allow the courts to decide the matter. Should they rule in your favor, then they'll be returned. Unfortunately, that will likely take some time, and time is a commodity that neither of us have in great supply right now. In my case, you're not my only guest. Others need my attention. And in your case, you'll be leaving here and not returning. I don't think I want you back. You break things, and not everything can be mended. That is my position. Would you like more coffee?"

"No, I don't want more coffee. I can and will make trouble for you."

"I'm sure of it, but not in this house ... not ever again."

"So now you'll have me thrown out?"

"Yes. It's been done before, I believe. I instructed Stanley to inform Cobb to help get your bags packed, and to tell Cobb specifically that his dinner invitation still stands. Harry will drop you at the train station. It's not far." I stood. "Perhaps we'll see each other again ... but maybe not. Goodbye."

I turned and was about to open the door when he yelled, "All right! All right! I'll tell you. Sit back down. I'll play your stupid game!"

I turned and said, "It isn't stupid. I think it's important that you say what you need to say, not for me, but for you. Who else is there to tell? Who will believe you? And who do you know that might want to?"

My father paused and glared at me. "Yes, in that you are correct. It's why I'm here. The question is, where do I begin?"

"At the beginning?"

"There are no beginnings, only introductions of different themes in an endless composition. Please. Sit back down and I'll tell you."

75

I sat back down and waited for him to begin. While he gathered his thoughts and poured some coffee, I considered our positions.

Letting my father speak was like opening the door to a vacuum cleaner salesman. It was not a question of whether I would buy, but how many I would own by the time he was done. To counter him taking the upper hand once again, I decided to control the conversation.

Before he could begin, I said, "Since time is pressing, perhaps you can simply state the reason you are here."

My father looked irritated again, but said, "I will be brief and to the point, as you've requested. It was my desire to use the idol to speak once more with Alice. There are methods. I understand that such an attempt may seem ridiculous to you, but this is the wish of a man who will not be around much longer. I did wrong by her, and she did wrong by me. Both of us require the other's forgiveness before either of us can move on. I know this to be true in ways I would rather not talk about. My telling you would make you doubt my sanity even more. Cobb is interested in such things as much as I am. It is why he's here with me—that, and to keep me alive as long as possible. I paid him well. The shares are his. It was our arrangement and our agreement. When Hugo told me that the idol was found, I knew I had this one chance. Now that I see that it is broken, I don't know what to do. You will likely think

I'm a fool for believing that speaking to the dead is possible. Perhaps I am. I've been a fool in many things, so being one now is as likely and no different. Now you know the reason I'm here, and given what remains of the idol, there is little more to be said."

"Thank you for being brief. You wished to use the idol and some other items to contact Alice in order seek her forgiveness. Is this correct?"

"Almost. She requires my forgiveness as much as I require hers. This I know without a doubt."

"I see. I understand your request now. Thank you. It has cleared up several issues in my mind, and because you have been so forthcoming, I would like to tell you three things, the first being that since the idol is broken, I cannot fulfill our agreement. I give you the option of either accepting the check back or giving me the funds to hold in trust for your grandchild. Bruni is pregnant. You did not know this."

"Is she now?"

"Yes."

"Well, congratulations. I'm happy to hear that. I suppose that will make me a grandfather."

"Yes, you will be a grandfather, and that is special. The second point I wish to make is that forgiveness and acceptance are not dissimilar. A wise lady told me that it is our willingness to accept what we've received that determines how we feel, and whether we are truly happy with it. Perhaps those words apply to the past as well. You will have a grandchild. All of what happened before was necessary for that to happen now."

My father nodded. "And what is the last thing?"

"Without getting your hopes up, I would like to explore an avenue that may help you in what you wish to accomplish, with the understanding that it may amount to nothing. For now, it is only a possibility."

"Really? What do you have in mind?"

"Be patient for a time, and I will let you know. One last question: if Cobb owns the shares, how could you have bet them?"

"You would have lost, so it didn't matter whether I owned them or not. I suppose now is a good place to end off for both of us. I will think about what to do with the check and let you know. I also must apologize for destroying the coffee service. I will see that it's replaced. I also wish to thank you for our talk—but before we go, a few words of advice, if I may."

"And what are they?"

"For all our sakes, stay away from gambling. You aren't suited for it, and lastly ... *never* bet against me."

I considered his words. "That's probably a good idea."

I got up and rang the bell for Stanley. Stanley arrived promptly and informed me that there were some decisions to make regarding the dinner tonight. I thanked him and excused myself from my father's company.

76

As we walked down the hall, Stanley asked me if the second half of the meeting went better than the first.

"It did, and you were correct. My father wants to contact Alice to ask her forgiveness and to forgive her. The broken idol unhinged those plans. Without going into specifics with him, I said that I might look into alternate methods for him to do that. Dagmar might be able to point me in the right direction, but I doubt she will have the time to tell me."

"She's quite busy, as you can well imagine. What I think is more significant is that you played your own game and avoided playing his. In keeping with that, I would do nothing about the matter you mentioned. You may feel that as a host, you have an obligation to look into it; however, he will take advantage of that willingness, and you will quickly find yourself ensnared once again. Do nothing is what I would advise."

"Thank you, Stanley. Now, I have to find Johnny and take that dog for a walk."

Stanley and I parted, and I found Johnny in the drawing room speaking with Maw. When she saw me enter, she handed Johnny the leash. Robert hadn't exactly smiled, but I sensed he saw a bout of freedom in his future. That anticipatory expression had been cut short when he noticed I was watching him. He turned his head away, as if to say, *you didn't see that.* To emphasize the point, he plopped into his sphinx position and ignored me. To my mind, simply because he looked and acted like a dog didn't mean he wasn't a hooligan underneath. Like the Sphinx, Robert had an almost unnatural patience and was as inscrutable when he wished.

Johnny and I walked Robert along the edge of the south lawn. Robert strutted beside Johnny on Johnny's left, not even straining against the leash. Maw had either taught him some manners, or he had gotten used to being on his best behavior around her. Robert, I was quite sure, had sufficient intelligence to know exactly which way the wind was blowing.

While Robert trotted jauntily beside him, Johnny listened to me and looked down at Robert from time to time. Johnny would smile, obviously thrilled at Robert's subservience. Certain that all was well, Johnny, in some misguided attempt to validate and acknowledge Robert for his good behavior, unclipped him.

Faster than the blink of an eye, I watched Robert become a fading speck in the distance, racing away in the direction of the tennis court. I shook my head in exasperation. I should have expected as much. Johnny observed Robert's vanishing trick like a child perplexed by a magician pulling quarters out of his ears or making candy disappear. After a few moments, Johnny said, "He wasn't supposed to do that."

"Really, Johnny? Of course he wasn't supposed to do that, but you unclipped him, so he most certainly *was* going to do that. Good heavens! Now we'll have to capture him. I hate having to capture him. I can't believe you did that."

Johnny sighed and then shrugged. "Not to worry. He should enjoy his freedom while he can. I'm sure he's been rather repressed lately. We'll follow at our leisure. He'll find some awful tennis balls that have seen a few winters and enjoy some canine ecstasy as he rips them to pieces. I'm quite sure he deserves that at the least. Now, where were we?"

"I rang for Stanley and we left my father in the library. I filled Stanley in on what happened. He seemed pleased with the results. I also mentioned my father's problem and said I would see what I could do. Stanley advised that I let the matter drop entirely."

Johnny and I continued walking in the direction Robert had taken.

"I suppose you had to offer your help since he's a guest," Johnny said, "but as Stanley pointed out, doing so opens yet another door, and that man can slip through the tiniest crack. On top of that, asking Dagmar might be difficult today, given the preparations that are going on. As an alternative, you might consider giving your father the flask containing Alice's tincture and tell him to take a couple of swigs. You might even give it to Cobb and let him administer it. Cobb can tell his lordship that he'll see more than Aunt Alice after consuming an ounce or two. Who knows? My flask idea might even work.

"Leaving that for a moment, I think you handled your father rather well, and that's saying a great deal. So, nicely done. I did speak with Bonnie. She told me that Cobb is doing his best to keep your father alive, but your father is a most difficult patient. Given that Cobb's the one who has the shares now, he's definitely been compensated sufficiently to make sure your father remains among the living. I also get the feeling that your mother is in negotiations with Cobb to get the shares back over to Hugo. That should be an interesting discussion. All told, we've made some progress, and from where I stand, it's all coming together rather nicely. I do have one question, however."

"And what's that?"

"How are the two hypotheses stacking up in your mind?"

"The Not Nice Hypothesis is still the most likely, but not overwhelmingly so. Acting the host, rather than a son, certainly allowed me to deal with him more effectively. I'll continue that approach going forward."

"That would be a good idea. Nonetheless, I think your father will show his true colors at some point. His plans are stymied for now, but I'm sure he hasn't given up. It's an obsession with him and likely what is keeping him alive. You haven't heard the last of him on the matter, I'm quite sure. Malcolm may be able to shed some light on what to expect. He went for a nap after lunch, and I haven't seen him since. I'll have a word with him before dinner and see what I can find out."

"Do that. We've done all we can for the moment. Right now, we must collect that dog. Do you see him anywhere? I would hate to think what might happen if we managed to lose him."

"Not to worry. I see the little bastard. He's behind the tennis court. I'll saunter up and put him back on the leash. It won't take a minute."

"That would be a refreshing change."

Forty minutes later, the three of us were headed back to the house. I'm not sure whether it was Johnny's pleading on hands and knees that did it, or whether Robert had simply grown bored with making Johnny run and leap about. In the end, it might have been pity. Johnny looked utterly exhausted, and we had a long night ahead of us. We parted in the drawing room, and I went looking for Bruni.

77

B runi was relaxing in the bathtub. I could hear her splashing about. I knocked on the bathroom door frame. "May I come in?"

"Of course. Good timing. You can wash my back … just don't get my hair wet."

I sat down on the edge of the tub and began to wash her back with a washcloth. It was a very smooth and attractive back.

"Don't get any ideas, Percy. Now tell me what happened with your father?"

I sat on the edge of the tub and told her in detail about my conversation.

When I had finished, she turned her head to look at me. "Good use of the whisper and nicely done on reframing the conversation into one between host and guest rather than father-son. That was smart. Cobb having the shares is an interesting twist. It was always a possibility but surprising, nonetheless. Cobb's obviously much cleverer than I thought."

"That he is, but he will have my mother to deal with. I think she wants to get those shares back to Hugo as part of a long overdue thank you."

"Really?"

"Johnny mentioned it as well. It's one of the reasons she's here."

"I hadn't considered that, but it does make sense. My only question is what, if anything, are you going to do to satisfy your father's wish? Before you answer, grab me a towel and help me out of this tub."

Bruni pulled the plug with her toe, stood up, wrapped the towel around herself, and allowed me to help her out. She felt nice and warm under the towel.

"Please focus, Percy. You get distracted so easily."

"And you have nothing to do with that?"

"I have everything to do with that, which is as it should be. Now, please turn your back so I can dry myself, and you can answer me without having to catch your breath every few seconds."

"I suppose that might work. I'll turn around. There. Anyway, I thought I would speak with Dagmar, but Stanley advised against it."

"One point you may not have considered is that Dagmar is aware of your father's situation, and that there's already a plan in place."

"You think so?"

"I do. She and I spoke about it."

"How did you manage that? Not even I can do that without an appointment."

"She likes me. What can I say? I'm welcome in her kitchen anytime."

"Really?"

"It's true. This afternoon I let her put me to work. She wants to teach me a few things, and she's most definitely someone to learn from. I'm considering being her apprentice whenever I'm here. Anyway, she mentioned that she was aware of your father's situation and that solving his issue with a tincture would be ill-advised. Besides, it would interfere with the end-of-the-evening surprise."

"There's going to be an end-of-the-evening surprise? That *is* news. What do you think she has in mind?"

"We'll have to wait and see."

"I bet she didn't tell you any specifics."

Bruni smiled. "She didn't. She told me instead to tell you not to worry, and that all is well in hand. I must say, that kitchen is a hotbed of intrigue, intelligence, and wagers of all sorts."

"It is, and you being part of that underworld might prove extremely useful. Are they making bets on the wedding?"

"Oh, yes."

"They're not wasting any time. Tell me."

"Unfortunately, I can't. That is also a 'need to know' subject."

I sighed, "Too bad. Stanley told Johnny and me that our participation would affect the odds, and since we were often the topic of the bets themselves, it would be unsporting. I'm sure the same applies to you."

"That was how it was put to me."

"Well, at least we're both in the same boat. I feel better. Now, have you figured out what you're wearing? You mentioned a new dress that you thought rather risqué. Was that last night's or tonight's?"

"Tonight's, only I'm having second thoughts."

"If you're having second thoughts, I can barely imagine what it's like … actually, I can, and that's the problem."

"Don't get too excited. The dress and I are talking it over. Now, why don't you start getting ready yourself. Aren't your things upstairs?"

"You're right, and my mother's in my room. Well, I best get going now. I'll be back soon."

"Please do. You'll be able to check out my dress, and we can make our entrance together. I'm definitely looking forward to this evening's celebration."

78

M y bedroom door was shut. Johnny saw me and motioned me into his room. "You should thank me. I managed to get your gear before your mother came up to get ready."

"Thank you, Johnny, and as compensation, here's some news: according to Bruni, Dagmar rejected the tincture idea. Apparently, it might conflict with what she's planned."

"Oh, I like that. I had my doubts about making it through the evening thanks to the antics of young Robert, but with this new information, I'll make it for sure. Excellent news. Now, let's get a move on. We can at least have a moment's peace before things start up in earnest."

Johnny and I were first down. My white tie and tails were reasonably comfortable. We both looked like we were from another century. Before I grabbed a flute of champagne, I mentioned to Johnny that I had to look in on Bruni. She was wrestling with a particular dress that might be too risqué for tonight's company.

Johnny looked horrified. "Well, I would definitely settle that. It happened to me with Laura Hutton. We attended this big to-do one evening, and since it was cold outside, she had on a long, elegant overcoat. Once inside, she removed it. I was already quite besotted and becoming overly protective. You can imagine the convulsions my brain went through thanks to some minimalist French designer when I saw what she was wearing underneath that coat. My face was red the entire evening, and people kept asking if I'd fallen asleep under a sun lamp. Laura was thrilled with all the attention. I wasn't. Please check on Bruni now while there's time."

I made my way to our apartment at a good clip.

"Well, what do you think?" asked Bruni as I entered.

The gown in question was made of patterned, dark blue silk and hugged her body like a second skin. Bruni observed herself in the mirror as she turned this way and that.

"At a much larger gathering, you would light up the room. At a more intimate one like this, you will outshine everyone else."

"My thoughts exactly. It's too much."

"What are you going to wear instead?"

"I have this black number. With some serious diamonds it will do quite nicely. You can unzip me now."

"I'm not sure if I dare."

"Fortune favors the bold, Percy."

We made it to the drawing room before most of the crowd. Johnny nodded his approval as Bruni went off to speak to her parents. Johnny said, "That took a bit longer than expected, but Bruni looks wonderful."

"Yes, and I can also breathe more easily."

"Always a plus. I've been waiting for the tall man to find out what he knows. If you feed him caviar to make him thirsty, and I keep him supplied with champagne, we might get somewhere."

"He is rather tall," I said. "I imagine four glasses should do it. There he is. Off you go. I'll join you in a bit."

My father had also entered the drawing room with Cobb. It was Cobb I wanted to speak to, but my mother slipped up beside me before I could approach him.

"Do you like my dress?" she asked. "Valentino Garavani made it for me."

I turned to look at her. Hers was made of thin black silk, but the way it was folded and wrapped around her made her look like she had stepped off a runway at a haute couture fashion show. Around her neck was a peculiar necklace of pale emeralds. She looked sensational.

"You could break many a heart without even trying."

"Fortunately, I've already done that."

"And more than once. How are negotiations going with Cobb?"

"I'm almost there. I need that little something to close it, and I think I know what that might be. Let's stand over by the bar. The light to the left is perfect."

She took my arm and guided me to the spot she wanted.

"Pass me a flute and stand to my right."

I handed her the flute and stood in the spot she had pointed out.

"Perfect. Look at me. Excellent. Smile and I'll smile back."

I smiled, and her face lit up. She really was something to look at.

"You're doing great, and here he comes. Kiss me on the cheek, turn, and welcome him. I'll take it from there."

I kissed her cheek, turned, and there was Cobb, gazing intently at my mother.

"Percy, why don't you get Angus some champagne."

I turned to do her bidding as she said to Cobb, "What do you think?"

I gave Cobb a flute and stepped away as he asked my mother, "Are they real?"

Her answer floated toward me. "You can discover that for yourself later this evening."

"I'd like that very much," he answered.

I didn't know what to make of that. I turned, and there was my father.

"May I offer you a glass of champagne?" I asked.

"In a moment. Have you made any progress on the matter you promised to look into?"

"Let's speak at the end of the evening. I don't mean to put you off, but I need to confer with others who are unavailable at this time."

"I imagine that cook of yours has something to do with that. Knowing her history, I wouldn't be at all surprised."

"Her history?"

"Everyone has a past, and she does, too. Some pasts are best left sleeping. Awakened, they can raise all sorts of questions."

"Is that a covert threat by any chance?"

"How do you mean?"

"I think you know exactly what I mean. You like to exert pressure to ensure things happen when, and in the way you want them to. I protect the people who work for me, and you making trouble for them would be ill-advised. Since I have no wish to threaten you, please do me the same courtesy."

"You think I'm threatening you?"

"Indirectly, yes."

"You can take it that way if you wish. I want to make sure that my request is *not* forgotten."

"I can assure you that it hasn't been. Now I have a question of my own."

"And what is that?"

"Do you plan to repair your relationship with Hugo, or simply let it fester?"

We were interrupted by Simon with hors d'oeuvres of Beluga caviar on circles of white toast.

I took one and then another. My father refused.

When Simon had moved away, I said, "You seem determined to not enjoy yourself."

"One person's enjoyment is another's irritation. Hugo has made no attempt to repair our friendship, and by not doing anything about it, he's the one who ended it."

"He, too, is upset, and you are correct. The absence of communication sends as clear a message as its presence, but such things work both ways. One of you must make the attempt. Do you wish him to act contrite and say that everything was his fault? Is that what it will take to ease the conflict between you?"

"I would appreciate an apology, but that's between us and doesn't concern you."

"If you manage to attend the wedding, I should think it would."

"He betrayed me."

"By not delivering the artifacts?"

"That is correct."

"Perhaps, but then again, you betrayed him by taking the shares. From where I stand, one cancels the other. Perhaps it's time to call it even, and for both of you to make an effort to fix things while you can. Now, I must welcome Mrs. Leland and her daughter."

I left my father standing in the center of the room. As I caught Bruni's eye, I realized that unless he chose to reconnect with the world around him, he would surely leave it—and soon.

79

Bruni glided up to me and took my arm. "What? No champagne?"

"I was speaking with my father. He's determined to have a bad time tonight."

"He's sulking. I'll take care of that while you grab a glass of bubbly and talk to Maw and Bonnie."

I took a glass of champagne and walked over to speak with them. Bonnie was in pale blue satin with a necklace of sapphires and diamonds, while Maw wore black with three huge emeralds around her neck that rivaled those at the Topkapi Museum.

"Champagne?" I asked as I motioned one of the staff over.

"Please," said Maw. "That walk must have been good for Robert. He's upstairs sleeping like a baby."

"I'm not surprised. He did a lot of running around. You both look heavenly, by the way."

John Sr. and Anne in a black Cassini joined us as I noticed my father holding a flute. Hugo and Elsa arrived. Elsa wore a black Dior with the same diamond necklace of the other night. All my guests were now assembled in the drawing room. They sipped champagne, and judging from the noise level, were filled with eager anticipation for what was to follow.

Several minutes later, Simon hit the drawing room lights, plunging our surroundings into darkness. Stanley opened the double doors to the brilliantly lit dining room. The long table was set with a white and gold tablecloth. All the glassware was of heavy red crystal and the red lips of the plates were reflected in the polished silver, as if flecked with ruby-colored blood. The table had been extended to accommodate the many additional glasses, pieces of cutlery, and plates, while allowing each guest to not feel overly crowded. I escorted Bruni to her place at the far end and seated her. She was between Elsa and Johnny. At my end I had my father to my left and Hugo to my right. Beside Hugo was Malcolm and opposite, next to my father, was Cobb with Bonnie beside him, followed by Anne and Mary next to Johnny. On the opposite side next to Elsa were Maw and John Sr.

It was an interesting arrangement. I wondered how often I would be required to act as referee, but I suspected that Anne thought it best to put Hugo, my father, and myself closer together in hope that I might be able to heal the rift between them in some way. I wasn't sure that was possible, but from the seating arrangement, I got the message that peace as well as food was on the menu.

I seated myself, looked around, and spoke to Hugo, my father, Cobb, and Malcolm. "There is only one rule tonight, gentlemen."

"And what's that?" asked my father.

"No dueling."

My father raised his eyes, while Hugo muttered to himself, "Too bad."

Cobb, once again sounding like an Oxford don, looked at me and said, "Food should always be consumed without upset. It would be best if we all adhered to that doctrine. I would also much prefer that I be addressed as Angus."

He looked at each of us at our end of the table. We all nodded.

"It's a pleasure to have you with us, Angus," I said. "You are an educated man. Perhaps you can answer a question for me. What is forgiveness, and how can it be achieved?"

Both my father and Hugo looked uncomfortable while Angus contemplated an answer. Before he could begin, the first course of Scottish smoked salmon was served on small plates, paired with a white Haut-Brion. Judging from the serving size and the number of utensils, there would be many courses to follow. What they would be was a mystery. By the time I looked up, most of my guests had finished.

"Perhaps I can answer your question now," said Angus. He looked about and saw that he had our attention. "As a definition, forgiveness is the deliberate untying of the strands that bind us to a particular offense. It is a personal decision that often requires time, reflection, and above all, willingness. Reconciliation, on the other hand, involves more than one party. One can forgive another and still not be able to reconcile. For example, death can intervene, or one party may decide to have nothing to do with the other for fear of further harm. Reconciliation in both cases becomes impossible."

I noted that Angus had one of those voices that was clear and articulate, even when set against the background noise of several people speaking at once.

He continued. "For what it's worth, the act of forgiving others is often cited as the key to a peaceful life. In my opinion, no single datum or precept is sufficient to encompass all of existence, and the decision *not* to forgive can be just as helpful."

He was interrupted by plates being whisked away and wine being poured.

Angus continued. "When I was in the ring, receiving a particularly vicious jab would make my blood boil, and I

399

would nurture and preserve that hurt to win the bout. Unwillingness to forgive was a most effective attitude. When I found myself acting that way outside the ring, such conduct proved unhelpful. By not forgiving, I found myself stuck in the past, and since the past didn't work out that well based on the need for forgiveness in the first place, the future looked more dire and less hopeful than it actually was."

I said, "Thank you for that. Did you ever forgive Stanley?"

Gales of laughter floated toward us from the far end. When the mirth had subsided, the doctor said, "Stanley did knock me out with a wine bottle, but a closer inspection of the circumstances showed his action blameless. I was at fault. I had deliberately given him several painful thrashings. On balance, we both gave as good as we got. Forgiveness becomes unnecessary in those instances. It is when there is an asymmetry, such as between unequal forces, or when one cannot respond in kind, that forgiveness can become an issue."

"You knew Stanley from before?" asked Malcolm.

"Yes. Certain people move in and out of our lives in unexpected ways. For instance, Lord Bromley is sitting at this table in this house. On the surface that would seem so unlikely as to be impossible, and yet here he is. Such things defy an easy explanation. What do you say to that, your lordship?"

My father looked sour and said, "Once all pertinent information is available, perhaps such things are not so difficult to understand."

We were interrupted by the next course of jellied consommé with a dab of crème fraîche served in small, white bowls on ice. Bruni's end of the table seemed far livelier than mine, with occasional hoots of laughter bubbling up from time to time. My end had a peculiar rhythm of eating in silence, followed by speech.

400

Angus started in again. "Even when we think we have all the information, we may not understand what has occurred. There can be hidden factors. The patient presents X that comes from Y, but it is Z, hidden beneath Y, that we must discover to resolve the matter fully. Sometimes we simply have no idea what the cause is."

"How often do you find that to be the case?" asked Hugo. They were the first words he had spoken aloud to anyone at the table.

"Medically speaking, in far more instances than one might think. Take the case of Mr. A. C. Peckover of London. On November 3, 1926, he awakened to find himself struck blind. He was taken to hospital. Coincidentally, his father was struck blind on the same day and was even transported to the same hospital. Both events occurred in different locations. What was the connection, let alone the cause? We don't know. Medicine is as much a human practice as a scientific one, and such inexplicable events happen from time to time. They make one wonder what exactly is going on? Science holds many answers but not all. Where do the others lie? If not in science, where?"

The next course was grilled salmon with a dollop of mousseline sauce. It was crunchy on the outside with a delicious delicate middle.

Hugo seemed to enjoy what he was eating. He was the first to finish and asked the doctor, "Regarding your question, are you serious about receiving an answer?"

"I assure you I am."

"Science has many answers," said Hugo, "but life is often more complex than we envisage. What commands our attention is not when everything goes according to plan, but when it doesn't, and the world no longer makes sense. We

401

don't want to know the reason scientifically. We want to know at a deeper level that means something to us. One can eat so many grams of protein, and science says we'll survive on that amount. What's missing from such a statement is the enjoyment factor, a concept we all can grasp instinctively. For instance, this salmon is utterly marvelous. It not only feeds the body but feeds the soul; and because it does, I wish to say the following:

"My dear Bromley, I'm heartily sorry that I didn't provide you with what I said I would. It's not that I didn't try. It's that I didn't succeed. The landscape changed. Perhaps it will change again. Both of us will be grandparents, which adds yet another factor. This dinner is hardly the place to say this, but it was always my intention that you would be successful in your quest. What I objected to most strongly was that you coerced me to do what I would have gladly done had you simply asked. In essence, that is my beef with you."

This last phrase was spoken into a pocket of silence. All eyes turned toward my end of the table and to my father.

My father sat back in his chair. At last, he nodded. "I was stupid. I let my obsession set aside everything, including friendship. I awoke one morning realizing that the time left to me was short. Soon, there would be no 'eventually.' That thought terrified me utterly, and I acted out of desperation, not sense. I do apologize for my conduct. It was atrocious. I was not myself."

Hugo looked at my father for a long moment and then nodded. "Apology accepted."

I dared not utter a word, lest I break the spell, but such moments cannot last. Shortly after, Stanley entered with a single envelope placed in the center of a silver tray. He stood with it until he had all our attention.

Having done so, he said, "I apologize for this interruption. Many years ago, and shortly before she passed, her ladyship gave me a series of instructions. The first was to deliver a particular letter. That task I completed not long ago. The second was to deliver this sealed envelope to Lord Bromley. Her ladyship's instructions were quite specific in that regard. It was to be given to him at my discretion on the last night of his visit and in front of witnesses. Further, that my possession of this letter was not to be revealed for any reason until the opportunity to deliver it presented itself. Lastly, that his lordship read it immediately upon receipt."

Stanley walked over to my father and offered him the letter. It might have been a poisonous snake the way my father looked at it. He hesitated. After several long moments, he reached out and took it from the tray.

My father held it in his hands as Stanley said, "I personally watched her ladyship write that letter and seal it. I can also swear that I have no knowledge of its contents. Having delivered it to you, my task is done. The rest is up to you."

Stanley handed the silver tray to one of the footmen and went back to his station by the Chinese screen in front of the kitchen entrance. He showed no emotion and looked into the far distance.

80

I watched my father as he held Alice's unopened letter in his hand. Perhaps he was debating whether to read it at all.

Hugo sensed that as well. "Open it, my friend. None of us will interrupt you. Take all the time you need."

In the silence, I overheard Elsa whisper to Bruni, "I love this place. It never stops."

My father finally nodded. Everyone in the room watched him tear open the envelope and pull out several handwritten sheets of paper. I recognized Alice's handwriting. At first, he simply read. After a time, he squirmed slightly and turned pale. By the end, his face was gray, and the doctor, sitting beside him, was concerned.

As he folded the letter and placed it back in the envelope, there was a muffled thud as something struck the double doors behind me with force. The sound in that silent room was loud and unexpected. Everyone jumped, including me.

I turned to look behind me, and then at my father, who had risen from his chair. Another loud blow struck the doors, and they swung open, revealing only the darkness of the unlit drawing room beyond. I stared into the blackness, disoriented and alarmed by its unnaturalness until ever so slowly, the white bulk of that miscreant, Robert the Bruce, took shape. He moved into the light with the stealth and quiet of a hooded cobra. I heard a choking cough and turned to see my father claw at his throat. He staggered, turned in my direction, and fell forward.

I watched the bridge of his nose strike the table edge and his forehead smack the rim of his plate. His head snapped back as the half-finished salmon with mousseline sauce was catapulted a foot in the air before my father disappeared beneath the table, and the plate came down on top of him. Everyone began to move and speak at once.

Robert snapped out of his trance and lunged toward my father, as did Angus. Both collided with a solid thud. Angus was knocked sideways as Robert disappeared underneath the table. I moved to help but noticed the letter my father had dropped on the carpet. I picked it up as the escaping Robert struck my legs and knocked me over. Robert held the half-eaten piece of salmon in his jaws as he vanished into the black of the drawing room, having never uttered a sound. I lay on my back and turned. The face of my father was a foot away. He didn't look at me directly but at something else. It took me a long moment to realize that he was dead.

81

Order was restored in a remarkably short time. My father's body was trundled up to his room by several staff, with the doctor leading the way. The bits of scattered food were swept up, his place at the table removed, and his chair placed against the wall. It was as if one moment he was there and the next, he had never existed. Other than the letter in my breast pocket, all evidence of his passing had been erased from view.

I considered halting the dinner, but my guests were hungry, as was I. The table remained quiet as we waited for the next course to be served. Stanley, too, had disappeared, perhaps advising the doctor on the procedures and protocols that were required should my father's death be confirmed. Whispered conversations overheard in snippets indicated that others entertained the idea that my father might have survived this latest episode. I was quite sure he hadn't. I said as much to Hugo.

Hugo nodded. "We should await confirmation from the doctor. That is all any of us can do at this point."

I looked up to see Bruni watching me. I gave her a half smile to indicate that I feared the worst but that personally, I was fine. She nodded and whispered to Johnny. The next course was filet mignon served with a fine Lafite. I tried to get into the mood, but that proved difficult. I wanted to go off by myself to read the letter that precipitated my father's attack and likely his death, but I was the host of this gathering.

I turned to Hugo. "What happens if he's passed on?"

"We bury him. I suppose he left instructions. Malcolm?"

Malcolm was picking at his food and hesitated before saying, "He did. His body will be shipped back to England. He is to be buried in the family crypt."

"I see," said Hugo. "With no indications of foul play, I imagine that such an evolution will be relatively routine. I take it you are the executor. Any surprises we should know about?".

Malcolm shifted in his chair. "I'm not sure. It's possible that amendments have been made, or codicils added, of which I am unaware. Angus will likely know."

At those words, the doctor entered through the drawing room and sat down next to me. He carefully placed his napkin on his lap. "Your father has died," he said softly. "I am sorry to be the one to tell you."

I whispered, "Thank you, Angus. I'm sure you did everything you could. I'll make the announcement now."

I rose from my chair and looked around the table. "The doctor has informed me that my father is deceased. In death, he has embarked on that particular journey that we all must undertake at some point. His death came quickly. It was not prolonged and filled with pain. We should be thankful for that.

"Given what has happened, I could put an end to this dinner to mark the moment, but doing so I feel would be unsatisfactory on several levels, and so I won't. Not everyone at this table knew him well, and I must count myself among them. Others knew him better. For now, I wish for you to raise your glasses and toast his farewell, wherever he might be and whatever his journey. If you have words to say to mark his passing, I invite you to stand during the course of this dinner and say them. I think that would be more appropriate than simply dispersing. For my part, I wish him well. Death is as much a beginning as an end. Please raise your glasses with me to one who has departed and to new beginnings, for him and for us all."

All rose and toasted my father's passing.

Once we were seated, the next course of glazed roast duckling slices with applesauce followed. Small amounts of mashed potatoes along with creamed carrots accompanied it. A superb chardonnay was poured, and between all four, my attention shifted away from the dark happenings of the last hour and the letter that felt like a weight above my heart.

I looked up to see my mother gazing at me from her end. It was hard to know what she was thinking. I really didn't know her that well, but enough perhaps to understand that she wished on me the strength these times required. I nodded and smiled back. I thought it would be wonderful to talk with her as we had done upstairs. I'd never felt as close to her as I had then. I wondered how my father's passing might have affected her.

At the end of the course, Malcolm stood and addressed the table. He towered over us before he cleared his throat and said, "I think I knew his lordship well but not as well as some. I have also known many of you, with a few exceptions, for some time. I appreciate your company now. I feel in need of it."

He looked around and continued.

"On the moors of Scotland, certain outcroppings, the tops of hills, and perhaps an ancient cairn beside a trail are landmarks that let us know where we are, where we've been, and which path will lead to where. When someone whom we have known passes, it's as if such a landmark has disappeared.

The landscape we had enjoyed is irrevocably changed, and we feel disoriented. I have felt that way. I feel that way now."

He paused.

"Lord Bromley may not have always acted in a manner that might be considered nice or even civilized, but act he did, and always according to what he thought best. He only cared about the opinion of a single person. She was his point of orientation, and yet a point of extraordinary blindness. Many have no such person in their lives, yet he did.

"His disregard for most everyone else was legendary. He stalked the Earth like it was his own, and because he thought so, it responded as if it were. I cannot live that way, but I admire those that can. With his passing, an era passes, too. He was a most difficult man, but I will miss him. He did what I could not, and because he could do such things, he earned both my respect and admiration.

"Death found him and ended him, or so it seems. Alice died years ago, and yet her spirit is still with us. I think she took him in the end. Was it revenge, or someone calling their lover home at last? I cannot tell you which. Now, both are gone. Perhaps with his passing, there will be peace between them and in their hearts. I hope so. Let us toast to that peace: to peace between them and between us all."

We raised our glasses and drank. Other small courses followed, one upon another. Small balls of pale lime sorbet had been laid before us when Hugo rose at his place.

He looked around the table.

"I have something to say about that man upstairs. The one who was here not long ago, the one who sat at this table. Some men are simply bad. They cast aside what should be kept, while holding onto things they shouldn't. They betray their friends, disregard those that might support them, and

409

generally ride roughshod over anyone that they deem to be of little use. They are incredibly thick-headed and equally thick-skinned. One grows fed up with them, and yet ..."

Hugo paused.

"It is that 'and yet' that forces us to confront a simple truth. Without such men, and Bromley was such a man, we would either not be here or not enjoying those things today that make our hearts sing. Such men do great good, but at tremendous cost.

"If not for Bromley, I would not be among you. My daughter would be dead, my wife would be a widow. Percy would not exist. Malcolm would be unemployed. Angus would be bored. Mary would not know happiness. Anne would not know John. John would not know Anne. Even Mrs. Leland would have missed the genius in her daughter, and her daughter would not have had a chance to shine—all because that man who lies dead upstairs failed to cause us trouble.

"I find this utterly unacceptable, irritating to the extreme, yet wonderfully appropriate. I was his friend. He wasn't always mine. He was a paradox. It is fitting that we mourn his passing. It is also fitting that we accept and embrace a future without him, although like his former spouse, his absence from our lives may be premature. We'll have to see. Please join me in drinking a toast to those who leave us in a better place for having troubled us. I, too, will miss him."

We all stood. While we were finishing the toast, Stanley entered and stepped toward me. He motioned me away from the table as everyone sat back down. He said softly, "Between the doctor and myself, all the necessary arrangements have been made. Your father's body will be transported to the funeral home in town. They should be here shortly to collect it. You needn't concern yourself with these matters now. Coffee and brandy should be served as usual. I suggest that you and I have a word in private before you retire. I will make myself available. Dagmar may also wish to say something, depending on the lateness of the hour. All the staff wish to express to you our deepest sympathies."

"Thank you, Stanley. We will talk tonight and ... thank you for your presence. It has been most stabilizing."

Stanley nodded and glided away. I looked at Bruni, who was watching me from the far end. I nodded. She stood and said, "Thank you all for your presence and for dining with us this night. I took great comfort in being surrounded by all of you at this time. That I needed that comfort was a surprise to me, and I am most grateful to you all for having provided it. Coffee will be served in the drawing room and brandy in the library. Please see me before you retire. I wish to thank each of you personally."

82

I moved to the bar in the library. Johnny was to my right. He poured a splash of brandy in a snifter and handed it to me.

"I wish there was something I could say, but I don't know how I feel at this moment. Perhaps it's the same with you?"

I turned to him. "It is. I don't know what to think either. His absence changes everything and nothing. Perhaps tomorrow I'll feel differently and know better."

"Me, too," said Johnny. "I wonder if that letter was the surprise that Dagmar had in mind?"

"Stanley wishes to have a word with me later this evening. I'll ask him."

I looked around the quiet room. Other than Johnny and I, who spoke softly, the other gentlemen present were silent, lost in their thoughts. They stood in a group by the fireplace, sipping on brandy or whiskey.

Angus stepped away from them, cleared his throat to get our attention. "I'm more comfortable speaking in male company, otherwise I would have stood up earlier. I wish to say a few words and ask one question. Would that be permissible now?"

He looked at me. I nodded. "By all means, Angus. Please do."

"Thank you. Allow me to express my deepest sympathies. Your father was unique. I didn't always like him. Frankly, I think that was true for most who knew him. He was difficult, fiercely independent, and yet he had a charm that dispelled our dislikes as often as he created them. He was also my patient, and that made for contentious moments. Several times, I thought I might be dismissed, and several times, I was determined to be rid of him myself. On each of those occasions, he would sit me down and speak with me. By the time he'd finished, I would sigh, having agreed one more time to carry on. Looking after him was never boring or uninteresting, and that may be why I continued."

Angus took a sip of his whiskey and paused before saying, "When a patient dies under one's care, one must make a survey of the course of treatment, scrutinize the decisions that were made, and review how the patient responded, all in an effort to discover if there were further avenues that could have been explored, or different approaches undertaken. I have looked at his history most carefully in my mind, and I doubt there was more that I could have done.

"His death was both expected and unexpected. In the end, his heart gave out. What precipitated that failure was either his reaction to the contents of the letter he received from his former spouse, or the untimely entrance of that dog. Whichever it was, or whether a combination of the two, I do not know. I am curious about that letter. He didn't have it on him. I would most certainly like to read it, and not merely for clinical reasons. Their relationship was always fascinating to me. Can anyone tell me what became of that letter?"

My guests shrugged their shoulders, except Johnny and Angus. I was quite sure they suspected that I had picked it up.

"I have it," I said into the silence that followed. "I retrieved it after he fell and have been debating what to do with it. The letter wasn't addressed to me, nonetheless we all witnessed his death. Given that, I think that I should read it aloud so all may hear what Alice had to say and that we might gain an understanding of what happened this evening. Whatever it reveals, knowing is better than being left with only the trauma of watching him die before our eyes. Do you agree?"

Everyone voiced their agreement.

I rang for Stanley. When he arrived, I told him what I had in mind. I asked that he join us as well. Stanley nodded and slipped out to gather the ladies and escort them to the library.

———————————

83

T he ladies accompanied by Stanley arrived and seated themselves in the available chairs while the men stood beside them.

Bruni whispered to me before she took a seat, "You were quick. I never saw you pick it up."

"I was bowled over by Robert as I did so. Where is he, by the way?"

"He's in the corner, over there behind Maw. She found him beneath the sofa in the drawing room, licking the carpet."

"Typical. The salmon was exquisite, so I'm not surprised."

She squeezed my hand. When the library quieted down, I invited Stanley to expand on what he knew about the letter before I read it aloud.

Stanley stood in front of the fireplace and said, "Ladies and gentlemen, please allow me to give you some context. I should warn you that what I say will likely stretch your credulity, and for that I must apologize.

"Her ladyship occasionally had visions. Some of you may be aware that she had them. They did not come while she slept, but rather when she was awake, and not all of them were about the future. The Sight, as she called it, was not only sporadic and unpredictable, but many times revealed only insignificant details when it came.

"For instance, she was shown a room in late afternoon that she had never seen before. The point of focus was some dust on a shelf beside a knickknack. In another, she heard a person speaking but was only able to perceive the lower half of their legs and their shoes. Her visions, she told me, had a peculiar logic, but not one that she could always follow.

"She had false visions and real ones. Real visions drained and tired her, often for several days. The more potent the vision, the greater the fatigue. She never understood what caused them, or why, or even what they meant on several occasions. She knew only that they happened to her and were important in some way. They were an affliction as much as a gift. This she told me.

"The day she wrote that letter, she rang for me from her study and invited me to sit with her. She had begun the letter I delivered tonight but hadn't finished it. It lay upon her desk with her fountain pen beside it."

Stanley pulled out a small notebook covered in dark blue leather and consulted it.

"She thanked me for my promptness and said, 'I've had a vision. I don't know what to make of it other than that I've had one. The seeing has worn me out, but I think it was significant. My first husband will return to this house at some point. I don't know when. I only know that he will. I've been writing a letter to him. I would like to finish it and seal it with you beside me. I wish you here, not only to be a witness to my having done so, but to explain to you how important these letters are. I've had right visions and wrong ones. This last I believe to be true, but the seer never knows for sure, other than by their strength, and even then, they might not come to pass. The future changes from time to time. Perhaps it is the choices that we make, or what others decide. If I am wrong, I would rather not have these see the light of day. If I am right, then … we will see. I should mention that I saw you there as well, and for that reason, I will entrust these to your care. The one to Percy you must give to him after he is twenty-five years old, and when the two of you are alone. He will have a decision to make, and he must read my letter by himself. The other, this one, is quite different. It must be delivered in front of several witnesses on the last night of his stay.' "

Stanley looked up. "She wrote for some time while I noted down precisely her words and her instructions. When she had finished, she sealed both letters and placed them to the side. She sat back looking at me and said, 'I know this is a lot to ask, given that it may be many years before you can complete these tasks. I'll be dead by then, and so you must be the one to deliver them. I have complete trust in you, but these are different. They are solemn documents. *Solemn* is a strange word to use, but that is what they are. They will require your utmost attention, not only to deliver them, but after, as you shall see.'

"She remained quiet for a time, lost in her thoughts, before she said, 'I know you well enough to be certain that you will attempt to read them at some point, but this last one you cannot. I don't wish to make an issue of it, but you mustn't. It's for your own good. After it has been delivered, you can, of course, but not before. Do I have your promise, Stanley, to do the things I've asked?'

"It was a strange moment for me. She rarely used my name when she would make me promise to do something important for her. That time she did, and with a peculiar emphasis. I recall being handed those letters. I read the one to Percy. I didn't read the second. Each time I thought to do so, I remembered that she had spoken my name in such a way that made me think again. Whether it was a trick that she had learned or a warning, I was never sure, and because I wasn't,

417

I never did. That is all I have to say. Thank you for your attention and for allowing me to speak."

He put away his notebook and moved to the side. He stood by the door, his face unreadable. I thought I detected a hint of curiosity for what was to follow. I took his place in front of the fireplace and pulled out the letter from Alice to my father.

84

Surprised to hear from me? I would be. I died years ago, yet here I am. Do you wonder if the dead are ever really dead? Conversely, I might ask, are the living ever really alive? Perhaps life and death are not so different, and it's all a matter of degrees. One can be alive and dead. One can be dead but very much alive. Like now. How very strange it is.

I cannot tell you how long it's been since last we saw each other. I see you in my mind's eye. I know what you're doing right now. You're reading this. You're wearing white tie and tails at a fine dinner, sitting next to Percy. Stanley stands by the Chinese screen, watching you. I don't know the date, other than you look much older, and that a doctor sits beside you. The picture is so clear to me, I could almost reach out and touch you, but I can't. You are not there ... not yet.

Visions are like that. They are moments out of sequence—temporal paradoxes that are disturbing. They make me anxious—not always from what I see, but from what I don't. I see what will happen, but not the when; or I see a point in time, but not the substance. I find myself yearning, craving to know more, and thus I am drawn inexorably into a labyrinth from which I can't escape. I can never know how it ends, and so I have no peace.

Enough about me; we have unpleasantness to tackle. You hate unpleasantness. I'm no great friend of it, either, but this can't keep.

Seeing where you are, and what you're doing, I have a bone to pick with you—two bones in fact—and one last issue, the one that hurts the most. I think you know what that is.

Squirm all you like, but squirming won't change what you have set in motion.

There were only two things I ever asked of you after we reconciled—only two, and you swore you would uphold them until the day you died. Shall I remind you of that perfect day, and the promises we made each other as we looked over that shifting blue-gray sea to the horizon far beyond?

The first was that you would never return to this house, and yet here you are. How did you manage that? You needn't answer. I know. You forced your way. It's what you do.

The second promise was to never involve Percy in your gambling or your schemes. This you swore to me upon that perfect day.

Now both your pledges lie broken at your feet. Did you think I wouldn't find out?

But those were only words—promises that you made. There is that one unforgiveable act you did, and I'm so enraged. How could you, after all we had and did together?

I had to stop and rest. I was getting too upset, and that is bad for me right now.

It's not only you I'm mad at, I'm mad at both of us.

I loved and trusted you! It grieves me to think of all we had, and that it's gone. Not once but twice! But those tragedies did not shatter my heart completely nor cause my soul to break. What you did sealed both our fates.

It was that copy that you managed to put into my hands. You know the one I mean. The sections I needed most, you removed. You did that ... knowing what would follow. All else I can forgive, but never that, and so I solemnly declare the following should my curse not be lifted:

What is mine shall be yours.

I will make one last attempt, and should I succeed, I will stay my hand, but should I fail, know that my torment and all its dark horrors will be yours. You will be locked away, underground, without light, suspended halfway between life and death.

By reading this letter at this time and in this way, know that what I write is real.

By breaking your oath to never set foot in this house, realize the magnitude of the power that I have called down upon you.

There are also twelve at the table with you who will know what you did and what will happen to you, and that includes your son.

My fate is sealed now and having read this, so is yours.

I will see you soon. I will.

— ALICE

85

We sighed as one like the tragic cries of some ancient Greek chorus echoing up the years. There were no words that could be said. Not yet.

Silence followed for a time until the library door opened, and Stanley announced that jasmine tea would be served, and that by inhaling the fragrance and sipping on occasion, we might feel partially restored.

I took a cup from Simon. It was small and white, almost Japanese. The yellow tea steamed. I inhaled the aroma and felt a calm. The taste was not quite bitter but having sipped it, I did feel more grounded. Bruni came up beside me.

She whispered, "Good Heavens! Alice certainly didn't mess around. Not even I could have come up with that! What an extraordinary woman! I wish I'd met her."

"Alice was in a league of her own. And my father ... what am I to say about him?"

"Later tonight we might discuss it, but not now. Let's work the room. I will start at the far end, and you, the opposite. Who knows what our guests are really feeling? Suppressed joy is what I'm getting. I could be wrong. We'll meet in the middle and compare notes."

"That's a smart idea. Thank you."

"You're welcome. Right now, we need to salvage what's left of the evening. I refuse to allow our first big bash to be anything but a roaring success."

I smiled at her. "Your mom is likely ecstatic and will count it among her most memorable evenings ever, so you have at least one who will agree. Let's find out." We kissed, and I went up to John Sr. and Anne who were standing to the side.

"Are both of you all right?"

"As well as can be expected," said Anne. "And speaking of unexpected: dear Alice. Dear, *dear* Alice, I just love that woman. Beneath all that elegance, is—was—who knows which it is—something of great quality and extraordinary strength. She had tremendous courage. I feel proud to have known her. I don't wish to cause you pain, Percy. He was your father, after all. There are few who deserve such a fate, but he was one. I'm happy to be rid of him. Speaking for myself, I say we break out the good stuff. It's time to dance on some tables. John?"

John smiled. "I quite agree. I'm relieved that he is gone. The messes he created can now be cleaned up once and for all, and without him, it will be much easier. Even the house seems happier ... calmer, and more joyous. Can you feel it?"

"Yes, I can," said Anne.

I looked at her. "Anne, what would you consider to be the good stuff?"

"Ask Stanley. He'll know."

"Of course."

And so I did.

Stanley smiled broadly. "Well, I do have this most unusual brandy that might suit."

"Please tell me it's not from Napoleon's cellar."

"Not his. Josephine's."

"Oh God. Well, it seems I may have misread the sentiments of my guests. Many seem in a celebratory mood.

423

You might as well bring up a bottle or two. Do you think we have enough?"

"It's very strong. The two bottles we have should do it."

"Okay then. I'll catch you before you retire."

"I'm looking forward to it." Stanley looked about before saying, "Make sure Cobb has a drop and don't be surprised if he starts singing. It's ghastly, but worth a listen. I'll return momentarily."

Before I moved on to Bonnie and Angus, I told John and Anne that, per their request, a very suitable something would be served shortly. Bonnie and Angus were deep in conversation.

"If I might have a moment?" I asked.

They looked at me.

"I have one question: Are we feeling tears of sorrow or tears of joy tonight?"

"Joy!" they said in unison.

"In that case, I have just the thing. Stanley will be around with what I understand is brandy from the cellar of Malmaison or thereabouts."

"Josephine's house near Paris?" asked Angus.

"That would be the one."

"Well, count me in. Bonnie, dear, would you care to raise a glass with me?"

"Only if it's more than one, Angus."

"Of course. What was I thinking?"

"Sign us up, Percy," said Bonnie. "I am sorry about your father. I really am, but there's an old saying I always keep in mind—rocky start, rollicking finish. The night's still young and so are we. If you're feeling blue, come join us. If you're feeling relieved, come join us. If you're not sure which it is, come join us. You'll soon discover which it is, and I think the word *better* will cover it. We'll be here."

"Thank you both very much. I do appreciate it."

I turned to Malcolm, who was staring at his drink.

"How're you feeling, Malcolm?"

"Well ... ah ... um ... like an accountant who's lost his best client. It's a peculiar mixture of relief and sadness. His lordship really was a pain, but he paid very well. The problem I find is when the client's a pain and *doesn't* pay well. Then one's simply elated, and of course you feel bad for feeling that way. I think I'm in between."

"Is that good?"

"Not bad, all told. I could go either way. I'm waiting to find out."

"I see. To help you with that, Stanley is bringing out some of the good stuff. It will be with you shortly: a rare brandy that Josephine drank when Napoleon was off traipsing about the rest of Europe."

"Well, the thought of that makes me feel a great deal better. Thank you for asking how I'm doing. The only one who ever did that was Alice. I'm sorry about your father. And speaking about Alice, she sure had a way about her, didn't she? Do you really think she ... ah ... cursed him and has him suspended in some limbo? Can she do that?"

"Malcolm, I have no idea, but given the circumstances, and what happened this evening, I wouldn't count it out. Not by a long shot."

"I know. I know. It's that possibility that keeps rattling around in my head. She really was an extraordinary woman. So very, *very* strong!"

"Very."

Johnny came up beside me with a snifter of brandy. "Try it. I think Hugo and I were had. It's either that, or Josephine really knew where to shop. This is a superb drop, and it's going fast."

I turned around. All my guests were mobbing Stanley and Simon.

"Good God!" I said, "This will get out of hand rather quickly."

"Oh yes," said Johnny. "It's all those pent-up spirits I've been sensing since that boisterous   lunch. This is going to be one for the books, I think."

"I think so, too. Bruni will be pleased. Angus sings, by the way."

"Really? I didn't know that. Well, when we hear his voice, we'll know the party has finally started. Care for a cigar?"

86

H ugo was swirling his brandy. I asked him, "Which is better? Napoleon's or Josephine's?"

He looked at me. "This one. Absolutely, this one."

"Excellent. How are you doing, if I may ask?"

"I am fine."

"I'm glad of that."

"I've been thinking about your father. Others will celebrate his passing. Instead, I give him my thanks. That being said, I doubt, we've heard the last of him ... or her, and that is of interest to me. Now, if you get me a cigar, I will have that drink with you."

"I will find one."

"Then be quick about it." He chuckled. "You'll need a thick skin where I'm concerned, Percy, so get used to it. I'll be waiting."

I went in search of the humidor and saw Elsa speaking with my mom. It seemed an unlikely association, but they looked like they were enjoying each other's company.

Elsa saw me. "There you are, Percy. I missed talking with you tonight, but I suppose that couldn't be helped. You are forgiven. I am also sorry about your father, although not completely. On another subject, I simply love your mother. We have far more in common than I expected. Isn't that right, Mary?"

My mother smiled. "Quite right, Elsa. Given half a chance, we'd rule the world."

We all laughed. I said, "I wanted to check up on you two, but you seem to be doing fine. I have to get a cigar for Hugo."

"Some advice, Percy," said Elsa. "The key to my husband is to do what he wants as quickly as you can but always kick him when you do. That way he will learn to temper his demands. That takes some time, but we have a wonderful marriage as a result."

"Oh, yes? Well, I suppose it's lucky that I'm not married to him."

"He's your father-in-law, Percy, or soon will be. It's much the same. By the way, Mary, we must discuss the wedding. I have some thoughts. I'm sure you do as well."

I left them to it.

As I searched for the humidor, a fine baritone voice broke out above the hum and burble of conversation. It sang an old English folk song with vigor, a cappella, and I knew that the party had officially begun. Johnny was staring at Angus in amazement. I stood next to him.

"You know, he's not bad," said Johnny, turning to me. "He and Jimmy Buckley ought to get together."

"Who's Jimmy Buckley?" asked Bruni as she joined us.

"An ex-handyman that Percy and I helped become an opera star. It's a long story and not suitable at this time."

"I see," said Bruni. "Perhaps later then. I must say this party is finally coming together. I think we may have actually pulled it off. Now, all we need is some music. Percy?"

87

After a quick consultation with Stanley, the drawing
room furniture was moved to the side, the carpet
taken up, and a dance floor prepared. While the
furniture was being rearranged, I managed to locate
the humidor in the library and pocketed two cigars.

Shortly after, I heard Burt Bacharach on the sound system
in the drawing room. Bruni announced that the party was
moving down the hall. I was about to speak to Hugo when
Bruni grabbed my arm and Elsa grabbed her husband's. The
ladies wanted to dance. We wisely agreed.

ABBA replaced Burt, only to be replaced by the Rolling
Stones. The volume was cranked to eight and then to nine as
the dancing went into high gear. My guests spiraled and
twisted about as couples were cut in on with abandon.
Everyone danced with everyone. I think I actually danced
with Angus for a moment, before Bruni replaced me with
Maw and got me to herself. She whispered that it might be
better if the doctor got to know Maw a bit better and vice versa,
but Johnny cut in on me before I could answer, and Bruni was
whisked away.

In a brief pause I managed to catch Stanley's eye, and we
headed for his office. I doubted either of us would be missed.
Dagmar had already retired before we passed through the
kitchen, yet the work of washing up and putting away was still
in full swing.

Stanley observed it for a few moments and nodded in satisfaction. He closed the door to his office, and we sat down. The noise from the music and the clatter of dishes faded away.

I looked at Stanley across the desk. "Stan, I do believe we survived."

"Percy, we did, and the house seems to be in a celebratory mood."

"It does. I'm not sure of the propriety of having an exuberant bash the same night as my father's death, but there it is."

"I understand, but considering the alternative, a party is better. Don't you think?"

"I do. There are still a few financial matters to sort out, but I think they will be put to rest before too long."

"Without your father's presence, I should think that will be fairly simple. Are you distressed that he's gone?"

"I suppose I am. It was both surprising and shocking to me."

"It was surprising, but not unanticipated. I kept my word to her ladyship, but doing so didn't mean that what she wrote was a complete surprise."

"I wondered about that."

"Sometimes it's necessary to know what's going on in spite of orders to the contrary. Her ladyship was very clear in regards my not reading what she wrote, but she didn't say that Dagmar couldn't, at least not specifically. I turned the letter over to Dagmar unopened, with the understanding that she do whatever she felt necessary and appropriate, based upon its contents. Dagmar never told me what it said. When we heard about your father's pending arrival, she reviewed the letter once again, and then made sure that events played out as intended."

"Dare I ask how she did that?"

"She controlled the menu and was able to create an atmosphere that was suitable: languid, but not too languid— excited, but not too excited. She also made sure that Cobb and your father were at the dinner tonight, white tie. The rest was up to her ladyship."

"Were you surprised by tonight's events?"

"I was, and more than once. Dagmar and I discussed this evening after I learned of his pending arrival. She warned me that your father might survive the dinner, but on the other hand, he might not. She suggested I be prepared for either eventuality. I took her advice and then waited to see what would happen. Standing there looking at him as he read her letter was like watching the slow turning of the handle of a jack-in-the-box. I didn't know what to expect and then bang. I watched him die and said to myself, 'She got him. Good.' I suppose that's rather crude, but that is what I thought."

"I didn't know what to think. I still don't, at least not fully."

"Yours was and is a more complicated relationship, and uncertainty as to what to feel *is* to be expected. Given time it will become clearer."

"It is my hope. You mentioned that you were surprised more than once."

"I was. The second surprise came while you were reading. They had been seeing each other intimately for years! I had no idea that was happening, although your father's ultimatum had me thinking along those lines. To me, it spoke of a monumental blindness on my part. How could I not know?"

"It isn't hard to understand. She played on many levels. If she chose to hide what she was doing when she was away, how could you have known, and even if you did, what then?"

"My thoughts exactly. And that leads me to the third

431

surprise of the evening, but before I tell you, I realized after hearing her letter that I wasn't the only one who underestimated her abilities. Her former husband did as well. Only an expert would have known that there were missing portions, but her ladyship really was such an expert. She must have realized what he'd done, and then suppressed all the turmoil she must have felt. I don't know when she found out, but obviously she considered her response carefully and made her preparations."

"Yes, the deliberateness of it shocked me."

"It was calculated and, of course, dramatic, but that was her style. Watching all of this play out over the years was as fascinating to me as observing a chess match between two grand masters. I followed every move as best I could. When her ladyship died, I thought that she had lost. For years I believed that, and then tonight, she pulls off a draw. It really was a surprise. It might even be construed as a victory given the odds against it."

"She certainly didn't lose, but I don't think I would go so far as to say she won. Based on the incidents with Sir Henry and myself, she's still trapped."

Stanley sighed. "You are correct. Still, the power and the force of what she did stuns me, and I do feel stunned. But that wasn't the biggest surprise for me tonight."

"What else could there possibly be, Stan?"

"It's odd, but I am free of her."

"Free of her?"

"I know that may sound strange, but it's true. I actually felt hurt when I learned of their reconciliation in that letter. She knew my feelings about your father, and knowing that, she hid what she was doing. There was no obligation for her to tell me, none at all, but there is such a thing as trust and friendship.

432

I think she knew that what she was doing was debatable, if not an outright mistake, but she couldn't face me, had she told me. That, too, was a choice she made. It's why she insisted I not read it. After you did, I felt a massive shift in my head. I stood about in shock, wondering what had occurred, and then I understood. The spell she had over my heart, if that is what it was, broke."

"That sounds wonderfully hopeful—is it?"

"It is more than hopeful. It's terrific!"

I recalled the cigars in my pocket and pulled them out.

"Stan, have a Cuban cigar, and I wouldn't refuse a drop of Hamish's stash to commemorate the moment. We have much to celebrate, even if we're a bit premature. We can always drink another round when the weekend has officially ended."

"I was about to suggest that myself, given how I feel, but with a fine Cuban cigar to accompany it, the moment is better than perfect. Allow me."

Two glasses of the truly good stuff were in each of our hands as Stanley raised his glass.

"To Hamish, to freedom, to enchantments, and to her ladyship, who made it all possible."

"To Hamish, to freedom, to enchantments, and to her ladyship, who made it all possible," I repeated.

We smoked and relished the brew. The combination was a small but no less extraordinary piece of heaven, as beautiful as a sunset and as profound as the very finest that human excellence could create.

When we had finished, I said, "That was momentous. Thank you, Stan."

"My pleasure. That brew really is sensational—and with the cigar … beyond description. But back to our discussion: I have a question. Do you think your father believed in the occult before he died?"

I considered his question.

"My father thought the occult a complete hoax at the beginning, at least according to the baroness. At the time he placed that abbreviated *Book of the Dead* into Alice's hands, I'm not so sure. He would have had to believe that removing certain sections would be damaging, or else why do such a thing at all?"

Stanley said, "We can't know why he did what he did. Perhaps he did it because he could. I'm sure he was a believer in the end. He lived in fear of what he'd done. I sensed that when he arrived. I also thought that it must have taken great courage to come here. Either that, or an extraordinary arrogance."

"Or desperation. Johnny commented that fear was where my father lived. Perhaps my father knew he hadn't heard the last of Alice and wished to dissuade her from what she had in mind. Maybe he realized that what he had done to her was reprehensible and wished to atone for it? Whatever it was it was, it galvanized him sufficiently to overcome any resistance to coming here."

"That may be, but a reconciliation, let alone absolution, wasn't going to happen with her. In the end, her ladyship ran out of time, and I suppose he did, too."

"I agree. Perhaps that happens to us all. Our endings catch us unprepared. I will speak with Dagmar in the morning. I'm quite sure Bruni and I will be staying on for a few more days. Dagmar wants to apprentice her when we are here."

"Dagmar mentioned that. They are an odd but most compatible mix. You and I have our friendship. Why shouldn't they have theirs? By the way, how did you resolve the matters between Bruni and yourself?"

"She told me about her past. The deaths of the nannies were not accidental—and with good reason, in my opinion. She'd told no one until now. Talking about what really happened seems to have released her, and me, too. Between the vision I had on that rock and her ministrations after, any doubts I had evaporated. Hers, too. We're joined, and that's a fact."

"I'm very glad to hear that. I should mention that Dagmar said that she had some thoughts about your visions. I will let her tell you. She thinks you might have a great gift, but that you will need a guide."

"A guide?"

"It's what she said, but what happened to you exactly? We didn't have the time for you to elaborate."

I told Stanley all that I experienced on the rock, including Bruni's story, and when I finished, he sipped his drink and thought about what I'd told him.

"Thank you for that, and excellent that you and Bruni managed to work out the issues between you. I am heartily glad. I should also reaffirm to you that whatever is said in this room remains here. Your fiancée has an inner hardness not unlike Dagmar's, or her ladyship's for that matter. In the meanwhile, the house has changed. You've changed."

"I have. The house and I are getting used to each other, and no small thanks to you. It feels like home now. I've also found a friend where I least expected."

"It's true. So much for knowing the future. I never saw it coming either. Now, one last puff and the tiniest of sips—I can't help it—and then we'll see how the world is dancing. What do you say, Percy?"

"Stan, that sounds terrific."

I awoke to an insistent knock on the door.

"Yes? Who is it?" I called out.

A voice answered, "Good Morning. It's eight o'clock. Breakfast is in an hour, and there is coffee outside the door."

"Thank you!"

Bruni stirred from under the covers and murmured, "Is that our coffee?"

"It is. I'll get it."

I got up, pulled the drapes, and opened our bedroom door. Sure enough, to the side was a tray with two mugs and a thermos. I picked it up and placed the tray on the table by the window.

Bruni sat up. "Tell me this isn't a much better way to wake up. Can you pour me some?"

"Of course, and yes, this is definitely a better arrangement. By the way, you looked beautiful last night. The party was wildly successful."

I handed her a mug. She sipped. "It was, but on a more somber note, will we have to do anything about your father's body?"

"I don't think so. Stanley said that all the necessary arrangements had been made. He will be shipped back to England. I don't know what's involved, but I'm quite sure that between Malcolm, Angus, and Stanley, they will have it figured out."

"I suppose we'll have to fly to London for the funeral."

"Yes, I think we'll have to. We should also set a date for our wedding."

"We must. After the funeral, we might want to visit the castle. Papa will be thrilled to show it off."

"I'm sure he'll want to. Let's start with some breakfast. Once I eat something, we can work out whatever we need to do, but only after."

"That would be perfect, and by the way, there's a meeting in the library between Papa and Mama, Bonnie, your mother, and Angus. I'll be there as well."

"The shares?"

"Yes."

"I hope the matter settles to everyone's satisfaction."

"It should, thanks to your mother and Bonnie. Poor Angus never knew what hit him."

"I'm not so sure of that. Likely it's going exactly the way he wants. My assessment of Dr. Angus Maxwell-Hughes has taken a serious upturn recently. I wouldn't underestimate him. Besides, he and Bonnie seem to be getting along. I'm sure you noticed."

"Yes, and I wasn't the only one. They do seem rather suited, and that's fine by me."

"I see. Well, let's get up and get going. Race you to the shower?"

Bruni, closest to the bathroom, won the race easily. While she showered, I looked in the closet for something to wear and thought about the end of the party after Stanley and I had spoken.

By the time I had rejoined my guests, the volume had been turned down and ballroom dancing had replaced the more modern arrangements. Bruni grabbed me, and we foxtrotted, waltzed, and on occasion merely swayed back and forth in time to the music. As our guests faded and made their way to bed, Bruni and I thanked each of them for the pleasure of their company, until only we remained. We took one more leisurely spin around the floor before heading off to our apartment. We had slept in each other's arms, and I had felt at peace.

Still feeling that calm, Bruni and I made our way to breakfast. As we passed into the drawing room, I noticed that the house seemed more at ease, the tensions less evident, and the darker undercurrents possibly more quiescent. Breakfast was also quiet, although Johnny, sitting beside me, looked a little worried.

He whispered, "Father wants to see me. You didn't happen to mention anything about that tab at 21, did you?"

"Frankly, I'd forgotten all about it, but now that you brought it up ..."

Johnny looked aghast.

"I never said a word," I whispered, "but I'm glad I can still rattle you on occasion. I think your father has a proposal for you."

"Really? You never told me about this."

"You were recovering from your excesses with Hugo. It would have added to your troubles."

"Troubles?"

"Troubles."

"What troubles?"

I had him at last, but I was mid-breakfast. I simply said, "Quite the opposite, so settle down."

"Well, I do feel a bit better now that you put it that way, and thank you for not taking advantage of me. You could have wound me up with no effort at all."

"I could have, and likely I'll regret that I didn't. Have a talk with him. A walk would be best. The library will be in use by almost everyone else as the disposition of the shares gets sorted out."

"You won't be presiding?"

"Thankfully, no. I'm going to speak with Dagmar."

"Interesting choice. I would keep an eye on that meeting. If all goes well, you will need to be available to lift that check from Hugo. He'll be in a good mood, and timing is everything in such matters."

"I'll keep an eye out. See you at lunch, and ... good luck."

"Good luck? Do you think I'll need it?"

I rose, nodded to everyone, blew Bruni a kiss, and made for the kitchen. Johnny looked suitably troubled.

439

89

D agmar was sitting at her table.

I asked her, "Is now a good time?"

"It is. I'm brewing some tea. It will be done shortly. Please sit."

"Thank you, Dagmar. Firstly, I want to express my gratitude. Without your help with the letter and your culinary skills, I'm not sure what would have happened this weekend. The only thing I'm certain of is that it wouldn't have turned out as well as it did."

"You are pleased, then?"

"Very much so. Are you?"

Dagmar nodded. "I am. Justice was served, and that is rare from what I've seen. It certainly took its time. Her ladyship had her say, and before twelve witnesses. Your father wronged her most severely. I apologize if that's not complimentary; I haven't asked you how you feel about him. Conflicted, is what I would imagine. Am I right?"

"Yes. I really didn't like him, although there were moments here and there when I must admit I did. My dislikes turned to likes and then back again."

"I'm sure he felt as topsy-turvy about you. No one is wholly bad, and of course, the opposite is true. Our intentions and what follows are often contrary, and that creates difficulties for us all. We mean well, yet the result is a stunning disaster. We act out of spite and the most wonderful thing happens. Time is what's required to gain the necessary perspective, and even then, more time may be needed. Now, I'm quite sure it's not your father that we should be discussing."

"Stanley mentioned that you said I needed a guide."

"Perhaps you do. I suspected that even before Stanley told me about your other experience. The tea is ready. Let us drink, and then I will speak."

Dagmar laid the service and prepared the tea. I sipped. It was soothing and most pleasant. After a time, she said, "There are stories of certain individuals who can travel places in their minds. Some have said they visited worlds different from this one. It is now in vogue to study ancient indigenous peoples and their beliefs. As a result, there are many recorded accounts, mostly from peoples of the North. Whether the stories they told were real, or simply exaggerated lies, we don't know. All we do know is what was written down by those who went in search of them.

"The majority of these reports form the source materials for shamanic studies, a field of great interest to her ladyship and myself. My interest was from the pharmacological side, rather than the mystical. You will find numerous texts on all aspects of the subject in the library, and voluminous notes written by both of us on related topics. Should this field be of interest, I think you will need a guide—not some hippie with long hair, and wampum beads, spouting new-age nonsense. I mean the real thing. Such people are extremely rare, but you will know them when you see them, and I wouldn't doubt that they will know you."

Dagmar looked at me critically.

"Perhaps you wanted me to say more about the details of what you saw and interpret them for you. I can't. I know a

441

great deal, but only along specific lines of research. I do not have your gift. You require someone who has the gift to teach you. For now, you must study what is available to you. Based on our rules for doing homework that we established years ago, we can talk more on this after you've put in some serious effort. Some of the answers are in that material. The others you must find elsewhere—that is if you wish to go further in that direction.

"On another matter, I will be teaching your fiancée some things in the kitchen. You should encourage her on this. Her mind goes a mile a minute. She must learn to use her hands to quiet it. The child might help, but I doubt it. What I will teach her will not solve her issues, but like you, it will give her the time to work out what she must. Stanley will direct you as to how to use the library. It's an extraordinary resource. Now, is there anything else?"

"Yes, you knew all this time what was in store for my father. How was that for you?"

"Difficult, but not too difficult. Keeping it from Stan was the hardest. Her ladyship gave your father plenty of room to avoid his fate. She didn't lure him, rather it was he who ran toward it. In the end, he did it to himself. Perhaps we all do that, believing that we don't. Do you have further questions?"

"I don't believe so, other than that I wish to give you my gracious and heartfelt thanks once again. Your meals were sensational."

I stood to hug her, and she rose as well.

"Well … I do appreciate your thanks. You are most considerate. To tell you the truth, I wouldn't have missed it, not for all the tea in China, and I imagine most of your guests feel the same. I'm glad it's over. Now, there is still a lunch to prepare, and I must get to work."

90

I ran into Malcolm coming down the stairs.

"Care for a walk?" I asked.

"By all means. Thank you for asking."

The morning was bright and sunny. We walked up the drive. Malcolm towered over me. Like most tall men walking next to those who are shorter, he slowed his pace to match my own.

"Have the necessary arrangements been made?" I asked him.

"Yes, for the most part. I will take the QE2 to Southampton and accompany your father's body to his supposed resting place. He may not rest at all. Who knows? Last night scrambled that for me. Once there, I'll make further arrangements. Will you come to the funeral?"

"I should, so yes."

"That would be appropriate. I'll telegram the details. While you're in England, I would like to invite you both to my country house."

"We'd like that. I understand you have an Aston Martin. I'd love to see it."

"I'll even let you drive it. It's the smell of the leather that does it for me. That and the sound it makes. There's nothing like it. Alice and your father visited there years ago on their honeymoon. It's where the accident happened. Had it not, I wonder how everything would have turned out. It changed him, you know."

"You mean there's hope for me yet, provided I don't fall on my head."

Malcolm laughed. It was deep and rich. I hadn't heard him really laugh before.

Malcolm continued. "Provided you don't. He really was quite different then. My father was still alive, so I was in the background, but Bromley and I spoke on several occasions. I always thought him considerate and kind. He never failed to say hello to me and was ever so polite. Alice, of course, was Alice. I fell in love with her the very moment I saw her. It wasn't unusual. The people she spoke to, and she met many, either loved or hated her. She never seemed to mind what they thought of her, although I thought that deep down, she did. We all need reassurance, and I doubt she was any different. She hid it better than most."

We walked, content to be a part of the morning.

"It was your father's former kindnesses that convinced me to work with him years later. I really didn't need to. After my father passed, there was sufficient money for me to while away my days in the Bahamas playing golf during the winter months and returning home in the late spring.

"Bromley was not the same after the accident, although I saw glimpses of his former self on many occasions. The change was in the volatility of his temperament. He grew less tolerant. The accident did that. I suppose what I am trying to say to you is that his darkness is not your darkness. Don't make it yours. You have Brunhilde, and she is truly marvelous. Make that last. I never married. Instead, I only gazed at the one I loved from afar. There have been ladies in my life, don't get me wrong, but I was always too ... big, too tall. I could barely fit in a bed. So here I am. I even have a nickname. I'm called the Tall Man."

"I am aware of that. Forgive me for asking, Malcolm, but are you feeling slightly adrift?"

"No need to apologize. Yours is a most perceptive question, but then the people here are all like that. They see things, and not only visions. Most have a keen sense of discernment. They can tell at a glance who you are, and what you might be capable of. Everyone is a threat of sorts, and when you move among the finest of minds, is it any wonder? Theirs is survival by mutual interest and with vast resources available to them, they feel more secure among themselves. Still, they are always wary of each other. I'm not like them. I never fitted in, not really. I've always been adrift."

We walked along the access road. The sun beat down through the trees.

"You cast a long shadow," I said. "You have been part of so many things that have happened here. Elsa joked that she is happy whenever you're around as something always happens. Why do you suppose that is?"

"It's true. Alice said the same, and even Bromley said it. Perhaps it's how I see the world. I'm drawn to knots. The threads of people's lives tangle and snarl in strange ways. Knots fascinated me as a child. They still do. I know so many, and they each do different things. There is purpose to them. It's not what they are made of that matters most, but their shapes and forms—how the loops bite and prevent movement in one part, while allowing movement in another. I suppose I'm drawn not to the substance of things, but to their arrangements. I love elegance above all, and so I worked for your father. I found obscure but beautiful pieces for him. Ours was a strange relationship. Left to my own devices, my life would have certainly run differently. But I loved Alice, and your father was kind to me. I followed them because I wanted to be with them. You are similar in that regard. You ask permission when others only command. It's why I'm speaking to you. I wouldn't otherwise."

"Thank you for saying that. I'm happy to hear my father wasn't all bad."

"He really wasn't. He was simply obsessed."

"With Alice?"

"With Alice, with money, with appearances, with himself. I, too, am obsessed, but then aren't we all? He acted on his obsessions. I never did. How can one trust an obsession? Left to seed, they quickly run riot. It happened to him. I never trusted mine. My life as a result hasn't been as dynamic as some, but I've been compensated. I've shared in so many critical moments. I've seen the world rearrange itself. If you're immersed in your own desires, how can you possibly see the patterns and the knots that develop? I am quite happy, all in all. I just hope that I might enjoy your company in the way I did his—and hers. I'm not too much trouble. I pay my way, and I see a great deal. It's really the reason why I'm tall. I have to be, to see so far."

We laughed. He was remarkably easy to get along with. I'd never known that, but then I'd never taken the time. We headed back.

We parted in the foyer. I thanked him for his company during our walk and told him that he would always be welcome here. I asked one more question as he mounted the staircase.

"What do you see, Malcolm, being so tall?"

"Everything, Percy. I see everything. I just don't know what it means."

He laughed and up he went, four stairs at a time.

91

Johnny must have heard us come in. He motioned me into the drawing room.

"How was the talk with your dad?" I asked.

"He wants to retire and turn the firm over to me, with you as my partner."

"That's good news, yes?"

"I hardly know what to think. Taking over from him is truly terrifying."

"I can't tell you the number of times I've felt the same, so welcome to my world. Besides, I'm sure your father will apprentice you. You'll do fine. It's what you were born to do, and I'll help you as your second in command. We'll have a terrific time."

"Well, that's unexpected, I must say. I thought you'd be a little more reserved in your assessment of the future, and that you would only agree to us being on an equal footing."

"You were always the senior partner, Johnny, and that works for me and for you. As to my happy assessment of the future, the alternative is far too awful to contemplate. Besides, anything less could have global consequences, so I go with the more empowering and more optimistic view."

"I agree. That would be a better choice. Was it Malcolm you were talking to?"

"It was, actually."

"Please talk to him some more. In fact, talk to him regularly. That will be my first order to you as senior partner. This will be great fun. And don't think for a moment I didn't notice that little comment as you left the breakfast table. You had me worried all over again. Perhaps I'll have you bring me coffee from now on to make up for it."

"Really, Johnny! Power simply goes to your head!"

"It does. Payback is so ... delicious, but not to worry. You and I will continue the way we've always done things. I won't have it any other way. I won't. Fifty-fifty it is, but I cast the deciding vote, of course. Now let's see if we can't get that check from Hugo before lunch."

We opened the door to the hallway as Maw was coming in with Robert.

"Oh, God," said Johnny.

"Not 'Oh, God,' Johnny. 'Oh, Robert!' The three of you could use some exercise. Now, off you go. Be back by lunch and don't be late."

Johnny and I looked at each other, and as we slipped out the French door to the south lawn with Robert in tow, Johnny said, "You know, just because one's supposedly in charge doesn't necessarily mean one is. Have you noticed that, or is it only me?"

92

W e walked toward the bordering trees to the south. "Johnny, you might as well let him off. You're going to anyway."

Johnny looked hurt and replied with some annoyance. "I'll have you know that I'm in excellent control over my impulses."

"I'm sure you are, but let's bow to the inevitable. Besides, I much prefer strolling at our leisure and stopping every now and again. Note the direction that creature heads in since we'll need to collect him eventually."

"Yes, and collecting him is usually where things fall apart, but you're right. I'll let him off."

Johnny reached down and unclipped the leash. Robert sped off, frolicking toward the edge of the lawn in giant leaps. We watched him disappear into the shadows beneath the trees and followed more sedately in his general direction.

Johnny said fondly, "I think the unclipping defines the nature of my relationship with him. He always looks so happy when he's free, and I love that."

"I know, and he gets even happier when you try and reattach him."

"That, too. He's a most peculiar dog. So strange! He made one hell of an entrance last night."

"That he did. Maw told me earlier last night that she had left him upstairs sleeping. I remember thinking that was a mistake."

"Leaving him alone for long periods is definitely not a good idea. I'm sure he got hungry. He also craves attention. One of the reasons I kept him in Stanley's office was that he learned to open every door in the house looking for me. That one he couldn't figure out, or maybe he chose not to. The kitchen was right there, and the nearness of all that food pacified him."

"He certainly doesn't like being alone, and he is peculiar. How did he know to butt that door at exactly that moment, and not once, but twice?"

"The twice is the easier to answer. It didn't open the first time. As to why he did so at that particular moment? That is a much more complex question that I'm still wrapping my wits around. Did you notice he was also doing that slow-motion moonwalk thing when he entered the dining room?"

"I did. He looked so ... unnatural. When I heard the door bang behind me, I turned with a start. The second time, the doors burst open, and the drawing room looked pitch black. I couldn't imagine what was happening, until I recognized Robert."

"God knows what your father must have thought. Do you think the sight of Robert killed him?"

"The thought did cross my mind."

"I think it crossed everyone's, but I don't think it was Robert who did the deed. The timing was too perfect, and that puzzles me. I was watching your father closely as he collapsed. He saw something. I know he did, and it scared him to death. He didn't die of heart failure directly. He died of fright."

"So, did Alice kill him, or was it what he thought he saw that did?"

450

Johnny looked away into the distance. "I think it was several things: the surprise of Alice's letter, and what she said, for a start. Robert's appearance at the precise moment in that exact way shortly thereafter helped to conjure up sufficient mystery, and something else besides. Something underneath it all that links the letter and the doors opening that I can't explain."

I considered that. "The timing was extraordinary. Perhaps there was some other factor involved. A more prosaic explanation is that my father's vanity was a contributory cause. He should have been wearing glasses but chose not to. Likely his vision was blurred, and he saw only what he imagined. People see patterns in random things. He saw something, and whatever that was, it killed him."

"I'm sure that's true to some degree. His fears materialized. Still, his death required all the elements we mentioned. I'm sure the fear that I sensed within him played a part as well. None of them alone was sufficient to cause his death. It was all of them acting together that killed him."

"It was certainly no accident."

"And if it wasn't accidental, then it must have been deliberate. But to solve the mystery fully requires that we open doors we would rather leave shut—death being one of them."

"I know. Malcolm doesn't know what to think, and he's the one who has to accompany the body to its resting place— that is, if there will be any rest at all."

Johnny smiled. "I suppose that's where the expression 'no rest for the wicked', comes from?"

"One of our favorite expressions, and speaking of which, it's time to collect that dog. Are you prepared?"

"I am. I've decided to change my tactics. I'm going to try whistling. I've never tried it, but I've seen it work."

"Well, that's suitably different. Give it a go."

Johnny gave a piercing whistle, and lo and behold, we saw the white speck in the distance turn in our direction and lope toward us. Johnny was in shock.

"Well look at that. It's a miracle! We're saved!"

I watched Robert skid to a halt in front of Johnny. Robert gave him an inquiring look and then took off again.

"I hate to say it, Johnny, but he wants you to chase him."

"I know. I know. Damn that dog! Come on! I'm not doing this alone!"

H ugo was waiting for us as Johnny, Robert, and I entered the drawing room. He motioned for me to follow him with a wave. We headed for the library.

The meeting must have dispersed, because it was only the two of us.

"Have a seat," he said.

I sat.

Hugo took a seat as well and asked, "Tell me why I should give you my check?"

"You shouldn't."

"And why not?"

"The original transaction was the result of a coercion, and because it was, you are under no obligation to complete it. You owe me nothing."

"I'm glad we agree."

"I'm glad as well. If you don't mind my asking, is the share business concluded?"

"It is, other than the paperwork."

"And to your satisfaction?"

"That, too. Your mother took care of it for the most part. Cobb owed her a hefty sum for some pieces he had purchased. He has quite a collection, apparently. She persuaded the doctor to part with the shares in exchange for what she was owed. She threw in an extraordinary emerald necklace to clinch the deal. Angus was pleased with the arrangement and readily agreed to transfer the shares to me. Everyone is happy, including Elsa."

"I'm very glad of that. My mother wanted to pay you back for what you did for her. I should thank you as well."

Hugo shrugged. "What is the price of a broken heart?"

"I don't know."

"I doubt anyone does. I accept what she did. I'll never forgive her, but that doesn't mean there hasn't been a reconciliation. The doctor was wrong. It is possible to reconcile yet not forgive."

"I suppose that's a good thing."

"I'm not altogether sure. For now, it is. Time will tell if it will be, or not. When are you getting married?"

"Soon."

"You keep saying that."

"We had other matters to contend with. By the way, your check never existed."

Hugo looked at me sharply and then smiled broadly. "Finally, a flash of brilliance."

He rose. "We might get along after all. I was beginning to wonder. I want a date before we leave. I told my daughter the same. I suggest you two have a powwow, as you call it, and tell me. You still owe me a cigar and a drink from last night."

"I do."

Hugo walked to the door and stopped. He turned and said, "And a dinner. You stood me up, and that is not easily forgiven in my world. You can tell that son of my oldest friend that I picked up the tab the other night in spite of his attempt to pay for it. Your brandy was better than mine. I kept that bottle there because it was secure, and I wanted it available for a suitable occasion. That evening qualified. Having drunk both, Josephine's was better. I'll remember that. Get back to me on that date before lunch."

With a wave he passed out of the library. I sat back in my chair and shook my head. Life with my future father-in-law might even be as exciting as living with Bruni. We did need to set a date. I got up and went in search of her.

B   runi was in our apartment changing for lunch.
      "There you are," she said. "You'll be happy to
      know that the share business is finally resolved, and
      that my father wants a date before he and Mama head
back to the city. He was most insistent. I say ten weeks from
yesterday. What do you think?"

"Is it auspicious?"

"I should think so, and if it isn't, we'll say it is. Besides, the
divorce will be finished by then."

"That would be a good idea before we marry."

"Now, I have some not-so-good news. I must head back to
the city with my parents. I must complete the paperwork on
the share transaction and collect my dogs. I will return with
them later this week. I did intend to stay on for a bit. Perhaps
I will when I return, but maybe not. There is your father's
funeral and the castle to visit in Austria. Likely there is more.
The list of what must be done seems to grow by leaps and
bounds, but that's how it is with you and me. The world
hurries on, and us with it. Will you come with me or stay
here?"

I chose to stay.

Lunch had come and gone. It was wonderfully relaxed. At the parting, I kissed and hugged them all, one by one, and thanked them. Four long limousines had lined up like so many train cars on a siding before they drove up the drive in a procession, turned right, and disappeared behind the trees that lined the access road.

Johnny had left with his parents. He had told me that his father had insisted that his apprenticeship begin Monday morning. I congratulated him but said that he would have to start without me. I needed some time. He had nodded in agreement. He told me that as senior partner he would give me a week to settle myself, but no more than that. I thanked him for being such an understanding and gracious senior partner. He whispered that if I needed more, he would consider it, but that too much self-absorption was unproductive. Further, that he would see what could be done about accelerating his father's return of the one million he still owed the estate. He was quite sure that suitable arrangements could be made, now that we were part of management. With the $750,000 from my father, Rhinebeck might even have more than enough. I had thanked him.

Angus had gone with Maw and Bonnie. He and I exchanged numbers. We would see each other at the funeral service. Bonnie had taken me aside. She had said that the

Pythia was spot on, and that she had a new necklace to prove it. Maw said she would see me in Austria. Hugo and Elsa had insisted she be there.

In private, Bruni had hugged and kissed me fiercely and said she would return as soon as she could. Elsa had squeezed me almost as hard as her daughter, but Hugo had outdone them both.

Malcolm and Mary had left together. Malcolm promised to telegram as soon as he had a date. He had invited Mary to accompany him on the voyage, since they had mutual interests to discuss now that he had room for another client. He also thought that they both could use some time to look at nothing but water rushing by. My mother pulled me aside and did what she did best. She melted my heart again and managed to extract a promise that Bruni and I would visit Florence before the wedding.

I had stood with Stanley, Dagmar, and the rest of the staff as we saw them off. Stanley mentioned after the cars had departed that Dagmar wanted a drop of the truly good stuff this evening and would I care to join them. I told him absolutely yes, and not to start without me.

I took a walk and stood at the top of the drive for some time, gazing back toward the house. The afternoon was bright and hot, and a layer of haze marked the edges of my world. I realized then that Rhinebeck was as much a summation of my fears as the realization of my dreams. Anything could happen here, even my wildest fantasies, Bruni being one of them. She had looked at me with some sadness when I told her that I had to stay. She had nodded and said that I needed time to consider what had happened, and that there were ghosts that needed my attention—Alice being one of them, and perhaps my father being another. Her words seemed odd at the time, but now I knew that she was right.

I could make Rhinebeck whatever I wished, and it would be that thing for me. And as for the ghosts, they jostled for my attention. They wanted a future as much as I did, but what it would be, I couldn't tell them.

I had tried to explain that the future lurks out of sight, like them, seen but not seen. It is a most implacable hunter and will always run us down. It's what the future does.

I would pay whatever was demanded, but whether it would be with joy or sorrow, I didn't know. I hoped it was with joy. I really did.

———❖———

THE END

ACKNOWLEDGMENTS

Writing is only one-third of publishing a book. The other two-thirds involve presenting the work for publication and then getting it out and into the world. It is an entirely different craft requiring a completely different skill set. Luckily, I've had a great deal of help in this area. I would like to thank Mary Jo Smith-Obolensky for spearheading that last two-thirds, Tom Hyman, for his wise direction as my editor, Nick Thacker for his superb cover designs, Joanna Cook for her detailed work behind the scenes, Michael Smith for his dynamic audiovisuals, Grid Graphics for their website creations, and the many generous readers who gave me vital feedback that made the story that much better.

LAST NOTE

There are limited avenues to spread the word about my stories, and reviews are a significant way to connect with potential readers. You can leave a review with your favorite store, library, social media, Goodreads, or even my website. Writing a review makes a difference.

I read every one of them, and appreciate the time spent sharing your thoughts and opinions. Please consider posting a review, whatever your experience. I welcome it.